BLACK OTTER BAY

BLACK OTTER BAY

VINCENT WYCKOFF

NORTH STAR PRESS OF ST. CLOUD, INC.
Saint Cloud, Minnesota

Cover photos © iStock/Getty Images

Author photo © Adair Soderholm

Copyright © 2016 Vincent Wyckoff

All rights reserved.

ISBN: 978-1-68201-026-6

First edition: May 2016

Printed in the United States of America.

Published by
North Star Press of St. Cloud, Inc.
P.O. Box 451
St. Cloud, MN 56302

www.northstarpress.com

For my best friend, Sybil

ONE

Abby Simon

"What do you think Dad will say when he finds out?"

It wasn't the first time this morning that eight-year-old Ben Simon had asked the question. But when it went unanswered yet again, he rolled over in the soft young tendrils of grass next to Big Island Lake and looked at his sister. Abby stood at the water's edge, her long black braid hanging down over her windbreaker. With avid concentration, she held her new telescoping fishing rod out in front of her.

This was the trial run for the new rod, and Abby had already told Ben that the one thing she'd learned early on about this "cheap crap" was that it didn't do a very good job of communicating what was going on at the "business" end of the line. The reason it had been so inexpensive, she'd discovered, was because it was made of plastic. And a hollow tube of plastic, as she'd explained to Ben, didn't have any life to it. Not like her good graphite rod.

Gently she worked the handle of the reel to take up slack in the line. She was sure a fish was mouthing the worm; she just couldn't feel it when it took a firm hold of the bait. Absorbed in the one-on-one game with the fish, she'd inadvertently inched closer to the edge of the lake, until now she felt the cold water seeping into her tennis shoes.

"You getting another bite?" Ben asked. He knew that when the fishing got this tough, his sister blocked out all outside distractions. Abby called it "being in the zone." The forest could go up in flames around her, but if she thought a fish was checking out her presentation, she'd ignore the fire and let the woods burn. She could fish as long and as hard as anyone Ben knew, and she usually caught more fish.

Ben poked at one of the rainbow trout they had lying on the grass. It was the only one he'd managed to hook and pull in by himself, the smallest of the bunch. Now, while his sister matched wits with another one, it was his job to splash water on the ones they'd caught to keep them fresh until it was time to go home. They only had the one pole, so they'd taken turns until Ben gave up in frustration at not being able to hook the wary little critters. Abby insisted on taking turns, however, handing the pole to her younger brother whenever she managed to hook another fish.

"Come on, Ben, your turn," Abby called. He looked up to see his sister leaning back, the pole arching high above her. Scrambling to his feet, he ran to her side and took the offered rod and reel.

"Keep the line tight now, Ben," she instructed. He knew how to do this part. Holding the pole straight up, he let the tension in the rod fight the fish. He felt the jerking vibrations as the trout ran back and forth. Abby had the drag set lightly for these small rainbows. That allowed the fish to pull out some line while enabling them to keep the hook wedged tightly in their mouths.

"That's good, Ben. That's good. Now work him!" Abby was a bundle of excitement bouncing next to her brother.

Ben felt the line go slack when the fish made a sudden run for the surface. Before he could reel it up tight again, the fish leaped out of the water and performed a stunning tail-walk in front of them. With a desperate flash of its shiny silver head, the trout spit the hook harmlessly to one side, and they watched as the remains of the worm flew high in the air.

"Dang it!" Ben exclaimed, shoulders slumping as he dropped the pole to his side. "I'm sorry, Abby. I tried to keep it tight."

He looked up at his sister, the adrenaline blush making her look older than her thirteen years. A broad smile accompanied her twinkling eyes. "Did you see it, Ben? Did you see that fellow tail-walking out there?"

"Yeah, I saw it," Ben responded, disappointment in his voice as he kicked at the soft mud along the water's edge.

Abby continued staring out at the spot where the fish had disappeared. "That was the biggest one yet!"

Ben handed the pole to his sister and watched while she reeled in the empty hook. Grabbing the line above the knot, she inspected the hook to see if it had been bent in the fight. Then she firmly yanked on the line to check for damage, and finally twisted the rod eyes to make sure none of them were working loose.

"I didn't hurt your new rod, did I?" Ben asked.

"No, of course not. It's just cheap junk, anyway. I guess it's like Dad says: you get what you pay for."

Last winter, while paging through one of her father's outdoor catalogs and daydreaming about fishing, she'd come across an ad for this telescoping rod. She'd determined right away that it would be perfect for carrying in a backpack. No six-and-a-half-foot rod tangling in the bushes on a trek into the woods. After talking about little else for the next two weeks, her father had prompted her to go ahead and buy it.

"You love fishing, Abby," he'd said. "And it doesn't cost much. Your allowance will cover most of it. I know you'll put it to good use."

"It telescopes down to only twelve inches," she'd explained.

"I know that, honey. You've told us at least a hundred times."

"And the cap screws off the handle to store hooks and stuff inside."

"That's great, Abby. Just buy the darn thing, will you?"

When it finally arrived in the mail, she spent hours inspecting it, telescoping it in and out, shaking the extended rod to feel the tension. She worried that it was too stiff.

"I guess the big test will be in May, then," her father had said.

Waiting for the fishing opener weekend had been nearly unbearable. Then, when it finally arrived, it was accompanied by a late-season Alberta clipper rolling in out of Canada. It dropped temperatures to the freezing point, as well as several inches of snow, erasing their plans for a weekend of camping and fishing. Abby's disappointment had been almost more than she could stand. This morning, when she'd looked outside to see the first warm, summer-like day of the season, she'd known it was time to go fishing. No more waiting. No more planning. She'd have to go today or she'd simply burst with anticipation.

But skipping school to go fishing without her little brother catching on would be impossible. She'd have to bring him along. After swearing him to secrecy, he'd hidden on the floor of the little school bus shelter while she'd explained to the bus driver that she had to stay home to care for her sick brother.

When the school bus finally pulled away, they grabbed their backpacks, which contained their lunches and Abby's carefully concealed telescoping rod. They dug a container full of red worms out of the backyard compost pile, and then climbed the path over the ridge behind town. A short walk through the woods brought them to the Superior Hiking Trail. When they reached Big Island Lake, however, they found ice floes still clogging the bays along the southern and western shorelines.

Spring had been late to arrive in this Arrowhead Region of northeastern Minnesota. Since the first heavy snowfall before Thanksgiving, winter had clung to the tiny village of Black Otter Bay on the North Shore of Lake Superior with an icy tenacity that made even toughened old-timers shake their heads. Lake Superior's massive body of thirty-five-degree water moderated temperatures along the shoreline, but over the pine- and cedar-clad ridge near Big Island Lake, several clear winter nights had seen temperatures in excess of thirty degrees below zero. The conifer forests had popped and groaned in the cold. Deer herds huddled close together under dense groves of white cedar during the frigid, fifteen-hour-long nights.

Known as the Snow Belt, this sparsely populated wilderness region had endured another winter that lived up to its reputation. According to local myth, every March a big snowstorm would blow in just in time for the Minnesota State High School Boy's Basketball Tournament. This year, the nearest team to be represented in Minneapolis had been from Duluth, fifty miles to the south, but the North Shore had received its blizzard anyway. Twelve inches of heavy, wet snow had fallen, followed by a week of below-freezing temperatures, during which time Lake Superior had buffeted the rocky coastline with twenty-foot waves, shoving huge mounds of floating ice up on the shore.

By early April, three-foot snowdrifts could still be seen deep in the woods, and ice fishermen angling for crappies on Big Island Lake had drilled through two feet of ice. While the Minnesota Twins were opening their summer baseball season, residents of Black Otter Bay were still getting around on snowmobiles. In the end, it had been a winter to try the patience of even the heartiest north-country denizens.

"Come on," Abby had told Ben, not about to let a little ice interfere with her fishing. "There's open water up on the north end."

Fifteen minutes later they came to a wide opening in the woods along the shoreline. An old two-rut road, leading in from the county highway behind town, came down to the water's edge here. At one time the road had serviced a boat landing, but the Forest Service had since taken control of the lakeshore and designated it a wilderness area. On rare occasions, someone from town would drive in to launch a canoe, and Rose Bengston retained her rights to trap minnows along the weedline for her bait shop in town. Her white plastic jugs, used as marker buoys for her minnow seines, were visible in the shallow water to the right of the old landing. For the most part, however, this was a deserted stretch of lakeshore. The small gravel parking area where trucks with boat trailers had once parked was now overgrown with tall grasses and scraggly bushes, making an ideal place for casting a fishing line. It was also the perfect spot for two kids playing hooky from school to spend the day.

Abby secured the hook into one of the rod eyes and reeled up the slack line. "Lets take a break and eat some lunch," she said. They wandered back to the grassy spot where their school backpacks lay near the row of rainbow trout.

Ben squatted at the water's edge to splash more water on the fish. "I don't think Dad will be very happy with us," he said, trying to sound nonchalant. He was still hoping for an encouraging word from his sister. "Even seeing these fish won't stop him from killing us."

Abby took her sandwich out of an oversized Ziploc freezer bag. Ben watched as she gently rinsed the trout in the lake water and then carefully laid them in the bag. She zipped it shut, placed it in the ice-cold water, then snatched a flat rock from the lake bottom to anchor the bag for safekeeping.

"There," she said, sitting back to eat her sandwich. "Just like putting them in a cooler full of ice."

Ben swallowed a handful of chips, and asked, "What about Dad? He's going to be really mad."

"Are you going to tell him?"

"No."

"Well, neither am I. He can't get mad about something he doesn't know about."

"He always finds out. What about when he sees the fish?"

Abby let her gaze roam out over the open expanse of water. Chewing slowly, she took in a medley of aromas: pungent, damp earth, the sharp tang of conifers, and the windswept, primordial smell of a new season of life beginning along the shoreline.

While studying the lake's namesake, Big Island, almost half a mile away, Abby said, "We'll get home about the same time we always get home from school, just after Dad gets off work. We can clean the fish and put them in the freezer with all the other packs of meat. He'll never know the difference."

Listening to his sister's explanation did little to calm Ben's fears. She was always so confident, so smart and sure of herself. Ever since their parents had divorced, he'd counted on Abby, looked up to her like another adult. He knew that other folks in town regarded her the same way. It was terrible to think of their mother living in Duluth with that creepy guy named Randall. Ben frowned at the thought of the long-haired owner of an art gallery in the East End of Duluth.

"Are you okay?" Abby asked.

Ben found his sister looking at him. "Yeah, sure. I was just thinking about Mom."

"Well, you better eat your sandwich." Abby turned her gaze back out to the water. "Mom's just a little bit crazy right now. Maybe someday she'll get better and come home, but for now, don't worry about her. Remember what Dad said? We just have to take care of ourselves right now." She looked at Ben and smiled. "Besides, you have me, don't you? And Dad will never leave us."

"Even when he finds out we skipped school?"

Abby smiled. "Listen, Ben. We just spent nine months cooped up in school. There are only a couple weeks left, so we're not even doing anything in class. How could we pass up a day like this?" She reached out to tousle her gloomy brother's hair.

Ben leaned back to get out of her range. He wasn't ready yet to feel good about their little escapade, much less to be coddled by his sister.

"Look out there at that water, Ben," she said, smiling and nodding wistfully over the mostly frozen lake. "No cabins or cars anywhere," she continued, "and not a cloud in the sky. Nobody around for miles." When she looked at her brother again, she was glad to see him taking in the panorama of virgin shoreline and deep, blue water. His expression softened slightly with her words. "Now tell me, little brother, would you rather be sitting in a a crowded, hot classroom, or out here in the fresh air and wilderness?"

Ben had to smile despite his lingering reservations.

"So enjoy it while you can," Abby concluded. "And if you say anything to Dad about this, you won't have to worry about him killing you, because I'll kill you first."

They sat in peaceful silence for several minutes, Abby pointing out a formation of northbound geese flying over, and a pair of loons fishing together out near the island. "It's uninhabited," she told Ben, "so it's a perfect place for them to nest."

So distracted were they by the new season of natural wonders, neither of them noticed a car idling into view on the access road. When Abby finally spotted it, she grabbed Ben's shoulder and shoved him down hard on the ground.

"What?" he stammered. "What's going on?"

"Be quiet! There's a car over there."

The children lay still, listening. Abby strained to hear anything over the soft lapping of waves at the shore and a breeze rustling the brush around them. Because they'd been sitting in the tall grass, she doubted the driver had spotted them, but it was disconcerting to think that a car sat just thirty feet away, and she hadn't heard a sound.

"Who do you think it is?" Ben asked.

Abby held a finger to her lips.

Closing her eyes to listen harder, she picked out a chiming noise. She knew the driver's door must be open, with the key in the ignition. Abby bit her lip, thinking. Maybe they had been seen after all, she worried, and their hiding spot was about to be revealed.

Motioning for Ben to stay down, Abby slowly raised herself to a kneeling position in the grass. It was easy to spot the vehicle: a big, shiny, black luxury car. The driver's door was indeed open, as was the trunk, while the driver stood near the hood looking out over the lake. A big man, she noted, with a clean-shaven dark complexion, wearing black trousers and shirt. His hair was cut close at the sides, but jutted straight up on top, like an overgrown crew-cut. Wrap-around sunglasses fit snug across his face.

To Ben, Abby whispered, "I think it's just somebody out for a drive. I've never seen the car before."

Ben started to sit up, but Abby stopped him. The man walked around to the back of the car. When he stopped at the trunk, he paused to look up and down the shoreline, and Abby dropped flat next to Ben.

"He's looking around," she whispered so quietly Ben could barely hear. "Don't move."

"We're going to get caught," Ben whined.

"Shhh!"

The fear on his face surprised her. She could feel her own heart beating fast, but it was more out of excitement than fear. They were only playing hooky, for goodness' sake! What was the worst that could happen? She reached out to place a reassuring hand on Ben's cheek. When he turned to look at her, she grinned and winked, but he only scrunched his eyes shut, cramming himself tighter against the ground.

Several quiet moments passed, until Abby finally sat up to take another look. The man stood near the trunk, awkwardly pulling on hip waders. A feeling of despair descended on Abby.

"Ben," she whispered. Her brother burrowed deeper in the grass. "Ben, I think the guy is a fisherman. We'll never get out of here now."

Ben finally looked up at his sister. "A fisherman?" he asked. "You mean he isn't trying to catch us skipping school?"

"Of course not," she whispered. "But he's an adult, and he knows we're supposed to be in school, so we can't let him see us."

"But what if he fishes all afternoon? We have to be home soon."

"I'll think of something," she said, patting her brother's shoulder while she rose to her knees for another look.

With his hip waders on, the man now leaned over the opening of the trunk. "He's taking out his fishing gear," she reported. But then the man bent even further, and with a lurching yank, pulled out a heavy bundle. Over his shoulder it went, and with her mouth hanging open in disbelief, Abby sat back hard on her butt.

"Holy . . ." she muttered.

Ben sat up beside her. "What?"

Abby studied the big man and his heavy load, trying to make it out to be something other than what she guessed it to be. Maybe it was a roll of carpeting, a rug, even a heavy blanket. The man strode directly into the water at the weedline, and when a hand, and then a forearm, slipped into view from the back of the bundle, Abby knew her worst suspicions were true.

Ben saw it at the same time, and Abby had just enough time to slap a hand over his mouth before he cried out. She pulled him down beside her.

"Ben, Ben!" she whispered harshly into his face. "You have to keep quiet." She held a hand over his mouth while imploring him to silence. His eyes were wide, wild, and his tears warmed her fingers. "It's okay, Ben. We just have to stay quiet. Please. We'll get out of here, you'll see. But you can't make a sound. Okay?"

They lay together in the tall grass, Abby's hand near Ben's face, ready to clamp down should he begin to cry out again. She worked her thoughts over the situation, trying to make some sense of what they'd seen. There could be no denying those images though, the flopping hand and lifeless arm. She had no idea who the man in the waders might be, much less the person hanging over his shoulder, but Abby was determined to find out.

When Ben finally relaxed against her, she moved her fingers away from his face and he emitted a whimpering sigh. Up to her knees she rose again, slowly lifting her face to the waving tips of grass. The man was well out in the water, still struggling with the weight on his shoulder.

"Ben," she said softly after lying down next to her brother again.

He interrupted. "Did you see what I saw, Abby?"

She nodded. "It's okay, Ben. He doesn't know we're here. If you stay quiet, he'll go away, and we can go home."

"That's all I want, Abby. I just want to go home." His voice rose again. "It's all because we skipped school."

Abby put her finger over his lips. "Quiet, Ben. It's not because of anything we did." She bit her lip and took another quick glance at the man in the water. "You stay here. I'm going to get a closer look at the car and the license plate."

Ben grabbed at her. "Oh, no, Abby!"

"Shhh! It's okay. He can't see you here, and he's way out in the water. I'll be right back. I'm just going to get his license plate number. He'll never know."

"Abby, please." Tears rolled down Ben's face.

"I'll be right back. Just stay quiet, and then we'll go home, okay?"

Ben answered by shutting his eyes and clasping his hands together in prayer. Abby smiled when his lips began moving in silent entreaties. She reached out to stroke his shoulder, and then turned to crawl through the brush toward the car.

Rocks poked at her hands and knees, but the car was even closer than it had appeared through the tall grass and in short order she was at the driver's door, the chiming ignition tolling like a funeral dirge. She rose up to look inside and saw plush leather seats, a folded road map, and a black sport coat on the passenger's side. Stretching higher, she peered over the dash and through the windshield at the man. From this range he looked even larger than before, his spiked hairstyle adding three inches to his height. Up to his thighs in water, his broad back arched up and outward from the close-fitting hip waders. They seemed too small for him, Abby thought, like they didn't belong to him, especially considering the fancy trousers and black linen shirt he wore. His right hand grabbed at the nylon rope attached to Rose Bengston's marker buoys, while his left arm still clutched the bundle draped over his shoulder.

Stealing a quick glance behind her, Abby gasped when she spotted Ben running for the safety of the woods. But another peek over the dash showed the man still in the water, his back to them. When Ben made the treeline, Abby relaxed in the knowledge that her little brother could find his way home through the woods as easily as a city kid following street signs.

She dropped to her knees to crawl to the back of the car. Completely hidden from view here, she turned sideways to look behind her down the neglected road. Weeds and rocks jutted up between the wheel ruts. That's why the car had appeared so suddenly, she realized. Like magic. The big sedan would have been barely moving over this rough terrain.

A flash of light reflecting through the trees interrupted her thoughts. A moment later, another flash, this one closer. Then she heard the rumble of a failing exhaust system and caught a glimpse of an old pickup truck approaching. Now Abby experienced her own heart-stopping panic as she realized she was about to be trapped between the man in the waders and the oncoming truck.

She grabbed the bumper of the car and lifted herself up to read the license plate. With the trunk still open, however, she discovered the license plate was over her head on the back of the trunk lid. Out of time now and acting on instinct, she stood up to get a better look, and came eye to eye with the man in the waders.

Returning to shore over the slippery, rocky lake bottom, he'd been watching the approaching truck when he spotted Abby as she stood up behind his car. The dark sunglasses obscured his expression, but his quiet, cautious steps became lunging splashes as he quickened his pace. Abby grabbed the trunk lid to look at the license plate, but all that registered was the fact that it was from Illinois. Then she was running, first down the road to put some distance between them, then into the woods just before the pickup truck rounded a veil of balsam trees and lurched into view.

Charging through the tall grass, Abby hit the treeline at a dead run. She heard the man yell, calling for her to stop, but panic had temporarily taken over, and she dashed through the woods like a rabbit before the hounds.

Running had always been a good tonic for Abby. She remembered family outings when, as a child, she'd raced her father through the woods, darting along winding forest pathways, the fresh air pounding through her lungs. And now, the harder she ran, the more her spirits lightened and her thinking cleared. She knew the man would never catch up to her in those waders. A grin spread across her face when she realized that if he stopped to take them off, well, he'd simply never see her again.

Leaping boulders, skipping over exposed roots, she flew through the woods like a breeze through the treetops. She thought the pickup truck looked familiar, but she couldn't quite place it. She'd be willing to bet it belonged to a local, though. Abby smirked with glee at the notion of someone from town asking the man from Illinois why he was wearing waders but not carrying a fishing pole.

Soon she spotted Ben up ahead. She knew they'd dodged a dangerous situation and successfully made their escape. Feeling just a little smug, she ran hard to catch up to her little brother, to let him know they were both safe. It would be a while yet before she remembered their backpacks lying near the shore of Big Island Lake, just a dozen or so steps from the big, shiny Cadillac.

TWO

Marcy Soderstrom

"I can tell you right now why summer finally got here," Red Tollefson stated from his seat at the counter in the Black Otter Bay Café. Red was a retired highway department foreman. He still carried his large frame with a confident, rolling swagger, even if he wasn't as solid as he'd been in his working days. Thick waves of graying red hair covered his head, and he still boasted the barrel chest and gnarled, workingman's hands common throughout the north country.

Turning sideways on his stool, Red shuffled a deck of cards while glancing outside, as if to confirm that summer had indeed finally arrived. Owen Porter reset the cribbage pegs, patiently awaiting Red's explanation. It was that quiet time of early afternoon when the lunch crowd had left but the regulars from the day shift at the taconite plant, in search of a cup of coffee and a card game, hadn't arrived yet.

Red squinted up at Owen, an extremely tall, lanky man perched uncomfortably atop his stool at the counter. Hunched over, Owen resembled a prehistoric insect, with his gangly limbs jutting out at odd angles. He was currently working afternoon shifts at the plant, so he'd be leaving soon for work.

The wrinkles around Red's eyes creased up with humor. He glanced across the counter to be sure Marcy was listening. "Summer finally got here because I wasted twenty bucks last Saturday tuning up my damn snowblower."

Owen suppressed a grin while drumming the fingers of one hand on the counter. "That's the dumbest thing I've ever heard," he said. "Nobody tunes up a snowblower in May."

"Hey, the way this winter was going, a fellow couldn't be too sure." As if suddenly realizing how ridiculous it sounded to be fixing a snowblower in May, Red shot a defensive frown at Marcy and added, "Anyway, at least it's all ready for next year."

Marcy folded the newspaper she'd been reading and dropped it on the counter. Grabbing a dishrag out of the sink, she swiped at coffee stains while directing her blue-eyed smirk at Red.

Marcella Soderstrom had worked in the café most of her adult life. In her mid-thirties now, Marcy's world seemed to revolve around the ebb and flow of customers. She opened the diner most days, started the coffee pots percolating while turning on the lights and heating up the griddle, then spread the bundle of Duluth newspapers along the counter for the morning regulars. She found something comfortable and affirming about this ritual. In a way, Marcy felt she played an integral role in the lives of the townsfolk of Black Otter Bay. The café gave her a sense of purpose, and she took pride in being there to greet the early-morning risers.

"How come you weren't out fishing for the opener instead of working on your snowblower?" she asked.

"Bah!" Red snorted. "The opener is for amateurs. All them yahoos from Duluth and the Cities with their fancy rigs. They just get in the way." He leaned over to Owen, as if about to impart some secret knowledge. "Water's too cold, anyway," he explained. "Walleyes haven't even spawned yet. I'll wait a couple weeks for the commotion to settle down a bit."

Marcy said, "I heard some of the lakes aren't even open yet."

"They would be if that clipper hadn't blown through. Day like today, though, they'll open up real quick."

Owen looked up from his cards. "Speaking of warmer weather, when are your folks coming home?"

Marcy smiled. "Who knows? I talked to them last weekend, but when they heard it was snowing again, they didn't mention anything about coming home."

Marcy lived with her folks. Since retirement, they'd been migrating to Phoenix for the winters, and it seemed they stayed a little longer with each passing year. They'd begun by heading south after New Year's. The next year it had been Christmas, then Thanksgiving, until last year they were gone by Halloween, and they never returned before the trees budded out and summer was in full swing.

"Well, you can give them the all-clear now," Red piped up. "Tell them I tuned up my snowblower, so it won't snow anymore this year."

Marcy laughed as she turned to stack dishes in the dishwasher. She was a tall, strong woman. What she lacked in beauty she more than made up for with personality and energy. She was big-boned, and that meant she constantly struggled with her weight. Her worst fear was that she'd gradually grow larger and dumpier as she aged. "Oh, Lord," she often prayed to herself. "Don't let me become like all the old, boring, workworn women of this town."

Her complexion was that of a fair-skinned Scandinavian and she had nondescript features. Her goals were as modest as her appearance, and she was more than satisfied with her job in the café. If she'd admit it to anyone (which she wouldn't), her greatest aspiration would be to one day own and manage the restaurant herself. Another thing she'd never make public is that she was convinced her Prince Charming would one day walk through the café door. She no longer daydreamed about either of these fantasies like she did ten years ago, but the conviction remained that in one way or another, her future was linked to her involvement with the diner.

While she took her responsibility to the café and the townsfolk very seriously, Marcy was part of that younger generation that changes hair color as easily as changing clothes. And not your normal, everyday colors, either. On St. Patrick's Day, you could bet her hair would be a brilliant lime green. Stripes of red, white, and blue for the Fourth of July. She'd painted hearts on her cheeks for Valentine's Day, and wore a Santa Claus hat on Christmas. The old-timers in town got a kick out of it. Anybody else and they'd say she was crazy, probably on drugs or something. But Marcy was one of their own, and they embraced her eccentricities as they would a favorite daughter.

"Hey, Marcy," Red had called out one time, loud enough for all the morning regulars to hear. "If I asked you to marry me, would you get a tattoo or dye your hair a special color for the wedding?"

"If I had to marry you," she'd retorted amid the catcalls and laughter, "I'd shave my head and join a convent."

Marcy glanced across the diner at the large picture windows facing Highway 61 and Lake Superior. It was the middle of May, but the trees along the highway had only recently leafed out. Their soft green hues glowed against the indigo blue background of Lake Superior. She acknowledged that Red had been correct about one thing: last weekend the café had been hopping with out-of-town fishermen. The small gravel parking lot had been packed with pickup trucks and boats.

The Black Otter Bay Café had been in existence in one form or another for over one hundred years, ever since Agda Hjemdahl began serving home-cooked meals to commercial fishermen outside her back door. By the turn of the last century, when the lumber business expanded across northern Minnesota, she'd added a small lean-to on the back of her house to accommodate the hungry foreigners passing through to the newest logging areas. A staunch Norwegian Lutheran, Agda wouldn't allow the bachelor Finns or Swedes, and especially the dark Slavic and Italian loggers, to take a meal inside her own house. When she served up kettles of stew in the little back room, however, the ribald roar of foreign tongues could be heard throughout the town.

By the 1920s, a road was punched through the woods from Duluth, and the tourist industry began in earnest. Worn out from long days of cooking and washing dishes as well as laundry for the bachelor laborers, Agda retired and sold the name of her café to businessmen from Duluth. In the terms of the sale, she'd insisted on a lifelong stipend, and thereafter Agda served graciously as the village matriarch until her death in 1968, at age ninety-nine.

Marcy maintained that Agda's spirit still occupied the premises. Whenever something turned up missing, or fell over for no apparent reason, or a door closed or a light suddenly turned on, Marcy jokingly blamed Agda. And even though she'd passed away years before Marcy was born, the self-reliant, hard-working founder of the café had been a mentor and spiritual colleague for much of Marcy's adult working life.

After buying the café from Agda, the businessmen erected a huge log structure with rooms to rent as well as a large dining area and saloon. The new establishment became known as The Black Otter Bay Roadhouse. During Prohibition, liquor arrived on boats from Canada, and the Roadhouse became a popular hangout for the rich and not-always-legal business community. Al Capone was rumored to have stayed there, and in the back rooms, business transactions and poker games went on sometimes until dawn.

In 1970, the old building burned down, and once again it became a legitimate mom-and-pop café and store. The rebuilt diner was modern and boasted state-of-the-art kitchen facilities. The décor was rustic but plush, the food hardy and reasonably priced, and soon the Black Otter Bay Café was a daily Greyhound and charter bus tourist stop. But that was four decades ago, and with no further updates or remodeling, the old furnishings were wearing out. The linoleum floor was worn bare, with hardly a vestige of its black-and-white checkerboard design still visible. Tables were scratched and further marred by cigarette burns.

To the local customers who ate at the café every day, however, the decline had been slow and unnoticed. The same patrons used certain tables and stools each day, as if reserved signs had been posted for their convenience. Tourists more commonly used the booths, although someone like Red might occasionally take a booth for a rare meal out with his wife.

Marcy's gaze swung back inside from the picture windows and landed on the giant lake trout mounted over the cash register counter. Weighing thirty or thirty-five pounds, the huge laker had hung on the wall for as long as Marcy could remember. A thick coat of grease and dust lined the back of the enormous fish, a fact that irritated Marcy to no end. Whenever she looked at it, she vowed to get the stepladder and climb up there to clean the old relic. So far, however, that task had gone undone. As the thought crossed her mind again, she spotted the county sheriff's squad car pulling into the parking lot. A moment later, Sheriff Marlon Fastwater stepped through the café's door. Red and Owen called out their greetings while Marcy grabbed a coffee cup and placed it on the counter in front of the sheriff's customary stool. By the time he sat down, Marcy was pouring coffee, and with a free hand grabbed a napkin to set near the cup.

"Afternoon, Sheriff," she said. "Who's winning the battle today?"

The sheriff smiled while trying to stick a thick index finger through the coffee cup's handle. Failing that, he grabbed the handle between two fingers and lifted the cup to drink. His massive hand made the cup look like a dollhouse accessory.

Marlon Fastwater was as tall as Owen Porter, and broader than Red Tollefson. When he placed his trooper hat on the counter, thick waves of glistening black hair highlighted the shimmer in his eyes, which were so dark they were almost black. At fifty years old, he'd been the sheriff of Black Otter County for over twenty years, ever since the time when, as a young police officer, he'd walked in on a late-night robbery of the local municipal bar. A transient had a gun pointed at the bartender. Fastwater locked eyes with the young man while instructing him to drop the gun. Most folks considered the sheriff's intimidating size and fearless, calm demeanor to be as effective a weapon as the .44 Magnum he carried in a hand-tooled leather holster on his hip.

After the incident, Fastwater reported that when he looked into the drifter's eyes, he knew the young man wasn't going to pull the trigger, even after the robber spun around to direct his aim squarely at the sheriff's chest. Instead of pulling his own weapon, however, Fastwater riveted his piercing black eyes on the would-be assailant. After closing the gap between them with a couple of surprisingly quick and quiet strides, he simply reached out and snatched the gun from the young man's hand.

The story made all the regional news media outlets, and Fastwater's picture even appeared on the front page of the Duluth newspaper. All the fuss seemed overblown to him. He'd been quoted as saying, "If a man pulls a gun and doesn't shoot you outright, well, you know he just doesn't have the heart for it." Shortly thereafter, he ran for county sheriff, winning by a wide margin, and he'd held the position ever since.

Fastwater's ancestors had lived on the shores of Lake Superior since long before the first white settlers arrived. When the Norwegian commercial fishermen, and later the farmers, loggers, and finally the miners came ashore, his family had been here to help them establish a community. In the early days, the fact that his people were Native Americans had never been an issue. Everybody was poor, and everyone worked together to survive in this beautiful, unforgiving country. It wasn't until the mining industry came in that life became a little easier. By that time, some of the native peoples had succumbed to the new white man's diseases, while others had moved to reservations, but as the sheriff would tell you, many of the settlers had died, too, or given up the struggle and returned to more civilized, populated urban areas.

Throughout it all, though, his family had stayed on. They were buried side by side with the white folks in the local cemetery up on the ridge. That's why Fastwater never saw any irony in the fact that he held the highest office in town while being the only non-white resident. He belonged here, and these were his people, no matter their color or nationality.

His older sister Arlene, a tireless, liberal, cause-oriented district attorney, lived in Duluth. Arlene was everything flamboyant and overstated that her brother was not. While Marlon earned respect with his commanding size and quiet self-assurance, Arlene was simply loud and large. She wore flowing, floral-printed caftan-style dresses, accented with bright, gaudy jewelry, and when she swept into a courtroom everyone sat up, compelled to take notice.

The men in the café turned to look at the door as the sheriff's nephew, Leonard, came in. Arlene's son worked part-time as a police officer in Black Otter Bay under Marlon's tutelage. Matthew Simon, just off his day shift at the taconite plant, accompanied him.

"Hiya Leonard, Matt," Owen said. All three had been classmates in high school with Marcy more than fifteen years ago. Even though Leonard lived in Duluth now, they remained close friends.

"Hey, it's Marlon Junior," Red called out. Leonard's father had run off soon after his birth, and folks often joked about how Leonard seemed to have inherited his character traits from his uncle rather than his own mother or father. Soft-spoken, tall, slender, and handsome, Leonard braided his thick black hair in a single long plait. Agile and strong, with big hands like his uncle, he devoted much of his free time to the study of spiritual and personal growth and harmony. He'd traveled far and wide, from remote Cree Indian villages in northern Canada to reservation outposts on the Great Plains, in search of spiritual teachers and wisdom.

One big difference between the two men was that while Marlon carried the heavy .44 Magnum everywhere he went, Leonard didn't even own a gun. He knew how to use one—he'd grown up hunting and trapping with his uncle—but as he'd matured into adulthood, he'd gradually left the guns behind, much to the chagrin of his uncle and others in law enforcement. Fortunately, in a quiet village the size of Black Otter Bay, with a population under five hundred, there wasn't much need for lethal firepower.

Leonard sauntered across the room, his lanky body fluid and graceful. "Afternoon there, Red, Owen," he said, nodding at each man in turn. His well-worn western-style boots alit softly on the linoleum floor. With hands in his denim jean pockets, he flashed the briefest wink at Marcy, his request for a cup of coffee. Above the blue jeans he wore an official police officer's long-sleeved shirt, with a badge pinned over one breast pocket and a photo I.D. tag clipped to the other.

Marcy set a cup and saucer on the counter, poured the coffee for Leonard, and turned to look at Matthew still standing by the door. He held his cap in his hands, formal-like, and stood just a few steps inside the room. She'd be the first to admit that Leonard could melt a girl's heart with his dark, virile good looks. Quite honestly, she'd found herself melting there before. But looking at Matthew Simon, she realized he commanded his own style of manly good looks. Standing in the doorway, his dark hair cut a little too long, he surveyed the room with large brown eyes set in a flawless complexion. She found herself smiling at him as he stood self-consciously in his lace-up work boots and faded blue jeans straight from the jobsite.

"Cup of coffee, Matt?" she called, holding up the pot.

"Ah, no thanks, Marcy. Just stopped in to say hi."

She couldn't understand how Jackie had walked out on a smile like that. If she had half the good looks Jackie had, she'd . . .

"I have to get home for the kids," Matt concluded, before turning for the door.

"Well, come back sometime when you can't stay so long," she called, laughing.

Sheriff Fastwater watched her, noting the color blushing high on her fair cheeks. He couldn't help grinning at her obvious infatuation.

Red called out, "Hey Matt. You and Abby got a plan for fishing yet?"

Matt stopped at the door and said, "Well, we had a plan, Red. But, hey, this is Minnesota. We got snowed out."

Everyone laughed, but Fastwater continued to watch Marcy's eyes following Matt's every movement. Finally, she stepped back, leaned against the stainless steel counter, and with effort redirected her gaze at the sheriff.

She could tell he'd been watching her, so to buy some time to cover her embarrassment, she turned around to place the pot back on the brewer stand. She loved to tease the big lawman, and for his part, he enjoyed his place on the receiving end, so when she turned back to face him again, he anticipated one of her smart-aleck remarks.

"How's Mrs. Bean?" she asked. Owen and Red perked up at the question. Mrs. Virginia Bean was the widowed postmistress in town. She and the sheriff were rumored to be an item, but that wasn't the sort of thing people would speculate about out loud. Except for Marcy. She often got away with outrageous comments, even ribald jokes, where someone else would get called to task for it.

The sheriff twisted on his stool to face Owen and Red, melting their inquisitive stares with a derisive glower.

The way Marcy saw it, Mrs. Bean had been widowed for twenty years, the sheriff had never married, and if they took some comfort in each other, well, more power to them. But harassing the sheriff had become a daily ritual for Marcy. It was just so easy. In some ways, the big man was a gentle giant: huge and ruggedly handsome, and always at a loss for words. Other than a modest grin, he seldom had a comeback for her jibes and jokes. Years ago, even before he'd become county sheriff, when Marcy was the star of the local high school basketball team, he'd attended all her games, all the way to the state tournament in Minneapolis her senior year. He'd been her biggest fan, and she'd never forgotten that. So even though she loved him like an older brother, Marcy figured it was his job to enforce the rules now, and her job to bend them, so it seemed only natural that they should remain close friends.

Fastwater's expression softened when he looked at Marcy. "Mrs. Bean is just fine. Thanks for asking."

"Did you have lunch together?" Marcy enjoyed making the big man squirm.

Fastwater smiled. "Yes, we did—tuna fish sandwiches. But she's pretty busy today, so I didn't stick around."

With no juicy gossip forthcoming, Red nodded his good-byes and headed home for his afternoon nap. Owen grabbed his boxed-up sandwich and prepared to leave for work. Marcy topped off the sheriff's cup while taking another long glance at the grime-covered fish on the wall. There should be just enough time to get up there on the stepladder, she figured, before the day shift regulars arrived.

A pair of swinging doors led to the back of the restaurant and the kitchen and storage areas. Cleaning supplies, tools, shovels, and the stepladder were stacked along the back wall. Now that the breakfast and lunch shifts were done, the cook had cleaned up and left for the day. Other than some leftover bakery items and boxed-up cold sandwiches, the diner didn't serve meals after the lunch hour. By late afternoon, the café would be closed.

Letting herself through the twin doors, Marcy stopped when her eye caught the outside screen door slowly closing at the rear of the building. The door worked on a mechanical closer, and took several seconds to shut tightly. It was only used as an emergency exit and to haul garbage out to the dumpster. She watched as the door silently swung shut.

A little unnerved, Marcy paused for a moment in the door-way. Thinking it over, she knew from experience that the closer mechanism was stiff enough to prevent a wind from blowing the door open. And no one had gone out, she would have seen them. That left only one alternative: someone must have just come in. The kitchen was a wide-open space, with nowhere to hide, and a quick glance revealed the room to be empty.

Facing the storage area, she called softly, "Hello?"

No response.

She knew there wasn't much reason for anyone to sneak in the back door. There wasn't anything of value back here to steal. Then she remembered the sheriff and Leonard sitting at the counter on the other side of the swinging doors, just fifteen feet away. Their presence bolstered her nerve, alleviated her fears. On a whim, she called, "Agda, is that you?"

Then she saw a child's hand on the floor, just at the back corner of a set of storage cabinets. As she watched, the hand disappeared from view. The intruder being a child brought a smile of relief to her face, but still presented a mystery. She stepped deeper into the room.

"Agda?" she said again, this time as a diversion so she could quietly approach the cabinet. "Come on out here, Agda."

Easing up to the edge of the counter, Marcy leaned over to peek behind it. A young boy knelt on the floor, arms covering his head as if that would magically make him invisible.

"Ben?" she said. "Ben Simon? Is that you?"

He didn't move, other than to shake slightly from crying. Marcy crouched beside him to rest a hand on the boy's arm.

"Ben? It's Marcy. Are you okay?"

Still no response. Marcy jumped when another form materialized from the shadows behind the counter.

"Abby!" she exclaimed.

Ben's sister knelt beside the cowering boy and put an arm over his shoulder. To Marcy, she said, "We skipped school today. He's afraid of getting caught."

"Oh, Ben," Marcy said. "Come on, I'm your friend. I won't tell on you." Kneeling on the other side of him, she stroked Ben's head, all the while looking at Abby. "So what are you doing here, then?" she asked. "Surely you didn't skip school to hang out in the café?"

Abby ignored the question. Instead, she urged her brother to raise his head and look at them. When he did, Marcy was surprised to see so many tears and a runny nose. Pulling a tissue from her work apron, she held it up to Ben's face until he took it himself and wiped his nose.

"Who's Agda?" he asked in a tear-stained, crackling voice.

Marcy laughed. Using a thumb to wipe away another tear at the corner of Ben's eye, she said, "Agda is a ghost. But she's a good ghost, and a friend of mine."

Familiar with Marcy's eccentric behaviors, Ben started to smile, but when he opened his mouth to speak again, Abby quickly interrupted. "We skipped school to go fishing today, that's all." She gave Ben a hard look as she continued. "We can't go home until after Dad gets home from work. He always gets home before us when we're in school."

Marcy nodded, still stroking Ben's head affectionately. "Well, he ought to be home by now. He just left here."

"We were going to get something to drink while we waited, but we saw the sheriff's car out front, so we snuck in the back door.

Ben asked, "You promise you're not going to tell the sheriff?"

"Of course not. You don't think you're the first ones in town to skip school, do you?"

Ben sat quietly, comforted by Marcy's tender attention. He'd stopped crying, but she thought he looked exhausted, with his glassy-eyed stare of shock. "I'll get you something to drink," she said. "Just sit tight." She glanced around their darkened hiding place behind the counter. "Where's your fishing gear?" she asked.

The loss of their equipment finally hit Abby. Now it was her turn to become silent and pale. And it wasn't just her new fishing pole, either. Their school backpacks were out at the lake, too, with her name and address in her notebook. Abby suddenly felt sick.

Then Ben piped up. "I think we left our gear out back of the restaurant."

Abby swung a dazed expression on her brother. She needed time to consider this new predicament, so Ben's sudden ability to think on his feet came as a relief, and could buy her the time she needed to make a plan to retrieve their backpacks.

Marcy smiled and patted Ben on the back. "Well, okay, then," she said. "Wait here. I'll be right back with some drinks."

Barging back through the swinging doors, Marcy saw the sheriff on his feet, talking on his cell phone. Leonard stood at the door, looking outside into the bright sunshine.

"We got a call," Marlon said to her, putting the phone away and reaching for his trooper hat. "Thanks for the coffee." A five-dollar bill stuck out from under his cup.

With their sudden departure, the café became eerily quiet. Marcy reached for the soda glasses, all thoughts of the giant lake trout once again gone.

THREE

Matthew Simon

It was Ben's turn to prepare dinner that evening. Of course, being only eight years old, he usually got help from his father or Abby, but he insisted on taking his part in the rotation of family cooking duties. Tonight, Ben had responsibility for the meal, Abby had clean-up, and their father had the evening off. Tomorrow night, Abby would be off duty, while their father cooked and Ben cleaned up. This system had served the family well ever since the children's mother left them over a year ago.

Matthew Simon had always stressed the importance of sitting down for dinner together as a family, even long before his wife had left. Over time, it had become a tradition that all of them looked forward to and valued. Taking turns with the cooking and clean-up chores gave each of them some ownership in the ritual. Even though his wife had missed many of these evenings together during the last few months she lived with them, Matt had been gratified to see that his children expected the family dinners to continue. If anything, he thought Abby and Ben had solidified the tradition by creating the rotating chores schedule, but they all used the time together to help each other fill the glaring hole at the table.

Abby had been sticking close to her younger brother all afternoon, worried that he might say something to their father. Aware of his listless attitude in the kitchen, she said, "I'll help you with dinner, Ben. Let's make taco goulash—it's your favorite."

And for a while, as the pasta boiled and Ben stirred in taco seasonings, the events of the day faded enough to allow his appetite to emerge. But it quickly disappeared when, with their father out of earshot reading the newspaper in the front room, Abby quietly asked, "How are you doing now, Ben? Are you feeling any better?"

His stomach flip-flopped and the butterflies resumed their sickening flights. "No, Abby. We saw a dead person today. I don't feel any better at all."

Taking a turn at stirring the hotdish, she said, "Well, you can't say anything to Dad. We have to act like nothing is wrong. If I can figure out a way to get back out to the lake and find our backpacks, in a day or two all this will be over."

Ben shook his head. "I don't think so. I don't think this is going to be over for a long time." Looking at his sister, he asked, "Who do you think the dead person was?"

Abby affected her most grown-up, sympathetic smile. "I have no idea. But the man we saw isn't from around here—his car had license plates from Illinois. None of it is our business. We just have to act normal until we get our stuff back. Can you do that?"

"I don't know."

Abby slipped an arm around her brother's shoulders and spoke softly. "You have to, Ben. Give me time to find our backpacks, and I promise everything will be okay. I know it's hard, and it's my fault for getting you to skip school. But if you keep quiet for another day or two, I promise I'll make it up to you this summer."

Ben twisted away from her arm. "I have to set the table."

"Ben?"

"I'll try, Abby," he snapped.

• • • • •

Matt couldn't take all the credit for the idea of eating dinners together. The household he'd grown up in had taken meals together, too, but whereas his children seemed to sincerely enjoy the ritual, he and his brother had tried every excuse imaginable to get out of it. In his parents' house, a small kitchen table took most of the available space in the cramped kitchen nook. His father had sat at one end, his back to the main kitchen, with his mother and Matt's older brother Daniel, at either elbow. Being the youngest and smallest, Matt had sat across from his father, jammed in against the back wall and blocked from escape by his mother and brother. One year they'd added an electric coffee pot to the table, and because the closest available outlet was on the wall behind Matt, the percolating, steaming machine had further crowded him in. But as bad as that was, it was a good deal better than his brother's seat, which was within a backhanded slap of the old man.

His father's drunken behavior and manic mood swings had crashed through their lives like an ill-tempered bull moose. And it never got any better, even after he quit drinking. If anything, without the alcohol to deaden some of the violent tirades, he became even scarier to the little boy sitting across the table.

The morning his father swore off drinking, the two boys and their mother were leaving for church. Matthew had been only five years old at the time, but Daniel, eight years older and a big kid for his age, had already begun showing some of the bullying traits inherited from his father. It was a frigid Sunday, with a blinding sun reflecting off a couple feet of snow. A northeast wind off Lake Superior whipped up whitecaps and six-foot breakers along the shore. The old man's pickup truck sat in the driveway, and as the boys drew near, they saw their father's face pressed up against the window where he'd fallen asleep after driving home after closing time at the bar. The windows were completely fogged over from his breath, with just a small clearing near his nose and mouth where he slept against the driver's side door.

Matthew hadn't even understood the significance of what they were looking at before Daniel ran up to the window and pounded on the glass. The old man jumped straight upright, a half-pint of Snowshoe Grog falling from his lap to the floor.

Daniel ran away laughing, but Matthew paused to look in at his father. A crusty layer of vomit spotted his faded, heavy woolen jacket. The boy worried that his father might freeze to death, but his mother quickly grabbed his arm and led him away.

Upon their return from church, the pickup truck was gone, and it was Matthew who spied the emptied bottle of grog in the crotch of a small birch tree in the front yard. The bottle remained there for years, no one daring to remove it. In one of his saner moments, his father told Matthew that he put it in the tree as a visible reminder to himself.

But the lack of alcohol didn't do anything to alter the old man's behavior. Looking back on it, Matt conceded that actual physical violence had been rare, but the constant threat of it had been very real, and anger and outrage were the main character traits Matt carried in his memories of his father. That, and the unpredictability of the old man's temper. He might come home from work singing at the top of his voice, or slam through the door swearing up a blue streak, but there was nothing anyone could do to either predict his behavior or change it. If Matt and his brother kept quiet and out of their father's range, he was likely to yell at them to quit sneaking around the house. And he'd just as likely ignore their loud fighting or roughhousing.

But for Matt, the hardest part had been listening to the late-night arguments between his mother and father. He'd lie in bed for what seemed like hours while the battles raged in the kitchen beneath his bedroom. Their old clapboard house had been built in a traditional North Shore style, with small rooms and low ceilings to better facilitate heating during the long winter months. Windows were at a premium for the same reason, so with the bedroom door shut tight against the loud voices, darkness was almost absolute.

Daniel shared the bedroom with Matt, sleeping against the opposite wall, but he claimed he never heard any of the arguing

from below. His father's individual words were generally indistinguishable to Matt, but the malicious intent was obvious.
Unable to sleep, he listened with alternating feelings of fear
and anger.

One night, after a particularly loud and vicious fight, Matt
heard the front door slam as his father stalked out. Daniel rolled
over in his sleep at the slamming of the door, but soon a deep
silence settled over the house. Matt listened to the dark, afraid
to move should he miss something. He thought of the first few
seconds after a shotgun blast, how his ears rang with the sudden
absence of sound waves. He listened for his mother. She would
be in the kitchen nook, where she often took breaks from the
household chores to drink a cup of tea. He wondered if she'd
be crying, or flushed with anger, or simply stunned into a cata-
tonic silence.

When the isolation of his thoughts and fears became too
much, he crept out of his room, down the dark, narrow wooden
staircase, to find his mother sitting in profile in the kitchen,
her chair tucked in, hands folded in front of her on the table. A
low-watt bulb over the stove emitted a meager glow, casting a
dark shadow across her face. For a long moment he stood in the
kitchen doorway, wondering if she could be praying. Then she
turned to look at him, and at first her dry eyes were a relief,
until he understood her shell-shocked expression of despair. He
felt his own tears then, and she reached out a hand to her son.

At six years old, Matt considered himself too big and old
for coddling, but he sat on her lap that night anyway. They
didn't speak for a long time, until finally his mother said,
"Matthew." It wasn't uttered as a question, but rather as a state-
ment, and Matt thought he must have misunderstood. Pulling
back to look at her, he was surprised to see that she still wasn't
crying. She said, "We really got it right when we named you."

Matthew's expression went blank. He had no idea what
she meant, but her tender smile calmed his young nerves, so
that once again he rested his head against her shoulder.

Using a hand to brush hair off his forehead, she said, "In Sunday school classes—remember reading about the disciple Matthew?"

He didn't answer, didn't move from the comfortable closeness of his mother's shoulder.

"Anyway," she continued, "Matthew was a tax collector. Now, back in those days, there were many tax collectors. It was a good job. Steady. And you needed an education, which not too many people had back then."

Matt listened to his mother's soft voice, accompanied by the familiar hum of the refrigerator across the room. He couldn't remember ever hearing about the disciple Matthew, but then, he didn't pay much attention in Sunday school, and he seldom read the Bible at all. It was too grown up and boring. So he couldn't say if his mother's story was a fairy tale she'd made up or not, but sitting in her lap, her soft voice next to his ear, he wished the story and the moment would last a while longer.

She continued, "Jesus picked Matthew to be one of his disciples because he knew a tax collector had to be a smart man. And Matthew had integrity. Do you know what that is?"

Again, Matt didn't answer. He didn't want to know about integrity or the disciples.

"It meant that Matthew was loyal. Jesus would eventually be mistreated and betrayed, but not by the tax collector. Jesus knew that through it all he could rely on Matthew, because he was loyal, honest, and sweet. Just like my little man here." She kissed him on the forehead.

That late-night talk in the little kitchen nook became a defining moment for Matt. So much of his life could be summed up in those few words from his mother. While Daniel spent his whole life escaping from the family and Black Otter Bay, Matt stuck around to help his mother maintain a semblance of order in the household. He wouldn't have called it loyalty. After all, someone had to mow the lawn and shovel the

snow. And later, after the old man died suddenly of heart disease, he taught himself how to replace leaking pipes and to
rewire broken fixtures. Matt didn't see how loyalty had anything to do with it. His mother couldn't fix the car, and Daniel
had been long gone by the time their father died.

Matt spent the summer of his tenth year scraping and re-
painting their small clapboard house. Daniel had proven himself useless for these kinds of jobs, preferring to chase around
the countryside with his pals, and Matt's father spent his time
either driving Euclids down at the taconite plant or lugging an
auxiliary oxygen tank for his emphysema around the house.
One morning, the town woke up to some new artwork.

Situated somewhat precariously on the face of the ridge
behind town, a huge wooden water tower boldly proclaimed
this to be the realm of BLACK OTTER BAY. In bright blue paint,
someone had added the word SUCKS. From a distance, the blue
paint blended in nicely with the black block letters on the
tower, so it took a couple of days for someone to comment that
the blue paint matched the new trim on the Simon house.

When Marlon Fastwater, just a part-time cop in town at
the time, stopped by to ask Matthew's father about the artwork,
even the old man knew his youngest son couldn't be responsible. By the end of the summer, Daniel had enlisted in the U.S.
Army, and he never looked back.

After his discharge, he worked the fishing fleets in Alaska
for a few years, about as far from Black Otter Bay as he could
get. He still came through town every two or three years. Each
visit would usually find him accompanied by a different woman.
He'd stay just long enough for the walls of the small town to
close in on him, long enough to attract the attention of Sheriff
Fastwater again. Then, without a parting word to anyone, he'd
be gone, just like the first time he'd left to join the army.

But the comings and goings of his brother meant very little to Matthew. They'd never been close due to the eight-year
gap in their ages, as well as the distinct differences in their per-

sonalities. In truth, he seldom considered his brother's welfare at all. If he had been the type to contemplate such things, he may have wondered why he gave so little thought to his own brother, but cared so deeply for these two children in his life.

Ben sat at Matthew's left hand, poking a fork at the mountain of taco goulash piled on his plate. Matt had suspected that something was wrong ever since the kids came home from school, and his suspicions were confirmed when the pile of food on Ben's plate didn't get any smaller.

"Not hungry tonight, Ben?" he asked.

"I guess not."

"Is everything okay?"

Ben looked at his sister before responding. "I'm just tired."

"I've never seen you too tired to eat taco goulash."

Abby spoke up. "I think we're just sick of school, and anxious for summer vacation."

Matt nodded while giving his daughter a long look. He'd noticed her reticence this evening, too, but had no idea how to get words out of her. To his way of thinking, there were events in a young woman's life of which a man his age had no concept. He certainly had no words for them.

His own childhood experiences had done nothing to prepare him for talking to his children in a meaningful way. On the other hand, he knew all about the confusion and fear that could dominate a young person's life. So, despite his inability to tell his children how much he loved them, and even though he couldn't get past the awkwardness of consoling them with hugs, he had determined from the outset to provide them a childhood free of fear and apprehension.

To Matt's practical way of thinking, it made sense that a parent should attempt to recreate the best aspects of his own childhood for his children. But there hadn't been much for him to borrow from his past. The old man had worked hard at the taconite plant, and provided good food and shelter for his family, even though Matt figured his father probably kept working just to stay away from the house most days. But Matt followed his father's footsteps down to the plant anyway, went to work every day, and provided a security for his children that they probably didn't understand right now, but would hopefully appreciate someday.

The other thing he'd borrowed from his childhood was this tradition of sitting down to dinner together. Even though his own experiences with it had been brutal, his pragmatic view was that the concept was sound. And with Ben and Abby's eager participation, dinnertime had become a highlight of Matt's day.

"It's my turn to cook tomorrow, right?" he asked.

Abby nodded.

"I'm planning to dig the grill out of the shed out back. It's time we get our summer going, don't you think?" He looked from daughter to son, but got no response. "Any requests for the first barbeque of the season?" He felt a little foolish putting so much enthusiasm in his voice. "Come on, someone must have an idea."

"Cheeseburgers," Abby finally said.

"Cheeseburgers. Good call, Abby. How about you, Ben? Any requests?"

"Cheeseburgers are good."

Looking at his son, Matt remembered last fall when Ben had found himself in some trouble in art class. The teacher had positioned herself on the edge of her desk, a book in her hands, reading to the class. The assignment had been for the students to draw a portrait of her as she read. They could use any style they wanted, from classical to cartoon. As far as she was concerned, they could put devil horns on her head or give her three eyes. The only requirement was that they couldn't show their drawings to each other while she read. They were to maintain silence and pay attention to the story.

Ben's drawing was really very good, Matt thought, except that he'd made his teacher's eyes crossed and the book in her

hands upside down. A classmate across the aisle saw Ben's picture and giggled out loud. Then others began looking and snorting, until the small cluster of students attracted the teacher's
attention. She pointed out to the whole class how Ben had
failed to follow instructions. Then she held his drawing up for
everyone to see, and the roomful of laughter added further to
his embarrassment.

A note had been sent home, accompanied by the picture.
It didn't help matters when Matt burst out laughing, too. The
note requested his suggestions for a suitable punishment. He
replied that he saw no need for any punishment at all. Further,
he added that his son should get an A on the assignment for
such a well-crafted, perfectly proportioned drawing. And if the
teacher didn't agree with him, he'd be happy to stop by to discuss it with her.

Ultimately, nothing more came of the incident, other than
Ben moping around the house for a couple of days. The drawing hung on the refrigerator until almost Christmas, when it
suddenly disappeared. Matt knew things like that happened in
a young boy's life, and a few days of embarrassed silence was
an acceptable outcome. Maybe that's all this was now. But then,
why was Abby acting so strange, too?

He looked across the table at his daughter. Whenever he
looked into her glittering dark eyes, pondered her thick black
hair and spotless, fair complexion, he hardly dared to believe
that this beautiful child was a part of him. People always remarked at how much she looked like him, and he agreed as far
as the fact that they both had black hair, large dark eyes, and
fair complexions. But whereas these things were a simple de-
scription of his looks, on Abby they came together to form
beautiful lines and exquisite features. She was growing up fast,
and soon she'd have her own trials and predicaments to deal
with. Matt knew he wouldn't have the words to help her
through it; a girl needed her mother for those things. That's
why he'd tried so hard to keep communications open with his

ex-wife, Jackie. Looking ahead, he'd admit that these mysterious adolescent years were going to be too much for him to handle alone. But Jackie had drifted farther and farther away, until the children hardly saw their mother at all anymore, and rarely even asked about her. So, while Matt diligently performed his duties as household provider, the role of parental confidante came to him about as easily as a foreign language on an alien planet. For that reason, he'd decided that if Jackie couldn't be there for her daughter, he'd ask Marcy to talk to Abby. She was great with the kids, and she'd do anything to help. She'd even been their babysitter at one time. But whenever he tried to see her, like today at the café, people surrounded her, and there was no way he could talk to her about Abby in front of others.

On the other hand, Abby had been his fishing buddy ever since day one. She'd ridden on his chest in a homemade sling while he walked the North Shore streams casting for steelhead trout. She rode along quietly for hours, her bright-eyed stare following ripples in the current, as if watching fish below the surface. When he'd hold up a thrashing trout for her, she'd giggle and poke at it. Even more than her brother, Abby begged her way in on every fishing excursion that came along. And now he hoped that passion could be his ticket out of this dilemma.

Reaching for the spoon in the taco goulash, he said, "I've been thinking about that lost fishing trip last weekend." He flicked a glance at both kids, but their eyes remained focused on their plates. Carefully, he scooped a second helping, then reached for the dinner rolls. "It seems that warmer weather is finally here. The lakes are opening up. If you don't have plans for the weekend yet, how about we wet a line? Maybe set up camp somewhere. You guys pick the lake. What do you say?"

Ben prodded his mound of goulash, but Abby sat back, eyeing her father. Matt could see the wheels turning. She'd never walked away from a fishing trip in her life, but she'd never been this age before, either—an age where fishing with your father would take a backseat to just about anything on her social calendar.

"What do you think, Abby?" he asked. "Can you get away for the weekend to try out that new fishing rod of yours?"

Her reply surprised him. "I vote we stay mobile. Maybe set up camp out by Lake Oja." Ben's head popped up, and Matt thought he looked as surprised at her response as he was. Abby explained, "That way, if the walleyes aren't biting, we can run over to Big Island. If nothing else, I bet the rainbows are active."

Matt had to smile. He never should have doubted her. She even had a plan. He said, "Well, how about Friday night, then? We'll drive up to Oja, set up camp, and get out on the water first thing in the morning."

"Ben and I'll dig some worms out of the compost," Abby offered. "We can stop by Rosie's Friday night for minnows."

By now, Matt was almost laughing. "What makes you think the compost will be thawed out? The frost only came out of the ground this week."

"Oh, the compost will be fine," she replied, as if she'd already been digging in it. "But if it isn't, I'd rather use minnows this time of year anyway."

Matt nodded. Turning to his son, he asked, "How about you, Ben? Are you in?"

It took a moment for Ben to look away from his sister, but then he shrugged and mumbled, "Sure. I guess so."

"Good, then. It's a plan." They discussed the details a bit longer, with Matt gratified to see some animation returning to Abby's face. Whatever had been on her mind had either been resolved or put away for the time being.

"You're on clean-up tonight, right, Abby?" he asked. "I have a union meeting, and I'll probably be out late. Round two of our cribbage tournament is after the meeting. Will you guys be okay here alone?"

"Of course," Abby said. "How late you going to be?"

"Probably after dark. You can stay up if you want. But have all your chores done." He looked at Ben. "You have any homework for tomorrow?"

The question seemed to catch him off guard. He looked at his father like he hadn't understood a word he'd said. Matt stood up, stacking dishes for a trip to the kitchen sink. "Go through your backpack, Ben," he said. "I'll check with you when I get home to see that your schoolwork is ready. Okay?"

Ben nodded, and Matt carried his load to the kitchen. When he returned, the children were clearing the rest of the table. "I'll see you later tonight, then," he said, passing through the room toward the front door. "If you need me, I'll be up at the Hall."

"Dad," Abby called after him. "Try to remember, you don't cut the cards in cribbage. That's poker."

Matt laughed. "You just get your fishing gear ready. I'm collecting a buck from each of you for first fish and biggest fish."

"You're on."

FOUR

Abby Simon

"You're crazy," Ben said when they were alone in the kitchen. "Did you forget that you no longer have a new fishing rod? And that I don't have any homework, or even a backpack anymore?"

"I'm going to fix all that," Abby replied, stashing leftover goulash in the refrigerator.

"When?"

"Can you do the dishes for me?"

Ben looked at his sister, dumbfounded. "You really are crazy. You're going back up there, aren't you?"

"The timing is perfect. It doesn't get dark until ten o'clock this time of year." She looked at the old round-faced clock above the sink. "That's a good four hours from now. If I cut straight up over the ridge, I can make the round trip in less than three hours."

"There's a dead person up there, Abby, remember?"

"I know. But our backpacks are up there, too. I'll be back before Dad gets home."

"I'm not staying here alone, Abby. I'm going with you."

"No. Absolutely not." Retrieving her Minnesota Twins cap from the hook at the back door, she fed her braid through the adjustable strap at the back, placed the cap on her head, then tightened up the rubber band securing the end of her braid.

"You can't carry both backpacks," Ben argued. His eyes strayed past his sister, through the kitchen doorway to the empty expanse of dining room beyond. Color dissolved from his cheeks as he looked into the deserted space.

"Come on, Ben. It's just a couple hours. Turn on the TV. I'll be back before dark."

"But we saw a dead body, Abby. And that big man carrying it over his shoulders."

"None of that concerns us. The only things I'm worried about are that stupid fishing pole of mine and our backpacks. We have to go to school tomorrow."

"But you almost got caught by that bad guy. What if he's still up there?"

Abby closed a cupboard door and looked at her brother. He seemed so young and vulnerable standing at the sink, hands hanging at his sides, fingers twitching with apprehension. "He won't be up there now, Ben. There's nothing to worry about. I'm just going to grab our backpacks and get out of there." She could see her words weren't having any effect on her brother, so she walked over to him and rested her hands on his shoulders. Looking into his eyes, she said, "The guy was some kind of city slicker. Did you see his big shiny car and fancy clothes? I'm sure he's long gone by now, but if not, he'll be keeping to the road, in his car. I'll be in the woods. Our paths won't ever cross. Besides, do you know anyone that can outrun me in the woods?"

She took his lack of response as a positive sign. "It'll be totally safe, Ben. Honest."

"I'm coming, too."

"No you're not." Looking at the dishes in the sink, another idea occurred to her. "Do the dishes for me tonight, and I'll take your turn for the rest of the month."

Ultimately, before Abby charged out the back door and into the woods behind their house, Ben had negotiated away not only his clean-up duties for the month, but his cooking chores as well.

Ten minutes after Abby left, there was a knock at the front door.

• • • • •

The ridge running along the backside of Black Otter Bay was no trifling little hill. Rising several hundred feet above the shoreline of Lake Superior, it boasted a steep craggy face with huge bedrock boulder outcroppings, as well as knarly old white cedars that had taken up residence there about the time of the signing of the Declaration of Independence.

Deer trails zigzagged the slope, although not too many animals chose to travel over this treacherous stretch. The Moose Lake Road cut over the ridge where it wound up from Highway 61 about a half-mile outside of town, but for someone on foot, and in a hurry, the ridge provided the quickest access to the lake district inland from Lake Superior. An old black bear might occasionally den up for the winter on this slope facing away from the prevailing Canadian northwesterlies, and the howling of wolves could often be heard in town when they hunted the ridgeline. But neither of these things worried Abby, even now with the sun behind the crest of the ridge and shadows growing longer by the minute. In a way, this wilderness remnant of the ancient Sawtooth Mountains represented home to her. She knew their geologic history, the habits of the wild creatures that lived here, and many of the plants and trees, including their useful attributes.

Over the top of the ridge she angled along an old animal path that soon intersected the Superior Hiking Trail. Roughly following the spine of the old mountain range, day hikers, as well as more serious long distance backpackers, used this trail all summer long. In the winter, cross-country skiers and snowshoers kept the trail open. Abby remembered hiking here as a young girl, exploring the woodlands behind their house with her father. One time, he'd cut across to the Trail while Abby stayed on the animal path. Looking back at her, he'd called, "I'll race you, Abby. Up to where the trails meet."

She took off running, her short little seven-year-old legs kicking out hard on the dirt track. Off to the side, she saw her father swinging his arms in an exaggerated fashion, showing off how fast he could run. But at the last instant she darted ahead of him to win the race.

Abby bragged about her victory for days, and couldn't understand why her schoolmates didn't see the wonder of it. Even her mother hadn't made much of a fuss over it. Of course, now she knew that her father couldn't have lost that race without letting her win. But at seven years old, she'd been convinced that she was easily the fastest creature in the woods.

And Abby still loved to run the forest paths. Even now, whenever the trail headed downhill, it was virtually impossible to keep from breaking into a run. So when she picked up the Big Island Lake Trail where it sloped away from the Superior Hiking Trail, she set a quick jogging pace for herself and let her mind wander.

Remembering that footrace with her father brought up images of her mother. Jackie Simon had never been the type to spend time in the woods. She'd gone camping with them a few times when Abby was very young, but at some point she'd given it up, and as mean as it may have been to even think about in private, Abby had to admit that camping was a lot more fun without her. Jackie always complained: it was too cold, or it rained too much, or the mosquitoes were going to eat her alive. The last time she'd gone with them, probably two or three years ago, she'd thrown her dinner into the campfire, exclaiming, "This is disgusting!"

Abby remembered getting mad about it, because she and Ben had worked hard to keep the fire going in the damp woods. And Ben had been just a little kid then. Stick by stick they'd built up the campfire, both of them getting soaked as they ranged far out from the campsite to find dry tinder under blowdowns or at the base of rocky outcroppings. But she'd felt especially bad for her father, the designated cook for these excursions. Dinner had been a freeze-dried stroganoff dish, but with a fire that was either too large and hot, or threatening to die out at any moment, the meat had been a little tough and the pasta undercooked. But, hey, Abby conceded, that's what

happened sometimes in the woods. As far as she was concerned, after portaging the canoe, fishing all day, and tending
to the campfire, she could have eaten the food straight out of
the vacuum-sealed pouch.

A day trip to the mall down in Duluth was a whole different matter for Jackie. She had a knack for finding the best
deals, just as Abby knew how to find fish in any given lake.
And while Abby could cast a lure all day, Jackie somehow
found the stamina to walk through dozens of shops while wearing high heels, taking breaks in trendy coffee shops, seemingly
able to reenergize herself off the artificial lights, or perhaps the
thrill of the hunt for a good deal. The trouble was that the rest
of the family had no interest in driving fifty miles to Duluth
just to go shopping with her. One time, Abby overheard her father say, "If I wanted to spend my free time hanging out in the
mall, I'd live in Duluth, or better yet, down in the Cities, where
they have that monster Mall of America place."

When Abby's mother discovered the casinos, however,
small-town Minnesota quickly lost whatever appeal it may
have had for her. Flashing lights, plush surroundings, and piles
of money—Jackie had finally found her true home.

Abby tried to be open-minded about her mother's decision
to leave, but she'd come to understand that sometimes a person's head and heart could have differing opinions. Last Au-
gust, for her thirteenth birthday, Abby's father took her on a
thirteen-day canoe trip into the Boundary Waters Canoe Area.
Every summer they went camping together, just the two of
them, each year venturing farther into the wilderness. With
every passing year they added one day to the trip in honor of
another birthday. Last year, they'd traveled well up into
Quetico Provincial Park in Canada. Jackie had moved out a few
months prior to the trip, and Abby's initial sadness had recently
been replaced by a simmering anger.

Looking back on last summer's canoe trip, she had to give
her father his due. He wasn't much for talking about himself

or sharing feelings, but in his taciturn, modest sort of way he'd attempted to reach a hand out to his daughter. Sitting by a campfire next to a nameless lake in the far north country late one night, their tent in the shadows behind them and the moon reflecting off the water before them, her father explained to her how the energy of the city called to Abby's mother.

"You know that your mother grew up in Chicago, right?" he'd said. "She's got that big-city blood in her, just like the mysteries of these deep, cold lakes course through you." Abby had liked that image, and the idea that she could somehow be related to this incredible wilderness.

"Your mother was actually pretty excited about moving up here when we first got married. I think she had some notion about how it would be. You know, like one of those Norman Rockwell paintings. I think she looked forward to a slower pace, and raising a family far away from gangs and violence."

Abby sat on a rock next to the campfire, poking at the flames with a long stick. She found it thrilling, and somewhat intimidating, to be having this grown-up conversation. She'd only just become a teenager, and it seemed like a whole world of adult emotions and passions was already opening up to her. She didn't dare speak for fear of sounding like the child she still felt herself to be.

"I'd say your mother knew that Black Otter Bay wouldn't work for her even before you were born. There's not much privacy in a small town. But you have to give her credit. She did try. Remember how she went fishing with us? And camping, too."

"Oh, sure," Abby pouted. "It was like babysitting the whole time."

Her father laughed. "But think about it. What if you suddenly found yourself living in Chicago? How would you feel about riding a crowded subway with all those strangers, or going to school in the city with thousands of other kids? It would be kind of frightening, wouldn't it?"

"I guess so," she replied.

"Well, your mother did it. She thrived on it, just like you thrive on a run through the woods."

"But she wanted to live here," Abby argued. "And then she didn't. It's not fair. Once you decide, you should stick to it."

"It's not always that easy. Sometimes people make mistakes. You wouldn't want her to stay here if she was unhappy, would you?"

Abby considered her father's words in silence for a while, until she realized that just thinking and talking about her mother made her angrier. She threw the poker stick into the fire, stood up, and stalked off down to the shoreline. Over her shoulder, she said, "Isn't it more unfair for her to make all three of us unhappy?"

Tears had threatened to erupt, but in the dark, gazing out over the placid lake, she managed to blink them back. Now, as she ran the Big Island Lake Trail, she let the tears roll. Letting her frustration push her even harder, she wondered aloud, "How can it be that I miss her so much when she makes me so mad?"

It was her mother's relationship with Randall Bengston that Abby had the hardest time justifying. With long, wispy, thin hair and shifty eyes, he gave Abby the creeps. Randall's mother, Rosie, owned the bait shop, but he had no interest in the business or small-town life. Jackie had found a kindred spirit in Randall. The lure of the city called to both of them, and when Jackie left Black Otter Bay for good, the two of them took up together in a small apartment on the eastern edge of downtown Duluth. Abby and Ben had spent a couple days with her after she was settled in, but they had no interest in going back. They saw their mother when she came home to visit, but she didn't make the trip up here much anymore. It was probably like her father said, Abby thought: Jackie didn't want to spend time in a tiny, rural town any more than Abby wanted to visit the big city.

Randall held minor financial interests in several small businesses in Duluth. He wore flashy suits, drove a small sports car, and Abby thought he strutted around like one of those hyperactive little dogs, a cockapoo or whatever they called them. If the man ever had to do an honest day's work, like her father did down at the taconite plant, it would kill him. Randall owned an art gallery, known as The Tempest, in the East End of Duluth. Jackie worked for him, dressing up in tailored business suits, greeting customers and, after getting to know them, showing select pieces she thought would be of interest to them. The prestige of her position appealed to her. The clientele was generally older and affluent, and Jackie's graceful bearing and knowledgeable conversation suited the job perfectly.

By night, she worked the dollar slot machines in the downtown casino. Recently, Abby had overheard some troubling talk about her mother. Rumor had it that she owed the casino money. She might even have a gambling problem. Her father wouldn't acknowledge the rumors, wouldn't discuss it with Abby at all, other than the one time when he'd said, "It's just a bunch of mean-spirited people saying these things. Don't you believe them."

Mean-spirited? Abby thought. Her own classmates were the ones doing the talking. When she considered her mother's behavior, she preferred to think of her as being temporarily insane. She'd come to her senses sooner or later. And Abby really didn't care what her friends said. She wasn't embarrassed about her mother leaving, but if she ever came home, she had some serious explaining to do.

Abby's pace never faltered as she covered the distance to Big Island Lake. Sure-footed and determined, she ran lightly, her thoughts carrying her past the burning in her lungs and the ache in her thighs. It helped that it was lighter on this western side of the ridge. There was more animal sign, too, and at one point she spotted a pileated woodpecker in its undulating flight through the woods. Deer tracks littered the forest floor, especially now with the snow gone and everything wet and muddy.

Dropping down off the hillside, Abby noted a large opening in the foliage ahead. It wasn't so much that she could see through the trees into the clearing, as that the existence of the opening was apparent to someone used to looking for such things. And an opening that large in this country signified one of two things: the site of recent logging operations or the pres-ence of a lake. Quickly scanning the terrain, Abby estimated her location. The abandoned road leading to the boat landing and Rosie's minnow seines wound in off the county highway about a quarter mile from the base of the hill. The trail she was on would take her to the iced-in side of the lake where she and Ben had first come this morning.

There wasn't much underbrush this early in the season, so after plotting an imaginary line through the woods, Abby jumped off the trail on a heading to cross the old roadway. Within minutes, patches of blue water flashed through the trees. The sun had dropped a bit but was still a long way from setting, and bright reflections off the water flickered through the early summer foliage.

To be on the safe side, when Abby came to the roadway, she followed it from just inside the treeline. She didn't expect to see anyone at this hour, but considering the events they'd witnessed that afternoon, there was no sense in taking chances.

Through a series of short curves, the overgrown roadway led Abby to the old boat landing. As she'd expected, no one was there. She paused for a moment at the water's edge to catch her breath. Scanning the lake surface, she saw that much of the ice had disappeared over the afternoon, with the remaining floes a dark gray and mottled with holes and standing water. Abby stood on the spot where the big fancy car had parked. Looking at the ground around her, it seemed as though the gravel and weeds were more disturbed than the passing of one car would warrant. Then she remembered the second vehicle approaching as she'd made her escape, the pickup truck she'd glimpsed through the trees. Studying the tracks, she wondered if the ground could have been dug up this much by just the two ve-hicles turning around in the small clearing. Finally shrugging off the mystery, Abby took another deep breath, and then turned into the brush to retrieve the backpacks.

Fifteen minutes later, she still searched. Nothing. Everything was as she remembered, except their belongings were gone. She even got on her knees at the exact spot where they'd first noticed the car. She found where the backpacks had been, where they'd started eating their lunches. Nothing. At the water's edge, she stood where they'd fished, looked back at the spot on the grassy bank where Ben had kept the fish wet. But other than a few places where the brush had been disturbed, a person could easily have thought that no one had been here since last fall.

Then she remembered the trout they'd caught. Scrambling along the shore, she came to the spot where she'd stored the freezer bag of fish. The anchoring rock was there, but no bag. She considered the notion of a bear wandering in and stealing the backpacks. And the nose of a bruin would have easily detected the bag of fish. But as she studied the vacant space at her feet, Abby's heart suddenly began pounding again. This time it had nothing to do with the run through the woods. In the mud next to her tennis shoe, she spotted the print of a large boot. Squatting for a closer look, even in her relative inexperience she could see that the impression had been made by a big man. Next to her own footprint, the indentation was huge and deep. It was smooth-soled, like a dress shoe, a style the big man in the fancy car would have been wearing.

Abby grunted in bewilderment, then hurried along the shoreline searching for any sign of their belongings. Her thoughts went to hip waders, how every pair she'd ever seen had thick-lugged soles. The man must have removed them, she decided, before searching the area. Scrambling back to the open boat landing, Abby stood still long enough to take a deep breath. She looked back up the road behind her, and out over the lake. The breeze had died down, making for a peaceful stillness at this early evening hour, but to Abby, the silence echoed with mystery. Things had happened here after her hurried departure earlier today, events with no witnesses. Big Island could have told her a few things if it could talk, or those loons calling back and forth to each other.

She wondered why the man had taken all their gear. There was nothing in the backpacks to interest a grown man. He'd even taken that stupid fishing pole, and the freezer bag of small rainbow trout. He'd taken everything, including their notebooks containing their names and address.

That was the factor that turned Abby aboutface and thrust her at a full run up the road. The man knew who they were. He knew where they lived. Ben was home alone, counting on her to fix this whole mess. She angled off the road into the woods, ducking branches, hurdling puddles and deadfalls, racing for home. Her mind whirled with fears and questions. What would the man do with the information? What could he do? They hadn't done anything wrong. He was the bad guy. She barely noticed the animal tracks she crossed, didn't really hear the ravens calling to roost above her, and ran right past a pair of white-tailed does watching her from under a copse of cedars.

Over the ridgetop she climbed, huffing, breathing deep gulps of fresh air. Lake Superior spread out to the horizon before her. A few rooftops in town became visible far down below. Barely able to check her flying descent, Abby dropped down the face of the ridge, grabbing tree branches along the way, using her knees as shock absorbers, all the way to the familiar landscape behind town and, finally, to the back door of their house.

"Ben?" she called. "Ben!"

Through the kitchen she ran, noticing the sink still full of dishes, and into the front room and the staircase to the bedrooms upstairs. "Ben?" she called, before leaping two and three steps at a time. By now it was apparent that her brother wasn't home. The rooms had a silent, vacant feel to them. "Where are you, Ben?" she called in desperation, as if by a strength of will she could make him be home.

Back downstairs. They always left notes for each other near the cordless telephone on the kitchen table. Nothing. Then she ran through the front room again, abruptly stopping in the front entryway. Their backpacks sat side by side on the floor inside the front door. Abby slowly approached, then squatted to inspect them. All her things seemed to be present: notebooks, pencils, books, even the plastic container of worms from the compost pile. Stuck behind her backpack was the telescoping fishing rod.

From her crouching position she contemplated the sudden appearance of their belongings until the phone rang behind her, causing her to cry out and nearly fall over. Lunging back through the house again, she grabbed the phone on the second ring. "Ben? Ben, is that you?"

Silence on the line, then a man's voice, deep and steady. "Hello, Abigail."

No one called her Abigail. It wasn't even her real name. She'd seen her birth certificate; her given name was Abby. Timidly, she asked, "Who's this?"

"I think you know who it is," the voice said.

"What do you want? Where is my brother?"

"Whoa, Abigail. Slow down. I thought perhaps you'd appreciate an opportunity to thank me for returning your school supplies."

Abby was getting mad. "What have you done with Ben?"

"Your little brother is just fine. And if you listen closely to me, he'll stay that way."

"He doesn't know anything. I'm the one you want."

"That's what I thought, too, Abigail. When I returned your belongings, I intended to have this discussion with you. But Ben said you weren't home, so I had to improvise. I think this new arrangement will work well, though. Ben's a nice boy, Abigail."

"Where is he? You better bring him home. When my dad finds out—"

"Abigail, please listen to me. Your brother is fine."

"Where is he!" she demanded, so mad that she stamped her foot on the kitchen floor.

Silence on the line again, then the voice. "Take a look out your front window, Abigail. You'll see that your brother is just fine."

Abby jogged back through the house, afraid of what she'd find outside. Pulling the front door open, she looked through the storm door window to see the big luxury car parked across the street. The man sat behind the wheel, cell phone at his ear. Darkened glass made it difficult to see, but she spotted Ben's head rising up in the backseat window. He looked so tiny and vulnerable, especially compared to the big man at the steering wheel. Another figure sat on the far side of Ben, but she couldn't make out anything of his appearance.

Ben's eyes, wide and round and scared, focused on Abby. From the phone she heard the man's voice. "Abigail."

When Ben slowly dropped out of sight again, Abby's heart rose up in her throat. But when she saw the figure next to Ben struggling to push him down in the seat, she lost her composure completely.

"Abigail."

The storm door flew open, the telephone crashed on the steps, and Abby exploded out of the front door. She ran at the car as hard as she could, heard muffled yelling from the driver, noticed frantic scrambling around inside, but before she even reached the edge of the yard, the car shot off down the street. She chased it a little way, until it turned the corner and headed south out of town on Highway 61.

Abby's adrenaline surge quickly dissipated. Walking back to the house, she used her lingering anger to scold herself. *Stupid! Stupid! Stupid!* Now Ben was gone for good. She'd blown what little chance she'd had to bring him home.

The only other house on the street was the Soderstrom place. No lights were on there, no one to witness her chasing an out-of-town car down the street. Marcy's parents were still in Arizona, and Marcy was probably down at the bar shooting a game of pool before going to bed. She'd have to be up early tomorrow to open the café.

Upon returning to the front door, Abby spied the discarded telephone lying in the grass. It began ringing, even with the back cover knocked off and the battery hanging out on its wire. "Hello?" she said, cupping the insides in her free hand.

"That was not the sort of behavior I expected out of you," the man said.

"Bring my brother home. He didn't do anything to you."

"That's just what we need to talk about, Abigail. If you can control yourself, I promise that no harm will come to him."

Abby went in the house, shut the door, took a seat in her father's chair, and watched the street out front. "What do you want?" she asked.

"It's really very simple, Abigail. You keep your mouth shut. You don't say anything to anyone about what you saw today. Can you do that?"

Abby didn't reply. All her strength was gone. She slouched in the chair, exhausted and discouraged. The telephone battery dangled against her shoulder.

The man said, "If you keep your end of the deal, Ben will come home in a few weeks."

Still no response from Abby.

"Do we have us a deal, Abigail?"

Abby finally found her voice. "When will he come home?"

"Probably six weeks or so. Fourth of July at the latest. Won't that be cause for a big celebration?"

"Why six weeks?"

"Do we have an agreement?"

"I don't know anything, anyway," she said.

"So there's no reason to discuss what you don't know. Not one word to anyone. Even this phone call. If anyone asks, it was a wrong number. Deal?"

Abby found it hard to think. The day had been too long. All she wanted was to crawl into bed, wake up tomorrow, and discover that this was all a bad dream.

"Abigail?"

"Okay. It's a deal." Silence on the line again. "Just don't hurt my little brother," she added, before realizing the line had been disconnected.

• • • • •

When her father came home half an hour later, Abby still sat in the chair. She looked at him, a solemn expression forcing the corners of his mouth to turn down. Matt switched on the entryway light and went to his daughter. "Why are you sitting here in the dark, Abby?"

She sat forward in the recliner. "Dad?"

"Listen, sweetheart," he said. "I'm afraid I have some bad news."

His words draped a mask of confusion over her face. How did he know?

"We just got word up at the Hall. It's your friend, Rosie. You know, from the bait shop? She drowned today working her minnow seines."

Abby shook her head. "Dad?"

"You know how high the water is now that the ice went out. And Rosie was really old. She shouldn't have been out in the cold water like that."

"Dad? Listen to me."

"Most of the rocks are still ice covered. It was just an unfortunate—"

"Dad!"

Matthew paused, seemed to actually see his daughter for the first time. Saw the disemboweled phone in her lap. "What is it, honey?"

"Ben's gone, Dad. Ben's gone."

FIVE

Mrs. Virginia Bean

The United States Post Office in Black Otter Bay sat about forty yards back from the curbing on Main Street near the center of town. Main Street was simply a narrowed stretch of Highway 61 where it passed through the city limits. The shoulder of the old highway in front of the post office had been converted into half a dozen angled parking slots for customers, with a series of five flag poles lining the front of the property. Every morning at six o'clock Mrs. Virginia Bean, the postmistress, raised the United States flag on the tallest, center pole. On days when the weather wasn't too disagreeable, she ran a Minnesota state flag up one of the other poles and a black-and-white POW-MIA flag on another one. After twenty-five years as postmistress, however, she still had no idea what the other two poles were for.

Several years ago, some local hooligans used the two outer poles for their pranks. Arriving for work early in the morning, Mrs. Bean found any number of odd items flapping in the breeze atop one of the poles. Usually, it would be a pair of men's underwear—sometimes long johns, other times briefs. One time, she found a high school letter jacket from Two Rivers, an Iron Range town seventy-five miles inland. She always suspected Daniel Simon to be the instigator, but Mrs. Bean had kept that suspicion to herself. She felt sorry for the Simon family, having to live with that abusive old drunk. Besides, Daniel always charmed her with his devil-may-care smile, while his younger brother Matthew usually tried to fix things by coming down to retrieve the fluttering garments.

Now, Mrs. Bean was no prude, but the morning she spotted the black lace bra and panties dangling high above the post office, she decided it had gone far enough. She cut the ropes off the two outer poles and posted a sign on them warning against vandalizing federal property. That was the end to the high-flying underwear, but she never knew if it ended because of her warnings or because Daniel Simon enlisted in the army.

The post office building itself was easily the ugliest building in Black Otter Bay. For years, Mrs. Bean had pleaded with post office headquarters in Duluth to do something about the rotting siding, sagging eaves, and mouse and chipmunk holes in the trim work. Finally, two years ago, a pallet of five-gallon buckets of paint and supplies arrived on the morning dispatch mail truck. Mrs. Bean advertised for volunteers to help repair, prime, and paint the post office, but, after inspecting the provisions, none of the local professionals would help. If they were going to volunteer their services, they said, the project should at least be suitable for a reference. In their opinion, attaching their names to this job could even hurt their reputations.

The problem was that the paint had been requisitioned through the federal government from Fort Ripley, 150 miles southwest of town, and consisted of three discontinued camouflage colors from the Vietnam War era. When the military's current color schemes went toward the desert hues of the Middle East, the forty-year-old jungle colors became obsolete. Sheriff Marlon Fastwater and his nephew finally came forward to help, spending much of their free time that summer working on the building. It was Leonard Fastwater who came up with the idea of mixing two of the three colors, providing over twenty gallons of paint for the siding, enough for two coats. The end result for the post office was that it now boasted a two-tone color scheme: a blended pea soup green siding with an olive drab trim.

For that reason, Mrs. Bean thought it a blessing that the building sat so far back on the property. Most of the other buildings in town were rough-sawn cedar-clad storefronts, or solid brick and stone edifices. When Red Tollefson heard about the paint fiasco, he joked that they had the only camouflaged post office in the state. "Folks driving through town won't even see it. It blends right into the woods behind it on the ridge."

On the Saturday morning three days after eight-year-old Ben Simon went missing, Mrs. Virginia Bean fed slab wood into the post office's barrel stove. It already radiated enough heat to warm the whole town, but she liked it hot. Over the top of the freestanding woodstove, she glanced at Sheriff Fastwater sitting next to her desk. Aligned in profile to her, one of his arms dangled at his side to scratch the ears of his dog, Gitch. A mixed-breed husky with plenty of malamute blood accounting for his formidable size, Gitchie Gami derived his name from the Ojibwe words for Lake Superior. Gentle by nature, yet ferociously loyal and protective of the sheriff, Gitch was known around the countryside for a unique physical trait: one of his eyes was a startling, opaque blue.

"Like shards of ice on the big lake," the sheriff had told her once.

Mrs. Bean always made Gitch welcome on his visits. She kept a stash of dog biscuits in a desk drawer, and a heavy ceramic bowl for water on the floor. For his part, Gitch exuberantly greeted her with a ninety-pound nuzzle, then made himself at home on the braided rug she provided next to her desk.

Over the last few years, the two of them had been stopping in almost every day. Mrs. Bean enjoyed the visits, and considered the sheriff to be one of the kindest men she'd ever met. For all his lack of words, she thought he communicated the sincerest forms of friendship. His late Monday afternoon visits, for example, delivered a much-needed boost to her morale, as well as dinner at the end of a long shift. Other than the day after a holiday, Mondays were the heaviest, busiest days in the post office. Years ago, the sheriff noticed how stressful the first day of the week was for her, and started bringing in dinner to

give her a break. At first, he'd share a pizza with her, or a take-
out sandwich from the café. Soon, he began bringing his own
homemade dinners: a grouse and wild rice soup, or venison
stew. For her part, Mrs. Bean hid a small set of dishes and sil-
verware in a supply cabinet. She even added long-stemmed
wine glasses, with a variety of red and white wines locked in
the bottom drawer of her desk.

This past winter, when daylight faded early, she introduced candles to the Monday evening dinners. She dimmed the
lights by turning off one bank of fluorescents, then covered her
desk with a linen tablecloth. Because Black Otter Bay was a
rural branch office, she wasn't required to wear a uniform, so
Mondays often found her in a floral print dress. Jewelry suddenly appeared at the end of the workday. Mrs. Bean's whole
countenance lit up with the arrival of her two friends, and the
dinner candles enhanced the delighted glow in her blue eyes.

On the other hand, Saturday represented a half-day of
work for Mrs. Bean, and, like today, the sheriff often stopped
in early to share a thermos of coffee from the café. She closed
and latched the doors on the woodstove, straightened up, then
brushed slivers of kindling off the front of her dress. Gitch was
sprawled out full length on the rug, his body tucked up tight
against the sheriff's boots. Mrs. Bean's blue eyes picked up the
black in her sweater, giving them an almost violet shimmer.
She planned to attend the memorial service for Rose Bengston
after work, so she'd avoided her usual bright colors for a modest
black shift and sweater. She wished she had the appropriate
words to comfort the sheriff. He was under enormous pressure,
and the sudden death of Rosie only added to his misery.

Fastwater rocked back on the rear legs of the chair, rolling
up his sleeves. As Mrs. Bean returned to her desk, he asked,
"Why do you always have to have a fire going? It's warm outside today."

"Helps my joints loosen up, Marlon," she said, smiling at
the man she felt so much affection for. "You should try handling

all this mail when your knuckles are swollen and your fingers won't bend. I know it's a short day today, but there's still a lot of mail to sort. Besides," she added while taking a seat across from the sheriff, "a good fire in the morning dries all the moisture out of the air. Keeps it cooler in here the rest of the day."

The sheriff knew her words were in no way meant as a rebuke. He looked across the room at the gurneys stacked with trays and tubs of mail, and a larger hamper overflowing with packages. He found it amazing that she could sort all that mail in just a couple short hours. As far as her need for a fire every day, he'd learned early on not to argue with her logic. If a fire somehow kept her cooler, so be it. He figured her reasoning came from her upbringing in eastern Maine. Marlon had never been to that part of the country, but he pictured the North Atlantic coastline as a generally cold, damp place. He imagined the natives there had developed their own techniques for dealing with the climate.

Mrs. Bean's husband had been an ironworker. A ruggedly handsome, virile man, Fred Bean had a gift for gab and a generous, fun-loving spirit. They married one summer after a brief, intense romantic fling. Fred had taken work on the wharves in Eastport, welding and repairing boats in the hard-working fishing fleet. Long days on the job perfected his iron-working skills, and even longer nights carousing around town cemented his image as a man among men. When his reputation suddenly became a little too risky, even by Fred's standards, he whisked his nineteen-year-old bride away from her strict parents and the sober, small-town existence that was rural Maine, to the austere lifestyle and severe weather of northeastern Minnesota. In short, not much changed for the new Mrs. Bean.

Technically, Mrs. Bean wasn't a missus anymore. Fred Bean died in a grisly one-car accident twenty-five years ago. With the construction job in Black Otter Bay completed, he had taken work on the docks in the Duluth harbor, commuting fifty miles back and forth to the jobsite each day. He could have found work in the taconite plant if he'd wanted, but true to his character, he needed to move on, try something new somewhere different. His wife, however, was perfectly content in Black Otter Bay, her new home away from home, especially after being hired on as postmistress. She'd made it clear early on that she had no intention of moving again.

Fred's job in Duluth was often dangerous, welding and repairing steel-girder crane structures high above the harbor. But it paid well, and with pockets full of cash and a spirit as free as the crashing waves beneath him, Fred Bean's drinking binges and carousing exploits took on an almost mythical status. The last episode ended with a call to the volunteer rescue squad in Black Otter Bay. At three o'clock on a Saturday morning, a caller reported taillights glowing in the woods down by Sheppard's Curves on Highway 61. Marlon Fastwater was one of the first to arrive on the scene. It was impossible to say with any certainty whether Fred had passed out at the wheel or simply lost control of the car. There was no question the man had been drunk. In the end, how it came to happen didn't really matter. At ninety miles an hour, the big Cadillac had cut a large swath into the woods, but ultimately it was no match for a three-foot diameter, two-hundred-year-old white pine.

Mrs. Bean had heard the call come in over her home base CB radio. Most nights she left it on for background noise, listening to the conversations of truckers and tourists passing through. Sitting home alone late at night, she appreciated the sound of fellow human voices, and once in a while engaged them in conversation, offering directions or suggesting local points of interest. Of course, Fred's name had never been mentioned over the air that night, but she'd known it was him from the outset, so when the sheriff knocked on her door at dawn, she was dressed and ready for the news.

By the time of Fred's passing, local folklore had him working jobsites across the state, crashing parties in every town from Minneapolis to Thunder Bay, and, among the blue-collar labor force, he'd taken on a Paul Bunyan-like image. For Mrs. Bean's part, however, the teenage infatuation had long since worn off. They'd never had children, and the twenty-five-year-old widow felt no need or inclination to move back east. She had the rocky coastline of Lake Superior here, which reminded her of the best part of her old home in Maine, and her job with the post office provided steady work and benefits. Besides, she felt plugged into the social gridwork of the townsfolk. People stopped in every day to get their mail, and Mrs. Bean had become the clearinghouse for community gossip and rumor.

Ever since her arrival in Black Otter Bay, the locals had known her as Mrs. Virginia Bean. She'd never been too happy with her given name, so the formal title had a new and exotic ring to it. After Fred's death, folks didn't know what to call her. Virginia, or worse yet, Ginny, just didn't seem appropriate for a young woman who'd lost her husband. So, even twenty-five years later, she continued to be known as Mrs. Virginia Bean, like the etched-metal placard on the post office counter proclaimed, and that suited her just fine.

Sipping coffee while absentmindedly rearranging papers on her desk, she asked the sheriff, "Are you going to the service later?"

Fastwater kept his eyes down, one hand in his lap, the other gently kneading the back of Gitch's neck. "I guess not," he replied. Nodding at the dog, he added, "We're going to head up to the perimeter of the search."

Mrs. Bean started to reach a hand out to him, wanting to comfort her friend, but his arms and hands were tucked out of the way. "Do you think you'll find him?"

He lifted his face to look at her, and she saw the answer in his eyes.

"What do you suppose could have happened to that boy?" she asked. The question might just as well have been rhetorical for all the chance it had of being answered by the sheriff. She knew he'd never discuss a case with her. He said she talked too much. His joke was that when he needed information or news spread around town, he'd tell the postmistress, and by the end of the day, everyone in town would know.

The last time she remembered him talking openly to her was six months ago, when his nephew's relationship with Marcy Soderstrom broke off. The sheriff took his role as mentor to Leonard very seriously, but this relationship business had him completely baffled. Leonard was hurting, and the sheriff had no idea what to say or how to help. Finally, on a chilly evening last fall, hunkered together around the woodstove in the post office, Fastwater mentioned the situation to Mrs. Bean.

"Are you looking for advice?" she asked, enjoying his discomfort while relishing the fact that he'd opened up to her. Of course, he had no clue that Marcy had been confiding in the postmistress all along, so she knew all the details of the break up.

"You have to keep these things simple, Marlon. They both care very much for each other, but Leonard isn't ready to commit to settling down yet. You know how he is, how he's always looking off into the distance. Now Marcy, on the other hand, well, neither love nor money could pry her out of that café."

The sheriff had stared at her like none of this had ever occurred to him.

"They're not kids anymore, Marlon. They know it takes more than physical attraction to make a relationship work." She didn't tell him that those were the words she'd passed on to Marcy: advice straight from her own experience. She'd patted him on the chest, brushed away imaginary lint from his shoulder. "All you have to do is let Leonard know you're there for him. That's all. They'll figure it out, but if he wants to talk, you listen."

Gitch rolled over and looked up at the sheriff, making it clear that he thought it was time to get to work.

Fastwater sat up straighter and cleared his throat, giving Mrs. Bean the impression that he might have something to say, but didn't know how to start. Finally, the sheriff said, "Nothing about this disappearance makes any sense."

"Do these things ever make sense? Is it ever fair? He's only eight years old, Marlon."

"I know. But things like this don't happen around here." Fastwater spun his thermos cup in his hands, a dark look on his face, and Gitch let out a sigh before lying down again.

Mrs. Bean could guess the real reason for the sheriff's sour attitude. Other than the missing child, the situation he disliked more than any other was a bunch of outsiders meddling in what he considered to be his business. And the town was full of outsiders now. She didn't know all of the agencies involved, but she knew the FBI by the insignia on the doors of their big, dark SUVs. Talk in town had referred to the state police, the BCA, and even the highway patrol.

The irony in the situation was that Fastwater himself had summoned the help. Immediately after learning of Ben's disappearance, he knew he didn't have the manpower to handle the situation. The boy was most likely lost in the woods, in which case the sheriff felt confident they'd find him in a day or two. But no one had witnessed the disappearance, so the child may have run away or, worse yet, been abducted by some sort of pervert. Fastwater couldn't afford to rule out any scenario. The bottom line was that time was the enemy, and with just a small local rescue squad and a few police officers spread around the county, he'd had no choice but to call in the cavalry.

As far as she knew, the story hadn't made the national news yet, but all the regional media outlets were in town. The sheriff's little office halfway up the ridge had been taken over. He still coordinated search teams in the woods, and he hadn't relinquished jurisdiction yet, but interrogations, data gathering, and overall strategy came from the outside.

"What has Abby had to say?" she asked. "Wasn't she the last one to see Ben?"

Fastwater snorted. "She's been questioned by everyone but the president of the United States. A bunch of suits in sunglasses asking the same questions over and over, as if she'll suddenly come up with an answer she didn't know two minutes ago." Fastwater paused, obviously upset. He took a slow, deliberate sip of his coffee from the thermos cup. "She doesn't know anything." Then he slid a glance up at Mrs. Bean. "At least, that's what she says."

"What do you mean? Do you think she's hiding something?"

He looked away again, scanned the hampers of mail and the metal cases where the letters would soon be sorted. She could feel his discomfort with the conversation. Finally, he said, "I don't know what she knows. Probably nothing. But she's scared. And I don't blame her for not talking to them."

"They're just doing their jobs, Marlon. They want to find the boy as much as you do."

He nodded, but she wasn't fooled into thinking he agreed with her. She knew how he felt. He was frustrated with all the law enforcement bureaucracy in town. The sheriff would be thinking he could get this settled much quicker if they'd just get out of his way.

"What about Jackie?" she asked. "I saw her in town yesterday."

"That's the first place the feds looked. But she doesn't know anything. She's just up here to make Matt's life miserable. Blaming him for being irresponsible."

"Irresponsible?" Mrs. Bean exclaimed, indignant. "Who's the one who walked out on the family?"

Fastwater ignored the question, glanced at his watch. Mrs. Bean reached for the thermos and poured herself another half cup. She knew his manners wouldn't allow him to leave before she finished her coffee. For the hundredth time she thought how much their early morning coffee sessions resembled an old married couple at the breakfast table, Marlon checking his watch before heading off to work while she prattled on, asking questions and giving advice.

"You don't think he's lost, do you?" she asked.

The sheriff swirled his coffee for a moment before responding. "You know, they had that fellow from Duluth up

here with his dogs. I told you about him. Followed the boy's
scent all the way out to Big Island Lake."

"That's where Rose drowned."

Fastwater nodded.

"You don't think the boy drowned out there, too, do you?"

"No. But just to be sure, they dragged the whole bay looking for him. The ice only went out a day or two before he
disappeared."

"Well, then, what do you think happened?"

Fastwater shrugged his shoulders. "The dogs picked up
several scent trails out there. There seemed to be a lot of confusion." The thing he didn't mention was that a scent trail
could lead in either direction, or both ways, if the person made
a round trip.

Mrs. Bean said, "But the dogs took you out there. Ben had
been there, right?"

Fastwater nodded. "And we found plenty of his tracks in
the wet ground to back them up. That's why so many of them
still think he's lost, and not abducted. But it just doesn't feel
right. I don't know what happened, but I don't think he's out
in the woods."

Mrs. Bean would be willing to bet the sheriff's feelings
were right. He had a distinct sense for these things, and everyone knew it. Since the time twenty-some years ago when his
intuition had told him that the man holding a gun in the bar
wasn't going to shoot and the sheriff had taken the gun away
by hand, folks had remarked on his gift. And before him, his
grandmother's powers had been legendary. Furthermore, having grown up in the woods, the sheriff was tuned into the pulse
of the natural world. If he didn't have a sense of the boy being
out there, then Mrs. Bean would say that chances were pretty
good he wasn't.

She smiled now as she studied the big lawman sitting
across from her. It wasn't often that he shared this much with
her. "Have you talked to Abby?" she asked.

"Sure. But Matt insists on being there. He's protecting her—wants everyone to leave her alone."

"Can't blame him, can you?"

"Not at all. But she's so used to repeating the same denials over and over that if she does know anything, it'll be impossible for them to get it out of her."

"So, you talk to her, Marlon. Get her away from all those other people."

He didn't respond right away, but cast his glance around the room again. She could see he was considering her suggestion.

"Do it, Marlon. She'll talk to you. You two are from the same mold: hardheaded maybe, but honest. You both want this thing to end soon, and end well. Talk to her."

Fastwater drank off the last of his coffee before screwing the cup back on the top of the thermos. Mrs. Bean could see the wheels turning behind his shiny black eyes. Giving him time to mull it over, she brushed a length of long, graying hair away from her face and reset the glossy red enamel barrette above her ear. Then, slowly leaning forward on her elbows across the desk, she asked, "Are you sure you can't get away to make an appearance at the service?"

When the sheriff stood up, Gitch jumped to his feet and loped to the dock door where Fastwater parked when they visited. The sheriff kept his eyes on the dog as he spoke. "If it turns out that I'm wrong and Ben is missing out in the woods, we need to keep after it. We can't afford to let up. We've been lucky with the weather so far, but each passing day adds to the danger."

Mrs. Bean walked with him through the cluttered back room. "Can I ask you something, Marlon?"

He didn't respond, but she was determined to ask anyway, knowing full well he wouldn't answer if he didn't want to. She clutched his arm to hold him at the back door.

"Why did you order the autopsy on Rose? She was almost eighty years old, Marlon. Doc Thompson said she died of cardiac arrest. Do you think something else happened?"

Fastwater opened the door for Gitch, and they watched the big dog carefully paw his way down the open wire mesh steps. Just as she'd suspected, the sheriff offered no response to her question. Gitch inspected the smells near the loading dock, then sniffed his way around the squad car. Mrs. Bean followed the sheriff's gaze up to the clear blue sky and got a whiff of an early morning breeze wafting up off Lake Superior. With such a beautiful start to a new day, it was hard to believe that one of the youngest among them was missing, and they'd be saying goodbye to one of the oldest in just a few hours.

Still holding the sheriff's arm, she said, "You know, some of the townsfolk are saying that the autopsy is unnecessary and disrespectful."

Gitch came around the backside of the squad car and raised a leg to pee on the tire. "Hey!" Fastwater yelled, bluffing a charge out the door. Gitch continued his business, unabashedly looking at the sheriff. To Mrs. Bean, Fastwater said, "I have to go. We'll see how the day plays out."

As he pulled away from her, she leaned into him, hoping for more words or a sign of affection. He took the hand that held his arm and gently squeezed it. Her hand disappeared inside the warmth of his big fist. He turned to face her, directing all his attention into her eyes. "I mean no disrespect," he said. "I just want to get this right."

And then he was out the door, leaving Mrs. Bean to wonder if he was alluding to the autopsy of Rose Bengston, or if his words were really intended for her.

SIX

Marlon Fastwater

In the spring of 1890, when the Canadian schooner *Madeleine* foundered and sank in a raging storm outside the sheltered inlet of Black Otter Bay, the village acquired one more permanent resident. Stephan Lecoursier, the sole survivor among his eight crewmates, found himself hurled onto the cliff-lined coast by a twelve-foot, ice-encrusted wave that had every intention of bashing his head into the rocks. Just before the moment of impact, however, Lecoursier was lifted clear by the floating wreckage of the mainmast and boom. The short section of destroyed mast broke the impact of his return to terra firma, but Lecoursier was knocked unconscious and only received deliverance from a watery grave thanks to the efforts of the brave townsfolk who'd witnessed the disaster.

Upon his recovery, the middle-aged, wiry little French-Canadian made two promises to himself. First of all, he swore he'd never venture out on that treacherous body of water again. *"Je suis battu,"* he declared. *"Le Lac Superior est la propre mer du demon et je l'abandonnerai pour toujours."*

The second promise had to do with the implement of his salvation: the broken mast and mainsail boom. Several days after his rescue, on a clear, calm day, with local fishing boats moving in and out of the harbor, Lecoursier walked the shoreline searching for debris from the wreck that might prove useful in this new phase of his life. The schooner had been small, a coastline hugger, and its cargo of barrels and crates of Canadian grain and eastern hardware had either sunk to the bottom of the lake or been smashed to pieces on the rocks. Debris lay scattered along the shore: broken furniture, hull planks, tattered pieces of sailcloth, and lengths of rope. When he encountered the remains of the mainmast, however, he fell to his knees in a state of shock. Anchored by boulders weighing hundreds of pounds, the heavy wooden beams that had conveyed him safely to shore resembled the biblical wooden cross. From his position on the ground, he studied the shattered section of mast and the crossing mainsail boom. The whole assemblage jutted out above him at an angle from the rocks, looking like the cross of Golgotha he'd seen in pen-and-ink sketches in a Jesuit church back in Canada. *Surely this is a sign,* Lecoursier thought.

He took up residence in an abandoned trapper's shanty on the ridge behind town. A well-worn path led up the hill, ending in a beautiful open meadow on the face of the ridge. With little or no topsoil anywhere along the shoreline, townsfolk had found this meadow provided the only available land to bury their dead. Even at that, tall rock cairns had to be piled on top of the shallow graves to protect the remains of the departed from prowling wolf packs. It was a quiet place, covered with bright yellow marigolds and red-orange Indian paintbrush blossoms in summer. The trapper's cabin was just beyond the meadow in the treeline.

Stephan Lecoursier came upon this hallowed ground about the same time he discovered the cross down on the shore. He knew what he had to do. On this restful piece of property, with its commanding position of dominance over the devil's own sea, he'd build a church to praise the God of his salvation, and the mainmast cross would be the focal point of the sanctuary. Such an important representation of his faith and adoration could be no mere log and sod structure; he'd build it out of the very stone that had been intended as the instrument of his demise.

Fortunately for Lecoursier, the townsfolk adopted him into their midst. They gave him food and good, warm clothing. They kept an eye on him, especially after it became obvious that something was very wrong with the man. Whether his eccentric behavior represented a lifelong disability or was simply a result of the shipwreck, they had no way of knowing. They couldn't understand a word he said. His teary-eyed monologues evoked sympathy and compassion, although children tended to run the other way when they saw him coming. He was, after all, a foreign French-Canadian, and the sole Catholic in a town full of Scandinavian Protestants.

With the help of Helmer Holien, Black Otter Bay's boatwright and blacksmith, Lecoursier refurbished a discarded handcart he found near the wharf and immediately set about hauling great quantities of stone up from the shore. There was an endless supply, all sizes, shapes, and colors, but he hand picked each one for a precise fit. He took long, rambling walks in the forest, and his hair and beard grew out in wild disarray, adding to his peculiar manner. One winter day, almost a year after surviving the shipwreck, a crew of timber men watched Lecoursier wander through the logging camp. They reported that he carried on a nonstop dialogue with himself, but no one could understand his words. A few months later, with spring lying soft across the forest, he set out on another walk and was never seen in town again.

It took a few days for word to get around that he was gone. Someone suggested that he'd probably decided to walk back to Canada now that the snow was gone, but most people figured he was simply lost. A search crew went out, but really, with an endless tract of wilderness beyond the ridge, there was little hope of finding him. An astounding revelation awaited them, however, when some of the townsfolk ventured up to the cemetery that summer. Lecoursier's stone church greeted them with an open door. Actually, the structure didn't have a door, and no roof, either, but the view from the empty doorframe covered fifty miles or more out over Lake Superior.

Everyone had known that Lecoursier was hauling rocks up from the shore; they'd seen him wheeling the loaded cart by hand through town. But his lack of tools and indecipherable speech hadn't prepared them for the primitive grandeur of his work. They found a single square room, twenty feet to a side, with rocks stacked and layered so tight as to make the eight-foot-high walls nearly impervious to wind or rain. The mast-and-boom cross stood in the corner.

For a while after that, when it was finally apparent that the stranger from Canada wasn't coming back, folks walked up the ridge path on Sunday afternoons to sit in the stone church's doorway and admire the view. At some point, tools were stored inside for use in the cemetery. A group of volunteers spent a weekend roofing the structure, and before long weddings were held there, as well as family picnics and civic celebrations. Young couples strolled up the hill to sit in the meadow among the marigolds at the edge of the cemetery. It was a quiet place, blessed with a cool breeze off Lake Superior in the summer.

As the years went by, the eccentric character of Stephan Lecoursier faded from the townsfolk's memory, and when the first roads and cars came to town, the little stone building itself became a neglected piece of local history. Even the cemetery was moved—at least, interments after the taconite plant opened in the 1950s were done in the new cemetery plotted out half a dozen miles up Highway 61. The old handbuilt structure became a hang-out for teenagers, a gathering place for beer parties, and occasionally a shelter for hikers using the nearby Superior Hiking Trail.

It wasn't until Marlon Fastwater was elected sheriff of Black Otter Bay County that the little structure found a new purpose. It was one thing for a part-time small-town cop to share office space in the local hardware store, but a full-time county sheriff needed his own place. Being the oldest continually inhabited town in the county, Black Otter Bay had been the county seat since its incorporation more than a century and a half earlier. The county itself had been named after the town. Time and circumstance had also contrived to make Black Otter Bay one of the smallest communities in one of the largest counties in the state. At more than 2,200 square miles, the county was a sparsely populated tract of wilderness, with nearly as many wolves in the territory as people. As for the town itself, its rich history and independently minded population insured its survival through economic booms and busts.

With state and county funding, the access path to the stone building was widened and paved into a driveway. A buried cable supplied electricity, and a cinderblock back room was added with plumbing for a bathroom. Stationary windows of hardened glass, double-paned against the weather, were installed, along with a heavy steel door. With the new metal roof, the place resembled a small fortress, impervious to fire, the vagaries of Mother Nature, and even most small arms weapons.

Sheriff Fastwater liked the office, especially the way it sat above all the other buildings in town. Just as Lecoursier had chosen the location to honor his God above all creation, Fastwater felt it gave the townsfolk something to look up to. Not that he'd ever think he was better than them, or somehow above the law himself, but it couldn't hurt to have the visible ideal of law and order presiding over the community.

But for him, the best part was watching the sunrise over Lake Superior. For that reason, Fastwater spent many nights in the office sleeping on an old army cot, Gitch camped out with him on the wide-planked wooden floor. Just before sunrise, with the distant horizon beginning to show pink, he'd lounge on his cot to watch the day begin. Above him, solid twelve-inch-thick rafter logs picked up the first hints of daylight, glistening with an antique lacquered sheen. Once the sun was up, however, there would be no more sleeping. Without blinds or shades, sunlight streamed straight in the office, glowing like flood lamps off the sealed mortar-and-stone walls.

He'd let Gitch out then, and usually accompanied the big dog on a short walk through the meadow to the old cemetery, where he'd greet his ancestors. His mother was here, even though she'd died after the new cemetery opened. His father was buried in Duluth, but everyone else was here: great-aunts and uncles and further back to where connections were not so clear. While Gitch sniffed around, Fastwater would pause at his grandmother's grave. Floating Bird had passed away before he was born, but many times as a child he'd heard the stories about her "medicine." His mother struggled to explain this strange concept to him, but made it clear that he needed to know about it. He remembered her saying, "Your grandmother could feel things. She told me many times that she saw shadows of events beyond our world. She could hear echoes of sounds beyond normal, everyday noises."

The outcome of all this was that Marlon, a quiet, shy, straightforward young boy, had understood exactly what his mother meant. He understood because those same things happened to him. Not very often, like his grandmother, but he'd had visions and insights as well. He couldn't call them up on a whim, but a few times, usually under stress or physical threat, he'd "seen" things not visible to others. Sometimes it was just a feeling, but those feelings spoke to him as clearly as a person talking beside him. That's how he'd known, all those years ago, that the man in the bar with a gun wasn't going to shoot. He could smell the incapacitating fear and "saw" the empty cylinder in the gun.

On the rare occasion when Fastwater needed to detain someone overnight, he simply padlocked the office door from the outside, and the large stone building became an overnight jail cell. With an understanding of the character of the local citizenry, he knew that no one would attempt to break one of his windows to escape. Folks around here didn't think that way. They'd never maliciously ruin a well-made piece of property like the sheriff's office. But just to be sure, drunk drivers sleeping one off or barroom brawlers cooling down overnight usually shared the jail facility with Gitch. It wasn't just the dog's intimidating size that promoted good behavior, but his glowering, opaque blue eye also helped them remember their manners.

The city of Duluth, with a population of nearly one hundred thousand, commanded the jurisdiction of Black Otter

Bay's neighboring county fifty miles to the south. A handful
of times in Sheriff Fastwater's tenure he'd transported potential
felony cases to the authorities in Duluth for safekeeping. He
wasn't fond of asking for help, however, and with his smatter-
ing of police officers spread around the territory, he generally
took responsibility for the county's law enforcement duties
upon himself.

Ever since the morning after Ben Simon went missing,
the road leading up to the sheriff's office had been lined with
the vehicles of volunteer searchers, the media, and law enforcement. Many years ago, the county provided Fastwater with a
sign that read RESERVED FOR BLACK OTTER BAY COUNTY
SHERIFF. Installing it had seemed like a joke at the time, but
now, as he eased the squad car past the line of parked vehicles
on the roadway, the only open spot in the gravel parking lot
was in front of the black-and-red-lettered sign.

Search parties on foot and driving ATVs had started out
before sunrise. Fastwater had been in the office early to orchestrate the morning search. After sending the crews out, he met
with law enforcement agencies still on site to compare notes.
At this point, there wasn't much to compare. Plain and simple,
the boy had disappeared. There were no leads, and no ransom
demands. All family members were accounted for, and known
sex offenders were being located and questioned. Fastwater
didn't like the feel of any of that, and now he paused before
getting out of the squad car to consider again Mrs. Bean's parting words.

From the very beginning he'd felt that Abby Simon held
the key to her brother's disappearance. Unfortunately, the
heavy-handed tactics and unfamiliar voices of investigators had
shut her up tight. He had to give the girl credit, though, he
thought with a smirk. If she didn't want to discuss it, there was
no way a stranger in a suit was going to get it out of her. Mrs.
Bean was right. He really needed to talk to Abby without in-
terference from outsiders, because he also knew a thing or two

about the case he hadn't shared with investigators. The way he figured it, those big-city hotshots with their high-tech gadgets could dig up their own clues. For himself, he'd trust his own instincts and keep his own counsel.

Fastwater adjusted his sunglasses and looked over at Gitch. The dog peered out the windshield, twitching with excitement at all the unfamiliar cars in the parking lot.

"Ready, pal?" Fastwater asked, patting Gitch on the shoulder. "You like all this commotion, don't you?" As he opened the door and swung his legs out, he added, "Well, all these people drive me crazy. Come on, let's get this over with."

Just then the office door opened and Jackie Simon emerged. Fastwater stood next to his car, holding Gitch close. He'd always been struck by the incongruities in Jackie's looks. Her nose was too long, and her lips too full, but combined with her thick dark hair, the features merged to create a very attractive woman. It was easy to see where Abby got her good looks, but the daughter brought another dimension to the equation: the vitality and energetic poise of youth. Jackie, originally from Chicago, could dress up and blend in with any select crowd in the world, but Abby, from little Black Otter Bay, carried herself with a stubborn resourcefulness sometimes found in young people. The look in Abby's eyes warned against underestimating her character. For proof, the sheriff thought, just ask the professionals camped out in his office, unable to get a word out of her.

Now Matt Simon came out of the office, too, and Fastwater became a spectator as Jackie turned on her ex-husband. "What you can't seem to understand," she yelled at him, "is that this is not about you. You no longer get to make these decisions."

Matt shot a glance at Fastwater before replying. "Please, Jackie, just calm down."

She stepped toward Matt and slugged him in the chest. "Don't tell me to calm down, you asshole."

"Jackie—"

"No! You listen to me, mister," she said, jabbing a finger at him. "Abby isn't some jackpine savage, as much as you may want her to be. She's coming home with me. It's not safe here for her. Obviously, you're incapable of seeing that fact." She turned to leave, but stopped to add, "I'm going to get a court order, and she's coming home with me."

When she finally stalked off, Matt remained in the office doorway, hands in his pockets, dejection and exhaustion stooping his posture. Fastwater and Gitch slowly stepped forward.

"I thought you went out early this morning with the volunteers," the sheriff said softly, in stark contrast to the sharp words from Jackie.

Matt gave him a brief look, then adjusted his gaze to watch Jackie walk down the hill. Fastwater turned to look after her departure, too. He knew Matt was aware that he'd overheard their argument, and as uncomfortable as that was, it would be even more awkward if he attempted to ignore it. So he said, "Have you thought about sending Abby down to stay with her for a few days? It couldn't hurt to get her away from this circus for a while."

Matt fixed his frown on the sheriff. He was tall enough to nearly meet the big lawman's eyes straight on. "No, sir, I haven't considered it. And I have no intention of doing any such thing."

Fastwater gave a last look over his shoulder at Jackie. She was halfway down the hill now, climbing into her car. Gitch loped around the parking lot, sniffing tires, marking territory. When the sheriff again faced off with Matt, he noted the extreme exhaustion in the man's eyes. It looked like he hadn't slept in the three days his son had been gone. He knew Matt had been the first one out in the woods each morning, and the last one back after dark. Fastwater wondered if he'd even taken the time to sit down for a meal. He was surprised when Matt spoke up again.

"I know that sending her away would be the logical thing to do," he confessed. "And I tried discussing that with Jackie.

I told her that I talked to Abby about staying with her for a few days. How am I supposed to tell her that her daughter doesn't want to come?"

With that, it was Fastwater's turn to stuff his hands in his pockets. There was a long pause, the space between them more than filled with exhaustion, frustration, and despair. Then Matt said, "He's not out there, Sheriff."

Fastwater nodded.

"Ben isn't the adventurous type," Matt went on. "I always told those kids, 'if you get lost out there, just sit down and wait. Someone will find you soon enough.'" Matt let his eyes wander out to the view over Lake Superior as Fastwater listened, studying the anguish on the younger man's face. "Now Abby, she'd never sit still. She could put on twenty or thirty miles a day, but then, she's too smart to get herself lost in the first place. She knows how things work out there. Ben, on the other hand, is too timid, too logical. He'd never go out there by himself, but if he did somehow manage to get lost, he'd do just as I taught him. He'd sit and wait for help."

"I think you're probably right," Fastwater said.

"Over the last three days I've tracked every goddamn inch of woods for five square miles. He'd be too scared to go farther than that by himself. We're wasting our time. He isn't out there."

"Well, I'm not calling off the search," Fastwater said. "Maybe the boy fell. Maybe you didn't see him because he was unconscious or sleeping when you passed by." The sheriff's expression was friendly and kind. "We have a boatload of volunteers, Matt. They need to feel like they're helping, so as long as they keep showing up, we'll keep sending them out."

Matt nodded and sighed.

The sheriff said, "Why don't you go home for a while. Take a nap. Everybody out there is wired together, so if anything breaks, you'll hear about it immediately."

Matt didn't answer, just kept staring far off to sea. Fastwater had the notion that he might start crying. He'd seen exhaustion and grief break bigger men than Matthew Simon. "I tell you what," the sheriff said, trying to work a positive inflection into his voice. "I'll walk you home. I'd like to see how Abby is doing."

"She insists on going to the memorial service for Rose," Matt said.

"Well, that's probably a good thing for her to do. They were pretty good friends, weren't they?"

Matt nodded.

The sheriff said, "You know, you said it yourself. There really isn't much point in going back out there. Let me walk you home."

When Matt finally looked at him again, Fastwater saw the tear silently sliding down the man's cheek, so he said, "This doesn't mean we're giving up, Matthew. We're just going to take a different look at it."

Matt took a deep breath and nodded.

Fastwater said, "I have to get something out of the office, then we'll take a walk over to your place. Abby is home, isn't she?"

"Yeah. She hasn't been to school lately, so she's doing make-up homework."

"Good." Fastwater stepped around Matt to go inside. "Excuse me for just a minute."

When he returned, he carried an old grocery bag under his arm, the top folded over several times like a large sack lunch. The two men followed Gitch as he trotted out ahead into the meadow. There'd been several inches of new snow here just a week ago, but with the recent warm, sunny weather, the sheriff could smell the earth waking up to another season. It amazed him every year to see the hardy local flora sending out new shoots and blossoms with reckless abandon, racing to establish a foothold in the rocky, acidic soil. With the short, chilly summer months here, plants took root as soon as the frost was out of the ground, often before the last of the snow had melted.

Passing through the meadow, they entered the old cemetery, where Fastwater paused near his grandmother's grave.
Matthew came back to join him. "Floating Bird?" he read.

"My grandmother."

"I've heard of her," Matt said, and the sheriff was pleased
to detect a tone of reverence and respect. Matt looked around
at the other gravestones nearby. Most of them were solid blocks
of granite, with names and dates professionally etched squarely
in the rock. The markers on the Native American graves, however, were a softer, black stone. Names were crudely scratched
in their surfaces, some so old and worn as to be nearly illegible.
When Fastwater realized that Matthew was noting these differences, he started to say something, then thought better of it.
The fact that all his family was here was enough for him.

"Come on, Gitch," he called. "Let's go."

They continued on the path through the woods, heading
generally downhill across the face of the ridge. The morning
light had a soft glow to it now, thanks to the sun rising higher
off Lake Superior. Woodpeckers rattled away overhead, and
yellow-shafted flickers bored new homes high up in aspen
trunks. The woods smelled damp and alive. It was hard to believe that in a peaceful setting like this, a situation of such omi-
nous gravity was playing out.

The path finally broke out on a paved street behind the main
section of town. Within a block or two it met the street where
the Simon family lived. The men walked side by side in silence,
the grocery bag tucked up under Fastwater's arm, and followed
Gitch into Matthew's front yard. The sheriff looked up at the
end of the street, a cul-de-sac turn-around a few hundred feet past
the Simon house. In the old days, a sawmill had operated up there
just beyond the cul-de-sac. In the decades before roads or rail lines
connected them with the outside world, logs cut from trees further inland during the frozen winter months had been stacked
there awaiting spring break-up and a float trip across Lake Superior to the populated areas on the southern shore.

But all that was gone now, nothing left of the old sawmill except two or three feet of compacted sawdust covering several hundred square yards. Antique hunters sometimes wandered over the area with metal detectors, digging in the spongy sawdust and dirt, uncovering well-preserved saw blades, bottles, tobacco tins, and even leather boots. With the forest grown back, however, a newcomer would have no idea of the extent of the labor and activity that had taken place here a hundred years ago.

As the men walked into the yard, the front door opened and Abby Simon bounced down the steps to meet Gitch. She knelt beside the dog, scratched his ears, and let him lick her face.

"Hey, there, Abby," Fastwater called by way of greeting. When she looked at him, he was pleased to see the smile remain on her face. They gathered around Gitch, Abby still on her knees, the men standing comfortably with hands in pockets.

Matt said, "How's the homework coming, kiddo?"

"Done. It's stupid, Dad. They're just mad because I skipped a day of school. Now they're making me jump through hoops to finish the year." With sarcasm, she added, "Like they wouldn't let me go to high school next year if I didn't finish the work."

Fastwater had to laugh. It was just the sort of comment he'd expect from her.

Matt shot him a stern look, but to Abby said, "Well, you did a great job all year on your assignments and grades. Might as well finish it off on a high note."

"How come you're not out with the search teams?" she asked. "Did Mom find you?"

Matt nodded, grinned, and toed a clump of sod in the yard. "Yeah, we talked."

"Bet you wished you were out in the woods, eh?"

Everyone laughed at that. To the sheriff, Matt said, "Can you stop in for a cup of coffee?"

Fastwater stepped toward the house, but hesitated with a glance at Gitch. Abby said, "He can come in, Mr. Fastwater. Right, Dad?"

"Sure."

The house seemed dark and close after the wide-open sunshine outside. They tromped single-file through the entryway and front room, with Abby and Gitch leading the way. When they reached the kitchen in the back of the house, Fastwater pulled out a chair at the table while Matt rummaged through cupboards for coffee fixings. Abby filled a bowl with water for Gitch, and then offered the big dog a leftover cheeseburger from the refrigerator. Gitch curled up under the table at the sheriff's feet, gently mouthing small bites of the unfamiliar treat. Fastwater held the grocery bag in his lap, but set his cap on the table and ran a large hand through his wavy hair.

Other than the custom .44 Magnum belted to his hip, the cap was his only piece of apparel that wasn't official uniform. Dark brown in color, tattered and frayed from years of use, it simply read SOO in orange block letters across the front. He'd begun wearing it years ago as a private homage to his Sioux heritage. If anyone had bothered to ask him which tribe his family descended from, he would have told them with pride about his Dakota warrior blood.

But no one asked.

Local white folks boasted about their Norwegian heritage, or Swedish, Finnish, or German; but to them, the sheriff was simply a Native American. Two or three hundred years ago, the Ojibwe had come down over the top of Lake Superior and pushed the native Sioux tribe south, out onto the prairies. The Ojibwe themselves were being pushed west by white settlers in the east. But Fastwater's family never moved. This had been their home since the first days. They assimilated themselves into the new tribe, helping the newcomers overcome the harsh realities of life on the north shore of Lake Superior. And when the white folks arrived, they assimilated again.

Together, but apart.

Of course, everyone in town thought his cap referred to the Soo Line Railroad, and again, if anyone had asked, he would have admitted that was probably what the cap had been designed for. But he preferred his made-up meaning, and the subtlety of it satisfied the sheriff just fine.

When Abby took a seat across from him at the table, he asked, "Are you planning to do any fishing this year?"

Her answer was evident in the abrupt change in her countenance: from a relaxed and easygoing teenager to an expressionless stare. Matt's coffee preparations suddenly resounded in the silence.

"Abby is the best fisherman in these parts," Matt said.

"I know that," Fastwater answered, holding Abby's stare. "Have you gone after any steelhead this spring?"

When Abby still didn't respond, her father said, "We haven't done much river fishing for a couple of years now. Abby tends to like lake fishing better."

Fastwater sat back, settled into his chair, and let a warm smile spread across his face. "You know, I remember when Leonard was just a little guy. I'd take him up fishing for rainbows." Abby's expression didn't change. Fastwater took off his sunglasses and carefully set them on the table. "I used to laugh out loud watching him try to hook those feisty little critters."

A trace of a grin showed up in the corners of Abby's eyes. "That's because their mouths are so soft," she said. "The hook just pulls through if you're too rough."

Fastwater pointed at her and said, "Bingo! But do you know the best bait for rainbows?"

"Red worms," she answered promptly, as if taking a test.

Fastwater nodded. "Red worms are good. But I know something even better." He leaned forward slightly, like he didn't want to be overheard. "A couple kernels of corn on a bare hook."

Abby looked skeptical. "For real?"

The sheriff grinned. He could see her thinking it through.

"Of course!" she exclaimed. "It makes sense. The yellow color would show up better in dark water." Now she began thinking out loud. "And rainbows locate most of their food by sight." Abby turned her avid concentration back on the sheriff. "I bet a fresh kernel of corn would stay on the hook better than a soggy old worm, too."

"That's right," Fastwater agreed. "But there's more to the secret, and Leonard is the only other person who knows about it."

Matt came to the table and set out cream, sugar, and an open package of store-bought cookies.

"Don't tell me about slip sinkers," Abby said. "That's about all I use. Best set-up out there."

Fastwater laughed and nodded. "Hey," he said, " if you're not fly fishing, then slip sinkers are a given for rainbows. But I'm still talking bait."

Matthew leaned against the counter, a smile resting easily on his face, enjoying the banter between his daughter and the sheriff.

Fastwater sat forward, Abby's attention completely his. "After you have that kernel of corn on the hook, and maybe just a piece of red worm for scent, you coat the whole thing in a thick gob of spit."

Both Matthew and Abby burst out laughing as the sheriff mimicked spitting on a hook. With a twinkle in his black eyes, he added, "Hey, it works. It's good luck, too. Just try it some-time when the fishing slows down."

Just then the phone rang and Abby jumped, letting out a startled "Oh!" Her reaction wasn't lost on Fastwater. Matt reached over to grab the cordless phone.

"It's Marcy," he said, walking to the other side of the kitchen.

The sheriff continued watching Abby. In an instant she'd gone completely pale, her half-eaten cookie forgotten. He calmly took the grocery bag from his lap and set it on the table between them. "There's another thing that's unique to fishing around here," he said. From the grocery sack he pulled out the freezer bag of fish. "I taught this one to Leonard, too. You bring your lunch with you in a zippered plastic bag, and after you've eaten, you use the empty bag to haul your catch home. Keeps the fish smell off your gear and clothes, especially when you're on foot." He pushed the bag across the table. "I believe these are yours. Leonard found them the day Rose died, not far from her minnow seines."

The insinuation couldn't have been clearer. Abby didn't move. That explained the footprints at the water's edge, she thought. Leonard always wore cowboy boots.

The sheriff spoke quietly, intimately. "I know that Rose didn't drown, Abby. And I believe you know that, too."

The tough guy stare was back.

Fastwater said, "It's too early in the season to seine minnows. Rose's stock of bait came from the wholesalers. It always has this time of year. Also, when I found her, she wasn't wearing waders."

Abby studied her hands resting on the bag of frozen fish. She vaguely recalled an image of the big man struggling to move in waders that fit way too tightly.

"Not even you would go out in the water this time of year without waders," the sheriff added.

"How did you find out Rosie was dead?"

"We got a call down at the diner." Before he could say more, Matthew returned to the table and handed the phone to Abby.

"Marcy wants to talk to you about the memorial service."

She took the phone, gave the sheriff a parting glare, and left the kitchen.

Matthew picked up the bag of fish. "What's this?"

"Abby was with Ben out at Big Island the day they skipped school. Looks like they had some luck. Leonard found the bag along the shore. I've been keeping it in the freezer in my office."

Matt took Abby's chair across from the sheriff. "She never said they went fishing."

"I think there's a few things she hasn't told us."

"Like what?" Matt's voice rose as he stood up again. "Do you think she knows what happened to Ben?"

"Sit down, Matt."

"I'm going to get her back in here. Abby!"

The sheriff stood up, cutting off Matt's access to the front room. He let his size take command of the situation. "Sit down, Matthew. Please. The one thing we know for sure about Abby is that she isn't going to tell anyone anything right now."

"But if she knows something . . . Sheriff, time might be against us."

"Listen to me, Matthew. Abby is one of the smartest and bravest kids I've ever known. If she had any knowledge of Ben's whereabouts, she'd tell us. I'm not sure what she knows. But the fact that she won't talk about it says she believes Ben is safe."

Matt's look was incredulous. "But if she knows anything—"

"I don't think she knows much," Fastwater interrupted. "But did you notice how she acted when you came home today? Think about it. I'm in charge of the overall search, and you've been spending eighteen- and twenty-hour days out there. All of a sudden, with no explanation, we both come home when the search should just be heating up for the day. Don't you think she'd want to know if we'd found something or had some news? But she went straight to Gitch—never asked anything about the search. I think she knows he isn't out there."

Matt sat down again, studying the sheriff, shaking his head. "She's just a kid. What you say makes sense, but if he's not in the woods . . ."

"He's someplace safe, Matthew. You'll have to trust me on this. Abby probably doesn't know where he is, but she has some reason to believe he's safe."

Matthew worked the bag of fish back and forth on the table, considering this new information. Fastwater looked at the coffee pot, spotted the mugs on the counter, and stepped over to pour a cup for each of them. When he sat down again, he said, "She took a couple of phone calls the night Ben disappeared. Wrong numbers. Remember?"

Matt fingered the cup. "Yeah. I wasn't home, though. The FBI asked her about them."

"Did they tell you the calls were traced to a cell phone out of Chicago?"

"Chicago?"

"It belonged to a man who died six months ago."

Matt shook his head. "I don't get it. What are you saying?"

"That I don't think they were wrong numbers. Abby is hiding something." Fastwater swung around in his chair to look through the kitchen doorway. At the far end of the front room, he could just make out Abby through the screen door, sitting on the front stoop talking on the phone.

"Whoever called here was using a stolen phone," he continued, turning again to face Matt. "They knew you were out when they called, which means they probably called from right here in town. They were calling specifically to talk to Abby. When they were done, they coached her to say the calls were wrong numbers. After all, she wouldn't know we could trace a cell phone call. She probably wouldn't have suspected we'd even know about the calls in the first place. If she had said a friend called, we would have checked it out, and known she was lying. This way, we can't know for sure."

Matt's eyes were wet, his voice soft. "My poor little girl—"

"She never flinched," Fastwater interrupted. "I was there. When the FBI suddenly asked her about the calls, she immediately said they were wrong numbers, like she expected the question."

There was a pause, then Fastwater said, "I thought maybe Jackie would know something. She's from Chicago, right?"

"Yeah. But that was years ago. Besides, she wouldn't pull a stunt like this."

"And the custody issue from your divorce hasn't changed?"

"No." Getting exasperated, Matt said, "The FBI went through all this, Sheriff. Jackie gave up custody—signed the papers and never said another word about it."

"Most abductions are by non-custodial parents."

"I know that!" Matt said through clenched teeth. "But Jackie would never do that to Ben. She wouldn't use Abby this way, either."

Another pause, and the sheriff asked, "But the kids have visited her in Duluth, right? Stayed with her there overnight?"

"Sure, but not for a while now. They don't like it there. Especially Abby."

Raising his coffee cup, the sheriff blew at heat vapors swirling above the mug. He heard the front screen door close behind him.

Matt shook his head, and said, "Jackie wouldn't take Ben. Not like this."

Abby sauntered back into the kitchen and dropped the phone on the table. She seemed to have regained some of her teenage swagger. "Marcy is picking me up to go to the service. We're going to walk."

Matt couldn't find any words. He looked at his daughter like he would a stranger, so Fastwater said, "That sounds great. You need to get out of the house for a while."

Abby picked up her half-eaten cookie. The sheriff watched as she studied her father, probably wondering why his eyes were moist, or could they just be bloodshot from lack of sleep? She said, "What were you guys talking about?"

Matthew still hadn't found his voice, so to fill the void, Fastwater said, "Leonard is coming up from Duluth with his mom, Arlene. I hope there's a good turnout for Rose."

Abby's countenance began to darken. She leaned against the counter, crossed her arms in front of her, and nibbled on the cookie.

Fastwater continued to carry the conversation. "Your dad and I were talking about going to the service, too. It should be okay to let the search go for a few hours, don't you think, Abby?" He had to give the kid credit. When she put on that insolent mask, there was nothing to be read in her face.

Ignoring the sheriff's comment, she said, "Okay, so really. I heard you guys talking in here. What's going on?"

Matt finally spoke up. "The sheriff thinks you know something."

"Like what?"

"Like maybe you know where Ben is."

Abby scoffed. Fastwater was surprised to see tears rise so quickly in her eyes. He seized the moment. "Or maybe you know the connection between Ben's disappearance and Rose's death."

Even Gitch jumped under the table when Abby stomped her foot on the floor. She stalked off toward the back door, then spun around and paced back through the kitchen.

Matt said, "Abby, please . . ."

She stopped and glowered at the sheriff. "Just what are you suggesting?"

"I'm not suggesting anything, Abby. I was just saying to your father—"

"Oh, my God!" she interrupted. "You think we killed Rosie."

Both men were shocked into silence. Abby said, "Is that why you ordered an autopsy?"

Fastwater tried to say something, but Abby's anger, punctuated with a nasty sarcasm, overrode him. "How about this one, Sherlock. You already figured out that we were at the lake, so I'll just tell you. My little brother killed Rosie, and then took off to lead a life of crime. I'm covering for him because he's only eight years old." She turned to leave the room.

"Abby, stop," Fastwater called. "That's not what I meant."

Abby grabbed the kitchen entryway and spun around. The rage flashing in her eyes looked to Fastwater like heat lightning on a summer night. When she faced her father, however, the despair on Matt's face seemed to diffuse her ill temper like sunlight through a thundercloud. He beseeched her with his stare, begged for a word of encouragement in this dark hour. Fastwater saw her softening. Abby dropped her gaze down to Gitch, and drew a deep sigh.

"Jeez, I was just kidding, you guys. Lighten up, will you?" She took a brief step toward her father, and said, "We'll get him back, Poppa. Ben will be just fine." She smiled at him, a smile so inspiring that Fastwater could only look on in wonder.

The silence following Abby's departure was complete. They heard her stocking-clad feet bound up the stairs to her bedroom. After a time, Gitch slunk out from under the table, and Fastwater reached out to scratch the dog on the nose.

Matt said, "She hasn't called me Poppa since she was about three years old."

"That girl thinks the world of you," Fastwater said. "I'm sure that if she knew anything she would've told us."

"I guess that means we're kind of back to square one."

Fastwater nodded, but not so much at Matt's comment as to his own thoughts. Abby may not have told them anything in words, but the sheriff was convinced now more than ever that Ben's disappearance and Rosie's death were somehow connected.

SEVEN

Arlene Fastwater

Sheriff Marlon Fastwater was indeed very happy with the turnout for Rose Bengston's memorial service. Little First Lutheran Church was packed, an especially gratifying turnout given the beautiful weather on this Saturday afternoon early in the fishing season. A small clapboard-sided structure surrounded by neatly trimmed cedar trees, First Lutheran Church exhibited the classic design elements so beloved in country churches: narrow stained glass windows, blonde oak woodwork, and a tall steeple topped off with an old cast iron bell.

Abby Simon, from her seat in the third row next to Marcy Soderstrom, watched the people as they entered. Abby wore a knee-length skirt with casual walking shoes and a button-up sweater. Her ever-present braid hung over the front of her shoulder. Out of respect to the church and Rose's memory, she held her Twins baseball cap in her lap. Marcy, on the other hand, wore black jeans and T-shirt under a black leather vest. Finishing off her "mourning" attire were black hiking boots. Abby thought that even Marcy's hair seemed to have a darker sheen to it than usual.

Matthew Simon stood behind the back row, directly behind the sheriff. Most folks stopped to shake his hand and to offer words of support for his missing son. Many of them had spent long hours in the woods and on the lakes searching for the boy. When Mrs. Virginia Bean arrived, Abby saw her face light up at the sight of the sheriff. She took a seat in the back next to him, patted his arm warmly, and said, "I'm so glad you decided to come."

Watching them, Marcy excused herself to join Matthew at the back of the church. She grabbed his hands, stood too close, and leaned into his height. Her conversation was animated, and Abby smiled to see her father responding with awkward smiles and conversation of his own.

The church filled up, with a comforting warmth settling over Abby, the cause of which was hard to identify. Sunlight through the stained glass windows cast a filtered glow over the room, while hushed voices and the familiar faces became a mellow backdrop. A collage of photos of Rose stood on an easel in the front of the church, with dozens of colorful, fragrant bouquets lining the sanctuary. The large turnout appealed to Abby's sense of pride. All of these people had known Rose. She'd been a dynamic character for many years in Black Otter Bay, and a particularly special friend to Abby. Rose had been one of those "fun" adults who appreciated the magic and wonder of the wilderness. She always made a big deal out of Abby's joy in fishing. To this day, a photograph of the little four-inch crappie Abby caught as a three-year-old was taped to the cash register counter in the bait shop. Whenever Abby and her father stopped in for minnows or tackle, Rose slipped a candy bar into Abby's pocket. "You have to keep up your energy," she'd say with a wink. "You never know when that big one will hit."

First Lutheran Church, located on Highway 61 about a mile north of town, backed up to the shore of Lake Superior. It was the only church servicing Black Otter Bay, although Immaculate Conception's gothic red brick Catholic Church and a modern evangelical Assembly of God served congregations in neighboring communities. Because of its location next to Lake Superior, easily visible from the highway, First Lutheran Church often hosted more out-of-town worshippers than local residents on summer Sunday mornings. Truth be told, Black Otter Bay wasn't a particularly religious community, but the little white country church beckoned to travelers with its nostalgic architecture, creatively cropped topiary, and the deep blue background of rolling breakers coming ashore on Lake Superior.

Randall Bengston entered the sanctuary then, his long, wispy thin hair resting on the shoulders of a corduroy sport coat. He wore a heavily jeweled watch on a turquoise band, with rings on all his fingers in an attempt to look arty and hip. But with his narrow-set eyes and thin-lipped scowl, Abby thought he looked more like an aging gangster. She shivered. After Rose's husband died, Randall had shown no interest in fishing or the bait business, but Rose had resolutely carried on.

Marcy finally returned, scooting into the pew beside Abby, and they watched Jackie accompany Randall up the aisle. She completely ignored Matthew, but held Randall's arm all the way up to the front pew. Jackie seemed to be glowing, with high color in her cheeks and a twinkle in her beautiful dark eyes. Spotting Abby and Marcy, she broke into a broad smile, and after they claimed their seats, she came around to speak to her daughter.

Acknowledging Marcy with the briefest nod, she took Abby's hand and asked, "Won't you come sit up front with Randall and me?"

"But I came with Marcy, Mom. I think I'll just stay here."

"Did you ride up together?"

"No. We walked."

Jackie was taken aback. "Walked?"

"It's only a mile or so," Abby said. "Most of it on the Superior Hiking Trail."

Marcy added, "It was a beautiful walk, Jackie. I'm really sorry about Rosie. We all thought the world of her."

The annoyance on Jackie's face was apparent. The two women were about the same age, but that was the extent of the common ground between them. In Jackie's opinion, Marcy was one of those small-town hicks she'd had to tolerate for the dozen or so years she'd lived in Black Otter Bay. To her credit, though, she managed to offer a perfunctory thank you.

Returning her attention to Abby and clasping her daughter's hand now with both of hers, she said, "You know, sweetheart, I really think you should come home with us. There's nothing here for you right now. Wouldn't you like to get away from all this for a while?"

Randall, sitting sideways with an arm draped over the back of the pew, watched their conversation.

"What about school, Mom?" Abby asked. "I still have another week to go."

"Oh, they're not going to say anything, honey. And Randall and I would dearly love it if you'd come stay with us this summer."

At a momentary loss for words, Abby again looked at Randall. She wanted to tell her mother that her boyfriend gave her the creeps, and that she couldn't bear the thought of being cooped up in the city for the summer. But what actually came out of her mouth was a complete surprise even to her. "I think Dad needs me to stay here."

Jackie flinched. Fortunately, just at that moment, Arlene Fastwater entered the sanctuary. She cruised up the center aisle like she owned the place, her son Leonard following in her wake. She wore a billowing, bright purple dress, and managed to carry her large frame confidently in matching purple heels. A huge straw hat, bedecked in flower blossoms like an Easter bonnet, made her look even taller and broader. Everyone turned to look.

"Well, think about it, Abby," Jackie said. "We'll talk more later." Just before she returned to her seat, she added, "You know, I need you, too, honey."

Color rose in Abby's cheeks, and she rolled her eyes at her mother's back. Marcy quietly let her hand rest on Abby's arm. "Don't worry about it," she whispered. "You do what you think is right. Besides, we all know it would break your dad's heart if you moved."

Just then Pastor John Petersen arose from his high-backed chair beside the altar. The reverend was a full-blooded

Norwegian, having immigrated to America with his parents while still a child during World War II. In a loud, heavily ac-cented voice he welcomed the congregation, and then read a passage from the Book of Psalms. Abby wasn't big on church sermons, but she found Pastor Petersen's accented speech to be tender and sincere, like a kindly old grandfather. He wore his short, steel-gray hair combed straight back. When he spoke, he held his hands out before him, as if showing off the length of a big fish he'd caught. His lilting Norwegian accent sounded like a character out of the nineteenth century.

He sang a hymn then, a capella and in Norwegian, so of course no one understood a word of it. It made the congregation a little uncomfortable. They looked at each other with raised eyebrows, safe in the knowledge that the pastor's eyes were closed as he sang from memory, his face and arms raised in praise toward the heavens above.

When he asked for friends and family members to come up to share stories about Rose, Randall was the first to stand up. No microphone was necessary, as the acoustics in the tiny sanctuary amplified every little sound. Facing the congregation, he thanked everyone for coming and invited them to stay after for a potluck luncheon. Then he looked out over their heads to the back of the church, and concluded, "You know, it was my mother's wish to be cremated. She wanted her ashes scattered over the aspen grove behind the bait shop." He stared directly at the sheriff. "I'm just sorry that the authorities took my mother away. This is her memorial service, but she isn't here, because someone decided an autopsy was necessary."

The congregation stole glances at the sheriff. Abby studied her hands in her lap. She couldn't believe Randall would chal-lenge the sheriff like that right in front of everyone.

The momentary awkwardness was broken when Arlene Fastwater stood up and walked to the front of the sanctuary. Abby wasn't even sure that Randall was done yet, but when Ar-lene stepped up to the altar and turned to face the congregation, all eyes were on her, and Randall quietly sat back down in the front row.

Arlene introduced herself, making sure everyone knew she was not only Marlon Fastwater's sister, but a successful attorney working for the city of Duluth. Her voice was big and rich, a full-bodied compliment to her plus-sized physique. Accustomed to speaking in front of people, her words rolled out easily, and Abby found herself enthralled by Arlene's voice and the sing-song inflections of her Native American heritage. At some point she even conjured up the image of an American Indian Aretha Franklin. Gaudy rings and bracelets flashed as Arlene worked her arms and hands for emphasis. Like an ancient sorceress, her words spun a web of mystery and magic over the assembled crowd.

• • • • •

"I've known Rose my entire life," Arlene began. "When I was a little girl, her bait shop was like a second home to me. As many of you know, my real home was an old log cabin up over the ridge. We didn't even have a road to our house, much less a car to drive on it. My brother Marlon and I walked down to Rosie's place to catch the bus for school.

"I loved that bait shop; all those bubbling tanks full of minnows and leeches. Rose kept the water in them ice cold. I especially remember the big sucker minnows, some of them up to a foot long. I'd stand over their tank for hours, mesmerized by the way they swam together in darting flashes, all in the same direction. Other than differences in size, they all looked alike. Sometimes I'd try to name them, like pets, but then they'd dart off again, and I'd lose track of who was who.

"Back in the old days, when Rosie's husband Henry was still alive, they raised rabbits in a hutch outside the bait shop. Rose paid me pocket change to feed the rabbits and keep their cages clean. I never tried to name them, however, because I knew that soon Henry would make rabbit stew out of them, and sell their furs to the Canadian buyers.

"As I sat on the edge of the minnow tank one day, a great sadness came over me. My fingers trailed in the water, flicking back and forth to agitate the minnows. It was getting deep into the fall, and a new school year was well underway. It wasn't until Rose came over to me that I realized tears had sprouted on my cheeks.

"'What's wrong?' she asked. When she placed her arm around my shoulders, I burst out crying.

"'My dear little Arly,' she said. That was her nickname for me: Arly. I don't know what she may have been thinking. Was something wrong at school? Did I have trouble at home? She knew we didn't have any money. I just looked at that cold, dark water, and all those wild minnows that thought they were so free and independent, when really they were just as dumb as the rabbits outside in the hutch.

"'Tell me what's bothering you, sweetheart. Let Rosie try to help.'

"It was difficult to talk about, because I wasn't even sure myself what was wrong. But Rose looked at me with her kindly brown eyes, and I just started talking. 'I wish I could be like everyone else,' I told her. 'Why do I always have to be the different one?'

"I mentioned the other children in school. They all looked like their skinny little Barbie dolls, all white-skinned and pretty, with fancy clothes and blonde hair and parents with cars. Then, here I come: a dark-skinned, chubby little Indian girl with straggly black hair. I didn't have a doll that looked like me. I didn't even have a doll that looked like them.

"'Oh, Arly,' she said, hugging me close. 'You have no idea how special you are. If I had been lucky enough to have a daughter, I'd want her to be just like you.'

"Well, of course, that was a very sweet thing to say, but I wasn't her daughter, and it didn't change the fact that I was different from everyone else. Then Rose said, 'You have been blessed with the gift of friendship from all of God's creation; the animals and plants, even the spirits in the rivers and lakes. None of those other children have that. They may have material things, like toys and cars and whatnot, but they don't have a clue about those other things. When you need them, Arly, your real friends will be there for you.' She squeezed my shoulders and kissed my cheek.

"We sat together quietly for a long time. Her words made some sense to me, but it was confusing, too. It was wonderful to have her arm around me as we listened to the water pumps filtering oxygen into the minnow tanks. Then, very slowly, we became aware of another sound, from outside, and we both looked at the open door.

"'What's that?' I asked, using a sleeve to wipe tears off my face.

"'I have no idea. Lets take a look.'

"Side by side, we snuck up on the open door of the bait shop. Together we looked outside, Rose's face peering around the doorframe about two feet above mine. Out on the gravel driveway stood a massive Canadian goose. He looked at us, and then let go with a series of powerful honks.

"'My goodness!' Rose exclaimed as I broke into a wide grin.

"We stepped outside, and Rosie said, 'Who are you, Mister? And why have you come to visit?'

"I felt a little like Alice in Wonderland. Did she expect the goose to answer her?

"Together, we took a couple steps toward the majestic creature. He made as if to stand his ground, but when we got too close, he turned and waddled off the driveway into the yard.

"'He must be migrating through,' Rose said. 'Maybe he's a little sick, or just all tuckered out and needs to take a break for a while.'

"I'd never been so close to a full-grown goose. He was huge! I spent the remainder of the afternoon watching him. He poked around the garden and yard, and spent long stretches just sitting in the sun. When I got home, I told my mother all about our visitor. The next morning, when I ran down to the bait shop to catch the school bus, my mother tied up a bag of wild rice for the goose. We'd just harvested the rice that fall, so it was unprocessed and quite fresh.

"I didn't know if he'd still be there, but I hoped so, although it would probably mean he was indeed sick or hurt. Crossing the highway down to the bait shop, I heard his great honking long before I actually saw him. Rosie wasn't around, so after taking out a handful of rice, I stashed the bag in my backpack and squatted in the driveway near the rabbit hutch. The goose eyed me from his resting spot under the cages.

"With my offering held out in front of me, I spoke softly to the goose. He immediately rose to his feet and honked. Then, making soft, clucking-like noises, he took slow, deliberate steps toward me. I suffered a few moments of apprehension when he drew near, because he stood as tall as me squatting in the gravel driveway. He looked ferocious up close, the thick white bands on the side of his black face like war paint. Then his long neck extended, and soon he scooped mouthfuls of food from my hand. When it was gone, I hastily grabbed my backpack for more while my tall, elegant friend patiently waited.

"He quickly finished off the food, and then followed me to the doorway of the bait shop. He wouldn't come in, but I retrieved a minnow bucket full of cold water and brought it out to his nesting spot by the rabbits. Coming back outside, I spotted Rosie in her kitchen window watching me. She smiled and waved, and I puffed out my chest with pride as I struggled to haul the heavy pail of water.

"This went on for several days. Before and after school, when I ran up the driveway to the bait shop, the goose waddled out to meet me. I even sat with him under the rabbit hutch, stroking his long wing feathers, and gently mussing the finer feathers along his neck. Occasionally, when a flock of geese

passed overhead, following the shoreline south, the goose became uncomfortable, strutting around the driveway while
honking like a crabby old man.

"The first weekend after the goose showed up, a boy from
school came to the bait shop with his father to buy minnows. He
saw me feeding my new friend and wanted to try it himself. As
soon as he drew near, however, the goose charged him, scaring
him back inside the bait shop. I just laughed and laughed. Of
course, he told all the other kids in school, but no one believed him.

"The next week, children got off the bus with me at the
bait shop to see my new friend. There were just two or three at
first, but by late in the week there were ten or twelve of us
hanging out at Rosie's. Fall was getting on, the nights were
cooling off fast, and snow could come any day. I found that by
taking turns, the children could feed my friend without him
getting too upset. But they had to be with me, because he
wouldn't approach anyone if I wasn't there. Suddenly, everyone at school wanted to come with me to the bait shop. They
sat with me at lunch. I even got invited to a sleepover at the
house of one of the girls from school. I overheard one of the
children telling the teacher that I had 'saved a beautiful wild
creature.' Well, of course, I had done no such thing. If anything, that wild creature had saved me.

"Then one day about two weeks after my friend arrived, I
ran down the ridge to the bait shop. Snowflakes fell in earnest,
swirling through the woods, ushering in a whole new season. I
clutched my bag of rice firmly in my hand. Usually I heard the
goose honking long before I spotted him, but this day all was
quiet. The snow whipped silently around me as I ran up the
driveway. My heart began to pound. Approaching the bait shop,
I saw Rosie in the open doorway, and my friend standing out
front. He made bobbing gestures with his head and neck, and
stretched out his wings like an athlete preparing to compete.

"I ran up to him. He stuck that great majestic head inside
my open coat, nuzzling me with his face and beak, looking for

his snack. I quickly fed him, noticing his distraction. It was easy to see what was happening. Then, from high overhead I heard the strangest noise. It sounded like a group of people laughing hysterically. I looked at Rose, who also heard the cackling laughter, but between the low winter clouds and the swirling fat flakes of snow, we couldn't see a thing.

"'Tundra swans,' Rose explained. 'Every time I hear them, I have to smile. They sound like a room full of kids laughing. But they're so beautiful. A swan is even bigger than your friend here, and pure white and so graceful. They fly very high, so against a blue sky they're almost impossible to see. But you can always identify that laugh.'

"Cupping my friend's food in my hand next to my stomach, I fed the goose the last of the wild rice. I scratched his head and neck. I knew he was leaving. For some reason I didn't feel sad. I was happy he felt better, and that maybe I had helped. Rosie stood in the bait shop doorway watching us.

"'Do you think he'll fly south with the swans?' I asked. 'Will they accept him?'

"'Of course they will. But he'll probably meet up with another flock of geese at some point.'

"Suddenly, he strutted away and startled us with several loud honks. He cocked his head to one side as if listening for a reply. Then, with a frightening lack of grace, he ran up the driveway as fast as he could and flung himself into the air. By the time he reached the highway, he was about ten feet off the ground. He swung out in a long loop and flew back. I ran to stand next to Rose. The goose looked down at us as he flew over. He barely cleared the bait shop roof, and we listened to his calls as he slowly gained altitude over the trees behind us.

"We couldn't see him, but through his regular honks we tracked his progress. Out over Rosie's boathouse on the shore, and then circling back. Tears pooled up in my eyes, but like I said, I wasn't actually sad. In fact, I hadn't been this happy in a long time. I just knew he was going to be okay, and that he would make new friends among the swans. Rosie held me close. He made another pass over us, much higher this time. I heard the rustling of his beating wings, and Rosie pointed at a fleeting glimpse of him, but I never saw him again. We could still hear the wild, crazy laughter from the migrating formation hundreds of feet above us. My friend looped out over the highway again, flew back over us one last time, and then he was gone."

EIGHT

Marcy Soderstrom

After the service, Marcy insisted that they stick around for the luncheon. Abby worried that her mother would corner her again about coming to Duluth, but Jackie and Randall were kept occupied setting out food and greeting folks. At the rear of the church, a drainfield extended, a narrow open patch in the woods where wildflowers and grasses grew in the summer. Marcy and Abby brought their paper plates here, away from the crowd, out into the sunshine and cool Lake Superior breezes.

"God, I'm just starving," Marcy said as they took a seat on the back steps of the church.

Abby wasn't hungry. The warm, communal feeling that had comforted her in church was gone. She knew the reason, and she let her thoughts go with it as she scanned the wide expanse of Lake Superior, extending out to the east beyond the horizon.

Marcy said, "I've always thought that cold cuts and cheese slices on dinner rolls are the perfect food. Throw in a couple pickles and olives and you have a complete meal." She looked at Abby. "Aren't you hungry?"

The young girl's thick black braid once again protruded from under her baseball cap. She had the brim pulled low to block some of the glare off the lake. Her meager helping of food sat beside her. She took a drink from her soda and replied sullenly, "Not really."

Swallowing another bite of her sandwich, Marcy said, "I thought that was a lovely service for Rose. She would've liked it, don't you think?"

Abby nodded.

Marcy set her plate down and wiped a napkin across her mouth. With a furrowed brow, she followed Abby's gaze out over Lake Superior. Taking a deep breath, she tried again. "I really liked Arlene's story. Rose was a wonderful person. She touched a lot of lives around here."

Abby got up and walked away.

"Abby, wait." Marcy grabbed a brownie off her plate and went after her young friend. Along the drainfield they walked, silently, Abby distracted by her thoughts and Marcy at a loss for words. The long, domed mound of the drainfield gently sloped into the woods, with the shore of Lake Superior just beyond. Abby picked her way through the trees until she could jump out onto the rugged bedrock shoreline.

Looking out to sea, Abby watched a thousand-foot iron-ore boat angling in toward the taconite plant a couple miles to the north. By tomorrow night the ship would be loaded and gone, returning to the steel-producing plants at the eastern end of the Great Lakes. She exhaled a long sigh. The plant kept milling out taconite pellets and the ore boats continued sailing the inland seas, but Abby felt like her own world had come to a complete stop.

The loud sigh caught Marcy's attention, and with concern she stole a glance at the girl. Abby wasn't the type to shed tears in public, so when Marcy saw her lower lip quivering, she stepped in closer. No one could ever accuse Marcy of being the quiet type, but she didn't know what to say to this young person who was obviously in a lot of emotional pain. Fortunately, Abby helped her out by saying, "Ben should have been here. It's all my fault."

That came as enough of a shock to free up Marcy's paralyzed tongue. "Your fault? Come on, Abby, don't be so hard on yourself."

"I told him everything would be okay. He believed me when I said I could fix everything. I'm so stupid." Abby stalked off across the rocks.

"Fix what?" Marcy called after her. She shoved the last of the brownie in her mouth and followed Abby to the water's edge. "What on Earth are you talking about?"

Abby didn't reply. Picking up a flat stone, she skipped it over the water. After several moments of silence, Marcy folded her arms across her chest against the cold. Standing next to Lake Superior was like standing in front of an open freezer door. "Jeez, it's cold down here," she exclaimed. "I'm not dressed for this, so hurry up and tell me what you're blaming yourself for."

After throwing another stone, Abby looked both ways up and down the shoreline. Following her gaze, Marcy identified several points along the coast, including the wayside rest and, farther to the north, the breakwater for the harbor at the taconite plant. To the south, the rock-lined shore continued unimpeded for half a mile or so to the two-hundred-fifty-foot high escarpment known as the Ramparts. Rosie's bait shop stood out of sight beyond that, about half a mile from Black Otter Bay.

Abby had secured several skipping stones now, and began firing them fast and hard across the water. Marcy stood back, watching, rubbing her bare upper arms for warmth. When the stones were gone, Abby turned and said, "Let's take the shoreline home. We can hike and climb the rocks. You'll warm up soon enough."

Marcy looked down the shore again. After such a long winter, it was a blessing to see bright sunshine glistening off the deep blue water. Seagulls bobbed on the waves and flew in soaring circles overhead. She wasn't much of an outdoors person, but Marcy had to admit it was beautiful here along the shore. "I'm not climbing over the Ramparts," she said. "And neither are you."

"We can get around it at the base. My dad and I did it last year. Even Ben made it."

To return home the way they'd come would require walking back up to the church, crossing the highway, and climbing the ridge to the Superior Hiking Trail. Marcy could see just a glimpse of the little white church through the trees. It would be warmer up there, but the shoreline offered a straighter shot back to town.

"Come on," Abby called.

Marcy stepped briskly to catch up to the athletic teenager striding confidently over the rocks. Something weighed heavily on Abby's mind, and if she wanted to talk about it, well, Marcy intended to be there for her, even if it meant spending the afternoon struggling over this ruggedly beautiful landscape.

The terrain was fairly level for the first twenty minutes. They set a leisurely pace, scaling small ledgerock cliffs and skipping stones over the water.

Marcy gratefully acknowledged that Abby had been right about the walk warming her up. And every time she steadied herself with a hand on a boulder or sat on a bedrock bench, warmth from the sun-drenched stone radiated into her bones. The experience—the fresh air, rolling waves, and indomitable rocks, the hiking, exploring, and stone throwing—elevated her mood like a natural high. Now, if only she could help her young friend.

As they neared the stark heights of the Ramparts, Marcy asked, "Did something happen to you and Ben the day you hid in the café?"

Abby stopped, leaned back, and looked up at the sheer rock wall ahead of them. Marcy got dizzy when she looked up, lost her footing, and almost fell over. She ended up taking a seat on the rocks a little more abruptly than she would have liked.

"Are you okay?" Abby asked, sitting down cross-legged next to her.

"Sure," Marcy replied, adding a chuckle at her own expense. "I know you're not supposed to look down if you have a fear of heights, but I didn't know you could get vertigo from looking up, too." She lay back on the bedrock to get a better view of the Ramparts. "I sure love these warm rocks, though," she added, spreading her bare arms out to the sides to capture as much of their radiant heat as possible.

When she sat up again, Marcy studied the jumble of rocks and boulders at the base of the Ramparts. The pile of slag had accumulated over many thousands of years, after being broken off the cliff face by the powers of wind, rain, ice, and a never-ending assault from the temperamental surf. She didn't see how Abby intended to get them across all that loose rock, penned in on one side by a 250-foot high wall of rock, and on the other side by the frigid, grasping waves of Lake Superior.

"Ben and I saw something that day you found us in the café," Abby suddenly blurted.

Marcy looked at her. Abby seemed calm, her dark eyes peering out to sea from under the brim of her baseball cap. She told the story then about the man in the big black car and the body rolled up in a blanket. "I know now that it must have been Rosie," she concluded.

Marcy reached out to her. "I'm so sorry, Abby. Did Ben see it, too? Are you sure it was Rose?"

Abby nodded. "We were fishing in the bay near her minnow seines. It was the only open water on the whole lake. They found her body there shortly after we left." She directed an intense stare at Marcy, as if willing her to believe what she said. "She was murdered, Marcy. The man wanted to make it look like an accidental drowning. Maybe a heart attack, I don't know. But the sheriff was right to request an autopsy. I just hope they find something."

"Who was the man?"

"I have no idea. The car had Illinois plates."

They sat for a few moments in silence, then, from her sitting position, Abby flung another rock at the lake. She said, "You know, I just remembered, when we ran away there was another vehicle coming down the road. A pickup truck. At the time, I thought it was a local, and maybe he'd confront the man with the body. I didn't get a good look at the driver. But I haven't heard anything more about it. It's almost like the truck never existed."

"You ran away?"

"Yeah. Ben was scared, but the man actually saw me. I had to get out of there fast."

Marcy laughed. "So you're telling me that you weren't scared, too?"

Abby stood up. "Hey, nobody can catch me in the woods." She eyed the mess of boulders ahead of them. "Come on, let's do this."

With a huff, Marcy pushed herself to her feet. The going was slow, but not particularly difficult. They climbed up and down over piles of rock. Abby set an easy pace, often hanging back to help Marcy over tricky stretches. A couple times, confronted by slabs of rock the size of small houses, Abby chose to scramble under them, and Marcy followed through the damp, cold, slippery openings. From time to time Abby stopped to scan the rocky escarpment beside them. Marcy had learned her lesson about looking up, but she couldn't help asking, "Why do you keep glancing up there, Abby? I hope you're not looking for a place to climb it."

"No way. At least, not without ropes and pitons. I just get nervous about some idiot up there throwing rocks over the edge. We have to be ready to take cover."

"Oh, my God," Marcy muttered, and when they set out again to finish the trek around the Ramparts, she worked even harder to keep up with Abby.

Once they left the trials of the natural obstacle course behind, they walked side by side again across the flat bedrock coastline. Summer cabins, some of them worth hundreds of thousands of dollars, came into view through the trees up on higher ground. They weren't generally visible from the highway on the other side, so even though she'd lived her whole life in Black Otter Bay, Marcy had never seen many of these homes. From the lakeside, gigantic windows reflected the sunlight, and massive decks provided owners with million-dollar views.

For a while they walked in silence, admiring the natural grandeur of the coast, as well as the stunning architecture. Then Marcy said, "I still don't get what happened to Ben."

Abby picked up and threw another skipping stone. Her arm was warmed up now, and she counted eight or nine skips. Then she turned to Marcy. "You have to promise that you won't say a word to anyone about this."

"Of course."

Abby studied her with a skeptical frown. "I mean it, Marcy. Ben's life may be at risk. You have to swear you won't say anything to anyone."

Marcy snapped to attention and held her hand up in a mock Girl Scout pledge. "You got it, Abby. I swear I won't say a word." She mimicked zipping her lips closed. "I just want to help if I can."

Abby paused, but soon Marcy figured she'd accepted her word, because the girl pursed her lips, nodded in agreement, and turned away so as not to make eye contact while she spoke. Scanning the stones at her feet for another skipper, she began, "We had to leave our gear behind when we ran away. That's why we didn't have anything with us when you saw us in the café. I went back later that night, but the man had already found it. He got our address out of the backpacks. When he came to get me, only Ben was home, so he took him as insurance."

"He kidnapped Ben?"

"Yeah. But I'm the one he wants. He called me later to say Ben would be okay if I didn't tell anyone what I saw at the lake."

"He called to blackmail you? And you believe him?"

Abby nodded. "Sheriff Fastwater told me the man used a stolen cell phone. I saw Ben in the car with him." She grimaced with worry. "Don't you see? I have no choice, I have to believe him."

"So, Fastwater knows all about this?"

"Of course he does." Abby told herself that she wasn't re-ally lying. She had no idea how much the sheriff knew, but he was aware of the phone calls, and he knew she'd been out at the lake. He'd put Rosie's death and Ben's disappearance to-gether, and for all she knew, he probably had even more facts than that to work with.

"But, Abby, if the man murdered Rose . . ."

"It means he'll kill Ben if he has to. I only hope something comes up in the autopsy."

Marcy shook her head, and with conviction said, "I have to talk to the sheriff."

Abby grabbed her by the vest. "You promised me."

Marcy pulled back. The look on Abby's face wasn't so much threatening as pleading. "This is way too big for you, Abby. The FBI is up there in town. They have all sorts of tricks and gadgets to catch people."

Abby shook her head. "The man said Ben would come home in a few weeks if I didn't tell anyone."

"And you believe him? Come on, Abby, you said yourself he's a murderer."

"That's just my point. Don't you see? If I go blabbing on about it, and the police somehow figure it out and close in, he'll dump Ben in a lake somewhere like he did with Rose. Then it's just my word against his."

Marcy's expression softened. "Abby, you can't be so naïve as to think he'll just let Ben go."

"What else do I have, Marcy? Even if I wanted to talk, I don't know who he is, much less where to find him."

"Let the cops handle it. They know how to negotiate these things. They get hostages free all the time."

"No way, Marcy. I can't risk it. I've thought all that stuff over a million times. If anything went wrong and Ben didn't come home, I'd never forgive myself." Having made her point, Abby turned and resumed the hike back to town.

Marcy quickly caught up. "If we could just figure out where he's keeping Ben, maybe we could do something."

Abby stopped so abruptly she almost tripped. "What do you mean, 'we'?"

"Well, jeez, Abby, now that you've told me the story, I'm kind of a part of the whole thing." And, she thought, making herself the girl's confidant might take some of the weight off Abby's shoulders. Besides, if any real information came out, she'd have no qualms about going to the sheriff with it. It was one thing to be a friend, but if Abby found herself in any real danger, Marcy wouldn't hesitate to run for help.

"Don't forget—you promised not to tell."

"I won't. But I don't think we can trust this guy to keep Ben safe. I mean, we have no idea who we're dealing with."

They walked at a slow, thoughtful pace for the next ten minutes. Marcy questioned Abby about the man, but other than the fact that he was tall and well built, with a tanned complexion, there wasn't much to discuss. "He was a white man, with short, dark hair that stood straight up on top, but he wore sunglasses, so I'm not sure I'd even recognize him again."

Marcy brainstormed ideas out loud. "The car was from Illinois. Maybe Chicago?"

"Could be. Seems logical."

"Maybe he's a gangster. I read one time that they have mafia in Chicago."

Abby laughed. "What in the world would the mafia be doing in Black Otter Bay?"

"Who else would have a reason to murder an old lady?"

"That's what I've been wondering. Why would someone want Rosie out of the way?"

"Maybe she knew something, like the name of a criminal."

Abby flashed her best teenage sarcastic look. "Again, Marcy, this is Black Otter Bay. What could she possibly have known?"

"First rule of brainstorming, young lady: no idea is a bad idea."

Marcy was happy to see a grin emerge on Abby's face, and it stayed there while they hiked in silence for a few more minutes. It was apparent that sharing her secret had been a relief to Abby, even though Marcy had no solid advice to offer her young friend. In fact, she really had no idea how she could be of help, but she was willing to listen, and at the first hint of danger, Marcy would run to the sheriff so fast . . .

Abby pointed. "Look, there's Rosie's old boathouse."

They were approaching the Bengston property, a five-acre slice of land between the highway and the lake with 600 feet of cobblestone shoreline. The old boathouse, a square-logged, hand-scribed structure, was more than a century old. Proof of that was inside, above the doorless opening facing the lake, where the year "1898" was carved in deep, thick numerals. The logs, lengths of twelve- and fourteen-inch-thick pine and cedar, were burnished black by years of abuse by waves and ice. The Bengstons hadn't utilized the building since the death of Randall's father more than thirty years ago. Henry Bengston had been the last commercial fisherman in the area. Over the past three decades, the shifting cobblestone beach had piled up against the boathouse, so that now it protruded out of the shore like a fortified beachhead. Several roof boards were missing, allowing enough light for Abby to point out the date etched over the door.

"Wow," Marcy said. "I never knew this was here. Did you?"

"Sure. Rosie brought me down here many times. She let me play on the beach. Ben and I used this place as a fort, or sometimes a castle, depending on what game we were playing."

When she looked around the small interior, Marcy noticed several huge spikes nailed into the logs. At one time used as hooks for Henry Bengston's fishing equipment, the spikes held discarded and long-forgotten marker buoys, rotting netting, and coils of rope. Even open to the sun and weather, the boathouse held a musty odor of decay and neglect.

As Abby ducked back outside, she said, "Rosie and I talked about jacking the place up and restoring it someday. I don't know what will happen to it now."

"It would be a shame to lose it. Can't you just see the old fishermen mending their nets in here?"

Abby stopped. "You really do believe in ghosts, don't you?"

"What do you mean?" Marcy asked with a laugh.

"Well, you told us about Agda, the ghost in the café. And now you're talking about the spirits of old fishermen. Sure sounds like you believe in ghosts."

Joining Abby outside, Marcy said, "I didn't say I believe in them. But I do like to keep an open mind."

Abby laughed. "Okay, whatever you say. Come on, let's go up to the house."

Marcy took great pleasure in seeing the smile on Abby's face and the lighthearted spring in her step. It felt good to think that perhaps she'd distracted the girl, for a short time anyway, from the worries of the past week.

A seldom-used path led up from the beach through a broad stand of tall birch and aspen trees. Straight as toothpicks, the trees held their crowns of fresh young leaves high overhead. It was quiet here, except for the soft rustling of a cool breeze wafting up from the lake.

An old barn-like structure soon came into view. A squat, fat building, the bait shop looked even shorter due to a heavy listing to one side. It appeared to be propped up by several cords of split firewood stacked along one wall. As they approached the building from the rear, Marcy was surprised to see so much junk piled up against the back wall. Scattered over the forest floor lay several old cattle troughs, once used as minnow tanks. Some of them now hosted full-grown aspen trees, their trunks growing up through the rusted-out, bottomless hulks. She identified old snowplow and tractor parts, and half a dozen overturned fishing boats with gaping holes in their hulls.

Silently, they made their way along the side of the building where neat rows of maple and birch firewood stood beneath
a tin-roofed lean-to attached to the building. The place had a
deserted feel to it, but Marcy found herself sneaking along behind Abby anyway.

Beyond the bait shop stood the clapboard-sided house. A
couple decades ago it had been painted white, with white trim,
but much of the siding had weathered to a bare gray, with
curled patches of peeling paint hanging in neglected disrepair.
Looking beyond the house, Marcy saw where the driveway
dropped off sharply from the highway, past a sign announcing,
Rosie's Bait Shop—Open 24 Hours. At the bottom of the
hill, the driveway split to make a circle around the house. Another homemade sign directed traffic to stay to the right. On
this right-hand side, a rubber-coated buzzer wire lay across the
driveway. It functioned like the ones used in old-time full-ser-
vice gas stations: when a vehicle rolled over it, a doorbell-like
chime sounded inside the house and bait shop.

But there were no customers here today. Abby crossed the
driveway to peek in the kitchen window. To Marcy, the place
had the overrun, weather-beaten look of desertion. Near the
side of the house was evidence of a long-ago garden bed. Having not been tended in years, it was now an overgrown jumble
of weeds and shrubs, highlighted by captured pieces of litter
that had blown in off the highway. A white plastic bag fluttered
against the house from its mooring on an aspen sapling sprout-
ing up next to the foundation. Bits of Styrofoam from broken
bait buckets stuck out like small patches of snow.

The windows of the house were covered with heavy
draperies against the recent cold weather, although many of the
first-floor windows were obscured by untrimmed vegetation.
The surrounding forest was quickly reclaiming what had once
been a lawn.

Marcy turned her attention to the front of the bait shop.
A single-stall overhead garage door was closed, as well as the

small service door next to it. On the plywood panels of the overhead door, a faded mural depicting a fisherman and his canoe could still be seen. A small sign tacked on the service door revealed it to be the home of ROSIE'S BAIT.

Abby recrossed the driveway and tried the small door. When it opened, she looked back at Marcy, and said, "Come on, let's take a look."

"We shouldn't go in there, Abby."

"Just for a minute. I want to show you something. No one's around, and Rosie wouldn't mind."

"It's trespassing."

"You wait here, then. I'll be right back." She scooted inside, but left the door open.

Marcy stuck her hands in her pockets and looked around the property again. It was peaceful and quiet, and the sunshine felt so warm and friendly here away from the lake. But it didn't take long for the stillness of the woods to work on her nerves. "Abby?" she called. Peeking inside, she found a large open room filled with shadows and, she guessed, cobwebs and little scurrying feet. The only light came from the open door. The minnow tanks hummed their insistent drone of life support.

"Abby?"

"Over here. I'm looking for the light switches."

Straight ahead, Marcy discerned the form of the cash register on the counter. Abby's voice came from behind it. "Okay, Marcy, I found it. Come on in and close the door."

Marcy did as instructed, only closing the door after the bank of fluorescent lights over the counter came to life. They emitted a pale, sickly glow, as if reluctantly, and didn't illuminate the corners of the room so much as enhance their crepuscular mystery. The building appeared much larger from inside. It extended well beyond the reach of the lights, where Marcy detected stacks of equipment and supplies, as well as Rose's old, dented and rusted-out pickup truck.

Abby came around the counter to grab Marcy's hand. "Look at this," she said, pulling her over to the cash register.

Abby pointed at a photograph from among dozens taped under the glass of the counter.

"That's me," she said. "Ten years ago."

Marcy looked at a picture of a grinning little girl holding up a crappie hardly bigger than her hand.

"And here's another one." Abby pointed at a photo of her family standing in front of the bait shop's mural. Ben and Matthew held a stringer of walleyes between them, while Abby and Jackie stood behind, looking on.

"Jackie doesn't look too happy," Marcy commented.

"She never liked fishing," Abby replied. "She didn't like camping, either, or the woods." Still holding Marcy's hand, she turned to look at her. "I'm sorry she was so rude to you today."

"It's nothing, Abby. I'm sure this whole episode would push anyone off center. Do you think she's happy living in Duluth?"

"I don't know. I guess so."

"I grew up with Randall. He's older than me, but I've known him all my life. He always was a little odd. It's weird though, seeing him with Jackie."

"Yuck!"

Marcy laughed. "Well, you have to admit, he's got some money."

"Sure. And he's also got pals in the casino business, which makes Mom really happy."

Marcy frowned and withdrew her hand. She'd heard the gambling rumors to which Abby alluded. Feigning interest in the photographs, she leaned over the counter while saying, "You can't be sure about that, Abby. People say all sorts of things."

"You sound like my dad now."

Marcy followed Abby along the length of the counter. "So, how's your dad doing?"

Abby stopped at the first tank of minnows. "I think this is killing him. But he doesn't talk much, so I don't know. He's been out in the woods every day with the search teams."

"You know, I grew up with Matthew, too. His older brother, your Uncle Dan, was Randall's age. Dan was everyone's heartthrob, but I always kind of liked your dad."

Abby continued on to the next minnow tank, then stopped to stare into the darker recesses of the room.

"Your dad and Leonard Fastwater were best friends in school. Did your dad ever tell you we went on a few dates in high school?"

When Abby didn't reply, Marcy figured it was because a teenager wouldn't want to talk about her father in that way. Looking at the girl's long, thick braid lying heavily against her back, Marcy concluded, "I think we were just too much alike."

Abby still didn't move, so Marcy stepped in closer behind. "Abby?"

"That's the truck," the girl said, staring into the darkened garage bay

"What truck?"

Abby turned to grab Marcy's hand again. "Out at the lake, when I ran away from that man. Remember? I saw a pickup truck coming in on the access road. That's the truck. I knew there was something familiar about it!"

When the bait shop buzzer suddenly rang, they both jumped. Abby ran back along the counter to peek out the window of the small door. "It's Randall," she hissed in a loud whisper. "And Mom."

By the time she returned to the shadows near the truck, they heard a car door slam and a voice raised in anger. "Quick," Abby said, nearly pushing Marcy up over the side of the pickup truck bed.

"The lights, Abby. What about the lights?" But before she could answer, the bait shop door crashed open, and they flattened themselves against the bed of the truck.

"I don't give a rip," Randall yelled into his cell phone. "We had a deal."

Amid the racket of things smashing to the floor, Marcy pressed herself as hard as she could against the truck bed.

"That's your problem," Randall yelled. "Tell them to wait."

Abby pulled herself up over the wheel well to spy on Randall as he ransacked drawers and shelves behind the counter. Tackle and supplies toppled to the floor.

"Screw you!" he bellowed. Then, following a long pause, he continued in a calmer, nearly normal manner. "Listen to me. We just had a memorial service for my mother. Now, I'm holding up my end of this thing, so you'll just have to be patient and back off. I need a couple weeks."

With one hand he extracted a small handgun from the till in the cash register drawer and held it up to the light. Abby watched as he used a thumb to pop open the cylinder. Satisfied that the gun was loaded, he slammed the cylinder shut with a deft flick of his hand, then grabbed a box of ammunition from the drawer and stuffed it in his pocket.

"That's right," he said into the phone. "Everything will be fine. If anything does go wrong, we'll just put it on Jackie. Either way, the deal goes through."

When he hung up, he stood still for a moment, staring straight ahead as if listening, or perhaps replaying the conversation in his mind. The gun in his hand hung limp at his side. He looked around, then at the counter and the floor. Slowly, his head tilted back until he faced the overhead fluorescent fixture. When he unexpectedly spun around, Abby ducked and closed her eyes tight against her arm.

"Damn it!" she muttered to herself.

The only sound beyond the pounding of their hearts was the suddenly amplified hum of the minnow tanks. Ears straining, they awaited discovery. Then the bait shop door opened again, and Jackie called, "Randall?"

"Shhh!"

"What is it? Come on, let's go."

"Shut up!"

Marcy grabbed Abby's hand. Over the humming tanks she heard the faint scrape of a hard-soled shoe on the concrete floor.

There it was again, closer, and then the loud click of the gun being cocked. Several seconds ticked off before Marcy sensed Randall standing at the driver's side door of the pickup, peering through the darkened window. He slid to the front end of the truck, and it was quiet again as he scrutinized the shadows in the back of the shop. The silence became so intense that Marcy involuntarily held her breath.

Jackie called, "Come on, honey. You probably heard a mouse or something."

Randall, returning to the counter, said, "Do mice turn the lights on, too?"

"You probably left them on this morning. Can't we just get out of here? I hate this place."

"Not as much as I do." Randall suddenly turned and fired a round at the back wall of the shop. The sharp report was deafening, like thunder right overhead, and surprised and hurt like a punch to the face. Jackie's yelp of surprise covered Marcy's cowering whimper. He fired again, the round whining over the truck bed to pucker into the side wall of the shop. Abby squeezed Marcy's hand as she scrunched up into a fetal position. Jackie ran for the door.

"Stupid idiots!" Randall yelled, swiping the contents of the countertop to the floor. He let out a string of epithets, knocked over a display of fishing lures, and then all the lights went out. "They think they can do whatever they want," he muttered through clenched teeth. The bait shop door closed, and Marcy opened her eyes to the comforting cover of darkness.

Car doors slammed and tires spun on the gravel driveway. Abby was up and over the side of the truck bed before Marcy even lifted her head. When she looked over the wheel well, she saw Abby framed in the light from the small door's window. The girl turned to face Marcy and quietly said, "They're gone."

Marcy collapsed in a flat-out heap on the truck bed.

"That fool," Abby said, running back to the truck. Looking in on Marcy, she added, "He could have hurt someone."

The absurdity of Abby's understatement ignited a chuckle in Marcy. The laugh felt good, so much better than the frightful river of tears that had been amassing. She let it all out then, a snorting belly laugh that ultimately released the tears anyway, a wall of tension flooded under waves of relief. Abby caught the mood and joined in. When Marcy finally managed to sit up, they hugged over the side of the truck, still laughing, still crying.

"Okay, help me out of here," Marcy said, climbing back to her knees. Abby helped her over the side, and then led her through the mess strewn across the floor. At the door, they looked out the window at the vacant driveway.

"I'm going to Duluth," Abby suddenly announced.

"You're what?"

"You heard him. Randall is in on this."

Incredulous, Marcy asked, "You think Randall killed his own mother?"

"I don't know. But I saw Rosie's truck at the lake, and she wasn't driving it."

"What about that other guy you saw?"

"I know, I know. But Randall is in on this somehow. I'm guessing he knows where Ben is." Suddenly Abby's mouth popped wide open, and she grabbed Marcy by the shoulders. "Of course!" she exclaimed. "That's it! I bet it was Randall I saw in the backseat of the car with Ben. That's why the man assured me he would be safe. Mom probably even knows where he is!"

"That's ridiculous." Marcy opened the door and cautiously looked up the driveway. "I have a better idea, Abby. Let's just tell Sheriff Fastwater what we know. Let him handle it."

"No. I told you, that's not an option. Mom wants me to come to Duluth, so I'll go. And while I'm there, I'll look for Ben."

Marcy pulled the bait shop door closed behind them. The air smelled so fresh out here, and the sunshine felt warm and

pleasant after the damp, terrifying darkness of the shop. Abby
led the way along the side of the building, back down the path
toward the beach. It was good to be moving again, to work the
tension out of taut nerves and muscles.

"I'll take you," Marcy said as they trotted down the slope.

Abby stopped so abruptly that Marcy collided with her
backside. "You'll do what?"

"You need a ride, don't you?"

"I'll take the Greyhound."

"And you're going to tell your dad about this? You think
he'll just let you get on a bus when his only other child is
missing?"

"What's the big deal?" Abby shot back. Marcy's questions
were interfering with her plans. She walked slowly down the
remainder of the pathway, stopping at the entrance to the cobblestone beach.

"You know," Marcy said, "I've never spent any time at
the casino. Never had any interest before." Abby looked at her,
puzzled. Marcy shrugged her shoulders. "Hey, these mafia
dudes could be connected to the casino. And they sure won't
let you in there."

Abby turned to take Marcy's hands. "Are you sure,
Marcy? What about the café?"

"Oh, please! I haven't taken a vacation in years. They'll
cover for me."

Sensing that Abby was close to agreeing, she pressed her
argument. "I'll get a motel down in Canal Park. That way, if
you have any trouble at your Mom's, you can just come down
there. In the meantime, I'll check out the casino and see if Randall has any connection to it."

Abby squeezed Marcy's hand, but turned to look out to
sea.

Marcy added, "Matthew—I mean, your dad—asked me to
help look after you. He doesn't have a clue about teenage girls."

Even in profile she could see the smirk on Abby's face.

"I'll talk to him, tell him we're taking a girl's trip to Duluth. We'll buy some clothes, hang out, and maybe get a makeover. Jackie wants you to visit. This way, your dad will be relieved that I'm spending time with you, and your mother will be happy to have you staying with her. And hey, if anyone asks, haven't I earned a few days off in Duluth?"

"Of course," Abby agreed, smiling at her friend. "And I promise it will only be a couple days. I'll figure out where Ben is by then."

"But there's one big condition in all this, Abby, and you have to agree to it." Clasping Abby by the shoulders, she studied the young girl's big brown eyes. It was hard to miss the confidence in her youthful expression. "At the first hint of danger, we're out of there. You understand? I'm a big coward, Abby, and I won't let you get yourself into trouble. First hint, we're gone."

After a brief, thoughtful hesitation, Abby slowly nodded. Marcy released her shoulders to pull her into a friendly bear hug. "It'll be fun, Abby. Hey, who knows? If things go well, you'll find your brother, and with some beginner's luck I just might win some money at the casino."

NINE

Jackie Simon

An antique feather duster got the job done about as effectively as any utensil she'd tried. Jackie Simon scoffed at comments about how silly and unnecessary it was to dust the whole gallery every day, because by the time she worked her way from the rear of the long, narrow building to the front of the shop and turned around in the light of the huge bay windows, she'd swear the freshened-up artwork seemed to jump out into the light. And the thing she'd tell all those ill-informed slackers is that when you're selling original oils and watercolors, getting the picture to "pop" is what it's all about.

Of course, she'd admit that sought-after art required, first and foremost, a gifted artist. And framing, the way in which a piece was displayed, was perhaps as important . But Jackie also knew the importance of lighting, knew that if any aspect of it was wrong, even the best work would hang in unappreciated neglect for months, or even years.

The Tempest carried some of the best artwork in the upper Midwest, and Jackie wasn't shy about taking credit for making that happen. She knew art, had a discerning eye, and worked hard to display the gallery's pieces to their best advantage. She currently had an original Oberg oil on the wall, although with the price the original commanded, a few numbered prints of the East Coast seascape were about all she could realistically hope to sell. Watercolors by Lars Hedstrom, the popular Canadian, meshed nicely with the Great Lakes theme of the shop. Local artists were represented as well, showing rugged Lake Superior landscapes in all seasons.

Whenever possible, Jackie displayed a dramatic, oversized painting of the sinking of the ore freighter *Edmund Fitzgerald*. She'd readily concede that, from a technical standpoint, these pieces didn't represent very good art. But around the upper Great Lakes region, the demise of the *Fitzgerald* carried a folk-lore-like mystique, and although the paintings weren't very valuable, she still found it surprisingly difficult to keep one on the wall.

After dusting her way to the front door, Jackie turned to look back through the narrow, cavernous gallery. Discrete, re-cessed lighting further illuminated specific highlights of the art on display. Ceramic and stoneware pots by local artists sprouted up on stands, arranged in such a fashion to slow the pace of browsers through the shop.

Unlocking the door, she stepped outside among the strolling tourists and window shoppers in Canal Park. It was especially gratifying to see so much foot traffic considering the fact that it was a Monday morning early in the tourist season, with a sky hanging low with clouds piling in off Lake Superior. Consisting of just a few square blocks of upscale shops and trendy restaurants, surrounded by lakeside motels and luxury condominiums, Jackie often called Canal Park the Navy Pier of the North. A native of Chicago, she'd spent many hours in the waterfront amusement park on Lake Michigan. Instead of a Ferris wheel, however, Canal Park boasted a one-hundred-year-old steel girder lift bridge. When the traffic horn sounded, tourists gathered along the concrete piers lining the canal to watch the bridge go up, allowing deep-water vessels, even ocean-going ships, to enter or leave the harbor.

Jackie waved at Camille, the owner of the bookstore two doors down. Just as Jackie dusted all the artwork in her shop every morning, Camille swept the sidewalk in front of the bookstore before wheeling out a cart of older hardbacks offered on sale. The lake was only a hundred yards from her door, close enough for Jackie to smell its cool freshness on the air, but far enough to be blocked from view by traffic and the two-story motel on the water's edge.

The Tempest was housed in a row of refurbished stone warehouses that at one time served the commercial needs of the Duluth harbor. Painted in flamboyant hues, with brilliant multi-colored trim work, signs, and doors, the shops were as unique as their owners and the merchandise within. Everything from tacky souvenir baubles to high-end baby boomer clothing was represented. The hip coffee shop on the corner always had a line of customers, and Camille hosted well-attended book clubs in her bookstore on an almost daily basis, but Jackie would argue that it was The Tempest that brought a classy atmosphere to the row of shops. All her efforts were directed toward elegance and beauty, and she considered the gallery itself to be a work of art.

A furrow wrinkled her brow as she thought of the commitment required to maintain that aura of effortless grace. Randall was useless. Of course it was his gallery, but since she'd come on board over a year ago it seemed more of the day-to-day management had fallen to her. Randall had his various business cronies, their luncheon meetings, and their private little business dealings. She'd never really understood exactly what it was that he did to lead such a privileged lifestyle, but it sure didn't seem to take any long hours or self-sacrifice.

Before she'd taken over management of The Tempest, the gallery was nothing more than a two-bit souvenir shop, selling western-style artwork, postcards, the usual run of snow globes and collector spoons made in China, and cheap birchbark and beaded Native American trinkets made in a factory in Illinois. What Randall couldn't seem to understand was that it took capital, a lot of capital, to run a first-rate gallery.

Her looming financial predicament darkened Jackie's countenance even further. Randall was so quick to blame her for the escalating debts. She argued that it wasn't her fault. She was doing what she had to do to make the gallery profitable.

She'd realized from the outset that The Tempest was her ticket out of Black Otter Bay—certainly the best, and perhaps her only means of escape. The men from the casino had been more than willing to extend a line of credit to her through Randall. It wasn't her fault that he'd never explained the timeframe to her, or the ridiculous interest rates they expected. It wasn't her fault that she'd hit a run of bad luck. But even as it continued to sour, hadn't she cut back on the hours she spent at the card tables? There were no more all-nighters, even though one good hand, or a lucky pull on a slot machine, could change all their fortunes.

When Jackie reached back for the door handle, her eye caught the approach of a large luxury sedan. It stuck out from the usual run of minivans and yuppie SUVs so common in Canal Park. It pulled up to the curb across from the gallery, and for a moment Jackie's heart froze at the thought that it might be one of those thugs from the casino. Through the darkened windows of the car she saw the driver glance at the gallery while talking on a cell phone. He said a few more words, slipped the phone into his coat pocket, and turned off the ignition.

When the car door opened, Jackie stood rooted in place as a tall man, large without being overweight, emerged from behind the wheel. She noted the casual way he buttoned his expensive sport coat with the fingers of one hand. When he paused at the side of the car waiting for traffic to pass, she was taken by the utter blackness of his sunglasses. She took another look at the sky. Dark clouds billowed overhead, tumbling ashore out of the vast wasteland over Lake Superior. If she hadn't known it was the beginning of June, she'd say it looked like snow coming. At the very least, it certainly wasn't sunglasses weather.

She retreated into the gallery. It was just so unfair, she thought, the way people ridiculed and blamed her. The situation should be obvious: good art commanded good prices, and eventually The Tempest would underwrite itself with a high-end inventory. But it didn't just happen overnight. She was confident she had the knowledge, but it also took time, effort, and a lot of money. She glanced outside to see the man crossing the street. "Leave me alone," she muttered to the artwork around her as she slid in behind the counter. A heated blush rose in her cheeks, and tears threatened to well up in her eyes. "I'm doing everything I can," she said to the pictures on the wall, as if trying to convince them, as well as herself, that none of this was her fault. "I'm risking everything, including the welfare of my children, to fix the problem."

And then it occurred to her, with a glimmer of hope, that maybe that was the reason for this stranger's sudden appearance: another stupid cop, with more questions about Ben, and nosy innuendoes regarding the divorce. If that were the case, at least she wouldn't have to make excuses for the money she owed. Those idiot associates of Randall's would never talk to the police about her debts. They had other means of collecting their money.

With shaking fingers, she distracted herself by arranging pens and papers next to the cash register. Then the sleigh bells over the entranceway jingled, and the sounds of traffic and voices and the wind accompanied the man through the door.

Acting nonchalant, as if too busy to notice his arrival, she even abandoned her usual smile and greeting. Seconds ticked by in which she expected him to directly approach the counter. She brushed away imaginary paper scraps and dust, rearranged the countertop items once again, and then in a fit of anxious energy grabbed the telephone and held it to her ear. The dial tone was so loud! He'd have to hear the incessant buzzing.

Finally, she stole a peek at the tall man in the well-cut suit. He stood in front of the Oberg, as far back as he could manage, to get the clearest overall view of the work. His head canted to one side in a thoughtful pose, with his gelled hairstyle standing straight up. On a younger man she'd say it was the early stages of a Mohawk, but he was too old for that, and with his deep tan and muscular good looks, she decided it was just his personal style. His sunglasses hung out of the chest pocket of his sport coat now, while his hands were casually slipped into his trouser pockets.

Jackie dropped the phone back in its cradle and turned to face the man. Still not ready to come out from behind the counter, she leaned against the cash register, a hand resting on her hip. "That's an Oberg," she said.

No reply, other than a soft sigh.

Jackie cleared her throat and stepped out from behind the counter. Still keeping her distance, she asked, "Are you familiar with Phillip Oberg's work?"

The man looked at her and smiled. "Sure. I've seen copies of this one before. I never thought I'd actually see the original, though."

Letting her guard down completely, Jackie approached the stranger, saying, "Phillip Oberg was from Massachusetts. He died just last winter." She found it refreshing to be in the company of someone who understood and appreciated good art. "Most of our inventory represents a Lake Superior theme," she continued, "or at least the Great Lakes. But Oberg is just so classic, you know?"

The big man extracted a pair of half-glasses from inside his coat pocket. Holding them over the bridge of his nose, he stepped up to the painting for a closer look. "Vermont," he said.

"Beg your pardon?"

Studying the painting at close range, scrutinizing the signature, he said, "Phillip Oberg was from Vermont. Many of his seascapes, like this one, were painted in Massachusetts: Cape Cod, Martha's Vineyard, Nantucket, and all that. For that reason it's been a long-held misconception that he was from Massachusetts." He turned to peer at Jackie over the top of his glasses. "But he was a lifelong resident of Vermont."

Jackie found herself grinning like a schoolgirl, but couldn't think of a word to say. Fortunately, the stranger continued. "Not a lot of rustic seacoast in Vermont to paint."

Jackie sidled up to the man to make her own distracted in-spection of the work.

The stranger said, "Oberg spent some of his early years up in Maine, but he said the whole coastline up there looked the same. Paint one scene, he contended, and you've done them all."

Now Jackie was chuckling, a spontaneous reaction to the release of tension as well as joy in the intellectual banter.

"Where did you get it?" he asked.

She wiped a hand across her face to erase the schoolgirl grin. Clearing her throat again and straightening up into a busi-ness-like posture, she started slowly. "It was over a year ago. I was in Chicago with the owner of the gallery when I noticed the Oberg come up for auction at an estate sale. I never ex-pected to bid on it. Really, I just wanted to see it." She held a hand out to the painting as if introducing it to a crowd. "It was beautiful." Looking up to the stranger, she concluded, "In short, somehow we were able to get it. It's the centerpiece of the gallery now."

"I'm sure it was a wise investment," he said, and with a smirk added, "Especially now that Mr. Oberg has passed away."

It was hard not to grin at this obviously fortuitous event. But Jackie maintained a straight face, commenting, "It's true that it's probably worth more than everything else in the gallery combined. But just think of all the beautiful work that will go undone with his passing. Phillip Oberg wasn't an old man by any means."

It became impossible to refrain from smiling when she saw the amusement on the stranger's face. Moments later, the obvious insincerity of her words invoked a quiet laughter, as when friends share an inside joke.

"So, you're confident this is an original?" he asked. "I've seen copies."

"I have a signed affidavit from the previous owner, and a letter from the artist that accompanied it."

The man nodded and smiled. Putting away his reading glasses, he turned to her, and in a casual tone asked, "If you don't mind, what were you doing in Chicago?"

The mood in the gallery had lightened considerably. Jackie barely heard the sleigh bells over the door as an older couple entered the shop.

"Actually, I'm from Chicago," she said. "I went to Northwestern for a couple of years before moving up here."

"My alma mater," he said. "Although several years before you, I'm sure."

Jackie blushed.

"Evanston was a great college setting," he said. "Right on Lake Michigan. I used to jog Lakeshore Drive."

"Don't forget the Magnificent Mile," she added.

"Remember the Drake Hotel?"

Then, in unison, "The Bookbinder's Soup?"

Both were laughing again. Jackie looked over at the couple who'd come in. They stood transfixed before the latest oversized depiction of the sinking of the *Fitzgerald*. It was hard not to roll her eyes when she shared the company of this knowledgeable gentleman.

When she looked at him again, however, the smile was gone, replaced by a cold, hard stare. All sign of their recent friendly chatter was gone. In an instant her fears and anxieties rushed back. He said, "How much do you think the Oberg is worth, Jackie?"

How does he know my name? she wondered. *We never introduced ourselves, how does he know?* She backpedaled a couple of steps, but he followed her, coming even closer.

"Let me put it to you this way, Jackie. How much are you willing to sacrifice for the Oberg?"

She shook her head. *This must be a misunderstanding,* she thought. Her mouth opened, her lips moved, but she couldn't manage a single word. Then the sleigh bells jingled again as Randall hustled through the door. Spotting them immediately, he rushed over. Jackie couldn't get her mind around this latest turn of events, standing transfixed under the bullying stare of the well-dressed stranger. Randall edged his way between them and said, "I got here as soon as I could."

His darting, shifty eyes bounced from the stranger to Jackie, to the couple across the room, and finally back to Jackie again. She'd always found it a little unnerving how his expression could mimic a predator one minute and an abject victim the next, but it was reassuring to see this aggressive, take-charge attitude now.

Rubbing his hands together as if working out a chill, Randall took a deep breath and said, "Why don't you help that couple over there, dear? See if there's something you can show them." His voice held steady and sounded calm, giving Jackie room to think that perhaps all this could still be okay.

The men withdrew to the small office behind the cash register counter. When the door closed, Jackie found herself wandering in that direction, too, but knew from experience that the thick stone walls kept conversations private. Even loud noises were muffled or distorted to the point of incoherence. When she stopped to think about what she was doing, she found herself once again rearranging items on the counter. She looked at the couple at the far end of the gallery. It seemed they had no idea something was amiss in the next room; they probably hadn't even noticed Randall's entrance. They stood close to each other, deep in conversation in front of the *Fitzgerald*.

Jackie took another moment to compose herself. Randall hadn't acted too upset. Maybe it wasn't as bad as she imagined. She pulled her hair back, held it up off her neck, and then let it fall in a wave over her shoulders. The stranger had been such a gentleman, so well spoken and knowledgeable. Surely he wasn't tied up in all this mess. Besides, she thought, her name was on the gallery door. He could've seen it there and assumed correctly it was her. She stepped around the counter and smoothed out her skirt. Walking toward the couple, she tried to put the incident aside, but the intensity of the stranger's glare had rattled her nerves right to their core.

It was her nose for a sale that finally snapped her out of it. Like a marketing machine, she made note of the couple's name-brand clothing, their pale skin, and soft hands. They wore high-tech, expensive outdoor wear, even though she guessed their most strenuous activity probably had to do with walking a pure-bred lapdog down the driveway. They were in their mid-sixties, she supposed, as the woman turned to meet her approach, clutching an expensive leather-grained purse under her arm.

"This is just the most amazing painting," the woman said, holding fingers with painted nails to her throat.

"Yes," Jackie replied, trying to drum up some enthusiasm.

"But it's all wrong," the husband said. "It shows the *Fitzgerald* breaking in two, but it wouldn't have broken up before going down."

Jackie looked at him in disbelief. *You've got to be kidding me.*

"There's no way you can know that," his wife countered. "I mean, were you there? What makes you an expert on shipwrecks?"

"So you're saying this artist was there?" her husband argued. "Does he know something the experts haven't figured out yet about how the *Fitzgerald* went down?"

Back and forth they went until Jackie wasn't listening anymore. Her eyes fixed on a small tag on the arm of the man's shirt. She'd seen one like it before. It explained that the material had been treated with an insect repellant, a high-tech fad for people with too much money. She stepped closer and cleared her throat. "You know," she said, "I think I have something over here that might be of even more interest to you."

The husband stood a little to one side, aloof, giving Jackie the impression that he was accustomed to being in charge. He was the boss, made the important decisions, and she would guess that he also controlled the purse strings. She threw him her best smile, and when he made eye contact with her, she demurely looked away. Leading the wife by the arm to the Oberg, she had no doubt he'd follow close behind.

Speaking intimately, as if privately to the woman, but loud enough for the trailing husband to hear, she said, "I believe this extraordinary piece is much more commensurate with your station." The wife looked a little confused, but Jackie saw the husband immediately step closer to make his appraisal.

"All I see is water," the woman said.

"Ah, but just look at that water," Jackie responded. "Look at the movement, the color. There's more going on in that painting than you think."

She suspected that the husband kept quiet out of ignorance as he stepped closer. They studied the painting in silence for several moments before she became aware of the background drone of voices coming from the office. She couldn't make out any of the words, but easily detected their short, staccato-like phrases uttered in anger. *Randall must be holding his own*, she thought.

"Is that supposed to be the sky?" the wife asked, pointing to the top of the painting.

"That doesn't matter," Jackie said, adding just a hint of impatience. She leaned toward the husband, explaining in a confidential tone, "See the lighting in the waves over here? Notice how much brighter it is than on the other side? It's nothing but chaos over there, and now here comes the light, perhaps even salvation, if you will."

The husband stood with arms folded, listening intently, watching Jackie's slender fingers pointing from side to side. When she looked at him, he nodded, as if all she had said was obvious.

"But there isn't a ship or a lighthouse or anything to look at," the woman whined. "Not even a seagull."

Her husband said, "Didn't you hear her? None of that matters. The story is all here in the water."

Jackie stepped back. This might be easier than she'd thought.

To her husband, the wife said, "In case you haven't noticed, Mr. Art Critic, there isn't a price tag on this thing. I bet that splash of water is going to cost you a fortune."

The office door suddenly opened, causing Jackie to jump. She turned to look. Randall held the door as the tall stranger stepped back into the gallery, buttoning his sport coat before pulling the dark glasses out of his pocket and settling them over his eyes. Jackie's breath caught in her throat when he walked straight up to her.

"It was so nice talking to you, Jackie," he said. "Randall found the artist's paperwork you told me about." He waved a manila envelope in front of her before folding it into his coat pocket. "I believe this arrangement will work well for everyone involved." And with that, he stepped between the elderly couple and reached up to lift the Oberg off the wall.

"But you can't," Jackie muttered.

Randall appeared behind her and placed his hands on her shoulders. She squirmed enough to feel his grip tighten, and realized he wasn't there to support her so much as to restrain her.

The husband said, "But we were looking at that painting, too."

When the stranger irreverently cradled the framed piece under his long arm like a stack of schoolbooks, Jackie opened her mouth to protest further. He paused for a moment to look at her, and even though his expression was hidden behind the dark glasses, his brazen behavior stunned her into silence. He turned his attention to the elderly couple, nodding in the direction of the far wall. "There's an interesting painting of the *Edmund Fitzgerald* over there," he said. "I think you'll like it."

The wife piped up, "That's what I thought, too!" Then she turned to lead the way back across the gallery, leaving Jackie behind to watch the Oberg walk out the door.

TEN

Randall Bengston

"How could you!" Jackie shouted, shoving papers aside on the desk so she could lean over to yell at Randall. "Do you know how much that painting is worth?"

In anticipation of her tirade, Randall had seated himself out of reach behind the desk. "The question is, my dear, do *you* know how much that painting is worth?"

"Argh!" she exclaimed, sweeping a small shelving unit to the floor. Through clenched teeth she said, "It's worth a damn sight more than what I owe the casino."

"It's not worth anything if it's just hanging on our wall."

Jackie had followed Randall into the office after the stranger walked out with the painting, leaving the elderly couple to ponder the sinking of the *Edmund Fitzgerald* on their own. She leaned over the desk now on white-knuckled fists. Frustration buzzed over her nerves like a spark along a fuse. Attempting to control her anger, she lowered her voice to say, "I was about to sell that painting to the couple out there."

"Sure you were. And the last time I dragged you away from the card table, you were about to sell my Miata for less than trade-in value."

Jackie swung a fist at him, missing by a good two feet as Randall leaned back in his chair. His self-righteous grin infuriated her. Sweeping a hand across the desk, she flung another pile of paperwork to the floor. Jabbing a finger at him, in a quivering voice she said, "The card tables and that painting are two different things. Meanwhile, your idiot friend out there is hauling an original Oberg around town under his arm."

"At least he knows what it's worth."

Jackie took a deep breath to draw in her anger. Just what did he mean by that? While Randall began reorganizing the trashed desktop, she studied the man who'd helped restart her life outside of Black Otter Bay. He hadn't shaved this morning, and it occurred to her that when she'd seen the stranger pull up in front of the gallery, it was Randall he'd been talking to on the cell phone. Despite everything he'd done for her, and the obvious fact that he adored her, Jackie knew better than to completely trust anything Randall said. He didn't generally lie outright, but sometimes he said things in such a way as to leave them open to interpretation.

She said, "What do you mean? You said he knows what the painting is worth. How would he know?"

Randall got up to retrieve the desktop shelf from the floor. "That 'idiot' you speak of has an MBA from Northwestern, but his undergraduate degree was in art history." After replacing the tray of shelves he looked at her and said, "He did his homework, Jackie. He knows what the Oberg will bring at auction."

"But it has to be more than I owe."

Randall nodded and shrugged. "The point is, my dear, we don't have what you owe, and now they're tired of waiting. The Oberg will buy us some time."

"Well, who is he?"

Randall sifted through a stack of receipts, not really looking at them as he eyed Jackie. She knew that look, and knew the next thing out of his mouth could mean almost anything.

"He's the oldest son of an associate of mine in Chicago."

"What's he doing here?"

Randall acted surprised. "Collecting on a debt, obviously."

"You said he majored in art history. He sounds more like a gangster to me."

"He's no crook. In fact, he'll soon be running their family business. The college degrees just mean he's no dummy." Now Randall's expression turned dour and serious. "He's no one to mess with, Jackie."

She remembered the severe look the stranger had given her, how cold and heartless he'd acted, even in the face of her vulnerability. She shuddered at the memory and decided Randall wasn't exaggerating much on this one.

She watched him carefully aligning things on the desk. Randall wasn't a big man by any means. Compared to the stranger, he was absolutely tiny. His unshaven beard sprouted thin and scraggly, and with wispy strands of prematurely graying hair hanging to his shoulders, next to the clean-cut physique of the businessman from Chicago he looked downright pathetic. In his late forties, Randall was several years older than her, but Jackie's critical appraisal softened when she considered the benevolent way he'd treated her. He was fair and kind, much in the way that Matthew had been good to her. The big difference was that he offered something her ex-husband and Black Otter Bay could never give: the chance to dream big. And she had to admit that it was very generous the way Randall considered her personal debts to be their shared problem. While he often made fun of her gambling, laughing at her for hanging out with the old folks and drunks at the downtown casino, he never made an issue out of the money. It was almost as if he thought of their relationship like one of his business deals: you agree to be my live-in partner, to accompany me on social outings, and I'll accept your gambling problem and agree to work through whatever debts you incur.

"How long have you been planning to use the Oberg?" she asked. Most of her anger was spent, but she wasn't ready to let it all go just yet. "Were you ever going to tell me, or was it more fun to watch my surprise when he took it?"

Randall paused in his straightening up to look at her. "It just came up this morning, Jackie."

"I thought you had a deal with them."

For the briefest moment a shadow passed over his face, and she felt a little sorry for reminding him of the circumstances of his mother's death. But his usual smirking grin soon returned. "Business deals ebb and flow, honey. They sort of have a life of their own. Over time they often change, especially when nothing is written down."

"What is that supposed to mean?"

Randall eased around the desk and took her hands. "Listen, Jackie. We still have the original deal on the table. Once the estate is settled, we'll see if we can get it done. You'll be able to buy two or three Obergs then. We'll take a trip, maybe New York or something. Take in some shows."

New York. About as far from Black Otter Bay as a person could get. The very idea caused her breath to catch in her throat. She stood up straighter and drew a deep sigh. Randall reached out and wiped a thumb over her cheek. She hadn't realized how many tears her anger had produced.

He said, "I think you should get out there and sell that *Fitzgerald* while you can."

Feeling emotionally numb, she was grateful for the warmth in his smile. Grabbing her purse out of a desk drawer, she retrieved a tissue to dab at her face.

"It's just a painting," Randall said, but when she looked at him, he clarified that by adding, "I mean the Oberg. There are many more like it out there. Even better ones. You'll find them in the future, and you'll handle them. You'll buy them and sell them and who knows, maybe someday you'll even hang one on your own wall."

She glanced at the mirror hanging on the back of the office door, wiped away another smudge in her makeup, and then reached for the door handle. When she turned to look back, it was her intention to leave him with a smile, but she was too worn out to manage it and ended up slipping out the door with no more than a modest nod.

· · · · ·

Well before dawn on a November morning in 1975, ten-year-old Randall Bengston awoke to the sound of his father's voice. "Randy? Come on, Randy. Time to get up. Let's go."

He rolled over with a groan and promptly fell back to sleep.

A short time later the old man was back. "Goddamn it, Randy. Let's go now, boy."

Randall looked up at his father's backlit form standing in the bedroom doorway. His heart sank when he saw the yellow rain slicker and knee-high rubber boots. He carried a lantern in one hand, a lunch pail in the other. This wasn't the nightmare Randall had hoped for. It was worse.

He quickly dressed and went downstairs to find the warmth in the kitchen. A stack of pancakes sat on a plate under a warm dishtowel on the kitchen table. Before he could sit down, however, his father tromped into the room in his extra large rubber boots. "You'll have to bring it along. You slept through breakfast again." He grabbed a paper sack from a drawer and sloughed it on the table. "We got to go. Barometer's been dropping all night. We got about enough time to get out and back before it sets up good to blow."

Randall grabbed the top pancake, folded it in half, and bit into it like a sandwich. Still warm, it emanated a comforting glow as it slid down his throat. Rosie's pancakes had achieved legendary status in Black Otter Bay. Some folks claimed they didn't even need butter or syrup, that's how light and moist they were. He dropped the remainder of the pile into the bag and followed his father out the back door. In the mudroom entryway he grabbed his raincoat and shoved the bag of pancakes in an oversized pocket. Unlike his father's yellow rubber boots, his were black with red soles, and so big they came up to the tops of his knees, making sitting down, or even walking, a hazardous undertaking.

Through the open door he heard his mother's laughter coming from the bait shop. A pickup truck with a boat and trailer was parked out back. A couple men wearing insulated coveralls stood in the driveway, the yard light illuminating them, hands in pockets, caps tilted up and back, a yellow lab sniffing around their feet. Rose was giving directions to some inland fishing lake. *Why would anyone do this?* Randall asked himself. Icy snow granules lit up as they shot past the flood lamp. It was the middle of the night. Why would anyone want to be out in this weather to catch a slimy old fish?

His father nodded at the fishermen and set his lantern on a table just inside the bait shop door. When he began pumping up the lamp's gas chamber, Randall seized the moment to grab another pancake from the sack. He stood out of the wind in the entryway. This was the way his Saturday mornings had begun since before he could remember. From early spring until late in the fall, while his classmates were sleeping in and planning football or basketball games, he was traipsing around half asleep in the cold and dark. As long as the shoreline remained free of ice, he helped his father with his commercial fishing nets.

He looked out at his mother chatting with the customers. She'd thrown on a woolen sweater over her housedress and apron, but it was easy to see she was getting cold as she lightly rocked on the balls of her feet, arms folded tightly under her breasts. She looked at him and smiled, but he wasn't about to leave this last bastion of warmth even one second before he had to.

The fishermen turned to leave, and Rose joined her husband in the bait shop. The lantern was lit now. Randall grabbed things off a shelf: a woolen stocking cap, a pair of light gloves he stashed in his pockets, and a heavier pair of lined leather choppers. The pancakes had settled warm and heavy in his stomach, returning his thoughts to the comforts of bed and sleep. Then his father called, and he stabbed around in the darker corners of the entryway to find his flashlight.

His mother met him halfway across the driveway. She took him by the shoulders and looked into his eyes. Embarrassed, he looked to the side to see his father's lantern heading toward the path around the bait shop.

"You be careful now, Randall," his mother was saying. "Don't stand up in the boat like your father does. You hear me?"

"I don't want to go, Mom."

She patted his coat pocket. "You have your pancakes?" They'd done this before.

"He doesn't need me, Mom. Please don't make me go."

Rose pulled her son closer. "But he does need you. And even more, I need you to be there to keep an eye on him." She reached out to pull his cap down snug over his forehead, and then zipped up his heavy raincoat. She said, "You understand what I'm saying?"

He nodded.

Rose placed her hands back on his shoulders and patted him one last time. "You do a good job now, Randall. That big boat will keep you safe. You make your father proud." And then she scooted around him to disappear into the warmth of the house.

He watched her leave, standing still in the driveway as the back door closed. Sometimes he hated her. Why couldn't she stand up to the old man? She ran the household with a military-style precision and kept the bait shop profitable all by herself. Everyone in town thought the world of Rose Bengston, but Randall knew she'd never challenge the actions of her husband. They were only a generation away from the hand to mouth, sustenance existence of the early settlers, a world where husbands were never questioned, even when it meant championing the safety or wellbeing of an only son.

When the yard lamp over the bait shop door turned off, he hastily grabbed for his flashlight. The backyard and driveway suddenly fell into a terrifying black darkness. Clouds filled the sky, covering up and blotting out any light emitted from the stars or moon. The combination of absolute darkness and shivering cold scared him, like one of the vampires in his comic books, threatening to suck the breath out of him. It frightened him in the same way that the dark depths of the big body of water out there scared him.

Far off through the woods he spotted his father's lantern bobbing between the trees toward the shore. Following the meager glow of his flashlight, Randall made his way around the bait shop and picked up the pathway to the boathouse. He'd hardly started out, however, before he stopped at a sound coming up through the woods. It took a moment to identify, and even after he did he couldn't believe his ears. A dull, intermittent roar rolled over the land, like a giant sea monster coming ashore. It was the surf pounding the black sand beach, pulverizing it with rhythmic violence. He couldn't remember ever hearing the waves so loud up here, so far away from the shore. He scrunched his head down to avoid overhanging branches and stumbled along as quickly as he could.

The only entrance to the boathouse faced the lake. Carefully edging his way around the building, the glow from Randall's flashlight reflected off wet logs on the front wall. "But it's not raining," he thought out loud, just as the spray from another wave crashed against their homemade breakwater, splashing over him and landing high up against the wall. The roar of waves pouncing on the beach sent a shudder through him, and fear prodded his boots over the boat rails and into the dim lighting and relative safety of the boathouse.

His father was in the boat arranging equipment and lashing down loose items like oars and his wooden box of tools. The boat itself was huge, eighteen feet long and made of thick slabs of white cedar over solid oak ribs. Hand-crafted by the Aasen Brothers Boatwrights in town, it boasted an extremely deep V-hull and a long-handled wooden tiller attached to the outboard motor. Randall's father bragged to anyone who'd listen that it was the most seaworthy boat afloat.

"It's a storm out there," Randall said, but his voice blew away in the roar of the surf.

"Hand me up my bucket," his father called, pointing to his lunch pail on the floor.

Randall lifted it over the transom, where Henry Bengston was tying down his seat cushion near the twenty-year-old outboard. With the boat resting atop the rail cart, the gunwales were as high as Randall's head.

Louder this time, he said, "Dad, it's storming out there."

His father reached over the transom to give him a hand up. "Hell, this ain't no storm, son. It's just loosening up. Give it a day or two and you'll see it blow."

Pulling on his father's arm, Randall climbed atop the rails and scaled the vessel's transom. The wide-open middle section of the boat was lined with narrow wooden planks running the length of the keel, used as a walkway and platform for nets and gear. The only seats were two wide boards spanning the width of the boat, one in back for the person running the motor and a smaller one up front. Using the long-handled tiller, a fellow could work his nets from the middle of the boat and still control the direction of travel.

Randall stepped out on the planking, but his father held him back. He draped a coil of rope over his head and cinched it up tight under Randall's arms. On the other end of the rope was a heavy snap ring. "Clip this on the eye of that cleat up there," his father said, nodding at the bow of the boat.

"But, Dad . . ."

"It's just a precaution," he said. "I promised your mother."

"But it's really bad out there, Dad. I've never heard it so loud before."

Henry Bengston knelt on one knee and made a show of going over Randall's work clothes, tugging on the raincoat's zipper and pulling his collar up tight around his neck. "It's not even raining yet, son. And this boat will take any wave that lake throws at her." He chuckled. "It's not like the old days when we went out in them shallow fourteen-foot skiffs. No, sir." He stood up and nodded toward the bow. "Go ahead now and get your seat."

Randall slowly made his way along the narrow floorboards, feeling like a pirate walking the plank. Behind him his father shouted instructions. "We'll not be wasting time sorting fish today. Everything comes in. It's time to mend nets, so in a day or two when this weather has blown over, I'll put them back out."

Randall took his seat in the bow facing the stern and his father. He pulled in ten feet of the rope tied around his torso and, taking hold of the slip ring, clipped it to one of the bow cleats. He hadn't done this since he was five years old, since that first season on the lake when his mother insisted that he be clipped to the boat. But he wasn't a kid anymore, and it would have been embarrassing if he weren't already scared to death.

Henry Bengston worked quickly now. Pulling an overhead cord disengaged the rail cart, and the heavy boat slowly trundled down the rails into the water. By the time it floated free, he'd started the outboard motor. The boathouse quickly filled with smoke as the two-cycle engine coughed to life. Backing out, Randall watched as his father reached up to hang the lantern from an ancient wrought-iron hook over the doorway. It was meant to aid in pinpointing their destination upon their return, but the boy knew it was just a throwback to the old days when fishermen used oars to row out to the nets and back to shore. The nets were smaller and often placed just a few hundred yards out back then. The men usually returned shortly after dawn, and the lantern could help in a fog or low light. In truly bad weather, family members built bonfires on the beach to aid in navigation. But Henry continued to hang the lantern every time he went out, perhaps out of habit, or as Randall suspected, as a nod of respect to the old ways.

The short breakwater of boulders gave them just enough time to get turned around and pointed into the swells before the first breaker crashed against the bow, spraying ice-cold water over Randall. He cringed, ducking low while tugging at his collar to better protect his neck. In the stern, his father burst out laughing. "Bet you're awake now," he shouted over the din of the storm.

Randall ignored him, instead twisting around to look out to sea. Everything was shrouded in darkness. Even the water itself was black and invisible. When the boat suddenly heaved up over the crest of another wave, a pale streak of daylight glimmered far off on the eastern horizon. Then they plunged into the trough of the next swell, and all was dark again. Meanwhile, Randall's stomach rose and fell with the motion of the sea. He looked back at his father, who yelled, "I ever tell you about the time we went out after your great-uncle Harold?"

Having heard the rescue tale dozens of times, Randall looked down at the floor of the boat and groaned. His stomach was going to be a problem. Henry started in on his story. "Storms back then were much worse than nowadays. Hell, I can't even remember the last honest-to-goodness November gale. I wasn't much older than you at the time."

Randall's stomach rose again. This time he tasted pancakes. Thankfully, most of his father's words blew away on the wind. "Harold went out by himself. He was like that, you know, preferred to work alone. We didn't miss him until after your grandpa and I returned. I tell you what, Randy, we gave them oars a workout that day. Nobody up here had motors back then."

The next wave lifted Randall right off his seat. As they dropped into the following trough, he slipped off the edge of the short bench seat and crumpled in a heap on the wet floor. With no time to spare, he reached up for the gunwale and pulled himself up to vomit over the side. Windswept spray splashed over him as he hung over the edge. His father roared with laughter, a demonic-sounding cackle, leaving Randall to pray that all this was just another aspect of his horrible nightmare.

A quick glance eastward again showed daylight dawning somewhere, but all around them the sky and water swirled in a maelstrom of madness. Henry's voice pierced the storm. "When we finally found him, Harold had tied his skiff to his net to keep from being driven out to sea. He'd busted an oar, and the fool hadn't bothered to stow a spare. He was taking on a lot of water, and another fifteen minutes would have put him under."

Randall vomited again, and then slumped like a wet rag on the cold, narrow floor. His stomach continued rolling as he panted for breath. He lay curled in a fetal position, clutching his stomach like a gut-shot soldier. He closed his eyes and let himself be tossed around by the waves.

His father's story was done, but Randall found himself thinking about his cousins and uncles. Of all the Bengston men who'd made a living off the lake, Henry was the only one left. It was a mystery to Randall why, when outsiders asked about the old days and working the lake, his father never had anything to say. And if he did speak up, he always downplayed the stories. "Oh, sure," he'd say, "we found Uncle Harold easy enough. Just broke an oar and needed a tow." Then he'd laugh, like it was nothing at all. But he loved to tell the stories to family and friends, and every time he did, the storms became larger, the catches heavier, and the fish themselves were mighty monsters from the deep.

Randall held himself tighter. *Damn them all,* he thought. *To hell with all the uncles and cousins and every last one of the Bengstons. To hell with the whole damn town.*

It wasn't until he saw his father up and moving about that he realized they were at the first of their two nets. The motor idled, but Randall couldn't hear it over the storm. Henry hooked the net buoy with a gaff and pulled the trailing rope into the boat. Seconds later he was cranking the winch, hauling in the net, holding himself steady by pulling against the rope. This was usually Randall's job, but with the weather worsening by the minute and the boy curled up in a ball on the floor, his father had decided to hurry things up by doing it himself. The tiller was wedged against Henry's thigh, while the weight of the submerged net held them in place.

Randall tried to get up. "Just stay there," his father yelled without bothering to look at him. Wind-driven waves washed over them, while his father rocked lightly on his toes against the torrent. Yard after yard of net came in with nothing but a few rough fish showing up. The nearby taconite plant, with its warm water tailings discharge, had so contaminated the water near shore that most of the game fish they were after now roamed a mile or two farther out to sea.

Without having to remove the fish or reset the net, it took only minutes for his father to pile the whole rig on the floor. Once again they were on the move. Every swell sent buckets of ice water gushing over the gunwales. From his perch on the floor, Randall opened his eyes to look into the gasping mouth of a two-pound sucker just inches from his face. He gagged and retched, but the pancakes were long since gone. He lay pale and limp on the floor, his head pounding while his stomach rolled. Faint and exhausted, he fell into a delirious sleep, visited by nightmares populated with sea monsters and vampires.

It was a rainy, pale gray dawn the next time he looked out. Heavy clouds tumbled overhead while the sea boiled and churned in discontent. His father was hunched over the tiller, the motor roaring full speed into the tempest. Henry's eyes and face grimaced against the blow. Sprays of water blasted across the bow in all directions. The boat tossed and turned like a carnival ride, while the wind howled a fury above them. Randall recited a prayer in silence, witnessed only by the glassy eyes of the suffocating sucker.

He pressed himself tighter against the bow, using the bench seat above him as a partial rain break. He tried to lessen the nausea by holding himself still, but the violent pitching of the boat offset anything he could do. Shivering almost uncontrollably now, and soaking wet despite his raincoat and boots, he perked up at the sound of his father's laughter. Henry had the second net in the winch, but needed two arms to crank it in this time. Fish came over the rail like on a conveyor belt in a processing plant. His father stood with legs spread wide apart, boots wedged between boat ribs, heavy thighs bracing him against the hull.

"Dad?" Randall called, weak and sickly. Unheard.

Again the old man laughed as a gusher of trout and ciscoes washed in over the side. Ten- and fifteen-pound lake trout flopped around them in a frenzy of energy. Henry began singing, but the wind was playing tricks with Randall's ears, or more likely it was that the words were from an old Norwegian folk song, because he couldn't understand a word of it. Henry looked down at him on the floor. "Must be some kind of a run," he yelled. "The storm must have them all moving. Haven't seen anything like this in years. Yi-hah!" He leaned into the winch, and the boat tipped precariously toward the net.

Randall rolled with the boat, closing his eyes against the nausea and headache. Sometime later, when next he looked around, his father was sprawled out across the pile of netting, his eyes as wide open and blind as the fish flopping all around him.

"Dad?" An image came to mind of a delirious pirate rolling in a treasure chest of doubloons. "Dad! What are you doing?"

Henry Bengston stared at his son. His mouth opened and closed like the fish around him gasping for breath. His Adam's apple bobbed with a swallow, and his tongue lolled around, but his eyes remained fixed on Randall, unblinking.

Kicking at a snarl of rope, netting, and fish, Randall dug his way out from under the bench seat. On hands and knees he slid over the wet, slimy pile to reach his father. "Dad!" he yelled. Grabbing the old man by the shoulders, he shook him hard. "Dad! What's wrong?"

Henry Bengston didn't move. Behind him, the tiller thrashed about in the waves. Water seemed to be everywhere. It blew sideways in the storm, the tops of waves sliced off by the wind and hurled across the deepening swells. The next wave loomed high over the gunwale before throwing Randall against the opposite side hull. "Dad!" he screamed, but the old man lay twitching in a pool of water and fish.

Pushing and shoving, Randall struggled to maneuver his father back on top of the pile of netting. It was horrible how the old man's jaw and lips hung slack to the side.

The boat suddenly pitched dangerously toward the net, knocking Randall off his knees at his father's side and back into the ice-cold slush on the floor. While using the starboard gunwale to pull himself up, he glimpsed the submerged net dragging them low in the water. Then the next wave washed over him, and panic thrust him back to his feet. "Dad!" he screamed. A thousand images flashed through his mind: the motor running but taking them nowhere, the tiller flailing about in the wind, the toolbox strapped to the hull, and the winch bending under the weight of the full net. Then he was airborne, carried over the portside rail by a fifteen-foot wave.

He found the real shock to being thrown overboard was how much warmer and quieter it was beneath the surface than exposed to the gale-force winds in the open boat. Then the rope around his torso yanked tight, instantly dragging him sideways through the water. The force of raging currents sucked off his oversized boots. Water was jammed up his nose and down his throat. He grabbed at the rope to pull himself upright, and when he finally broke the surface he was once again assaulted by the noise and mayhem of the storm. The boat dipped sideways into another swell, giving him an opportunity to grasp the gunwale, and when they rode up the face of another wave, he clambered back aboard.

Lying in the bottom of the boat, coughing and panting for breath, he was horrified to see how much water they'd taken on. The additional weight of the nets and fish caused the boat to ride even lower, where it listed dangerously to the side toward the submerged net. Randall knew immediately what he had to do. Slipping and scrambling, he crawled over the pile of netting and fish to reach the winch. The strap-metal braces securing it to the hull were bent like a child's erector set. He found the handle jammed against a rib in the hull. The whole mechanism buckled and creaked under the strain of the fish-laden net. Try as he might, he couldn't budge the handle.

Desperate now, he made for the toolbox in the stern, for-getting about the rope still lashed around his torso. His feet flew in the air when he was thrown backwards to the floor. Cursing and crying at the same time, he worked at the rope with frozen fingers. Wet and caked in ice, the knot felt like rock against his numb hands. The next wave smashed into them, and once again he crashed into the hull. His father's body rolled with him, and Randall watched as sloshing water flowed in and out of his slack-jawed mouth.

Randall crawled over him, fighting his way to the bow, where he unclipped himself. Returning through the swishing quagmire, he pulled his father back up on the pile of nets, and then crawled his way back to the toolbox. His frozen fingers ached opening the latch, but the first item on the top shelf was a heavy hunting knife with a six-inch blade.

Back to the winch now, he perched precariously on the gunwale at the lowest edge of the boat, hacking and slicing and stabbing at ropes and netting. Everything was wet and frozen, causing the knife to slip off-target time and again. Waves and spray battered him, until he wrapped an arm around the winch to support himself, and with the other hand worked the point of the knife deep into the ropes. Digging and wedging, he fi-nally made a cut, allowing room to insert the knife farther. With renewed hope he used both hands again, forcing the knife with all his might, until the next wave rolled high over the gun-wale and threw him across the boat, cracking his head against a hull rib.

Eyes closed against the searing pain, for a moment he rev-eled in the concussion-induced silence. As the sound of the storm slowly returned, however, he vaguely wondered what had happened to the knife. It seemed to be his only chance for survival. Fully conscious again, he decided he had to find it, and opened his eyes to once again look face to face into the unblinking stare of his father. The old man had come to rest on top of him. Randall couldn't move, splayed out on his back with the weight of Henry Bengston's torso across his chest. He gasped for breath in the swirling slush-pile on the bottom of the boat, his right arm twisted painfully underneath him.

It can't possibly end like this, he thought. He hadn't even wanted to be here. He'd begged his mother, hadn't he? And now here he was, drowning in this fucking boat, and he couldn't even move. Tears sprang out on his cheeks. "Goddamn boat!" he yelled, kicking at the only thing his legs could reach: the strap-braces holding the winch in place. Pain in his bootless, frozen feet shot up through his legs, further igniting his anger. He kicked the winch again, his frustration welcoming the pain. "Fucking shit-ass lake!" And then he let loose, kicking and cursing with all his might, while his father's blank face stared at him. He cursed his parents and his life in Black Otter Bay. He stomped out his hatred for the lake and the fish that swam there. And then he heard a loud crack, a splintering of wood, and just when he thought the boat was breaking into pieces, he saw the winch catapulted over the gunwale by the weight of the net. The boat immediately rose on the waves as the heavy net unraveled back into the sea. Fish and rope and netting went overboard, yanked out from under him. His father was dragged across the boat and dumped in a heap on the spot where the winch had been.

Randall got his arm out from under him and rose to a knee to look over the rail. No longer anchored low in the water by the submerged net, the boat raced over the surface, propelled in its newly acquired buoyancy by a ceaseless battering of waves. Half stumbling, half crawling, he reached the tiller and steadied himself into the rear seat. He knew how to run the motor. He'd done it many times with his father on quiet, calm days.

Sitting up now and getting his first good look around them, Randall saw how truly wild the seas were. He felt the wind buffeting him from every direction at once. He couldn't believe they were still afloat. Maybe his mother had been right when she said the big boat would keep him safe. Then he took an even wider look around them and realized that all he could see was water. In every direction, as far as the horizon, nothing but a black and white fury of waves, whitecaps, and sea spray.

He twisted the throttle, revved the motor, and the boat shot out at an angle up the side of a wave, nearly flipping over on itself. He backed off the throttle and used the tiller to run them high and dry before the wind. He had no idea which way to go, but following the swells seemed like a good plan. At this point, he figured, one direction was as good as another.

He looked down at his father gently rocking against the hull, his mouth opening and closing, his throat swallowing, but his eyes maintaining their vacant stare. "We're going home, Dad," Randall called out loud, as much to himself as anyone.

For several minutes they ran fast with the swells, until he surveyed a low-lying band of dense fog out past the point of the bow. To the young man driving the boat, it looked every bit like the very edge of Earth itself. And then, above the fog, looking like a protective angel, appeared the faint outline of a tower. Randall blinked and rubbed his eyes at this miraculous apparition. Just before the little boat disappeared into the fog, he recognized the familiar steeple over First Lutheran Church.

He held the tiller steady, letting the motor and the waves carry them swiftly through the blinding fog. Looking back on it, Randall knew the danger he'd run in making that decision. It could easily have resulted in a bone-crushing collision with the rocky shoreline. And it was especially foolish because he'd already spotted the church and knew they were so close to land-fall. But it seemed his luck had finally turned. The enormous surf carried them over the first barrier of jagged boulders and ran them safely aground atop the flat bedrock shore. The propeller howled its outrage against the rocks before the motor died. The next wave eased up against them and gently tipped the boat on its side, but they were back on shore. Just before Randall closed his eyes in exhausted relief, he glimpsed Pastor Petersen in his flowing black robes running toward them down the path from the church.

• • • • •

In the office of his appropriately named art gallery, The Tempest, Randall sighed and shook his head at the memory. Everything he'd done since that day had been in preparation for leaving. By the time he was in high school, he'd begun hanging out in Duluth, working minimum wage jobs in fast food restaurants and motels. The summer after graduation, he rented a fleabag apartment in the West End. With an eye always open for opportunity, his part-time jobs soon led to various connections and better paying positions. He learned to negotiate the fine line between legal and illegal business transactions. That's not to say he became a hardened criminal, or even aspired to it. But he paid close attention to money—where it was, who had it, and how best to ensure he had enough of it to keep him as far from Black Otter Bay as possible.

His father had suffered a severe stroke that November day, and died a few weeks later. No one ever blamed Randall for what happened, but no one ever praised him for getting them back to shore, either. Doc Thompson, however, hinted that if Henry Bengston had gotten medical attention sooner, perhaps they could have done something for him.

Randall suffered his frostbitten fingers and toes in silence. He accepted the ongoing nightmares as punishment for his ineptitude and lack of skill. But he never went out on the big lake again, and adamantly refused to have anything to do with the bait shop. Never again did he ask his mother for anything. But that little nugget of anger he'd discovered while lying on his back in the bottom of the boat became his best friend. He nurtured it and got to know it well. In his newfound life in the city, it helped him level the playing field when he dealt with richer, more powerful men.

Over time, the makeshift breakwater down on the shore began falling apart under the constant battering of ice and waves off lake Superior. The boat rails and rail cart were still there, but the boathouse itself was deserted to the whims of Mother Nature. As an historical example of the disappearing Great Lakes commercial fishing industry, the tough old eighteen-foot open boat was hauled into town and put on display for tourists outside the Black Otter Bay Municipal Bar. And a day after Randall's deliverance from the storm, the 729-foot freighter *Edmund Fitzgerald* sank in 530 feet of water in thirty-five-foot waves just outside Whitefish Bay.

• • • • •

He looked up from his desk when Jackie returned to the office. It was good to see the smile on her face. She must have resolved her disappointment over losing the Oberg. That was good, he thought as he returned her smile, because he had something even tougher to discuss with her now.

"Guess what?" she asked, all perky and happy. "We sold the *Fitzgerald*. Got a damn good price, too." She placed a charge account receipt on the desk in front of him. He picked it up, looked it over, and nodded his approval.

Randall got to his feet, his usual mousey-looking self on the outside, but comforted by the rising anger within. He took a couple of short paces behind the desk, then turned on Jackie while the smile still lingered on her face. "How's Ben?" he asked. "Did he call this morning?"

Jackie's lighthearted demeanor immediately disappeared. Replacing it was her recent, more familiar countenance of haggard hand-wringing. "Ben's fine," she replied, wary. "Why?"

Randall shrugged. "He's having a good time, right?"

From Jackie's point of view, they were back on treacherous footing where it was best to say little and listen closely. "It sounds like you know more than I do. Why don't you tell me how he's doing?"

Randall said, "Come on, Jackie. He's having the time of his life. He's got Disney World right in downtown Chicago."

Other than glowering across the desk at him, she didn't respond.

"He's eight years old now, right?"

She stared at him, wondering where this could be going.

"Eight years old," he repeated, chuckling, "and he's convinced he's in Florida. Lake Michigan is the Atlantic. You have to admit, Jackie, this is a good one."

"Listen to yourself. You're proud of deceiving an eight-year-old. He's just a shy kid, Randall. When did you decide to stoop so low?"

He threw his hands up defensively. "Hey, at least nobody's getting hurt. It could have been a lot worse. Navy Pier may not be Epcot, but what does an eight-year-old know?"

She hated that sarcastic smirk of his. He paced behind the desk like a caged badger. *Or more like a weasel,* she thought. But when he stopped pacing and turned to face her again, she worried at the cold glint of anger in his eyes.

"People are getting nervous," he said.

"So what? We held up our end of the deal."

Randall nodded. "Of course we did. But like I said, deals have a way of changing over time." Now he looked her hard in the eyes. "It's Abby, honey."

"What about her? She hasn't said anything."

"I know, I know. And as far as I'm concerned, that's good enough. But with every passing day, the chances increase that she'll say something."

Getting nervous now. "No, she won't."

"She might not even mean to. It could be an accident, an offhand comment. Bottom line is, you need to bring her to Duluth."

"Why, so you can send her off on some phony trip? She's nobody's fool, Randall. Abby will eat you alive."

He slammed a fist on the desk. "Do you have any idea who you're messing with here? These are some of the richest real estate developers in the country. These are the big guys, Jackie, the major leaguers." He began counting off on his fingers. "They have connections everywhere, from the building trades to casinos and five-star hotels, condos, and restaurants. They select political appointees around the country to back them up. They own a little bit of most everything." He pointed a finger at her. "And, my dear, they own a pretty good sized piece of you."

Jackie felt her anger dissipating. She quit listening to his tirade, thinking instead about her children and wondering how she'd managed to screw things up so bad. Other than a handful of short camping trips, Ben had never even been out of his small town on the North Shore. And now he was a pawn in a financial scheme that she'd helped orchestrate. It was never her intention to bring the children into this; their involvement was all a horrible mistake. But her problem with the casino was certainly to blame for launching this whole mess.

She turned her attention back to Randall. "Will Ben come home if I bring Abby to Duluth?"

Randall seemed to lose a bit of his edge. He looked down at the desk and picked up the receipt again before responding. "We just want Abby nearby so we can monitor who she talks to."

"But what about Ben? You won't need him anymore if you have Abby."

Randall didn't respond right away. He carefully placed the receipt on a stack of papers, as if distracted, and then straightened the whole pile.

"Oh, my God," Jackie said. "Ben's not coming home, is he?"

"Of course he is, when all this is done. For now, you just need to get Abby down here."

"She'll never come of her own free will. And in case you haven't noticed, she doesn't exactly get along with you."

"Then talk to Matthew. He's reasonable."

"Matt would never make Abby do something she doesn't want to do."

"Then I guess we'll get the court order."

"Oh, for God's sake, Randall. What judge is going to give me custody?"

Randall's smirk returned. "You're her mother. And in terms you'll appreciate, mothers trump everything."

Jackie shook her head. "It'll never fly."

"Of course it will. What do you think all those connections are for?"

As the meaning of his words came clear, she looked up at him to see an unexpected expression of surprise on his face. His gaze was fixed over her shoulder, at the door behind her. She watched the slow return of his sardonic smile. She turned around, and in unison with Randall, proclaimed, "Abby!"

ELEVEN

Red Tollefson

Red Tollefson pushed his empty lunch plate across the counter. Rubbing his well-fed, portly stomach, he said, "Tracks as big as pie tins, eh?"

Owen Porter said, "Yep, up off the Moose Lake Road. You can see them yourself if you know where to look."

Red reached for his coffee cup. "No, I believe you. And I'm sure it's an impressive animal. But I've seen bigger."

With Marcy taking a few days off from her job in the Black Otter Bay Café, Anna Eskild, the owner of a plant nursery and greenhouse up over the ridge behind town, had arranged to cover for her. Anna had been the café's full-time waitress for several years, only cutting back on her hours after getting married and starting a family. But she still knew her way around the café, and before Red's cup was half empty, she appeared before him at the counter with a fresh pot.

"What I'd like to know, though," Red said, winking in confidence at Anna, "is what kind of pie tins we're talking about here." Holding his hands out wide in front of him, he said, "Now, do you mean the homemade Thanksgiving dinner type of pie? Or some mass-produced little thing like you'd get at a McRonald's?"

"You mean McDonald's," Owen corrected.

"Is that your idea of big?"

Anna said, "Sounds like someone is still hungry."

"You got any pie back there?"

"Dammit, Red," Owen interjected. "We're talking about a moose, not pie."

"Well, the discussion is whetting my appetite. What you got there, Anna dear?"

"Apple. And we can do it à la mode, if you'd like."

"See how she talks to me, Owen? Like she doesn't know that Marcy is my girl."

Even Anna had to laugh at that. "Okay, mister, no ice cream for you."

Red patted his belly. "I think we'll pass on the pie, too. If my middle gets any tighter, something will have to give."

Owen said, "I'm just curious about something. I've never seen such big tracks before. My guess is they belong to a huge bull moose, but is that possible so early in the year? I mean, they haven't had time to regain the weight they lost over the winter. And this guy had to be not only big but heavy, too, to make such deep prints."

"Could be a pregnant female," Red offered. "They'll be dropping their calves any day now."

Owen leaned back on his stool, a thoughtful look on his face as he folded his long arms in front of him. He was so tall that, even sitting at the counter stool, his feet rested flat on the floor. "Well, all I know is, I'd sure like to get a look at the animal that left those tracks."

The café had emptied out considerably since the lunch rush ended. Anna wound her way through the room collecting dirty dishes and napkins in a plastic tub. Her strawberry-blonde hair was held back with tortoise-shell barrettes. Red thought she carried her motherhood well, with a healthy glow in her freckled cheeks and a mature cast to her blue eyes. He waited for her to return behind the counter before he asked, "I ever tell you two about the moose I saw up Highway 1 a few years back?"

"Was this the time you'd been out drinking all night?" she asked.

"Hah, hah, very funny. As it so happens, I was working that day." Red took a drink of coffee, and Anna had to smile

looking at the pair of them. She couldn't help picturing Laurel
and Hardy sitting at the counter. Owen Porter was tall, quiet,
and slender, while Red Tollefson was short and chubby, al-
legedly the brains of the pair.

"The first time I heard that story I was working here full-
time," she said.

"What moose?" Owen asked. "I never heard you talk
about a moose."

"Maybe I will take a slice of that pie," Red said, squirming
on his stool to get comfortable. "And cut one out for Owen
here, too. I don't want him interrupting my story."

Anna set out the slices of pie, adding fresh napkins and
forks. Then she started rinsing the tub full of dishes for stacking in the dishwasher, and with the clinking of plates and cups
in the background, Red began his story.

• • • • •

"We were repaving that low stretch of highway up past the
Finn town. It was pretty late in the year, probably October or
early November. Whenever it was, the moose rut was in full
swing. I sent the crew home at the end of the day, then spent
some time securing all the equipment. When everything was
safely locked away and ready for another day of work, I went
back to my pickup to drive home. Unfortunately, I'd left my
lights on all day, and the battery was dead.

"I had no way of jump-starting it, and this was before cell
phones were common, so in the end I decided to take the Kenworth home. That was the flatbed rig we used to haul our heavy
equipment around. In just a couple minutes I had the D-9 Cat
chained down tight on the trailer, fired up the big Cummings
diesel, and soon thereafter I bounced the heavy rig through the
ditch and up onto the blacktop.

"In retrospect, I should have unhooked the trailer, but my
thinking at the time was that it would be just my luck that

some fool would come along in the middle of the night, hook up to it and steal the whole rig. So anyway, I ended up taking all eighteen wheels home with me.

"It was still light out but getting on to dusk. Definitely suppertime. I wound through the gears, noting the total absence of traffic. Of course, that's not so strange way out there on a weekday evening. Anyway, I'm coming down the highway just fine when I see this enormous animal walking down the middle of the road, following the center line like a drunk trying to prove his sobriety. I slowed down as I got closer, and the creature turned out to be the biggest bull moose I'd ever seen. His rack had to be better than four feet across.

"Well, this was just the most incredible thing ever. He sauntered along at a leisurely pace, head wagging from side to side, drool dripping off his face, walking right down the center line. He had white stockings on three of his legs—that is, from his knees down the course hair was pure white. Otherwise, his fresh winter coat was thick and black. Despite the drool, I have to say he was one of the handsomest critters I've ever seen. It was neat following him in the Kenworth because I had such a great view from up in the cab. I wondered where he was going, and why he used the highway to get there. He sure wasn't in any hurry, though, just sashaying down the road the way he did. I idled along behind him for ten or fifteen minutes, until my belly started growling and I remembered it was suppertime.

"I eased in closer behind him, looking for room to pass. You know how there aren't any shoulders out there, just boulder-strewn rough ditches, and then the woods. I nudged up on his right side, but with the long flatbed trailing behind, there was no way to get around him. I tried his left side, too, but it was just too tight. I suppose I could've made it in a pinch, but with my luck the outside trailer wheels would've dragged me into the ditch, or I would've cut it too tight and taken out the moose.

"So once again I settled in behind him. He paid me no attention whatsoever. I tell you, I could've crawled down that road faster than he walked it. I opened my window and yelled at him, but all I got was a shake of his big, burly head. About this time, my stomach began doing most of my thinking for me. It was getting dark, I was hungry, and I really wanted to be home. So, in a fit of impatience, I reached up and gave a blast on the air horn.

"Well that got his attention. I had to stomp on the brakes when he suddenly stopped and turned to face me. I tell you, I don't know if it was the low lighting or just my eyes playing tricks on me, but when he looked up at me in the cab, that angry old bull was the scariest looking thing I'd ever seen. Like I said, thick gobs of drool hung from his mouth and beard. Heavy strands of swamp weeds clung to his antlers, and his eyes were so wide and crazed-looking that I could see the whites all the way around them. It was just reflex that made me hit the air horn again.

"Bad idea. He backed up a step or two, and then charged the Kenworth like a nose tackle off the line of scrimmage. The whole truck shook from the impact. Two or three times he head-butted the grill, and then so fast I couldn't believe my eyes, he turned around and started kicking with his hind legs. My God, that old boy was pissed off! He put all his weight into it, rocking the cab with the fierce pummeling.

"Steam soon appeared over the hood, so in desperation I again rolled down the window to yell at him. In a split second he charged around the front end to lunge at my door. I dove across the seat as one of his antlers jabbed through the open window at me. The other antler caught on the metal bracket holding the outside rearview mirror. Thrashing about to free himself, he yanked and heaved with all his might, rocking the cab from side to side, until the whole mirror unit tore right off the truck. Then he turned and started kicking again, the mirror and bracket flopping around on the end of his antlers. He kicked my door so hard I thought for sure it would fall off.

"Well, fortunately for me, about that time another vehicle came along from the opposite direction. It must have been a tourist, because I didn't recognize the little pickup truck. By now my mirror was shattered across the highway, and thick plumes of steam billowed out of my hood. I had to shut the rig down when the temperature gauge pegged out in the red.

"Anyway, this new guy saw right away what was happening. He tried to help by pulling up and laying on his horn. Well, you can guess what happened next. The old bull took one look at that little runt of a truck challenging him and went after it like a bully in the schoolyard. By now it was pitch dark. If I hadn't been so upset, it would've been funny as all get-out to watch that little truck retreating in reverse down the highway, the moose in hot pursuit. Headlights flashed back and forth from ditch to ditch as the driver made hasty corrections in his retreat.

"It wasn't long before peace and quiet settled in over the highway. I had to climb out the passenger side because my door was too battered in to open. The stars were out, and I stood in the middle of the highway looking at my truck. It's hard to picture a big rig like that Kenworth sitting broken and forlorn in the middle of the road. Steam hissed from the punctured radiator. The headlights were on, but in the early evening darkness and fog the tall cab looked like a giant ghost truck. It was like a Hollywood movie set, or the scene of a horrible accident, with shattered glass everywhere and brackets and hardware strewn across the highway.

"Unaccustomed to the sudden quiet, I watched down the roadway for a minute, but the moose and his new victim were long gone. At least, I hoped for the stranger and his fancy little truck that he was long gone. Like I said, this was before everyone had cell phones, so I just stood out there waiting, hoping someone else would come along to lend me a hand.

"Then I had an idea. I climbed back in the cab and turned on the CB radio. Of course, there wasn't much chatter on the air, but I put out a call on the trucker's frequency for Black Otter Bay information. I tell you what, it sure was nice to hear

Mrs. Virginia Bean respond to my call. You know she monitors the airwaves from her home base in town. I remember her handle back then was 'Thunderbird.' She often sits up at night listening to the truckers talking on their way up and down the shore between Duluth and the border.

"Turns out, she was playing cribbage with the sheriff, so Marlon Fastwater got on the air and I gave him my location. I didn't tell him what had happened, just that I was broke down up on Highway 1. He called out a wrecker to help pull the Kenworth off the blacktop. You know, I never did see that little pickup truck again, but I'm glad to say I didn't see any more of that moose, either."

· · · · ·

Anna Eskild leaned over the counter and jabbed an index finger against Red's chest. "You're a big fat liar, Red. No way is a moose going to shut down an eighteen-wheeler."

The retired crew foreman sat back in shock. "Liar? Anna, honey, you've never seen an animal like that moose. He was so big, he nearly looked me eye to eye through the windshield of that Kenworth."

Owen Porter guffawed. "Come on, Red. He'd have to be at least ten feet tall to do that."

"Well, that's what he was, then."

Owen snickered while stealing a look at the door as Sheriff Marlon Fastwater entered the café.

Red, unaware of the sheriff's entrance, continued his argument. "You're talking measly pie tins, Porter. The fellow I saw left tracks the size of trash can covers."

Anna said, "You know, Red, you can't blame us for being a little skeptical. That's a mighty big story you're telling there." She was pouring Fastwater's coffee, and Red had yet to notice the sheriff's arrival. She grinned at Owen. "Maybe we should get another opinion, or ask an expert to confirm the story."

Red spun around on his stool to argue, then eased up when he suddenly spotted the sheriff sitting next to him.

"Confirmation on what?" Fastwater asked.

"You remember that moose up on Highway 1?" Red asked. When the sheriff didn't immediately respond, he added, "You know, a few years ago, Marlon. Remember how that moose smashed in my Kenworth?"

The sheriff took his time, sipping his coffee, looking at the three of them bunched up at the counter.

"Remember how I called you and Mrs. Bean on the CB radio?"

Fastwater finally nodded. "Yep, I can confirm that."

Owen Porter spoke up. "But the moose, sheriff. Red says he was as big as the cab of his truck."

"I never saw any moose." Fastwater winked at Anna.

"Ah, Sheriff," Red complained. "Come on. You saw the damage to my rig."

Again Fastwater nodded. "Sure, I saw the truck. The grill was busted in and the door was dented and scratched. About what you'd expect after working way out in the country like that. Could've been a run-in with a tree or a mistake with the backhoe, but again, I never saw any moose."

Owen laughed. "There you go, Red. At least I have some tracks to back up my story."

"I can't believe you people," Red proclaimed, getting to his feet. "I get attacked by a moose the size of a small house, and all you can do is laugh. I could've been killed out there."

"Now don't go away mad," Anna said. She wore a look of sincere contrition. "If you want, I'll believe you."

"Don't bother." Red slapped some cash on the counter. He wouldn't stay mad for long, and they all knew it. By this evening, the whole thing would be forgotten.

Owen said, "I'll tell you where I saw those tracks, Red, and you can go see them for yourself."

"Shut up about the tracks, Owen. I've already seen the biggest moose there is to see. Who cares about some stupid tracks?" He headed for the door, adding over his shoulder, "I need a nap. All this moose talk wears me out. I'll probably need an antacid, too."

Anna covered a laugh, while Sheriff Fastwater grinned into his cup of coffee. As Red went out the door, Leonard came in, accompanied by Matthew Simon. Leonard's shiny black hair hung in a loose braid from under his sheriff's department cap, and Matt was fresh off a day shift at the taconite plant. While the two men strolled up to the counter, the sheriff signaled Owen closer. When the bearded, rangy man awkwardly leaned toward him, Anna stepped in close on the other side of the counter, too. Fastwater took a quick glance behind him at the door to insure that Red had left, and then turned his attention to the pair of listeners, saying, "After we got the truck towed off the highway, I stayed behind to clear debris off the blacktop. I swept up glass and bent pieces of metal and hardware. At the far side of the road I found the biggest moose antler I've ever seen. Just the one," he added, holding up an index finger. "But it was firmly entangled in a bracket from a rearview mirror."

Owens's eyes went wide. "Wow," he said. "No kidding, Sheriff? Kind of backs up his story, doesn't it?"

Anna laughed. "Don't ever let Red know that. We'd never hear the end of it."

"So you knew about this, too?"

Anna smiled, but Leonard interrupted to answer for her. "Hell, Owen, we all knew about it. Keeping it an inside joke is the only way we can tolerate listening to that moose story over and over."

Owen looked at the sheriff. "I can't believe you never told him."

"No reason to. It doesn't prove anything."

"And it's more fun this way," Anna added.

She held up the pot of coffee for Leonard, and when he nodded, Matt said, "Make it two." They took seats at the counter next to the sheriff.

"But you said the mirror bracket was still attached to the antler."

"Owen," Anna said, still wearing a broad smile. "We've been friends a long time. But don't you dare say a word about this to Red."

Owen opened his mouth to argue, but she set the coffee pot down and leaned across the counter to place a finger over his lips. "Don't you dare, Owen. We've kept this secret for ten years now."

Matt said, "Now that Owen is in on it, is it still a secret if everyone but Red knows?"

"Everyone in town is in on this?" Owen asked, incredulous.

"Well, it's been at least ten years," Leonard said. "You know how word gets around in a small town."

Owen had to smile. He felt a little smug now that he was in on the secret, even if he was the second to the last person to know. "I guess it is kind of funny," he said to no one in particular. "Red always has an answer for everything." He laughed and looked at Anna. "He sure has some bad luck sometimes, though. Did you hear about his snowblower? Instead of fishing for the opener like he always does, he spent the day and twenty bucks tuning up that old beast of a machine. Then he put the wrong gas in it by mistake and screwed up the carburetor."

Everyone laughed. "Just goes to show," Leonard said, fingering his coffee cup. "He needs to keep his priorities straight. Fishing always comes before chores, right?"

Anna said, "Okay now, Owen. Red never told us about wrecking his snowblower. I'll tell you what we'll do. You keep quiet about the antler, and I'll never let him know you told us about using the wrong gas."

The sheriff was still grinning as he sipped his coffee. He looked at Anna and said, "It's good to have you back in the café. It's been long time."

"Yeah. Other than a few hours here and there, little Christopher and the greenhouse keep me pretty busy."

"Where's Marcy? She's not sick, is she?"

"No. She just took a few days off. She asked me to cover for her."

Owen Porter got to his feet. "Well, if Matt's here, I guess the day shift is over. Time for me to get work." He took his boxed-up sandwich from the counter and nodded his farewells to everyone.

Anna cleared away his dishes and said, "I think Marcy was going to Duluth. She said something about hitting the casino."

Fastwater grunted. "She's never gone to the casino before."

Matt suddenly spoke up. "She's kind of doing me a favor, Sheriff. She took Abby to Duluth to stay with Jackie for a few days."

"Abby?" The sheriff leaned forward to look down the counter past his nephew in order to skewer Matthew Simon with his black-eyed stare. "You said she didn't want to go."

Matt slowly twirled his coffee cup and shrugged. He looked at Anna, but she was busy with the dishwasher again. "She's a young girl, Sheriff. She's at that age where she needs a mother's counsel. I'm hoping Marcy will either make that happen, or help her out herself if she can."

Fastwater contemplated the nicked-up countertop in front of him. He raised his coffee cup, then set it down again. "How long will they be gone?"

"Just through the weekend, I imagine. It is a little odd, I guess, the way Abby suddenly decided to go for a few days. But Jackie has really been bugging her for a visit, especially since all this happened with Ben. And Marcy told me she needed a break from the café, so it all just sort of worked out."

Fastwater didn't like the sound of any of it. "Is Marcy staying with them?"

"No. I'm sure she'll be seeing them, but she booked a room in Canal Park. It's like Anna said, she wants to try her luck at the casino."

"When did they go?"

The sheriff's excessive questioning finally attracted Leonard's attention. He studied his uncle, saw the tension in the clenched line of his jaw.

Matthew said, "They just left this morning. Abby decided to go after seeing Jackie last weekend at Rose's memorial service. She went to school the last couple of days to make sure all her work was done for the year. But she's a good student, Sheriff. They let her go, no problem."

Fastwater dug some change out of his pocket and placed it on the counter. Leonard could see the wheels turning and understood that they were leaving even before his uncle stood up. Gulping the last of his coffee, Leonard twirled on the stool to face his friend. "We'll be seeing you, Matt. Your house is going to be kind of quiet for a few days. Let me know if you want some company."

"Thanks, Leonard, but I'll be fine. Abby promised to call every night."

Sheriff Fastwater paused to listen to their exchange, and then patted Matt on the shoulder before heading for the door. "Thanks for the coffee, Anna," he called, flashing her a thumbs up. "You still got it."

Once outside, he strode to the back door of the squad car to let Gitch out. He followed the big mixed-breed husky around the rear fender and leaned against the trunk to gaze off across the highway at the rolling expanse of Lake Superior. He folded his arms across his chest and waited for his nephew to join him. Gitch sniffed around the gravel parking lot, then stopped to point his nose into the crisp, fresh breeze. Everything was fine in Gitch's world, but the sheriff didn't see it that way.

As Leonard approached, Fastwater turned to him, saying, "I need you to go back to Duluth. To keep an eye on Abby."

"She's with her mother, Marlon. What harm can there be?"

The sheriff's pragmatic outlook and indomitable size had created his reputation for calm self-assurance, so Leonard took notice when a scowl appeared on the big lawman's face. He followed his uncle's gaze out over the lake and took a moment to consider his orders. The sheriff wasn't the type to overreact. Either he had some information that he wasn't sharing, or that extra sense of his was warning him about Abby's welfare in the city. The one thing Leonard knew for sure was that he'd never get anything out of his uncle that the sheriff didn't want to share.

"What am I supposed to be looking for?" he asked.

"Just keep an eye out. Try to not be obvious. See who visits them. Maybe look for something out of the ordinary at the art gallery."

"You mean you want me to spy on them."

"Damn it, Leonard," Fastwater snapped. "Either someone in this investigation is lying, or there's a cover-up going on. Probably both. I need an extra pair of eyes and ears in Duluth."

"Why not the FBI? That's what they do."

When Fastwater didn't respond, when he didn't even break off his viewing of the majestic scenery before them, Leonard figured he knew the answer. His uncle preferred to handle local incidents on his own. He didn't like outsiders getting involved in the townsfolk's personal business. The sheriff considered it meddling, and so far as he could, he'd keep the investigation quiet and within the confines of the community. For Sheriff Marlon Fastwater, it was simply a matter of respect.

"There must be someone down there who can keep an eye on them," Leonard said.

"Well, the feds assigned an agent," Fastwater said, "but he's working the business end of this thing. And he's undercover, so let's keep it between you and me."

"Undercover?"

"That's what they tell me. They found someone who knows the area and people. But his focus is Randall's business dealings and associates. It's a federal investigation, but it might tie into Ben's disappearance."

"So you still think he was kidnapped, and it's tied to Rose's death?"

"Absolutely. And Abby knows something. Depending on how much she knows, she could be in danger."

"What about the autopsy?"

Fastwater looked at his nephew and allowed himself a short sigh, perhaps hinting at an inner disappointment. His eyes followed Gitch around the parking lot while he collected his thoughts. Leonard stood at ease with his hands in his pockets. The sheriff said, "Nothing of value showed up in the initial bloodwork." He dug his toe into the soft gravel and emitted the briefest chuckle. "At least now we know that Rose wasn't a drug addict, and she didn't overdose on her medications." He fixed his gaze on Leonard again. "Rose died because her heart gave out, even though there's no sign of coronary disease. It seems like there has to be something there, like we're missing something. Rose was a tough old gal, she doesn't just drop over like that. Anyway, I know this guy in the lab down in Duluth. He's going to do another work-up for me, a chemical analysis of the blood. But it's going to take a while, so in the meantime we need to keep Abby safe."

"I don't know, Marlon. It seems kind of weird. I've never even been on a stakeout before."

Fastwater called Gitch back from the edge of the road. The big dog looked at him, then slowly sauntered across the parking lot in a wide arc, as if returning to the squad car was his own idea. The sheriff walked around to the back door and held it open. To Leonard, he said, "I'd go down there myself to look around, but my presence would really make them suspicious. Just don't make a big deal out of it. You're hanging out in Duluth for a few days, that's all. Randall's apartment is in the East End, and the casino and Canal Park are both within walking distance. There's a coffee shop just down from the art gallery."

Gitch jumped into the squad car and Fastwater closed the door. "Make a note of traffic in and out of the gallery. There's no way that little place clears enough to cover the high-priced real estate it sits on."

Leonard stood rock solid in the parking lot, but his expression betrayed his confusion and dismay. "I don't know, Marlon. I think this is a little beyond a part-time cop."

The sheriff put his hands in his pockets and walked back to the rear of the car. He gave a look up and down the roadway, then turned his attention back out to sea. From a distance, the movement of the waves appeared in slow motion, a phenomenon that always had a calming effect on him. So he took a moment now to suck it all in, then, drawing a deep breath, he slowly began. "You know, other than Jackie, I've known everyone involved in this case their entire lives. That fact alone gives me a little insight. For instance, Randall is withholding information, but then, he's always been that way. He's a loner, and it's not in his nature to share anything more than he has to. That doesn't mean he's guilty of anything, but it doesn't mean he isn't, either."

Leonard started to speak, but Fastwater held up a hand to stop him. "Now Jackie, on the other hand, is a different matter. She's not from around here, so she's harder to read." He raised an eyebrow, as if to ask, "Know what I mean?" Then he continued. "I agree with you that she's Abby's mother and that alone should be enough, but something tells me she's not the safe harbor Abby needs right now."

It wasn't in Fastwater's nature to carry on such long conversations, and now he paused for a moment to watch the roll of white-capped breakers coming ashore. Leonard could feel his uncle's discomfort. When the sheriff spoke again, his voice was hardly more than a whisper, and his open expression seemed to plead with his nephew to go along with him on this. "Up to now," he said, "I haven't been able to bring Ben home, and I'm stumped as to how all this went down, but I'll tell you what I think. I'm convinced the kid isn't just lost in the woods, that his disappearance is somehow tied to Rose's death, and we aren't

going to find the answers here in town to put it all together."
He drew himself up straighter and looked at Leonard with a
wry grin. "You saw how the feds pulled out of here all of a sudden? Now they tell me they have someone working it from the
inside in Duluth. So it seems to me they probably have an idea
what happened but they're handling it themselves, which tells
me it's some kind of a big deal. Now, I can't just leave here to
go snooping around Duluth for answers, but you can."

Leonard toed the gravel and nodded. "Okay, Marlon. I'll
do it."

"Good," Fastwater said. "It's only a few days. They know
you live down there, so it won't raise any suspicions if you're
spotted, or if you decide to drop in on them." He laughed. "If I
suddenly showed up, Randall and his buddies would scatter like
cockroaches in the light."

Leonard cracked a smile and looked down at his boots. "I'll
call you, what, every evening?"

"Call whenever you want, several times a day. You have
my cell. I want to know everything you hear and see." He allowed his expression to soften again as he concluded, "I'm sorry
to be so circumspect. You know I prefer going straight after
something, but I don't even know what we're looking for. Until
something breaks loose, we have to keep an eye on everything."
He frowned self-consciously. "You know about Jackie's gambling thing, right? We don't need people digging around in that
and embarrassing the whole family. Remember, you're there
primarily to keep Abby safe."

Leonard nodded. "Okay, Marlon. I'll do what I can." He
cleared his throat and shuffled his feet. "What about Mom?"

"Arlene?" Fastwater laughed. "Now there's an idea. Right
now, though, we need to be discrete. When the time comes to
barge in head-on, believe me, we'll call in your mother." He
slapped Leonard on the back and started around the car to the driver's side. "I still have a few things to look into around here, but
I'll be waiting for your call. Thanks for doing this, and good luck."

"Sure," his nephew said, even though Fastwater had already climbed in the car. He watched him pull away, disappointed that his uncle had misunderstood his question. He'd meant to ask how he was supposed to reconcile the time off over the next few days with his mother. Arlene was too observant not to notice he wasn't going to work, and too nosy not ask about it.

Leonard stood in the middle of the nearly vacant parking lot. This was the first assignment of real significance his uncle had entrusted to him, and now, like the sheriff himself often did, he stared out over the wide vista of Lake Superior. Ultimately, he conceded that dealing with Arlene's questions would be a minor inconvenience compared to the task his uncle had placed before him. He closed his eyes and inhaled the sweet, cedar-clad aroma of the forest around him. Then, turning to his old pickup truck, he shook his head and scuffed at the gravel beneath his boots before opening the door to make the fifty-mile drive back to Duluth and home.

TWELVE

Jackie Simon

The fast-moving cloud formations reminded Abby of a time-lapse sequence on a PBS program. Rolling in off the lake, thick white cumulus clouds billowed and tumbled over each other coming ashore. The lake itself wore a regal cloak of indigo blue, with a strip of royal purple trim farther out. On the eastern horizon, where the sun was shining, the water reflected a brilliant aquamarine, almost inviting in its cheerful transparency, but deadly in the darker recesses of its ice-cold depths.

"I have yet to encounter an artist capable of capturing all those colors," Jackie commented, following Abby's gaze.

The light breeze off the lake still wielded a wintry bite, so Abby's hands were fisted up inside the pockets of her hooded sweatshirt. "No," she agreed. "But then, it doesn't even look real, does it? It reminds me of the artwork in one of Ben's comic books."

With that, Jackie turned around to look up the steep hill facing the lake. In the foreground rose the narrow stretch of Duluth's downtown buildings, with Superior Street and London Road following the shoreline here at the headwaters of Lake Superior. From their vantage point on the lakewalk, Jackie could see homes and condos and parks climbing the ridge all the way to the top, where Skyline Parkway wound along the crest. Duluth's existence had always seemed fragile and temporary to her, perched as it was so precariously at the base and, to a lesser extent, along the face of the ridge. True, there was much more to Duluth on the other side of the slope, including an international airport, but from here a person could almost envision the huge lake rising up one day to swallow these puny manmade edifices.

Jackie looked back at Abby, who still stared out on the great inland sea. This was the biggest difference, she thought, between her hometown of Chicago and her adopted residence here in Duluth. Chicago was so large and cosmopolitan that it dwarfed the warm, calm waters of Lake Michigan, humbling it into a friendly park and poolside-like attraction. And the city was old enough that it had already burned down once before Duluth had really even gotten started. But looking out at Lake Superior, with its vibrant colors, bottomless depths, and temperamental reputation, it was easy to see who the real master was at this end of the Great Lakes.

Jackie stepped up behind Abby to cup her hands over her daughter's shoulders. Then she deftly fingered the girl's braid, holding it up to feel its thickness and weight. "You have such beautiful hair," she commented. "Why don't you ever wear it long and unbound?"

"It just gets in the way when I'm doing stuff."

Jackie grinned to herself. "Well, I bet the day is coming soon . . ."

Abby turned around and smiled at her mother. "Remember when you used to brush it out for me?"

Jackie burst out laughing. "Of course. You hated it. You screamed and yelled the whole time."

Abby grinned self-consciously. "I remember. But I'm not a kid anymore. Maybe you could brush it out for me later."

"I'd love to."

Then they took a few more moments to study the vivid colors splashing across the water. Jackie embraced her daughter from behind, resting her chin on her shoulder. Abby said, "You know, I don't think anyone would buy a painting from an artist using those colors. I mean, it doesn't look real, does it? People would think the painter was hallucinating."

Jackie stepped back, laughing again. "That's a great observation, Abby. And you're probably right. Maybe you have a career as an art critic."

They continued their walk, Jackie's arm around her daughter's shoulders, following the lakewalk through re-emerging flowerbeds and gardens. When Abby had suddenly appeared that morning in The Tempest, Randall had volunteered to watch the shop while Jackie and her daughter went out for a bite to eat. Abby said, "Somehow I have a hard time picturing Randall working in the art gallery."

"Actually, he does pretty well with customers. Randall is no slouch. The man knows enough about art to talk a good game. Besides, he wants to catch up on paperwork this afternoon, so it worked out fine."

"Well, he has his work cut out for him. Your office was mess. It looked like a windstorm had blown through or something."

Jackie hesitated before replying. The fight with Randall flashed through her thoughts, the way she'd swept stacks of papers and shelving to the floor. She said, "Well, we're changing some files around and doing some reorganizing. You just caught us at a bad moment."

"Are you sure it's okay for me to hang around for a few days?"

"Of course, sweetheart. I'd love it."

"What about Randall?"

"He's thrilled that you're here. Believe me, Randall is quite fond of you. In fact, he's going to offer you a part-time job working with me in the gallery."

Abby stopped her mother by grabbing at her arm. "I'm only here for a few days, Mom. Seriously. Marcy is picking me up this weekend."

"And then what are you going to do? Spend the summer sitting around that dead-end town while your father works all day?"

"I'm going to find Ben."

Abby watched the rosy glow from their walk disappear from Jackie's face. Clearly upset, her mother's eyes shifted left and right before she asked, "What makes you think you can find him?"

"Why not? He's got to be somewhere. Why can't his sister find him?"

"Because you have no idea what you're doing." Jackie huffed in frustration. Looking around, she took a deep breath, struggling to soften her expression. Starting over, she said, "Abby, sweetheart, don't get yourself hurt any more than you already have been. The FBI can't find him. We don't even know if he's still alive."

"He's alive, Mom, and you know it."

"What do you mean by that?"

"I just mean that if anything really serious had happened to him, you'd know it."

They were approaching Sir Reginald's, a deli and restaurant across Superior Street from the lakewalk. A kid on a skateboard passed them, his smile and open jacket revealing his satisfaction with the summer day. They crossed the street, and Abby stopped in front of the restaurant. She said, "I just totally believe that when something really horrible happens to a child, the mother senses it. Somewhere down deep, she knows."

"I'm not so sure about that, honey." Jackie reached out to stroke Abby's arm. "I don't think that's the kind of mother I've been to you kids. I doubt I could feel what you're describing."

"Of course you could, Mom. I mean, if Ben was dead, you'd know it, and you wouldn't be going off to work every day, or going shopping or out to lunch if you'd just lost your son." Abby held her mother's gaze with her steady dark eyes. There was a note of challenge in her voice. "Really, Mom, if you thought it was even remotely possible that something terrible had happened to Ben, you wouldn't be standing here right now like this."

Jackie touched Abby's cheek. "You give me much more credit than I deserve." Then she paused to collect her thoughts, looked out at the lake again, and said, "But I suppose you're right. And if nothing terrible has happened, then I pray Ben will come home soon."

Abby smiled. "He's all right, Mom, and he will be home soon, because he's my little brother and I'm going to find him."

Almost timidly, Jackie took a last look into her daughter's confident dark eyes, but she couldn't bring herself to hold the stare. It was like looking at herself more than twenty years earlier, the innocence and idealism of youth. When she turned to open the restaurant door, a weight of sadness and remorse bore down on her, so that she had to catch her breath for a moment to hold back the tears.

• • • • •

When her father left, he took most of Jackie's prospects for a comfortable and successful life with him. Of course, she didn't know that at the time; in fact, she had no solid memories of her father at all. There was the feeling that he was a dashing, handsome man, but that could have come from the small handful of photographs of him that her mother had kept. All in all, she had few specifics she could ascribe to her father. He came from a wealthy family boasting a family tree firmly rooted in Chicago's Near North. She also knew that his family had been thoroughly and utterly opposed to his union with Jackie's mother. In a deal quietly negotiated with their lawyers, he was given a beautiful brownstone residence in Oak Park in exchange for a signed contract promising to never actually marry this dark-eyed little diversion.

Within a couple of years her father had come to his senses, just as his parents had foretold. He found the routines of family life tedious and boring, and constantly berated Jackie's mother for her awkward attempts at mingling in his upper-class society. When he finally walked out, the only thing he left behind was a court-ordered eviction notice giving them six weeks to vacate the premises. Her mother moved them into a tiny apartment above a coffee shop across the tracks from a stop on the "L."

The history of all this had never been openly discussed between mother and daughter. At an early age, however, Jackie worked out the chronology. She believed her mother had been pregnant before they even moved into the brownstone. She liked to think that her father had initially wanted to do the right thing, but she had to admit that, with no word from him in years, that probably wasn't the case. And knowing her mother, she believed the pregnancy could have simply been a trap. Either way, as a child Jackie convinced herself that her existence had ruined her parents' chances for happiness, and that she'd probably inherited the worst traits of both of them.

But she had to give her mother some credit. With limited resources and abilities, she'd provided what she could for her daughter. Their apartment, though small and embarrassingly tacky, was nonetheless still in Oak Park, which put Jackie into a decent public school system. Her mother worked long hours in the coffee shop downstairs, giving Jackie a supervised place to hang out and play. When she started school, her mother hired out as a house cleaner, using the "L" to get to the homes of clients. And that was about the time Jackie's grasp of the reality of her mother's situation became a little fuzzy, even though memories of strange men in the apartment were very clear. Most of the time they'd suddenly show up in the morning when she shuffled into the kitchen for breakfast. Still groggy and half-asleep, dressed in pajamas, she'd encounter a stranger sitting at the kitchen table, drinking a cup of coffee from downstairs while reading the paper.

The first few times this happened she'd been thrilled with the notion that her long-lost father had finally come home. But then she'd quickly realize that the man sitting at their shabby kitchen table didn't nearly match up to the fictional image she had of her handsome, world-traveling father. That's not to say that all these strangers weren't kind to her, even if her presence seemed to make them a little uncomfortable. One time, she came home from school to find a man smoking a cigarette and lounging on their sofa. This was the time a new pink and purple two-wheeled bicycle appeared, complete with sparkly streamers hanging from the handlebars.

By the time she was Abby's age, Jackie despised her mother for the way she used people, yet admired her wily ability to keep going and make ends meet. She grudgingly admitted that her mother was a survivor, and from her she learned firsthand about employing God-given talents to stay afloat. Some people were blessed with the brains to excel in life, while others worked hard and studied. But if your personal strength happened to be a shapely body or pretty face, well, you had to use whatever tools were at hand.

When Jackie started working in the coffee shop, she found that a friendly smile could often double her tip, especially among the male customers. In high school, and later in college, she learned how to raise her grade point average by perfecting an open yet vulnerable feminine charm. She didn't see any ethical dilemma here. After all, it wasn't her fault. If her father hadn't left, she would have been working with a whole different set of tools.

· · · · ·

"Tell me again how you and Dad met," Abby said when they were seated in Sir Reginald's.

Jackie sipped from a glass of Chardonnay while following Abby's gaze around the restaurant. Low wood-plank walls, almost like stalls in an old barn, sectioned off the dining area. Unfinished paneling lit by cast-iron wall sconces gave it a medieval feel. A cobblestone fireplace near the kitchen held huge four-foot-long pine logs. The walls were decorated with suits of armor, old family crests, and colorful paintings of castles and English gardens. It was easy to picture themselves in fifteenth-century Europe, especially with the mounted head of a wild boar staring at them from across the room.

"I've told you that old story about meeting your father, haven't I?"

"You told me the little kid version, Mom. Tell me again."

Jackie smiled. Their tomato basil soup arrived, and then grilled cheese sandwiches. "Speaking of little kids, these used to be your favorite," she said, pointing at her sandwich.

"I know, Mom, and they still are. But tell me about Dad."

Jackie finished off her wine and set the glass aside. Stirring a spoon through her soup, she let her thoughts drift back to a suitable starting point for her story. "You remember your Uncle Dan, don't you? Your father's brother? Well, I actually met him first."

Abby stopped, her spoon halfway to her mouth. "You went out with Uncle Dan? Where did you meet him?"

"In Chicago. I was at the university, and met him at some club downtown. He was older than me, but he sure was handsome. And fun?" Jackie laughed. "Let me just say, your Uncle Dan liked to have a good time."

"I've heard stories. Dad told us how he used to run underwear up the flagpole at the post office."

"Yeah, well, that's not all he used to do, believe me. I don't remember why he was in Chicago, but he always seemed to have money. It was fun to go out with him." Jackie's thoughts turned inward for a moment, or maybe it was just that the reminiscing came hard for her, but Abby noticed her mother's expression tighten up a bit. "It wasn't the best time in my life, you know. School wasn't going well, I didn't have any money, and I had no clear idea of what to do with my life."

"So, how does all this lead to Dad?"

"Well, your Uncle Dan told me he was going home for a few days. I'd never heard of Black Otter Bay before. It sounded so exotic, like some Indian village up on the tundra." Jackie used her knife to slice off a corner of her grilled cheese. Grinning now, she said, "So I asked to go along. Knowing your uncle, I figured it would be an interesting adventure. Besides, I needed to get away for a while to consider my options."

"I bet it was weird coming up here. I mean, being from Chicago and all."

"Weird doesn't begin to describe it. In my whole life, I'd never been out of the city. But it was beautiful, it was summertime, and everyone I met was so nice. I met your father, and something seemed to click."

"You mean, like, 'love at first sight'?"

Jackie demurred. "No, I wouldn't say that, especially for your father. I think he hardly noticed me at all. But, like I said, I had no money, and no clue about the direction my life should take. Your father worked at the plant, earned a good wage, and seemed like an honest, sincere man. He wasn't like the men I'd met before. He wasn't like my father, who I couldn't even remember, and he certainly wasn't like any of the men my mother knew. He was even night and day from his own brother."

Abby pushed back from the table to pull off her sweatshirt. The fireplace was ablaze with pine logs popping and crackling. She looked at her mother, trying to envision her as a college student. She'd heard a lot of this before, but she was old enough now to picture the events in a totally different fashion. Reaching for the grilled cheese, she asked, "How did you get Dad to come around?"

"Well, it certainly didn't happen overnight. In fact, I wasn't even sure about it myself. I mean, I'd never had a real family life. I wasn't sure how the whole thing was supposed to work. All I knew was that when I thought about that little town so far away, so far away from my life and all my stupid problems, I got a warm spot in my heart."

"So what you're saying is, you didn't actually love Dad."

Jackie gave her daughter a wry smile. "To be honest, I'm not sure. But I was definitely in love with the notion of settling down in a safe place, starting a family, and working toward a normal, secure life for once." She paused to emit a brief chuckle. "One time I drove up with some friends to visit your

father. You should have seen Black Otter Bay the night a car-
load of co-eds from Chicago showed up. We sure were popular,
even though the only place open was the Municipal. Sometime
later, after I'd been seeing your father for a while and we'd decided to get married, it was those same girlfriends who convinced me I was doing the right thing."

Incredulous, Abby asked, "You mean you married Dad because of advice from your friends?"

Jackie took her time replying. "You know, Abby, it's hard
to have this conversation when your bias is so set against me.
It's like you're not even hearing me, or that what I say isn't
important."

"Okay then, Mom, tell me. I'm listening. Why did you
marry Dad, and then leave us?"

Jackie sighed, her thoughts jumbled up in old memories
and emotions. She reached for her sandwich, but ended up
grabbing her napkin to dab at her mouth and wipe her fingers.
"I suppose it's terrible to admit, and it won't help your opinion
of me, but all my friends were jealous. I had this tall, handsome
boyfriend and a secure future. I'd never had that before, Abby,
and no one had ever been envious of me. It was a good feeling.
I was actually proud of the way my friends gossiped about my
good fortune." She shrugged. "So, even though it was for all
the wrong reasons, settling down with your father just seemed
like the right thing to do."

Abby frowned at her mother while taking the last bite of
her sandwich. Brushing crumbs from her fingers, she said,
"You know, I just don't think it's fair. You should have known
that it wouldn't work before you got the rest of us involved."

Jackie raised an eyebrow. "That's a mean thing to say,
Abby. Did your father tell you that?"

"Of course not. But it's obvious."

"I tried to make it work. Honest. I wanted to raise my
family in a safe community, with no gangs or violence. I
wanted to have enough money to give my children a good start

in life. I'd never had any of that, so it was very important to me. Your father had a good job with a steady income, and he had some notions about raising a family, too. I wanted to teach you about the finer things in life, the arts and theater." Jackie paused to look down at her plate, reached for the wine goblet, but set it down again when she realized it was empty. When she again looked at her daughter, all the sadness of her failed marriage shown in her face. "But there are no arts or theaters in Black Otter Bay. There isn't even a library."

Abby had no intention of letting her mother off the hook. Her feelings of betrayal had been festering for over a year now. She said, "All that theater and arts stuff is what you wanted. All we wanted was a mom."

Jackie shook her head as if unable to believe what she was hearing. "But you've got me, Abby. Don't you see that? I'm right here. I just can't live in that town any longer."

"Why? Why can't you, Mom? Your family is there. It's not right."

Tears rolled silently down Jackie's cheeks. She tried to speak but couldn't find her voice. Then she blurted, "I was suffocating."

"But Ben needs you. We all need you."

Jackie shook her head again, and then held her napkin against the tears sliding down her face. She said, "It was like living in a fishbowl. Everyone knows your business. Whenever I'd leave the house, people wondered, 'where is she going?' They'd even watch to see if I turned onto the highway toward Duluth." She paused for a few moments, sniffling, slowly regaining some measure of control. Then a flame seemed to ignite in her eyes, and she drew herself up straight to look at her daughter. She held a hand up as if to stop the conversation, and said, "I can't believe this. I simply can't believe I'm trying to justify my life to you. You want to talk about unfair . . ."

Abby had been saving up for this fight for a long time, and she was glad for having finally said what was on her mind.

She'd stood up for Ben and herself, and her mother's tears seemed to prove that her points were valid. But it had never been her intention to make her mother cry, so instead of pushing her advantage, she sat back and returned Jackie's glare from across the table. The one thing she knew for certain, however, was that her father's heart had been broken when Ben left, and if she moved to Duluth now, it would probably kill him. She said, "You want me to spend the summer in Duluth. Do you think that would be fair to Dad?"

"It's just the summer, Abby. I want to share some of my life, some of my interests, with you." Jackie leaned forward with newfound enthusiasm. "Do you know that just this morning I sold an oil painting for one thousand dollars?" She rapped her knuckles on the table. "Just like that, Abby, one thousand dollars." Her rapid chatter signaled the recovery of her composure. "In all honesty, sweetheart, your father is a sincere and good man. I knew that from the beginning. But he deserves someone who appreciates living in a small town. That's what's right for him. I just can't do it."

Abby nodded. "That's pretty much what Dad said, that you shouldn't have to live somewhere that makes you sad."

"Well, not sad, really. It's just that I'm used to more. I love the city, the energy, and all the opportunities and things to do." She sat back, took a deep breath, and brushed a length of hair back from her face. Looking at Abby again, a bashful smile rose on her face, and she asked, "Want to hear a poem I wrote a few years ago?"

Abby doubted it, but in the spirit of rebuilding their relationship, she dipped her head in a half-hearted nod.

Jackie sat up straighter and cleared her throat. "Okay, good. Here goes.

"When did I realize you didn't like poetry,
And that art wasn't important to you?
Why couldn't you see the grace in a skyscraper,

Or know that city lights don't always block out the stars?
Why were you always the leader,
And when did I stop following?"

Abby flashed a tentative smile. "That's pretty good, Mom."

"I wrote it in the car on our way home from one of those horrible camping trips."

Abby laughed. "Did you ever share it with Dad?"

Now it was Jackie's turn to wear a shy smile. "No. I think writing it was therapy enough. I guess I've always been more of a silent rebel."

For a few quiet minutes they mulled their separate thoughts. Abby finished her grilled cheese and pushed the plate away. Looking at her mother, she said, "I like that, Mom. The 'silent rebel.'"

Jackie broke into a broad grin. "Well, there you have it, then. We finally hit on the one thing my daughter appreciates about me."

Abby laughed. "It's a start, Mom. Now, if we could just get you to take up fishing."

THIRTEEN

Marcy Soderstrom

Despite its location on the main drag in downtown Duluth, just blocks from the trendy, upscale Canal Park, the two-story Native American–owned casino seemed straight out of a 1940s B movie. Flashing neon lights, even in the light of day, harkened a garish come-on, like a cheap whore under the corner lamppost. Transients and panhandlers squatted against the outside walls in full knowledge that anyone going in probably carried spare change. Security personnel at the narrow front entrance maintained an obvious, rigorous appearance, even on this weekday early in the evening.

For the first several minutes after her arrival, Marcy Soderstrom was pleasantly surprised by the admiring glances and double takes she received. But then she realized she was probably the youngest female in the building, surrounded by a cadre of senior citizens and ne'er-do-wells. Among the three or four dozen sedentary video slot machine players, her spirited presence seemed to invoke the question, "What are you doing here?" So as she strolled through the aisles, she held her head high and added a slight swagger to her step, as if to reply, "I'm here because I choose to be."

Everyone smoked, to the extent that the rank smell of cigarettes permeated everything—not only the carpets and furniture, but in short order Marcy's clothes and hair as well. She was struck by how the unhealthy pallor of the patrons seemed to reflect the flashing lights from the machines in front of them. The incessant clanging of bells in the background sent a ringing vibration through her ears, causing her to come to the

quick conclusion that this place and these people weren't exactly her style.

She kept moving. The reason for her being here was suddenly lost in the cacophony of bells and whistles. Stopping in
front of one of the video slots, as if deciding whether or not to
play, she stared at it while getting her bearings and collecting
her thoughts. Abby was convinced that Randall was involved
in Ben's disappearance, and many of his business associates had
ties to the shadier side of the gambling community. Therefore,
Marcy had volunteered to visit the casino to look for any of
those connections to Randall or Ben. But what exactly was she
supposed to be looking for?

"Buy you a drink?" Marcy jumped at the voice, which was
too close beside her. She turned to face a backwoods-looking
character grinning at her through yellowed teeth. He held out
a tall plastic cup of beer.

"I don't drink," she said too quickly, obviously lying.

The man's grin became even larger. "That's okay," he said,
as if accustomed to rejection. "I have two hands." Then he held
up a second glass of beer, pointed it at the machine in front of
them, and asked, "Are you looking to play this thing?"

"No. No, I'm not. Actually, I'm meeting someone here
soon." Marcy looked at the vacant spot on her wrist, as if checking the time.

"That's okay," he said again, ignoring her blunder. "These
machines are a waste of good money, anyway. The house stacks
the odds against you. Even a big winner on a nickel slot won't
pay you much. The only real chance you have is at the card
table, and then you'd better be either really good or really lucky."

Marcy thought of Jackie and her rumored problem with
gambling on cards. She glanced around quickly, and then asked,
"Where are those tables, anyway?"

"Upstairs. I'll show you, if you want."

She took a closer look at the man, at his Duluth Outfitter's
T-shirt and camouflaged cap. His thick arms were covered in

tufts of hair, and the twin cups of beer were grasped firmly in wide, battered, calloused fingers. His smile was simple and friendly, not unlike most of the young men who frequented the Black Otter Bay Café, so when he stretched an arm out to point their direction down the aisle, she gave in and set out beside him. At the end of the aisle, the man turned to lead her to the stairway in the rear corner of the building. As he did so, she reached for one of the beers he carried, and with a laugh he held it out for her.

Marcy had never been to a casino before. Her only concept of them came from stories her parents told from their winter excursions out West, or from Hollywood movies with scenes of Las Vegas. She had a notion of glamour and fun among well-dressed, wealthy patrons. What she'd found so far was just the opposite. There was a sense of desperation about the place, a clanging, flashing persistence that seemed intent on bashing its way to fulfillment and happiness. She sensed sadness in the room, as if all the bright lights and noise were no more than an empty gesture, or a cheap sleight of hand.

Marcy's inherent upbeat disposition had deflated considerably during the short tour of the casino. She found it impossible to think of Jackie hanging out here. Abby's mother, who dressed with such flair and style, who carried herself with a grace Marcy had never before seen in Black Otter Bay, couldn't possibly have fallen in with the mindless drones sitting at these machines. In the end, she decided the stories were nothing more than mean rumors. She just couldn't picture it, but the effort to do so had distracted her from the comments of the man at her elbow. "I'm sorry," she said. "You were saying?"

When he introduced himself again, her fretful reticence dumped a weighty silence into the air around them. At the top of the stairs they came out on another room with a tall ceiling, filled with more clanging slot machines. Even the ones not in use were flashing and ringing, as if pleading for attention. Every outside wall around the second floor housed a bar serving drinks. Following her new friend, Marcy once again found herself passing through an aisle lined with the thumping, clanging video slot machines.

At the end of the row they came upon a small area cordoned off for card tables. Of the half-dozen or so tables available, only one was in use. Marcy's friend nodded at it and said, "There you go, sweetheart. Blackjack."

Marcy studied the small area of play. A handsome, long-haired Native American stood behind the table. As the dealer, he was well dressed in slacks and black, western-style boots. A black leather vest topped off a long-sleeved white shirt, but the item that made the biggest impression on Marcy was the bolo tie clasp at his neck. Made of pipestone and highlighted with smaller bits of turquoise, it was an amazing, eye-catching piece of jewelry. It was huge, and just flamboyant and gaudy enough to bring a grin to Marcy's face. The dealer caught her looking at him when he glanced her way, but soon returned to the business of dealing cards. Three somber, hunched over card players sucked on cigarettes while squinting through the smoke at their cards.

Her new friend squeezed her arm. "How about it, honey? Go ahead, take a seat."

"Oh, no, no," Marcy said, stepping back. "I've never played before. I'd rather just watch for now."

The man grinned and shrugged. He tipped his cap back, and said, "Well, maybe I'll give it a go, then. I bet you're good luck, eh?"

"Oh, I doubt that," she replied, but was relieved when he stepped over to the table.

He took a seat and motioned for her to join him. She slinked around behind him, almost picturing herself in one of those Las Vegas movies. Unfortunately, the dingy atmosphere of the place had churned a pit in her stomach. And her nerves were on edge, so that just a couple swallows of beer brought on a light-headed giddiness. She rested a free hand on the man's shoulder, but jumped in alarm when he acknowledged it with a friendly pat of his burly fingers. Looking around, it was a relief to see that no one paid them any attention. The few slot machine players sat transfixed by their flashing lights and the idle, bored bartenders carried on conversations among themselves.

Then, down the aisle they'd just walked, Marcy spotted a big, well-dressed man just reaching the top of the stairs. He moved like an athlete, she thought: agile and solid. He didn't look at all like the other patrons of the place. This man fairly glowed with a smug confidence. His black sport coat looked tailored, and his collared black shirt was pressed and fresh. With his dark sunglasses, spiked flat-top haircut and black clothing, he would have been one of the bad guys in Marcy's Las Vegas movie. He appeared to be alone. At the top of the stairs he cast his glance around, as if wary of enemies, she thought, and strode off with a purpose. Marcy followed his progress as he passed the far ends of each aisle. Then, he suddenly disappeared.

She couldn't have said why exactly, but Marcy abruptly leaned over her friend's shoulder and said, "I'm going to the ladies room. Be right back—good luck." She gave his shoulder a companionable rub, but he ignored her, already engrossed in the cards in his hand.

She made her way down the last aisle she'd seen the man cross. On either side, slot machines called to her, the coin-fed automatons unaware of her passing. Marcy told herself she wasn't doing anything wrong, but her heart began racing anyway, and even though a nervous sweat had erupted over her brow, her hands were ice cold, especially the one holding the beer.

At the far end of the aisle she slowed, easing her way into the open. Glancing both ways, she found no sign of the man. It seemed he really had disappeared. Stepping across the open space at the end of the aisle, she placed her beer on the bar and looked around again, still puzzled. Then the bartender was there, a middle-aged matronly woman asking her what she needed.

Both of them eyed Marcy's nearly full glass of beer. "Well, nothing really," she stuttered. She glanced behind her, and then said, "Actually, I was wondering, did you happen to see . . ." But then, thinking better of it, she paused, looked at the woman again, and asked, "I mean, could you tell me where the ladies room is?"

Not even attempting to hide a snicker, the woman looked over Marcy's head at a sign protruding from the wall, barely five feet away. WOMEN, it read.

Marcy followed the bartender's gaze until the stupidity of her request became apparent. "Well, duh!" she mumbled, and then giggled at the straight-faced woman.

She turned to leave when the bartender stopped her, asking, "You want that beer?"

"Oh, yes, of course," Marcy said, grabbing the cup while avoiding the woman's snide grin. Finally walking away, she berated herself, thinking, *What an idiot! I'd be the world's worst detective.*

The entrance to the restroom was through an open vestibule. Just as she entered, Marcy noticed another door right next to the entryway. It was painted with the same geometrical designwork as the walls, effectively disguising its existence while not really hiding it. She decided that it had to be the door through which the stranger disappeared.

Inside the vestibule, Marcy stopped to look back. No one could see her here, as the one visible aisle of video slots was vacant. At the far end, the card players were too involved in their blackjack game to notice. Marcy leaned against the wall, working to calm her breathing and slow her heart rate. She took several moments to get herself together, then took a deep breath and eased back to the entrance to look at the bar around the corner. The bartender was gathering a tray of drinks for a customer. Screwing up her courage, Marcy stepped out of the vestibule and grabbed the handle of the painted door. If it opened, and she got caught, she could always claim the overhead restroom sign had confused her. Besides, she was just a dumb country hick, right? And she wasn't actually doing any-thing wrong, was she?

The door was locked. She stepped back, looked at the solid steel door and metal handle, then reached out and vigorously yanked on it again. This time it opened, but from the inside, and as Marcy jumped back she glimpsed a luxurious corner of-fice with soft lighting, flanked by floor-to-ceiling windows overlooking the street. She jumped back as the tall man in sun-glasses came through the door.

"Excuse me," he said, in a tone of voice closer to meaning, "Get out of my way." He lowered his glasses to peer over them at her, and the cold contempt in his stare froze the breath in Marcy's lungs. His expression of utter disregard reminded her of black ice on a lake in late spring: it may be interesting to look at, but take a few steps out there and it will kill you.

"No, excuse me," she stammered in a shaky voice. "My mistake."

The stranger reached back for the door handle, pushing it shut. Marcy stumbled backwards out of his way but he bumped against her anyway, knocking the plastic cup of beer from her fingers. It splashed across the floor, sloshing up on the man's trousers and shoes.

"Oh, my God!" Marcy cried. "I'm so sorry."

The stranger's stare turned dark and menacing. Marcy's heart pounded with such a fury she thought it might explode. Her breath fluttered erratically, making her feel powerless and weak. "I'm really, really sorry," she said. She couldn't look the man in the eye for fear of fainting dead away under his threat-ening glower.

"Do you think perhaps you've had too much to drink?"

"What, me—to drink? Oh, no. I was just, I mean, you know, the ladies room . . ."

"This isn't the ladies room," he said with a scornful tone of superiority.

"Of course. I'm just so sorry." Before she could make a move to get out of his way, the man signaled to a security guard at the far end of the bar near the top of the stairs. Marcy couldn't think. She stood helpless in front of him, her mouth hanging open, unable even to swallow.

Then, another voice behind her. "Is there a problem here?" A hairy arm draped itself around her shoulders, and she turned to see the camouflaged cap beside her.

The man in the sunglasses asked, "Who the hell are you?"

Marcy saw the security guard talking on his radio as he approached. Another uniformed guard bounded up the steps. As they drew near, the man beside her tensed up and said, "I asked you, mister. You got a problem?" Then he noticed the spilled beer, stained trousers, and wet shoes. He laughed. "You should learn to control yourself."

The two security guards were there then, with more of them flowing up the staircase. The man in the sunglasses looked at the guards, then nodded toward Marcy and her friend.

Her companion turned, his arm around her shoulders, pulling Marcy with him. "Come on, sweetheart. Let's play some cards."

"Excuse me, sir," one of the guards said.

The heavy arm slid off Marcy's shoulder as her friend looked at the guard. Then he abruptly turned to face the man in the sunglasses. "What's your problem, man?" He took a step toward him but was instantly set upon by security. They grabbed his arms and twisted them behind him, at the same time wrestling him around to face in the direction of the stairs.

Marcy cried, "Stop it! We haven't done anything wrong!"

Her friend kicked out at the man in the sunglasses, but missed, and soon there were half a dozen guards restraining him in their powerful arms. He yelled and cursed, his cap went flying, and Marcy watched as a sinister grin appeared on her tormentor's face. "You can't do this," she yelled. "We haven't done anything wrong!"

The man calmly replied, "We have you on video tape. Don't ever come back." And then he left, leading the way down the stairs.

Another security man, dressed as a regular casino employee, took a firm grip on Marcy's arm. Her friend thrashed against the guards, yelling like a fiend in a nightmare. They carried him spread-eagle between them, feet first, his flailing body and the determined captors an undulating mound of violence. A few paces behind, Marcy's escort led her down the stairs. Like an animal caught in a trap, she warily looked around, and spotted the man in the spiked hair and sunglasses striding quickly across the foyer toward the front entrance.

Near the bottom of the stairs, a security guard holding one of her friend's legs suddenly stumbled. The whole pile of bodies crashed forward. For an instant, she saw a fist the size of a paver stone at the end of a thick hairy arm lash out. The guard at her side jumped into the melee, and soon order was restored as the tussling mass of arms and legs once again headed toward the door.

Marcy followed, this time alone, until she stopped among a group of onlookers watching the excitement. She slipped into an aisle of video slot machines, peeking back around the corner to watch as her friend was forcefully ejected from the building. She felt weak in the knees, sick to her stomach. She knew that if she were thrown out now, she'd feel obligated to help the man who'd stood up for her. A shudder bounced up her spine. How had all this happened?

Her hands were shaking when she looked around the corner again. Most of the security men were returning now, laughing and high-fiving each other. Flashing lights through the lobby suggested a squad car out front. Were they really arresting him? For what? Would they come looking for her, too?

She ran down the aisle, passing an older Native American woman sitting at a slot machine three or four seats in from the end. Marcy passed her and climbed atop the next stool, using the woman to help block her from view. Once again she found herself staring at a flashing, ringing machine. It was useless trying to focus on the instructions. Trying to control her racing heartbeat, she looked at the woman next to her and was surprised to find her staring back, as if she hadn't seen this much excitement in years. Embarrassed, Marcy averted her eyes and fished her coin purse out of her pocket. Fumbling it open, she hunched over on the stool like all the other mindless gamblers, keeping her back twisted toward the far end of the aisle, as if by not looking at the security men she could somehow hide in plain sight.

Besides her driver's license and a credit card, there was a small wad of cash in her coin purse. Grabbing the money, she thumbed through it, at the same time locating the flashing slot in the machine to feed paper money. She snuck another quick peek behind her, past the old woman, just in time to see a couple more security men walk past the end of the aisle.

Marcy fed a five-dollar bill into the machine. Bells rang and lights flashed in thanks as it swallowed her money. She tried to calm herself with several deep breaths, and then climbed off the stool and crept back to the end of the aisle. Looking toward the entrance, she saw a crowd of people standing around talking about the incident. Past them, through the lobby, she noticed the lights of the squad car intermittently glowing through the descending darkness. Her eyes were trained now to spot security, even those in plain clothes, and she saw a guard at the front door, like a doorman, and another one standing out on the sidewalk. When she looked back down the aisle, she spotted the woman still watching her, apparently finding Marcy's dilemma more interesting than the machine in front of her.

Back in the lobby, she saw the outside door open and a woman enter. Marcy couldn't believe her eyes. Jackie strode through the door and into the lobby, smiling graciously in greeting to the doorman. Marcy ducked back into her aisle as the fears and queasiness came rushing back. "You stupid idiot," she hissed at herself. "Why didn't you leave when you were supposed to?"

She chanced another peek around the corner. Jackie stood in the lobby, her hands in the pockets of a dark woolen coat, reading flyers on the bulletin board. Marcy shook her head. *If she comes this way, I'm toast.* She hustled back to the slot machine, noting the old woman still watching her with a placid, expressionless stare. It was the same vacant look she'd seen on so many of the customers, like addicts awaiting their next fix. Marcy hunched over in her "hiding" position atop the stool. Her mind reeling, she attempted to read the instructions before her. Then, bewildered, she reached around the side of the machine, slapping at it with the palm of her hand. Turning to the woman beside her, she asked, "Don't you even pull a handle on these things?"

The old lady didn't respond, and acted like she hadn't even understood her words.

Marcy said, "I thought they called them 'One-Armed Bandits.'" She sighed in frustration as another scene from her Las Vegas movie was erased.

Sitting forward for a closer look at the machine, she was startled when the old woman suddenly leaned in at her side. With a fragile, crooked finger, she pointed at buttons in front of Marcy. She mumbled something completely incoherent and pointed at more buttons, but Marcy was too distracted by Jackie's arrival to pay attention. She scrambled down off her stool and, using pantomime, motioned for the woman to take her seat.

Returning to the head of the aisle, she peeked out to the lobby again and was surprised to see Jackie departing through the front door. Why was she leaving so soon, and where was she going? Marcy wanted to run after her, maybe follow her into the night, but before she could make a move, she heard her machine go crazy.

Looking behind her, Marcy saw a miniature light show going off in her aisle. The machine whistled and clanged. Her first thought was that somehow she'd broken it. With a frown,

Marcy took a step down the aisle toward it, but then abruptly turned around and made a dash for the lobby.

At the door, she spotted a charter bus parked at the curb. Along the side of it she read the name of another casino outside of town, a much larger establishment than this one, with a hotel and restaurants attached as well as a theater for live entertainment. She watched as Jackie climbed the steps and disappeared into the bus.

Marcy ran back inside. People looked at her as she hustled through the casino to her aisle. When she rounded the corner, however, she stopped in her tracks. The light show still exploded across the far end of the aisle. The old woman had taken Marcy's seat, and the machine in front of her buzzed and clanged like a New Year's Eve noisemaker. Whistles shrieked and bells rang. Strangers ran into the aisle, attracted by the noise, so Marcy eased her way forward with them. People were laughing and cheering, patting the old woman on the back, oblivious to the fact that this was Marcy's machine. After all, to the best of her knowledge, no one had actually seen her sitting there.

Marcy wormed her way up the aisle to stand beside the woman's stool. She wondered if the machine had short-circuited or something, but then the woman turned to look at her. The lifeless expression had been transformed into one of joy and good humor, causing Marcy to finally realize what had happened. The woman started to climb down off the stool, but Marcy put a hand out to stop her. "Please," she said, pointing at the machine. "It's yours."

The woman broke into a laugh and suddenly reached over to pull Marcy into a hug. "Oh!" Marcy exclaimed, surprised by this sudden act of affection. But then a security person was there, the very same guard who'd escorted her down the stairs. His attention, however, like everyone else's, was focused on the machine, waiting to see how much it would pay out. Marcy pulled back into the crowd of onlookers. She struggled against the flow of curious well-wishers to make her way to the end of the aisle.

When she finally returned to the lobby, she paused at the spot where Jackie had stood. On the wall was a schedule for bus departures to the neighboring casino. Now it started to make sense. Of course Jackie wouldn't be caught dead hanging out in a place like this. Or, perhaps it was true that she did have some gambling debts, like rumor suggested, and her credit here had been cut off. Either way, she had a free ride to a bigger, classier place down the road. To Marcy's way of thinking, a place probably much more suited to Jackie's style.

She had no more use for this smoky, noisy, depressing place. The one thing she remembered the man in the camouflage cap saying was that even on a good day the nickel slot machines didn't pay out much. The old woman could have it; coaxing a smile out of that wrinkled old face was good enough for Marcy.

She offered a sweet smile to the doorman as she left. Outside, the temperature was dropping under the darkening sky over the harbor. She gulped fresh air while shaking off the creepy claustrophobia of the casino. Even the acrid aroma of the paper mill over the ridge in Cloquet, wafting down to the waterfront, was a delight to her deprived senses. With her mood quickly rebounding, Marcy dropped a few quarters into the outstretched fingers of a panhandler squatting against the building, then quickened her pace at the stoplight to cross the street. The warmer, friendlier lights of Canal Park were just a few blocks ahead.

Marcy strode down the hill toward the harbor, thinking back over her bizarre adventure. At least the man with the camouflage cap was gone. She felt a little bad about that, about how he'd stood up for her and she hadn't bothered to go outside to see if he was okay. But then, he had the look of someone familiar with the harder side of life, and she decided he'd probably be just fine.

All in all, Marcy figured she hadn't learned much of anything that would be of help to Abby, although she'd certainly
learned something about Jackie. She held herself tightly against
the enclosing chill, almost jogging now, putting the dark gray
stone buildings of downtown behind her. She felt exhilarated,
and burst into laughter at the memory of her beginner's luck.
It would be fun to tell Owen and Red about it when she returned to work in the café. She still couldn't believe how much
noise that machine had made, and on her very first try, no less!
So engrossed was she in her thoughts, and so glad to be putting
the whole escapade behind her, Marcy didn't notice when a
shadow slipped out from a darkened office doorway. She wasn't
aware of it trailing along beside her, either, just across the street.

FOURTEEN

Abby Simon

Randall never did come home that evening. When Abby and Jackie returned to work after lunch, he was still busy in the office, and Abby couldn't help but notice his secretive behavior as he tended to his paperwork. The office door remained shut, further piquing her curiosity. Earlier, when she'd made her surprise appearance, she'd managed only a brief glimpse into the room because Jackie happened to be blocking most of the doorway. Now Abby learned that the room was virtually soundproof, and with no windows and just the one solid steel door, absolutely impregnable. The absurd notion that the office would make an ideal holding cell immediately wormed its way into her imagination, to the extent that it created an obsession of sorts for her get inside.

While Abby's admittance had been stymied, Jackie entered the office several times to talk to Randall. After the first of these meetings, the change in her mother's behavior had been obvious. Jackie chattered nonstop as she bustled about the gallery. She joked and laughed with enthusiasm, using outrageous, dramatic hand gestures while describing the artwork on the walls. Something had happened, Abby was sure of it, and the answer was in that rock-walled fortress of an office.

Dinner that evening was Chinese take-out they picked up on their walk home. Randall had finally left the gallery late in the afternoon, but the office door was locked tight when Abby quietly gave it a try. When he didn't show up for dinner, Jackie observed, "He does this all the time. He has his business buddies, you know. I think it's just an excuse to hit a few happy hours. Suits me just fine."

Her mother's inane chattering kept up while they ate, until Jackie suddenly looked at her watch, stood up, and said, "I have to go out for a while."

"What do you mean? I just got here. I thought we were going to hang out."

Jackie whisked a stack of take-out containers to the refrigerator. "Tomorrow, honey. We'll work the gallery together, then we'll do something fun tomorrow night."

Abby looked around the uncluttered, ultra-modern apartment. She didn't even see a TV. She hadn't wanted to be here in the first place, and now she was going to be left alone? Finding clues about her brother's whereabouts had been the motivation for coming to the city, but now she was being deserted by the two people she suspected might know something about Ben's disappearance. Besides, she thought, getting angry again, she wasn't even done with their conversation from earlier in the day at Sir Reginald's.

Jackie stood in front of the hall mirror to put on her black woolen coat. She took a brush from a drawer in the entryway table and swept it through the ends of her thick black hair. Abby said, "I thought you wanted to brush out my braid tonight."

Jackie found her daughter in the mirror and said, "Not tonight, honey. You've had a long day. I really need to make this appointment."

Abby watched her mother's fingers shake as she prepared to leave. She couldn't hold her daughter's gaze in the mirror, either. She watched as Jackie leaned toward the mirror for a closer inspection of her face, then stood back and straightened her coat. With a critical eye still on the mirror, she said, "Just relax tonight, sweetheart. Tomorrow will be a busy day. It'll be just you and me, with the whole city out there waiting for us."

Abby grappled with her anger. She knew her mother was lying, or at the very least holding something back. Without considering her words, she blurted, "What happened at the gallery today?"

Jackie's departure plans were temporarily interrupted. When she finally looked at her daughter, neither one of them could muster up a smile. "What do you mean?"

Abby shrugged. "Something happened. After lunch, when you talked to Randall, all of a sudden you were all happy and stuff. Like you got some good news." Jackie stared at her daughter, but concern now furled her brow. Abby realized her shot in the dark had hit something. "I thought maybe you'd heard something about Ben."

Jackie's expression softened. She crossed the room and took both of Abby's hands in hers. "My dear little girl," she cooed. "Is there anyone in the whole wide world as loyal and faithful as you?" She led Abby to the couch where they sat together, close upon each other, the young girl sitting up as straight and tall as her mother. "Abby, you have to give this a rest. We discussed it earlier. It will only lead to more heartache."

Abby shook her head. "He's my brother, Mom. How can you ask me to let it go?" She saw no reason to confess that she felt responsible for Ben's disappearance.

"But Abby, there are good people working on this, people who know more about this stuff than we do. They're experts, trained to solve these kinds of things. We have to leave it to them to bring Ben home safe. Otherwise, who knows, you might just get in the way and make it worse."

For the first time Abby had the feeling her mother was telling the truth, or at least not out-and-out lying, so she asked, "Well then, if there isn't news about Ben, what happened today that made you so happy?"

Jackie slapped her daughter on the knee and stood up. "Well, nothing really that will mean much to you, but the Bengston estate has been settled. Randall officially inherited everything, including the bait shop property." She walked back across the room to study herself again in the entryway mirror. "You know he never felt any attachment to that old place." She looked at Abby, still sitting on the couch. "So he already sold it, signed over the papers today. Now we'll be able to do some really big things with the gallery."

Abby felt small tucked into the corner of the sofa, like a little girl again, with big people saying things that she didn't really understand. It had only been a matter of weeks. She wasn't even used to the idea of Rosie being gone. Now the bait shop was going, too? "Who's buying it?" she asked. "Will it still be a bait shop?"

"Oh, dear, no," Jackie said, laughing. "No one could make a living selling bait there. Not even Rosie. They'll tear down those old buildings and haul all that garbage away. It's a beautiful piece of shoreline, though."

"I know. But it won't be the same without 'Rosie's Bait.'"

Jackie turned to reach for the door. "Oh," she said, looking back again. "There's a TV in the den, and some movies, too, I think." She noticed Abby's glum scowl. "Hey, sweetheart, I know how difficult all these changes can be. But just think how beautiful Rose's place will be when they get the luxury condominiums put up. I think they even plan to build a marina where Henry's old breakwater used to be." She offered Abby the warmest smile she could manage while still avoiding her gaze. She opened the door. "Get some rest, Abby. We have a big day ahead of us tomorrow. It'll be fun, you'll see."

Abby continued to slouch on the sofa after her mother left. She didn't believe any of that crap about having a meeting tonight. The idea to follow her mother crossed her mind, but she still couldn't believe Jackie had taken an active role in Ben's disappearance. She probably had an idea of what was going on, and Abby still firmly believed her mother knew that Ben was okay, but she couldn't imagine Jackie actually kidnapping and hiding her own son. Besides, her mother was right, it had been a long day, and she was tired.

Without much enthusiasm, she finished clearing the dinner table and ran water to rinse the dishes. Then she spotted the ring of keys on the kitchen counter. She knew those keys. She'd seen them today in The Tempest when her mother had used them to lock up the gallery. Abby stacked the plates and glasses in the dishwasher, but her gaze kept slipping over to the key ring, three or four keys bound together on a metal hoop. Her heart fluttered when she realized one of those keys would probably open the fortress of an office she'd been unable to enter.

The cleanup went much faster after that. She told herself it would only take a few minutes to run down to The Tempest, use the keys to get inside, check out the office, and run back. She'd be home long before her mother, and she'd rid herself of the nagging mystery of that locked room. She quickly finished straightening up, pulled her hooded sweatshirt over her head, and fitted her Minnesota Twins cap over her braid. Then, just twenty minutes after Jackie left, Abby slipped out the door to join the early evening pedestrian traffic on Superior Street.

• • • • •

Because of the height of the ridge running behind Duluth, darkness fell quickly over the harbor when the sun set. A chill in the air moved Abby briskly along the sidewalk. Shops on both sides of the street were open, so many that she was overwhelmed by the amount of lights and people and commotion. All the shops and businesses in Black Otter Bay wouldn't cover a single half-block here in Duluth. The tail end of rush hour traffic still clogged the street. Abby dodged away from the curb when a large charter bus, bearing the name of a popular casino south of town, accelerated past.

She turned downhill toward the harbor and Canal Park. Abby found all the activity startling and unfamiliar, in some ways even unnerving, because it was impossible to keep track of everything going on around her. Cars honked, a truck climbing the hill roared through the gears, and foot traffic scurried past in both directions. A man suddenly appeared out of a darkened doorway. He approached, staggering and careening too close. Abby jumped aside in time to avoid contact with the vomit discoloring the front of his jacket. She lurched into a jog then, down the hill to the tangled mass of freeway overpasses shunting traffic around the heart of downtown. The puzzling network of ponderous slabs of concrete, as well as the megalithic stone and brick buildings of the city swirled overhead, and it was then that she realized her mother had been wrong: the city really did block out the stars. In the woods, when the mysteries of the night awoke, her father had taught her to count on the cheerful guidance of moon and stars to find her way. Their presence on a dark night would calm and reassure her, in much the same way that their absence from the city skyline added to her unease.

Still jogging, she left the noise and confusion of the freeway behind and entered Canal Park, a well-lit, friendlier section of the port city. She slowed to a walk here to match the casual pace of window shoppers out for an evening stroll. Some of the stores were closed, but the ones that were still open, as well as all the restaurants and bars, were abuzz with customers. On the corner she passed the mellow glow of the neighborhood coffee shop, its clientele logged into their laptops or thoroughly engrossed in conversation. Next came Camille's bookstore, which had just closed for the day, and then she was at The Tempest. A few lights inside threw haunting shadows across the artwork. She spotted the little red light on the security system winking its one-eyed glow of surveillance. With the alarm system activated, she knew that no one was inside. Abby took a deep breath to collect herself, then continued walking past the gallery and turned into an alleyway cutting through the block.

It was even darker here in the narrow passage between tall brick buildings. Her tennis shoe–clad footsteps emitted a scuffling echo on the sand-covered concrete alley. Abby was grateful for the covering darkness, but the unfamiliar noises and chaotic nightlife jangled her nerves. How was it, she wondered, that she could walk for miles alone through the woods at night without a thought for her safety, but a few blocks in the heart of the city scared the devil out of her? She turned at the end of the alley, where it emptied into the parking lot in the middle of the block, and a few more steps brought her to the back door of The Tempest.

She climbed a couple of open-mesh iron stair treads and turned around on the landing to peer down the length of the block of businesses. While the storefronts were well-kept and painted in vibrant colors, here in back everything was dark and dingy. The parking lot was a potholed gravel bed with no markings, but more than a few mud puddles. Cars were parked in a haphazard manner, sharing space with storage sheds, electric power lines, and overflowing dumpsters. From across the way Abby heard the amplified sound of a rock and roll band, and voices and laughter filtered through to her between guitar riffs. It was well lit over there, too, which made it seem even darker on this side of the block. The row of back doors was quiet and hidden away in the shadows, and a sense of mystery or suspense seemed to hang in the cooling night air. Then she heard footsteps down the alleyway behind her.

Abby pulled the key ring from her pocket. Her heart was racing, but it was her fingers that caused her problems. They were frozen by the surge of adrenaline, and shook like lifeless twigs. She had no idea which key opened the door, so she jabbed blindly at the deadbolt with the first key her fingers managed to manipulate. The footsteps were running now, nearing the corner. Desperate, Abby turned the key upside down and tried again, but her fingers were useless in the dark. As the footsteps rounded the rear corner of The Tempest, she backed herself into a dark shadow on the door and stood completely still.

"Marcy!" she cried when she saw her friend race around the corner.

Her sudden call caused Marcy to scream, stopping her dead in her tracks. "Where are you?" she demanded, squinting around in the dark.

Abby bounced down the steps. She could breathe again. She ran to Marcy and asked, "What are you doing here?"

"I saw you from across the street. I was going back to my motel. Wait until you hear what happened to me." The cool night air and excitement painted a brilliant blush on Marcy's cheeks. "What on earth are you doing sneaking around back here?"

Abby held up the ring of keys. "I'm going inside to look around." From under her smile of joy at the sight of her friend, Abby feigned a glare of anger and swatted Marcy on the shoulder. "You scared me half to death, Marcella Soderstrom!"

"Sorry. But that's what you get for sneaking around in the dark." Marcy scanned the parking lot, the puddles, and all the trash. "It's spooky back here," she said. "Does your mother know what you're doing?"

Abby rolled her eyes and returned to the stairs.

"That's what I thought," Marcy called after her. "Speaking of Jackie, I saw her a little while ago. I'm sure she has no idea what you're up to."

Abby stopped on the landing. "You saw my mom?"

Marcy climbed the metal steps behind her. "I was up at the casino. She came in, but just to check the bus schedule. She got on the charter headed south."

"Did she see you?"

"No. Why?"

Abby worked with the keys again. She saw no point in telling Marcy that her mother had lied about her plans for the evening. "You're in my light," she said, hipping Marcy to the side.

It took a few tries, but the door finally opened. "Wait here while I shut off the alarm system."

"You know, I won a bunch of money," Marcy called, but Abby was already deep inside the darkness of the gallery. In the sudden stillness, the sounds of music and laughter from the bar wafted across the parking lot, but here on this side not a soul could be seen. Marcy peered into the dark corners and hiding places in the parking lot. She'd meant it when she'd said it was spooky out here. She didn't like standing alone on the landing, but just as she turned back to the door, Abby grabbed her arm and pulled her inside. The door slid shut with a click behind them.

The Tempest was dark and still, long and narrow like a cavern, with a brooding silence that could be hiding almost anything. Abby held Marcy's hand when she asked, "So, how much money did you win?"

"I don't know. I gave it to some old Indian woman. I had to get out of there because security was after me."

"Security?"

"It's a complicated story."

Abby shook her head. "You're crazy, Marcy. But I'm glad you're here. Come on." She led her friend through the maze of artwork to the office door.

"There was this guy in the casino," Marcy explained, following close on Abby's heels. "A big guy. He looked to be in charge or something. Actually, he looked like a gangster, like he should be in *The Sopranos*."

Abby paused at the office door and looked at her. "What's *The Sopranos*?"

"Well, you know, like the mafia or something. A gangster."

"Is he the guy who threw you out?"

"Oh, no. He's more important than that. He called security on me because I spilled my beer on him."

Abby's eyebrow went up.

"I know, it sounds crazy. But this guy really scared me. He wore dark sunglasses, even inside the casino, and a flat top haircut."

Abby's eyes narrowed. "A flat top? You mean like a crew cut?"

"Yep."

"And it stuck straight up on top?" Abby held her hand several inches over her head. "Kind of like a Mohawk?"

"Yeah, I guess so."

The girl thought about it, and then asked, "Was he wearing a suit coat? Like a black blazer or something?"

"Yes! Exactly! And a black shirt, too. How did you know?"

Abby hesitated before answering. "I think I've seen him before. I think he's one of Randall's business partners."

"Oh, that's bad, Abby. That's real bad. This guy is not someone you want to mess around with."

Abby ignored her, instead holding up the ring of keys to inspect them.

Having told Abby about the man in the casino, Marcy's fear flared up again, so she tried another argument. "I really don't think we should be here."

"It's okay. We're not doing anything wrong."

"You want to tell that to Randall? Remember that gun of his?"

"We'll only be a minute. I just want to see what's in the office."

The door before them was completely shrouded in darkness. Abby knew where the lights were but feared attracting attention by using them. Once again she struggled with the keys, and with Marcy crowding up tight against her back, Abby's frustration quickly mounted. She finally gave up, banged on the door with a fist, and then pressed an ear against it to listen. "Ben?" she called in a hoarse whisper, even though she knew her voice couldn't be heard inside.

A small light suddenly appeared on the door, and Abby turned to see Marcy holding a miniature LED penlight. "Girl Scouts," Marcy explained. "Always be prepared. Mrs. Bean was our scout leader. I always thought she did it because she never had children of her own."

Abby's expression glazed over in pure confusion. Marcy's words were so out of the moment that they came at her like a foreign language. Finally, she shook her head and held the keys up between them. "Hold that light over here."

Marcy watched as Abby fingered through the ring of keys. "What were you saying about Ben?" she asked.

Abby didn't answer. In a moment the door quietly eased open, and Abby stuck her head into the darkened room, calling softly, "Ben?"

The room was pitch black. Abby snaked her hand along the wall until she found the light switch. "Come on," she said, pulling Marcy inside with her.

After closing the door to hide the light, Marcy locked it, and they stood side by side looking around the office. The room was actually quite large, just as Abby had imagined, but it was only the one big room, with nowhere to hide—and more importantly, with no sign of her brother. She walked around the desk, opening and closing drawers, feeling the futility of her efforts mounting.

Marcy clicked the computer on while Abby wandered over to the file cabinet. Marcy asked, "What are we looking for?"

"Ben," Abby answered, yanking the top drawer open.

"What?"

"We're looking for signs of Ben." She fingered through files with labels for artist information, billings, contracts, and sales receipts. She pulled out the file of receipts and laid it open across the top of the drawer of files.

Marcy said, "If I knew the password, we could look at their books. I always wondered how this place made enough money to stay in business."

"Oh, yeah, like you know anything about bookkeeping."

"I beg your pardon," Marcy said, smirking. "Who do you think keeps the books for the café?"

Abby found herself grinning at her friend. "Really?" She had to admit that Marcy looked comfortable behind the computer. She studied the monitor with a gleam in her eye, clicking away on the keyboard like she knew what she was doing and belonged there. Abby returned to the file and found the latest receipts, including the one her mother had bragged about at dinner. She paused, staring at the receipt, and then over her shoulder blurted, "Try Fitzgerald."

"For a password? Really? Okay." And than a moment later, "Nope, too long. Six characters or less."

"How about Edmund?"

Marcy typed away. "Oh, my God, Abby. That's a bingo, girl!"

Abby smiled. She didn't expect Marcy would find anything in the computer, but it was amusing to see her settling in behind the monitor, concentration wrinkling her brow. Abby returned to looking through the files. She pulled out the most recent receipt, the thousand-dollar credit card transaction for the *Fitzgerald* painting. Fingering through the rest of the file revealed only a few small purchases over the last several weeks.

"Wow," Marcy sighed, studying the ledger on the computer. "I had no idea this stuff was worth so much."

Abby grabbed her file and walked over to the desk. She watched as Marcy scrolled through the entries. "Look at this one," Marcy said as she brought up the current transactions. She read out loud. "Phillip Oberg, *Deep Water Passage*. Oil on canvas, framed." She pointed to a column on the far right side of the monitor, and whistled, "Fifteen thousand dollars."

Abby was stunned. "Mom never mentioned that one. She told me about selling a painting of the *Edmund Fitzgerald* for a thousand dollars. She made it sound like that was a big deal."

Marcy scrolled down, and read, "*Sinking of the* Edmund Fitzgerald. Oil on canvas, framed." She looked up at Abby standing over her. "Sold today for ten thousand dollars."

"No way," Abby declared. "It must be a mistake." She dropped the file on the desk and opened it to the charge account receipt. "Look here, Marcy. One thousand dollars. Randall must have entered it wrong in the computer."

"There's a big difference between one thousand and ten thousand dollars," Marcy said. "It would be hard to make a mistake like that." They studied the numbers on the monitor and the smaller numbers in the file. Then Marcy slowly sat back and looked at Abby again. "Unless . . ."

"Unless what?"

"Unless he didn't make a mistake. He could be cooking the books."

"What?"

"I don't know, Abby. I don't know. But he might be using the gallery to launder money for his buddies, like that mafia guy I saw in the casino." She reached over to turn on the printer sitting on a tray table next to the desk. It buzzed and beeped, and when it settled down, she hit the print function on the computer and the machine went to work. "Your file there only goes back a few weeks, right?" she asked. "These computer records go all the way back through last year. I bet if we look closer, we'll find bank account deposits to match the higher figures on the computer."

"Can he do that?"

"As long as he doesn't get audited. But I'm guessing that when you consider the characters he hangs out with, an audit is probably the least of his worries."

"But what about these receipts?"

"He'll keep most of them, but the ones he alters in the computer probably get shredded. That's why there are so few of them, and this way he doesn't leave a paper trail. Anyway, I'm only just guessing. We need to get these files to someone who knows about this stuff."

Abby's thoughts whirled through what they'd discovered. She didn't know exactly what Marcy was talking about, but she didn't need to. This could be the connection between Randall and that horrible fellow she'd seen out at Big Island Lake, the man carrying Rosie's body over his shoulder. The same man who'd come looking for her, but took her little brother instead.

Then they heard a key in the office door lock.

Abby froze. Marcy calmly canceled the print command and snatched a small pile of printed pages out of the tray. In one smooth movement she shoved them into the file folder of receipts and closed it, looking up just as the door opened.

"Randall!" Abby exclaimed.

He looked genuinely surprised to see them, but downplayed his reaction. "What are you two doing in here?"

His voice may have sounded calm, Abby thought, but she could sense the monster lurking within. And she had no doubt that he carried the handgun on him somewhere. She looked at Marcy, who held Randall square in her field of vision while quietly typing away. They hadn't responded to his question yet, so Abby shut the file cabinet and said, "I'm just trying to learn my way around here. You know, getting used to the filing system and stuff."

"Uh-huh," he said, obviously not believing a word she said. "If you're not up to anything, why is the door locked?"

Marcy continued typing, silently pressing keys while watching Randall, ready at a moment's notice to shut down the computer.

Holding her breath, Abby took a step toward him to buy some time. His eyes were bloodshot, and his hair hung in limp strands along the side of his face. A mottled-gray sport coat hung loosely over a pale blue button-down shirt. He licked his lips, and with his long, narrow nose, Abby pictured a poisonous lizard confronting them. "It's scary in here at night," she finally answered. "And we're not used to all the strange noises in a big city."

He stepped quickly around the desk to look over Marcy's shoulder at the computer monitor. A game of solitaire was underway on the screen. To Abby, he asked, "Where's your mother?"

"She went out. Said she had a meeting. I was bored, so we decided to come down here."

Randall snickered, then looked down at Marcy again. The knuckles on her hand holding the mouse were white. "Move," he said. The smell of alcohol and stale cigars clung to the air around him.

Marcy rocked sideways out of the chair, leaning over the desk while sliding the manila file folder along with her. Randall shook his head as he fell into the chair. "Dear, sweet Jackie," he said, chuckling, as if no one else was in the room to hear. "We just get you solvent again, and it's off to the card tables with you." He closed the solitaire game, and brought up his work files. He turned an evil grin on Abby. "Sorry to tell you this, young lady, but your mother isn't at any meeting tonight."

Abby stood her ground near the file cabinet. She noticed that the power light on the printer was still on, and now that she'd seen it, it seemed to glow like a beacon in the room. Meanwhile, Marcy backed away from the desk, slowly, her hands behind her back clutching the file folder.

Betraying a trace if belligerence, Abby said, "Well, Mom said that you were at a meeting tonight, too."

Marcy winced. The room was completely silent while Randall studied the computer monitor. After a few tense moments he seemed satisfied that his files hadn't been compromised. He looked over at Abby again and laughed. "Jackie. You got to love her, don't you?" Then the smile disappeared, and he added, "I mean, if I didn't love her, why would I put up with all her crap?"

Now it was Abby's turn to get mad. Lately, she hadn't been so fond of her mother herself, but that didn't mean she would listen to snide comments about her from the likes of Randall. She looked over at Marcy, standing wide-eyed and frozen in the middle of the office floor. She seemed to have some sense that Abby was about to speak, and tried to will her to silence with a glare and a barely perceptible shake of her head.

Abby turned her attention back to Randall. While her fear may have subsided, the feeling that they were close to some answers rendered her temporarily speechless. She didn't want to jeopardize the information they'd already uncovered. Besides, even though she wasn't so scared right now, she certainly hadn't forgotten about Randall's gun, nor his wild shots in the bait shop.

Just as the silence in the room became awkward, Randall spoke up again. "The thing about Jackie is, everything with her is about money." He leaned back and pulled a stray length of hair away from his face. "She thinks I care about the money." Now he laughed, a sour-sounding cackle, and swiveled on his chair like a little kid proud of himself. Another pocket of stale, alcohol-scented air floated past Abby.

She looked at Marcy, who by now had backed her way across the office to the doorway. Abby gave her a slight shrug, as if to ask, "Why is he telling me all this?"

"I mean, it's only money," Randall continued. "What's the big deal? Money is the easy part. It's like I tell her: it's the relationship that's important. Money comes and goes, but you take care of each other in a partnership. Hell, I don't care about Jackie's gambling." He took a moment to refocus on Abby, waving a drunken hand of dismissal through the air. "No, sir, the gambling doesn't mean a thing to me. What your mother does have is an eye for class, which is something that is important to me. She has a knack for style, and she likes to have a good time."

Randall stared into the computer monitor again, his sudden glassy-eyed silence making Abby uncomfortable. Was she supposed to say something? Was he going to pass out?

"No, it's not about the money," he finally concluded. He sat up straight and pointed a wobbling finger at Abby. "I promised Jackie that I'd do everything in my power to keep Ben safe."

Abby bolted to attention, standing up straight. "What have you done with him?"

Randall snickered. "I hope you're not going to screw this up for your mother."

She was standing by the corner of the desk now, and noticed the difficulty he had in focusing on her. His breath once again assaulted the room. Marcy no longer tried to hide her feelings. She emphatically wagged her head in the negative while making faces at Abby, who saw her theatrics out of the

corner of her eye, but wasn't about to back off from this particular discussion.

"I'm not going to screw up anything," she said. "I promise.
Just tell me where he is, and I won't say a word to anyone."

Once again Randall emitted his devious little cackle.

"Come on," Abby pleaded. "You can trust me. I haven't
told anyone anything yet, have I?"

Randall turned a questioning eye on Marcy, as if wondering how much she knew. Then he looked at Abby again, and
said, "You know, if it hadn't been for you, none of this would
be happening. The whole thing is your fault."

Abby stepped back, stealing a glance at Marcy. This latest
revelation had left her friend's mouth hanging open in shock.
Then Randall said to Abby, "And now, for your mother's sake,
I've had to argue on your behalf, too. Fortunately for her, I've been
able to keep you two kids safe. You messed up everything for us,
but so far I've managed to fix it. Now Ben is on his way home."

There was a tremor in Randall's voice that warned her to
be careful. She could feel his anger rising again. But it was
Marcy who spoke up first. "So you really do know where he
is? Ben is coming home?"

"Well, not exactly straight home," Randall said, puffing
up like a child who's proud of owning some privileged information. "But he'll be found soon, and if you two behave your-
selves, this whole wretched mess will be over."

"What do you mean, 'he'll be found'?" Abby asked.
"Where is he?"

Randall put the computer to sleep and rolled his chair back.
Instead of getting up, however, he leaned back and put his feet
up on the desk. He studied his shiny black loafers and swiped
at a stain on the leg of his trousers. He looked at Marcy, standing silently again by the door, then swiveled back to Abby.
Scrunching his face in thought, he scanned the ceiling for a moment. Then an almost friendly smile spread across his face as
he said to Abby, "I hear you're quite a fisherman."

Once again his words caught her off guard. She looked hard at him and thought how at this particular moment, in his casual attire and slouching posture, he could fit right in with any of the other middle-aged men from Black Otter Bay.

"I used to be a fisherman, too," he continued. "In fact, I probably caught more fish by the time I was your age than you'll catch in your whole lifetime."

Abby had heard stories about the commercial fishing done by the Bengston family, especially Randall's father Henry, and his uncles. The tales were near-legend around Black Otter Bay. Unfortunately, Henry had died before Abby was born, and Randall himself had no interest in the business, so the closest she'd ever come to seeing the operation was an inspection of their old handmade boat on display outside the municipal bar in town. But she didn't want the conversation to be sidetracked by fishing, so again she asked, "Where is Ben?"

Randall looked at his hands in his lap, ran a thumb over his fingernails, and then reached for the cell phone in his pocket. After checking for messages, he tossed it on the desk, sat back, and slowly swung his gaze up to Abby. "Anyway, we're both fishermen, right, Abby?"

She had no idea where this was going. Was it just more drunken rambling? She didn't want to be fooled by his calm familiarity. In some ways, he was like the Great Lake he used to fish: friendly and serene one minute, and a raging gale the next. But with nothing to say, she gave a brief nod in answer to his question and waited for him to continue.

Randall picked up his phone again. Before dialing, however, he said, "A real fisherman never gives away his secrets. Isn't that right? I mean, would you go around telling everyone exactly where you caught a stringer full of fish?" He turned to Marcy. "How about it, Marcella? You ever have out-of-towners come into the café telling where they just caught a boatload of fish? Hell, most times they won't even admit that they caught a fish, or what kind of bait they used." He punched numbers into the phone. "So I'm sorry, ladies. I know where the fish is, but I'm not going to tell you. Chances are, it probably won't make much difference now, anyhow."

He held the phone to his ear, a clever, smug look on his face, like he was pleased with his fishing metaphor. A moment later he spoke into the phone. "Yeah, I have some company up at the office." He listened, nodded and smiled, then changed the phone to his left ear while his right hand reached behind him under his sport coat. He nodded. "Sure, no problem." Then he abruptly hung up and dropped his feet to the floor. The phone clattered across the desk. He sat up straight, his soft, drunken expression suddenly pale and tight. Looking past Marcy to the doorway, he rested both hands on the desk.

Abby asked, "What do you mean? Why doesn't it matter anymore?"

Randall didn't respond, just stared across the office at the doorway. When she finally followed his gaze, the sight of Leonard Fastwater leaning against the doorjamb came as a shock.

"Leonard!" Marcy announced.

"Hello, Marcy," he said. He nodded at Abby, adding, "Good evening, Abby."

Randall still hadn't found any words for his newest visitor. Leonard pushed off from the doorframe and took a few steps into the office. He stood tall and easy in his western boots. The solitary braid at his back was tied off with a wide strip of rawhide. His hands were huge for such a tall, slender figure, and they rested at his side with thumbs hooked into the pockets of his blue jeans. "I saw the lights on," he said, looking at Randall. "And the door was unlocked, so I thought I'd come in and see that everything is okay."

Randall made a face. "So, what, are you a cop here in Duluth now, too?"

"No, sir. Like I said, I just wanted to see that everyone is okay." He looked at Abby, an inquiring expression on his face. "Everything is okay here, isn't it?"

Abby noticed Randall fingering his cell again, like he wanted to make another call, but not in this crowd. Then Marcy said, "Actually, Leonard, we were just leaving." She gestured with a nod for Abby to follow her.

Randall glared at Leonard. "You just happened to be walking by, eh?" His sarcasm was so thick that to Abby it sounded like a challenge. She remembered now that Leonard never carried a gun, and she wondered if Randall knew that.

"It's a beautiful night," Leonard replied, soft and friendly. He glanced at Marcy, and said, "I took a stroll up by the casino, and then thought I'd come down here by the harbor for some fresh air."

When she saw Marcy inching into the doorway, with the file folder still behind her back, Abby started across the office floor to join her. "I guess it's getting late," she said, even though she had no idea what time it was. "And it's been a long day."

Randall manufactured a cheerful voice, calling to Abby, "Remember about the brotherhood of fishermen."

When she paused to look back at him, she felt sickened by the phony smile on his face. Averting her eyes, she offered him a brief nod.

Marcy flashed a more-than-friendly smile at Leonard, and then impetuously skipped over on tiptoes to kiss him on the cheek.

Leonard smiled. "Good night, you two," he said, winking at Abby.

Marcy led the way out the door and through the darkened gallery to the back entrance. Abby heard the men's voices behind them, but couldn't make out their words. When they were outside, Marcy paused on the back landing, where she held the file folder over her head like a trophy, exclaiming, "We got it, Abby! We got it!"

Abby gave a final thought to the men in the office while Marcy danced a jig on the landing. Then she grabbed Marcy's arm, and asked, "What did Randall mean when he said that it doesn't matter anymore about Ben? I mean, he told us he knows where my brother is, but he said it probably won't make any difference now what we know."

Marcy stopped her ridiculous gyrations. Abby's somber expression dissolved her giddiness and wiped the grin from her face. "I don't know, Abby. He probably just meant that Ben would soon be home safe and sound. What we know or don't know won't change that." She held the file up again. "But this does matter, Abby. This matters a lot." Then she bounded down the steps and headed for the alleyway between the buildings. "Come on," she called.

Somewhat reluctant, as if she had missed an important piece of information, Abby descended the steps to follow her friend. Marcy's explanation seemed too simple. If that's what Randall had meant, he could have just said it, instead of talking in riddles about fishing and keeping secrets. The one thing he had made clear, however, was that he expected them to keep quiet until Ben got home. Following her friend around the back of the building, with all these thoughts and worries running through her mind, she didn't notice the big, black, idling sedan in the parking lot behind them, and wasn't aware when the headlights came on as she turned into the alleyway.

FIFTEEN

Marcy Soderstrom

"I don't want to hear any more about it," Marcy argued. "We're taking this to the police."

They rounded the corner out of the alleyway and burst back into the real world of tourists, restaurants, and bars. Moonlight glistened between the steel girders of the Aerial Lift Bridge, casting shimmering reflections across Lake Superior as it rolled dark and cold into the harbor. The early summer evening had blossomed out soft and mild, signaling an end to winter, and it appeared that the whole city had turned out to celebrate the change of seasons. Most of the retail stores were closed, although by mid-summer, at the height of the tourist season, many of the shops would stay open as long as potential customers filled the sidewalks.

Abby caught up to Marcy and grabbed her arm. "But we can't, Marcy. You heard Randall, we can't say anything."

Marcy stopped abruptly and turned on her young friend. "Listen to me, Abby. Randall knows where Ben is. He said so, and that means he lied to investigators." She held up the file folder. "And we know he's laundering money or something. This is a big deal, like federal-type offenses. It's gone way beyond what we can simply keep to ourselves."

"But Ben is coming home," Abby pleaded. "Can't we just wait until he's safe?"

Marcy drew a deep sigh while scanning the crowd with a furtive eye. She started to speak, but changed her mind, instead putting an arm around Abby and pulling her into a walk. Leaning into her, she said quietly, "I don't like the way any of this has gone today. I feel like we're in over our heads, like we might be in danger. There's just no other way, Abby. We have to get help."

She led them toward her waterfront motel, wending their way through the throngs of people in Canal Park. The Great Lakes Nautical Museum was closed, but dozens of people filled the park around it anyway, enjoying the moonlit evening. Clusters of college students milled around, playing hacky-sack or tossing Frisbees under the light of streetlamps, while lovers strolled hand in hand along the concrete pier out to the lighthouse at the entrance to the shipping canal.

Abby ducked out from under Marcy's arm and stopped her once again. "We're not in any danger," she said, her youthful confidence adding a tone to her voice. Then she lightened up a bit. "I mean, as long as we don't tell anyone what we know, there's no reason for us to worry."

They paused across the street from Marcy's motel, where the crowd had thinned out into small groups of people, some drinking beer, others just hanging around, enjoying an evening outside without parkas or boots. Marcy spoke softly, but with an impatient urgency not typical in her voice. "You know, Abby, ever since that day I found you and Ben hiding in the café, you haven't been exactly open and honest with me. And who knows what Randall was going on about with all that talk about fishing. But for me, the main thing is that I'm getting a bad vibe from all this. Plus, your dad asked me to keep an eye on you." She stood up straight and scanned the crowd again, like a secret service agent looking for trouble. Then she leaned over Abby, saying, "So, this is what we're going to do. We'll run up to my room, call the police, and when they get there we'll turn over this file and tell them what we know." She bent down face to face with Abby. "And I mean *everything* we know."

Abby shook her head. "No."

"Abby, please, it's our only choice."

"No." And then she reached out and grabbed for the file folder.

They struggled, but Marcy was bigger and stronger, and with a grunt she yanked it out of Abby's fingers and clutched it close with both arms. Marcy had a reputation for her easy-going personality, but the nerve-wracking events in the casino and gallery had set her on edge, and now Abby's challenge finally provoked her to anger. She fixed her young friend with a wild-eyed stare. "You listen to me, young lady. Do you think Randall let us go out of the goodness of his heart? Huh? Do you?"

Abby stepped back, shocked by this outburst of anger.

"The only reason he let us go was because Leonard showed up. Think about it. You want to know why Randall said it doesn't matter anymore what we know? Because he had no intention of letting us go. The phone call, Abby, remember? He was alerting his friends that we were there."

"But he said that Ben . . ."

Marcy waved her off. "He would have said anything to keep us there. And he had a gun, Abby. I'm sure he was reaching for it when Leonard came in." She looked around again, shaking her head with a grimace. "Leonard must have seen me up at the casino. He was watching us to make sure we were safe. But we're on our own now, so we're going to do the right thing." She took a moment to study the motel across the street, then reached out and grabbed Abby by the shoulder of her sweatshirt. "Now, come on," she said. "If you want, we can call Sheriff Fastwater instead. He'll know what to do."

They stepped off the curb, instinctively striding into a jog, with Marcy holding tight to Abby's sweatshirt. Then the street suddenly lit up from the headlights of an approaching vehicle. A full-sized sedan bore down on them, coming much too fast. Marcy dragged Abby back by the collar as the car's tires screeched, finally skidding to a stop broadside in front of them. The driver's window came down, and Abby froze with dread at the sight of the man in sunglasses just four feet away. The same man she'd last seen on the shore of Big Island Lake.

"Come on!" Marcy yelled, pulling Abby around the rear fender of the car to race across the street. Another driver, approaching from the other direction, blasted his horn at them and swerved into the curb. Then they were running, across the street and into the motel parking lot. Behind them, Marcy heard the big sedan accelerating, wheels squealing on the damp asphalt. They ran between parked cars, dodging people, racing for the entrance of the motel. All around them was a maze of lights, shadows, pedestrians, and traffic.

The big luxury car roared to a stop under the valet parking awning just as Marcy and Abby reached the glass front doors. Through the lobby they ran, past the concierge desk and down a wide, brightly lit hallway to a bank of elevators. Marcy held the file folder tight against her, making her run in a lopsided, lurching fashion, with her hair bouncing and swinging across her shoulders. Abby chanced a quick look behind them, just in time to see the man with the spiked haircut barge through the front doors.

Past the elevators, Marcy turned into a side hallway, lengthening her stride to run full speed down the carpeted aisle. A father and mother, fresh from the motel's swimming pool, towels draped over their shoulders, pulled their young son to the side as Marcy charged past. Abby kept her eyes on her friend. Marcy's desperate, headlong flight, and her sudden burst of speed, sent her own athletic response into panic mode. She yelled, "Where are you going?"

"Just run, Abby, run!" Marcy called. Then she hit a side entrance, an emergency exit door. When she crashed through it the security system erupted, blaring down the hallway like a fire alarm. Abby followed so close behind that she cleared the exit without even touching the door. They burst out into a side lot of the guest parking area, a dimly lit expanse of asphalt reaching right up to the boulder-strewn shore of Lake Superior.

"Come on!" Marcy yelled, but Abby was already passing her. She'd spotted Marcy's old Buick sitting alone at the back of the parking lot, as if its rusty rocker panels were a contagious disease to be avoided by other vehicles. Abby reached the passenger side first, and Marcy called, "It's open. Get in." Then both of them tumbled into the car.

Abby felt around in the dark for the door locks, barely hitting the switch before Marcy started the engine. Looking over at her, Abby watched as Marcy sat back behind the wheel, drawing a deep breath, giving herself a moment to pause while focusing her attention on the man sprinting at them across the parking lot.

"I never lock it," Marcy said, as if reading Abby's mind. "And I always keep the keys under the seat." She finally looked over at Abby and grinned. "Hey, what can I say? I'm a small-town girl." Then she grabbed the steering wheel with both hands, tromped down on the accelerator, and the big V-8 lurched to life.

Abby held on, bracing her feet against the floor. Marcy hadn't turned the headlights on yet, but Abby was certain she saw reflections off a gun carried by their pursuer. Now a second man joined the chase, but trailed several yards behind the first guy, his figure barely discernable flickering through the shadows. The Buick ripped out across the parking lot, tires throwing sprays of sand and grit as Marcy hurtled the car at the men. Abby yelled at her to slow down, but Marcy showed no sign of backing off. She pointed the car at the men like aiming an oversized handgun at them. Abby grabbed the armrest and seat, bracing her legs for impact, but at the last possible instant the men split up, diving out the way to either side.

Abby twisted around to look behind them, but all she saw was a thick cloud of dust swirling out from the Buick's wake. Then Marcy spun the steering wheel, careening them around the front of the motel, and Abby rolled across the seat. With tires squealing, they roared over the exit, sparks shooting out from under them as the Buick bounced off the driveway ramp into the street.

Speeding away from Canal Park, Marcy put a block or two behind them before turning on the headlights. Abby finally dug out her seatbelt, keeping her feet planted firmly on the floor. "Where are we going?" she asked, as Marcy pushed the car hard up the narrow hillside streets of Duluth. Twelve or fifteen years ago the old Buick probably provided a smooth, quiet ride, but tonight the worn-out passenger compartment and chassis no longer held out the rattling road noises of an old engine and tires.

Marcy hadn't responded to her question, so Abby stole a sideways glance at her. Grasping the steering wheel with both hands, she drove with the intensity of a NASCAR racer. She'd back off a bit at intersections, but her concentration never faltered, and she kept a constant vigil on her mirrors as if anticipating pursuit. She seemed to be randomly picking a course through the East End neighborhoods, making sudden turns as if trying to lose a tailgater. She obviously hadn't heard Abby's question over the noise in the car.

Louder this time, Abby asked, "Marcy! Where are we going?"

"To Arlene's," she answered, without taking her eyes off the road.

"Arlene Fastwater?"

Marcy grinned and leaned slightly toward Abby. "You got a better idea where we can get rid of this folder?"

Abby returned Marcy's smile. "Perfect," she said, nodding her agreement. Then after a thoughtful pause, she asked, "So, do you know where she lives, or are we just going to drive in circles all night?"

"Hah!" Marcy laughed. "I dated Leonard for over a year. I guess I should know where his mother lives."

They entered a residential neighborhood and Marcy slowed down so as not to attract attention on the quiet, deserted streets. After a few more turns, and a couple more anxious looks over their shoulders, she suddenly stopped on a side street at the edge of a large corner lot. A split-level home, situated all alone on the hilltop, commanded a view over the harbor on the lakeside, and the ridge and woods behind.

Marcy didn't waste any time. Glancing up at the house, she shifted into park and said, "The lights are on. Come on." And then she was out the door and jogging up the wide front lawn to the breezeway door.

Abby stayed close, keeping an ear tuned to the street behind them while looking up at the huge, stately house. Marcy led them into the insufficient glow of a low-watt bulb outside the screen door of the breezeway, which was attached to the house on one side and a three-season porch on the other. The exact color of the house was indistinguishable in the dark. Through oversized picture windows she spotted floor-to-ceiling bookshelves, all of them stacked to overflowing with fat, leather-bound books. A tuck-under garage was mostly hidden from view in the dark.

Marcy didn't stop at the door. Instead, she simply rang the doorbell before letting herself in. They dashed through the breezeway, and just as Marcy reached for the inside door, it swung open before them. Arlene Fastwater stood in the doorway, looking even bigger and more imposing than Abby remembered. Her hair was piled up on her head, some of it in curlers, some of it secured in place with pins and barrettes. She wore a flowered print housedress, huge and shapeless, but the smile she bestowed on them was pure small town friendly.

"Hello, ladies!" she exclaimed, arms open wide in welcome. "My goodness, isn't this a wonderful surprise!"

Marcy barged straight inside while Abby hung back, a little shy in front of this legendary woman. Arlene waved an arm into the room. "Well, come on in, Abby," she said, an amiable impatience in her voice.

Abby stepped inside. Marcy stalked over to the wide windows overlooking the lakefront and the street below, while the

high ceilings and spacious styling of the large front room captured Abby's imagination. Arlene said, "Miss Abby Simon, to
what do I owe the honor of this unexpected visit?"

A side table covered with animal figurines had drawn
Abby's attention. She stood before the three-foot high table
looking at porcelain statues of elephants and tigers, stone carv-
ings of monkeys, horses, and fish, and elegant, antique wooden
duck decoys. The largest figure by far, at life size, was a somewhat abstract, grisly caricature of a goose. Abby leaned over
for a closer inspection, a conflicted expression of intrigue and
disgust on her face. The goose looked like something a child
might accidentally create, primitive and simple, but with
enough lifelike contours to give the grotesque features a frightening appearance.

"Leonard gave me that one," Arlene said. "An Indian up
in Manitoba carved it." She laughed. "For a while there, just
after I put it out on the table, I had nightmares about the thing."

"It is kind of scary," Abby said. "But it's beautiful, too."
She turned to look at Arlene. "It made me remember your talk
at Rosie's memorial, that story you told about when you were
a little girl, and the goose coming to visit you at the bait shop."

Arlene's smile broadened and she stepped closer. "Bless
your heart, Abby. Leonard grew up with that story, too, so he
brought this goose home from one of his journey quests up
north. He says the goose is my spiritual guardian, and this carv-
ing will protect my house from evil spirits." She laughed.
"With a look like that, I don't doubt it."

She clasped her hands together and looked from Abby to
Marcy, her unabashed grin proving her joy at seeing them.
"One minute I'm sitting at my desk, bored to death, going over
case reports and reading briefs, wondering just how it is that
people can get themselves into so much trouble." She clapped
her hands in delight, as if performing a magic trick, and said,
"And suddenly I have friends visiting from back home. This
is just so wonderful."

Marcy left her window perch and crossed the room with her head down. "Actually, Arlene, we're sort of in trouble ourselves." She braved a look into Arlene's strong face. "I didn't know where else to go."

"Trouble?" Arlene's expression turned serious. "My goodness, Marcy, you look like you've seen a ghost. Okay you two, I'm going to get us some refreshments, and then you're going to sit down and tell me what this is all about."

SIXTEEN

Arlene Fastwater

Arlene returned to the living room with a tray stacked with teacups, cookies, a pitcher of milk, and a ceramic teapot emitting exotic aromas of the Far East.

Marcy took the cup offered to her and returned to her station at the window, her protective senses still on high alert. "Could we turn down the lights? It's possible that we're being followed."

Arlene stepped over to a dimmer switch and lowered the lights. "Okay, now out with it. What's going on?"

Abby helped herself to a couple of cookies and joined Marcy at the window, but as far as she could see there wasn't any traffic outside at all. Off to the right she saw the rear end of Marcy's Buick parked around the side of the house.

Marcy said, "Boy, do we have a story." She paced across the room again, nervous energy giving her movements a stiff, robotic-like stride. She sipped from her teacup, and then spun around and pitched an anxious glance at Arlene. "Starting with the fact that Randall Bengston knows where Ben Simon is."

Arlene's head snapped up like she'd been slapped. "He told you that?"

Abby stole a peek at her, watching as Arlene went to Marcy to lay a hand on her shoulder, leading her back to Abby's side. With her other hand she reached out to gently stroke Abby's cheek, a calm reassurance in her touch. "Please, you two. Sit down. You're safe here."

They sat on the long, wide sofa, Arlene between them, the animal figurines looking over their shoulders. "Now," Arlene said, patting a thigh on either side of her. "Tell me this story of yours."

And so they did, or at least, Marcy did. Abby still wasn't ready to reveal her secrets. Marcy talked about Randall, and how he'd startled them at the gallery. She described his drunken dialogue and his cell phone call. "He was telling his friends we were there. And he had a gun."

A sharp intake of breath. "He held a gun on you?"

"Well, no. But he would have if Leonard hadn't shown up."

"Leonard? He's supposed to be up home working with Marlon tonight."

Marcy shook her head. "Not tonight. He was keeping an eye on us. I bet Sheriff Fastwater told him to. Anyway, he saw me up at the casino, and followed me down to The Tempest."

Arlene's eyebrow went up. "You were at the casino?"

Marcy glanced at Abby. "Yeah, well, I was just looking around." She went on to relate how she'd been thrown out at the hands of a big gangster-looking dude.

"Thrown out? Where was Leonard when all this was going on?"

"Probably outside keeping watch." She told about seeing Jackie, and how she'd boarded the bus for the casino outside of town. "When I left I spotted Abby, and joined her down at the gallery. Oh, yeah," she added, "I won a bunch of money at the casino, but I gave it away."

Arlene shook her head, overwhelmed by all the information and unable to make much sense out of most of it. She didn't know what to believe, or which pieces of the story may have been enhanced by Marcy's vivid imagination. And, she wondered, how did any of this have anything to do with Ben's disappearance? She looked at Abby for clarification, but the young girl was finishing off a glass of milk and seemed oblivious to Marcy's story. Arlene had years of experience questioning people, as well as reading their reactions and emotions, and the primary thing she'd picked up on so far was Abby's reticence. She reached across with her free hand and gently stroked the girl's face, tucking loose strands of hair behind her ear. She asked softly, "Do you think Randall really knows where Ben is?"

Abby shrugged.

Marcy said, "He told us not to say anything, and if we're quiet, Ben will be home soon."

Arlene continued watching Abby. She could sense the tension beneath the teenager's implacable demeanor.

Then Marcy jumped up. "Oh, hey, we found out that Randall is doing some creative bookkeeping at The Tempest. Like laundering money or something. Show her the file, Abby."

"You have it, remember? You wouldn't give it to me." The bitterness in Abby's voice wasn't lost on Arlene, either.

Marcy looked around, as if she could make the file folder magically appear. "It must be in the car. I'll run down and get it." She started for the door, but stopped to ask, "May I use your bathroom first?"

"Of course, dear," Arlene said. "You know where it is."

After Marcy left the room, Arlene continued to sit with Abby, sharing her silence for a few more moments. Then she said, "It sounds like you've had quite a day."

Abby nodded and broke a timid smile.

"You really miss your brother, don't you?"

There wasn't a need to respond to the question, but Abby's eyes glistened with tears.

"Of course you do, dear. And you want to help him, or protect him if you can."

A single tear spilled over to run down Abby's cheek.

Arlene put an arm around her and held her close. "It's okay to cry a little," she said. "It's okay to cry, because we can't always be strong all the time. Sometimes we need a break, and other times we need some help."

Abby responded with a sniffle.

"One time when I was about your age, maybe just a bit younger, I went on a scavenger hunt with a group of friends from our church youth group in Black Otter Bay. It was Sunday evening, which is not a good time to have a scavenger hunt, but we were doing pretty good, although the other team was doing well, too. By nightfall, we only needed one more item to win. Unfortunately, that item was a light bulb." She squeezed Abby closer. "Do you know how hard it is to get a light bulb at suppertime on a Sunday in Black Otter Bay? All the stores were closed, and most everybody in town had gone inside for the night. We were frantic, knocking on doors, but no one would answer. Then, in desperation, my best friend Lindsey ran up to a garage and unscrewed the light bulb."

Abby lifted her face to look into the shining brown eyes above her. "That's right, Abby," Arlene said. "Lindsey stole the light bulb for our team. We ran back to church, turned in all the items on our list, and got hot fudge sundaes for winning. The next day, the owner of the garage called the church to say a light bulb had been stolen. He'd even witnessed the theft, and he claimed that 'the Indian girl' had done it. Pastor Petersen walked out to our house for a long talk with my mother. She was waiting for me when I came home from school."

Arlene looked down at Abby cradled in her large, warm arm. When the girl returned her glance, she smiled and continued. "You can imagine how shocked I was. But I couldn't very well squeal on my best friend, could I? We'd had so much fun the night before, and now this guy wanted 'that Indian girl' to pay for a new light bulb. I was so mad, but I was scared, too. I mean, come on, it was just a light bulb."

"So, what did you do? You had to tell the truth, right?"

Arlene sat back and laughed. "Well, no way was I going to tell on my friend. And I refused to pay for the light bulb. That would be the same as admitting that I stole it. Sort of like you telling the investigators that you don't know where your brother is; it's not really a lie, but not completely honest, either." She cupped Abby's chin and made her look at her. When she was certain that her point had been heard, her expression softened, and she concluded, "So in the end, I misled my mother and told her I found it."

Abby scrunched up her nose. "You lied to your mother?"

"Well, it wasn't exactly a lie, now was it? I mean, after all, we did find it. I just didn't tell her that Lindsey found it screwed into a light fixture on a garage."

Abby looked skeptical. "Did she believe you?"

"I don't know. I really don't know what she thought. But she asked me over and over if I stole it, and I kept saying no, we found it, and so finally she called the reverend and told him I didn't steal it."

Abby said, "You must have felt horrible."

"I'll say. My mother said, 'You're my daughter, Arly. If you tell me that you didn't steal it, then I believe you.' Turns out, she intended to stand up for me."

"So what happened?"

"Well, the reverend asked us to come down to the church after dinner. He said we'd discuss it. In the meantime, I went to my room in tears."

Abby gave her a thoughtful look. The memory of that long-ago event put a strain on Arlene's face, matching Abby's somber expression.

"My brother Marlon finally came home. You know he's always been kind of a loner, and never a big one for words." She chuckled. "Unlike me, the one in the family that never shuts up. Anyway, he knew something was wrong, and eventually I told him everything. It felt really good to unburden myself, Abby. Gosh, I was crying and sobbing, and all the time begging him not to tell on Lindsey."

It was quiet for a moment until they noticed Marcy leaning against the wall, arms crossed, listening to Arlene's story. "Well?" Marcy asked, impatience in her voice. "What happened?"

Arlene drew a deep breath, and then turned it into a yawn. The smile returned to her face, along with a soft blush from the fond memory. "Fact is, my big brother Marlon fixed it."

Abby leaned away, surprise on her face. "Really? How?"

"Well, he ran down to Erickson's—you know, the hardware store—and bought a few dollars worth of cheap light bulbs. Then he snuck out behind the garage and scattered them in a growth of weeds and bushes. It was near the garage, but off the man's property at the edge of the woods."

"Why, that sneaky Marlon Fastwater," Marcy said. "Wait until the next time I see him in the café."

Arlene pointed a long, wide index finger at her. "Don't you dare say a word to him, Marcella. He saved my rear end that day."

"They believed you?" Abby asked. "It worked?"

"Well, they couldn't very well not believe me. Marlon went with us down to the church, and then we all trooped up to the scene of the crime. Marlon made it look accidental, but he led them straight over to the pile of light bulbs. He'd even broken a couple of them so they looked like they'd been there for a while. The garage owner came out and said he'd never seen the pile of bulbs before, but he swore he'd seen 'that Indian girl' steal the one off the garage. You know what Marlon said then?"

Abby looked at Marcy, but neither of them had an answer.

"My brother was pretty big, even back then. He stepped up to that fellow and said, 'Maybe you just don't like Indians.'"

Abby gasped.

"I tell you, Abby, that pretty much ended that discussion."

"So, what you're telling her," Marcy interjected, "is that it's okay to lie."

"That's not at all what I'm saying." Arlene patted Abby's thigh. "And this young one knows that. This is not about lying, is it, Abby?"

Abby stared at her, a blank expression revealing her confusion.

"Whatever," Marcy said, waving a hand in the air. "But it sure sounds like lying to me."

Arlene ignored the comment, focusing her attention on Abby. "As an attorney working in the DA's office, most of the time in the public eye, I've learned a couple of very valuable lessons over the years. You know how everybody repeats the old maxim, 'know thy enemy'? Well, the reality is that enemies come and go over the course of a lifetime. Our friends, on the other hand, and I'm talking about the type of friends that you can count on when you need them, are often around throughout your life. Like our mutual friend Rose, for instance, whose friendship meant so much to me when I was a child, or my mother, who took my side even though she must have had her doubts. And I'm telling you that a person couldn't hope to find a more loyal friend than my brother, Marlon."

Arlene took a moment to reseat her large frame on the couch, snuggling in close to Abby. Marcy had started for the door, but Arlene's dialogue delayed her departure so that now she lingered in the entryway, listening. Leaning in close to Abby, with an intimate voice, Arlene said softly, "Another thing I've learned is that it isn't so much the answer to a question that counts, but rather, it's the question itself that's important. For instance, in my case, instead of asking me if I stole the light bulb, they should have been asking who stole the light bulb." She cocked an eyebrow at Abby. "See what I mean?"

Abby nodded. "I guess."

"With the right question, it becomes an open-and-shut case; either you lie or you don't." She scrunched herself around to better face Abby. "Now," she said. "Do you want me to start asking the questions?"

Abby shook her head, a movement so short and quick as to be nearly imperceptible. She stood up and poured herself another glass of milk, keeping her back to Arlene while looking at the array of animal figures on the side table. Marcy took a step toward her, but at a look from Arlene stopped in mid-stride.

Arlene said, "I admire your loyalty, Abby. Ben couldn't ask for a better sister."

In a voice hardly more than a whisper, Abby said, "It's my fault that they took him."

"Well, I really doubt that," Arlene said. "But the fact is, you know what happened to him, even if you don't know where he is." She paused to hold a hand up at Marcy, again stopping her from going to the girl. "I'll tell you something else, Abby," she continued, still talking to her back. "The sheriff has spoken to me several times about the case. He knows you haven't been telling him everything, but the big galoot is too kind to press you on it. And you can thank him for keeping the federal investigators off your back. Now, don't get me wrong. Sheriff Fastwater knows which questions to ask. He just doesn't want to hurt you anymore."

With that, Abby turned around to face her. She saw the truth all over Arlene's face. She remembered her talk with the sheriff at the kitchen table shortly after Ben disappeared. Now she understood what should have been obvious: the sheriff had tried to give her an opening to let him help. He'd led her right to it, but she'd been too stubborn to see. Acknowledging the possibility that good people like Arlene and her brother could share her burden opened the spillway to her emotions. She stood in an exhausted slouch, trembling gently with her tears. She faced Arlene, but cast her looks and thoughts inward. Marcy finally broke free to come to her, wrapping the distraught girl in a protective bear hug.

Arlene rose to her feet with a grunt. She moved slowly, stretching her neck and back while clearing her throat. With her hair pinned up and the flowing, colorful housedress billowing about her, Abby pictured a Native American opera singer preparing to perform.

"You need to go home," Arlene said. "Right now, Abby. Tonight. I'll call Sheriff Fastwater to let him know you're on the way." She cleared her throat again, narrowing her eyes to a confidential squint. "There are unsavory elements infiltrating our local law enforcement, and they could present a danger for you. Until we figure out who Randall is working with, it's not safe for you in Duluth."

Abby tried to think, tried to focus on Arlene's words, but exhaustion had stolen her ability to concentrate.

Adjusting a couple of the large, flashy rings on her manicured fingers, Arlene said, "We're pretty sure the Chicago mafia is here. Of course, for years they've worked the trade unions and the harbor, but they were always quiet, staying in the background. Lately, we've been hearing about sums of cash paid out for cooperation—politically, legally, and in the network of small local businesses. Randall Bengston has shown up on our radar, but so far we don't know who is involved, or why." She paused to soften her official bearing with a gentle smile. "Bottom line, Abby, is that I wouldn't trust your welfare to anyone in Duluth right now. You need to go home, and you need to talk to my brother."

Marcy said, "Speaking of Randall, I'll run down and grab that file folder for you. It might point a finger at some of these bad guys you're talking about."

Arlene nodded her agreement, and when Marcy left she took her place at Abby's side.

"What about my mother?" Abby asked.

Arlene shrugged. "I really don't think Jackie is a player in all this. I mean, she must be involved, but I really doubt she's calling any of the shots." She sighed and gave Abby a squeeze. "Your mother is a tough cookie, Abby. She can take care of herself. On the other hand, we don't know Randall's Chicago connection, so we're just watching and waiting to see who comes around."

From outside came the sound of muffled voices, but Abby was thinking about Big Island Lake and a black luxury sedan. She said, "On the day Rosie died, I saw a car with Illinois license plates. I think the man driving it was one of the guys chasing us tonight." Before she could explain further, however, the voices outside turned into shouts, and in the next instant Abby broke free from Arlene's grasp and darted to the window.

Down below, off to the right, the big sedan had Marcy's car cornered against the curb. As she watched, Marcy came sprinting up the front lawn, arms pumping wildly, the file folder flapping from her fingertips. Behind her, the two men from the motel gave chase.

Arlene finally joined her at the window. "Oh, my God," she muttered, stepping closer. "That's . . ." She grabbed Abby by the arm. "Let's go!"

They ran to the entrance off the breezeway, but as she opened the door for Marcy, Arlene pushed Abby across the room. "That way, Abby, through the kitchen. Run! Downstairs."

Abby did as she was told. She didn't have time to admire the large kitchen with its flagstone flooring or the racks of stainless steel pots and pans hanging from the ceiling, because halfway through the room the lights went out. Beside her, the refrigerator clattered to a stop. Her momentum took her across the open space, and then, more than seeing it, she sensed the wide stairwell opening into a pitch-black chasm before her. Gingerly, she eased herself forward, located the hand railing, and lowered herself into the void. Behind her she heard the breezeway door slam and the deadbolt latch.

It was cooler at the bottom of the stairs. Behind her, she heard voices and footsteps crossing the kitchen floor. A light suddenly flickered around the stairwell, and then Marcy appeared on the steps above her. Arlene came next, wielding a flashlight and pulling the kitchen door shut behind her. Soon they were all standing on the concrete basement floor, Arlene's new hybrid sedan waiting silently in the shadows on the far side.

"They cut the power," Arlene cried, breathless. "Come on, this way," she panted, pointing the flashlight beam at the car.

They'd hardly set out, however, when the whole house shook from a thundering crash upstairs. And then another smashing impact, this time with splintering aftershocks as the breezeway door gave way. "Run!" Arlene yelled, and they were moving, dashing between stacks of boxes, garden tools, and old furniture.

The flashlight briefly illuminated the obstacle course that made up Arlene's storage room. The light bounced around helter-skelter as she ran, revealing the haphazard stacking arrangements of a pack rat. The ceiling hung low overhead, causing Marcy to run crouched over like a soldier darting through the trenches. A lone garage door stood at the far end, with the hybrid tucked in snugly behind it.

"Go! Go!" Arlene called, running to the driver's side of the car. Abby dove into the backseat just as Marcy swung too wide around the front fender, toppling a stack of boxes containing giveaway clothes. Climbing back out, Abby swiped a pile of clothing off the hood, and then reached a hand out to help Marcy up.

The hybrid electric motor hummed to life, immediately followed by the crushing explosion of the stairway door above them in the kitchen. Abby directed Marcy into the front seat, and as she reached for the back door she once again saw the flicker of flashlight beams in the stairwell. She ducked into the car, the headlights came on, and Arlene reached up to push the overhead garage door opener. Then she pushed it again, and then a staccato rhythm of frantic jabs as she proclaimed, "It doesn't work! There's no power!"

"I'll get it," Marcy called.

"There's no time!" Arlene yelled before Marcy could even grab the door handle. Arlene put the shifter in reverse and, bracing herself against the steering wheel, floored the gas pedal. "Hang on!"

Abby spotted the glint of a flashlight playing over the car before she flew head first into the back of the front seats. Marcy caught herself against the dash, and then there was an ear-shattering explosion when the blunt rear end of the hybrid blew the old wooden garage door to pieces. They emerged on the other side, bounding recklessly downhill in reverse on the long concrete driveway.

A deafening screech pierced the night as Arlene fought to maintain control. A section of the splintered garage door had lodged under the vehicle, grinding against the driveway and jerking the car around at odd angles. Abby slapped her hands over her ears until she was thrown against the ceiling when they bounced out of the driveway into the street. Arlene swung the steering wheel around and stomped on the brakes. A moment later they shot forward, and with a clatter and jolt the garage door panel was ripped out from under them. Finally free of its anchor, the spunky little car quietly shot out into the dark.

"Yee-haw!" Marcy yelped, bouncing like a rodeo rider in the front seat.

Abby tried to look behind them at the house, but Arlene soon turned a corner, and with the house completely lost to view, the wide panorama of the harbor and Canal Park lit up before them.

"I've been meaning to replace that old door for years," Arlene said. "Never got around to it, but I guess I will now."

Marcy laughed, offering up a high-five across the front seat.

"Give me your cell phone," Arlene said.

"I don't have one."

Arlene opened the storage space between them, but slammed the lid after a quick inspection. "Damn it, mine's back home in my purse. We have to get in touch with my brother."

Abby caught her eye in the rearview mirror. "Who was that guy back there? You know him."

Arlene focused on her driving, turning onto Skyline Parkway and aiming them for the expressway north. "It was dark, Abby. It could have been anyone."

"But you saw him. You know him."

Arlene suddenly swerved into another turn, throwing Abby across the backseat. They entered another tree-lined residential street. "I guess I'll just have to take you to my brother myself," she said, changing the subject. She checked her mirrors, looked around to get her bearings, and to Marcy said, "We'll take the back roads. They won't be but a couple of minutes behind us. I'll never outrun them on the freeway."

Abby studied the lights and skyline and harbor spread out for miles below them. It was beautiful, and at this distance looked peaceful and safe. She moved over against the door, avoiding Arlene's sightline in the rearview mirror. Now that the adrenaline rush had passed, she felt the heavy cloak of exhaustion wrapping itself around her. Ultimately, it didn't matter who was chasing them. Arlene was in charge now.

Abby let her head loll against the seat, half-heartedly picking out landmarks in the dazzle of lights below. As beautiful as it was, she'd had enough. She closed her eyes, rocking against the headrest and door, her thoughts moving forward in anticipation of the relative safety and familiarity of the great forests back home.

SEVENTEEN

Marlon Fastwater

The postmistress laughed and tossed her crib cards at the cribbage board. She'd won again, making whatever points she might have in the crib meaningless.

"I swear, Mrs. Bean," Sheriff Fastwater declared, "your luck is absolutely unconscious." The outcome may have already been decided, but he picked up the crib cards anyway just to see what was there, "Look at this," he said. "Another eight points." He threw the cards down, shaking his head in disgust.

"Now, don't start in with your whining," Mrs. Bean scolded, eyes twinkling as she gathered up the cards. "What is it that's so upsetting, the fact that you've been playing for about thirty years longer than me? Or is it because I'm a woman?"

He scoffed. It irked him when she talked like that. "It's your unconscious luck, that's all. You have no strategy, but then you get all the cuts anyway."

"Well, don't forget you're the one who taught me to play." Mrs. Virginia Bean slid an index finger along the cribbage board to count up her margin of victory. "Thirty-one cents, Marlon," she announced. She moved some of her dinner dishes out of the way to locate her bank, an old cough lozenge tin full of coins. "You barely made it off Third Avenue this time," she added.

Ignoring her last smart-aleck comment, the sheriff opened the middle drawer of his desk and counted out change from the pencil holder. "I'll have to write you an I.O.U.," he said, fingering the coins. "There's only eighteen cents here."

"I broke the bank?" Mrs. Bean clapped her hands and laughed. "You know, you really shouldn't be gambling if you can't afford to lose."

At the sound of her clapping, Gitch got up from his rug beside the desk and walked a slow lap around them. He ended up at the door, looking back at Fastwater. The sheriff eyed him while commenting to the postmistress, "Even Gitch is happy to have his office back. I don't know how many times his tail got stepped on when this place was overrun with federales and volunteers. What a circus."

"I think we're all grateful for a little peace and quiet," she said.

Fastwater got up to let the dog out. The crock-pot on the desk still emitted the glorious aroma of meatballs in barbecue sauce, even though they'd shut it off some time ago. Gitch had eaten a fair share of them himself, probably adding to his lethargic behavior this evening. When the sheriff stepped away from the desk, Mrs. Bean did a quick straightening up, collecting napkins and paper plates for the trash.

Standing in the doorway, Fastwater inhaled the fresh breeze off Lake Superior, letting the cool night air caress him. Gitch plodded into the parking lot, keeping his nose down as if some exotic scent had captured his interest. The sheriff knew this game, and resigned himself to letting it play out. The big dog moseyed along, occasionally swinging his head far enough around to keep an eye on the sheriff to make sure he wasn't being followed. He sniffed along the side of the squad car and then paused near the rear wheel, lifting a leg to do his business against the tire.

"Real funny, you old mutt," Fastwater called. "Just see how many meatballs you get next time."

Gitch gave him a last look, then wandered off to inspect the perimeter of the parking lot. Fastwater continued standing in the doorway, hands in his pockets, the door propped open against his shoulder. Behind him, Mrs. Bean asked, "What do you hear from Matthew? He hasn't picked up his mail in a day or two."

The sheriff took a final deep breath of the cool, damp air, and then rejoined the postmistress inside. "I think he's just trying to focus on work and staying busy. They say that can help."

"That's a load of you-know-what," she said, suddenly standing up and becoming more animated in her housekeeping. The sheriff stood back, watching while she stuffed the trashcan and used a napkin to scrub at spilled barbecue sauce. "I can tell you what that man needs," she continued, as if talking to herself. "He needs someone to look after him, and I don't know why he can't see Marcy standing right there in front of him."

"Now, Mrs. Bean . . ."

She waved him off and turned to face him with a withering glower. "All you men are just alike, so macho and self-sufficient. I suppose he expects Abby to keep that place running."

"Matthew does a good job with those kids."

Mrs. Bean glared at him, but didn't dare utter the thought that came to both of them. She seemed to back off then, and took her seat beside the desk with a sigh. "I'm sorry, Marlon. I just feel so bad for them."

"Well, we all do."

"I know, I know. It's just that Marcy could be such a comfort to him right now. And Abby—who is she supposed to turn to?" Mrs. Bean paused to take a breath, looking a little lost amid the clutter of the sheriff's office. "All I'm saying is, Matthew and Marcy belong together. They're just alike, and neither one of them will ever leave this town. She's not like Jackie, who was trying to get away from here as soon as she arrived."

Fastwater remembered the looks Marcy gave Matthew in the café. Maybe Mrs. Bean was right about them, but he doubted that Matthew had a clue. "Now, don't be so hard on Jackie," he said. "You know that Abby is staying with her for a few days."

"In Duluth? Are you kidding me? Abby hates Duluth."

"Well, it was her idea."

"And Matthew is okay with it?"

Fastwater shrugged. "I suppose. What's he going to do, forbid her from visiting her mother?" He started for the door again, but stopped to add, "Marcy took her down there. She and

Abby convinced Matthew that it would be okay. They're kind of hanging out together."

It took a moment, but the smile finally bloomed on Mrs. Bean's face. She started to speak, but the sheriff cut her off. "Now, don't go making more out of it than it is. Marcy is just trying to be a good neighbor, and a friend to Abby."

The postmistress closed her cribbage coin tin, a self-satisfied grin lighting up her face. Fastwater could see her mind whirling as she adjusted items on the desk. He couldn't stop the rebuke. "All you women are just alike, so conniving and meddling."

She pulled her woolen postal sweater off the back of the chair and draped it over her shoulders. Flipping her hair away from her neck and out over the collar, she sat up straight and fixed him with her merry blue-eyed gaze, as if everything was once again right with the world. "Okay, Marlon, fair enough. Touché."

He shook his head and went back to the door to watch for Gitch. For the most part he enjoyed the evenings he spent with the postmistress. She could be a little pushy at times, perhaps a bit too opinionated for his quiet nature, but the fact remained that he looked forward to sharing a dinner with her, or a walk down along the shore. He appreciated her companionship, and the intimacy of sharing their daily exploits and gossip. He even had to admit that as irritating as it was to lose to her, he enjoyed their cribbage games over his desk in the office. She'd picked up on the subtleties of the game very quickly, and although he'd never admit it to her, she was a good player.

He spotted Gitch sitting by the entrance to the parking lot, gazing down the hillside toward Lake Superior. The dog tipped his nose up, as if picking up on a scent or listening to a strange sound beyond the sheriff's ability to hear. A sudden gust of wind blew past, and a chill rattled down Fastwater's spine. He shook himself as goosebumps rose on his arms. Peering into the darkness around the side of the office, up into the woods and the graveyard beyond, his intuition warned of ill tidings roaming the forested countryside. Whatever it was, evil motives or just bad news, he knew that it was coming his way.

And then the phone rang.

He jumped and turned much too quickly. He could see in Mrs. Bean's face that his reaction had startled her more than the ringing of the phone. Striding across the room, he held his breath in an attempt to compose himself. He allowed his shoulders to slump in apparent disregard, while his thoughts coalesced around the certainty that this was no ordinary phone call.

"Sheriff Fastwater," he said into the phone.

"Hey, Marlon. I wasn't sure you'd still be up at the office."

"Ike?"

"Glad I caught you. I'm on my way up. Can you stick around for a while?"

Earl Eikenberry was a forensic pathologist in Duluth, and a good friend of the sheriff's. Fastwater looked at Mrs. Bean, and when he noted that she was studying him with a curious eye, he turned away, and said, "Of course, Ike. Come on up." He lowered his voice and mumbled, "You got something?"

"As a matter of fact, I do. But you have to see it. I'm already on the road. I'll be there in thirty minutes."

Fastwater's thoughts blurred over. He held the phone to his ear like a small dumbbell, nearly crushing it in his hefty palm. He directed his attention to any spot in the room other than Mrs. Bean's eyes. Ike had found something. What did this mean?

"Marlon? You still there? I'm not interrupting anything, am I?"

"Yeah. I mean no, you're not interrupting," the sheriff blurted, unaware that he was nodding into the phone. "I mean, yeah, I'll be here."

"Okay, buddy. Ciao."

Fastwater put the phone down. He wanted to move, needed a physical outlet to override the premonitions of dread and ill will.

"Was that your friend Earl?" Mrs. Bean asked, as if reminding him that she was still there.

"Yeah, Ike. He's going to be stopping by." Trying to hide
an involuntary shudder, the sheriff flashed on a picture of
Floating Bird, his grandmother, and then shook off the remnants of his intuitive vision. Abruptly, he was all business,
stalking to the door to call Gitch while running his fingers
along his belt in an unconscious inventory of equipment. Back
at his desk, he picked up his cell phone. No messages. Should
he call Leonard?

"Well, I should be getting along anyway," Mrs. Bean said.
"Tomorrow is another day in the post office."

"I'll walk you home," Fastwater said, his thoughts still
reeling. He had no idea what Ike may have found, but he
trusted his intuition enough to know that it was important.
"Just let me finish clearing away the trash, and I'll take the
garbage out on our way." He could feel the postmistress watching his every move, and even Gitch seemed to have overcome
his lethargy. He paced around the room with renewed energy,
anticipating the walk that he knew was coming.

When they'd finished picking up, Fastwater tied off the
garbage and took a last look around the office. His gaze finally
fell on Mrs. Bean, and he couldn't help but return her smile of
affection. That was another thing he appreciated about her—
she seemed to know when to back off. She'd get all the gossipy
news out of him soon enough, usually before anyone else, but
when he was in the middle of it, she allowed him his space.

"Come on, Gitch," the sheriff called. "We're on escort
duty tonight."

The big dog bounded up to Mrs. Bean, nosing her hand to
hurry her along, and then trotted over to the door.

"Okay, Gitch. I'm coming," she said, smiling at his impatience. She hooked an arm through the sheriff's, and then the
three of them stepped outside into the mellow glow of the parking lot's flood lamp.

• • • • •

A short time later, when headlights flashed through the parking lot, Gitch ran to the window to see who was coming. The
sheriff didn't often get visitors arriving by car, and Gitch usually recognized the few vehicles that did pull in. He never
barked at them. When Gitch spotted a friend approaching, his
tail began wagging and he'd whine in anticipation. On the other
hand, when a stranger pulled in, the doge would strike a rigid
pose at the window, his front paws on the sill, and emit barely
audible, deep-throated growls.

But it was dark out now, and the headlights made it impossible to get a glimpse of the car, so Gitch assumed his position at the window and emitted a growl, all while trying to keep
his tail from wagging. The growl soon rolled into a whine, and
then he looked back at the sheriff sitting at his desk.

"It's okay, Gitch. That's our friend, Ike."

Fastwater came out from around the desk and the two of
them went to the door. The sheriff let the dog out, and Gitch
bounded into the parking lot to greet their visitor.

Earl Eikenberry was a tall man with an athletic build, and
a smile full of large, white teeth that lit up under the glow of
the flood lamp. His teeth were crooked, but only slightly so,
and not enough to be homely. Instead, they seemed to enhance
and accentuate his virile, masculine good looks.

"Hey ya, Marlon," he said, reaching out a hand to shake.
"It's good to see you." In his other hand he carried a soft-sided
canvas bag, like a toolbox. "And here's my pal, Gitch!" The big
dog stood on his hind legs to nuzzle the offered chin, while Ike
wrestled him into a staggering bear hug.

"Come on in," the sheriff said, holding the door. He wished
this was a simple social visit. He'd offer his friend a beer, maybe
a shot of something stronger, and they'd swap some stories and
jokes about the old days. But Ike was here on business tonight.
He had news to share, and Fastwater was anxious to hear it.

Ike marched straight across the office to the sheriff's desk, but paused when he spotted the crock-pot and cribbage board. He gently settled his bag into a cleared-off spot and turned to Fastwater. "The postmistress was here, wasn't she?"

The sheriff quickly gathered up items from the desk, depositing them on the tops of file cabinets. "She was leaving when you called."

"So, what's the story with you two, anyway?"

Fastwater ignored the question. Instead, he adjusted the chair next to the desk, pointed to it for his friend, and then took his own seat. "What have you got, Ike?"

The smirk remained on Ike's face while he took his seat and opened the bag. Gitch settled in on his rug next to them. Fastwater's impatience glittered in his black eyes, but the big lawman sat in stoic silence, waiting.

Finally, Ike leaned forward on the desk and said, "So you know, Marlon, your friend Rose Bengston was in exceptionally good shape considering her age. I don't believe she took any sort of medications, and that's quite remarkable for an eighty-year-old." He pulled a thin sheaf of papers out of the bag and quickly thumbed through them. "I know you're familiar with the results from the official autopsy, which showed there was nothing of note out of the ordinary. In fact, I completely agree with Doc Thompson's diagnosis of cardiac arrest." He paused for a moment to scan the paperwork again, and then continued. "That is, technically at least, the poor woman's heart gave out on her. To be totally accurate, though, I would have stated the cause of death as 'unknown.' Of course, we have to consider the fact that she was outside in the cold, working in freezing water, so a heart rhythm disturbance, or arrhythmia, would naturally be the most likely culprit. That would certainly be expected in a person her age, and one not likely receiving regular medical attention. So, all that said, cardiac arrest would be an accurate diagnosis."

"But she had no reason to be out in the water," Fastwater interjected. "There's no minnow seining up here this time of year, and she would have known that."

Ike held a hand up to stop him. "I know, Marlon. You told me that before. But I've also heard that her mind had been slipping. Folks that knew her said they'd worried about her this past winter, living alone down there on the shore, burning wood for heat. People were concerned that she'd either freeze to death or burn the house down."

Now it was Fastwater's turn to lean over the desk. When he spoke, his voice was soft, but deep and full. "She wasn't wearing waders, Ike. Not even you could walk out there in thirty-two-degree water without waders."

Ike sat back, nodding. "I know, Marlon, I know. And that was what convinced me we needed more information. So I worked up a chemical analysis of her blood." He shook his head and made a face. "I have to tell you, buddy, there are people down there who wouldn't go anywhere near it. I ran toxicology tests, but there was nothing: no drugs, and no medications of any kind. And then orders came down to stop the investigation."

"Stop it? Why?"

"Because it was deemed frivolous and unnecessary."

Fastwater's excitement began to fade. That sounded like Randall's words at Rose's memorial service, or the opinion Mrs. Bean had shared with him, voiced by some of the townsfolk. He studied his friend across the desk. He'd been so sure . . .

Ike said, "You know me, Marlon. Orders are orders, but loyal friendships trump all that administrative crap." He dug in his bag again while a sardonic grin rippled across his face. "So I did some work at night, after hours and on my own."

The sheriff sat back, still eying his friend. "And?"

"Well, basically, I just put some time into taking a closer look." He pulled out a handful of photographs, lining them up on the desk. "There were a few bruises, but I have to be honest with you, Marlon, old people bruise very easily. You can look at these pictures and make an argument for a physical confrontation, but I can just as easily explain them away as bumps against the woodwork, or a load of firewood cradled in an arm."

Fastwater skimmed over the photos depicting pale white skin, slack and wrinkled, with purple and yellow blotches. He thought it a blessing that he'd never recognize this as the body of his friend, Rose.

"She wasn't diabetic," Ike continued. "Although, if she was, we have no medical records to support treatment. But looking further into the chemical makeup of the blood samples, I found an extremely low level of serum glucose."

The sheriff shook his head. "What does that mean?"

"She didn't have any sugar in her blood, or very little, at any rate. It's something we might expect to see in a case of diabetic shock."

"Diabetic shock?"

"But again, she wasn't diabetic. So I checked her insulin levels, and they were sky high." He bit off a chuckle. "It would take the pancreas of a fifty-foot giant to put out that much insulin. I couldn't believe it, so I ran the test again, with the same result." His expression turned serious as he mirrored the sheriff's stare. "That much insulin had to be administered externally."

Again Fastwater shook his head. "So, what are you saying?"

Ike looked at the last photograph in his hand, but before flipping it over on the desk, he explained, "Diabetics inject themselves with doses of insulin to regulate their blood sugar. The dosage is strictly monitored—too much and the patient can slip into a state of shock, eventually triggering organ failure, a diabetic coma, or even death."

"But you said she wasn't diabetic. How does all this apply to Rose?"

"Because somehow she had lethal amounts of insulin in her system. Now, with a person her age, working under severe weather conditions and physical strain, the probability of a cardiac event would be increased, and I believe her heart did indeed fail her, but not because of the strain. Like I said, she was in good physical shape. Instead, it was due to the insulin in her system preventing her body and organs from functioning properly. Listen to me, Marlon. You were so sure of something more than a simple heart attack that I had to follow up on any anomaly that stood out—in this case, the low serum glucose. Now, to administer insulin, most diabetics simply inject themselves through the abdomen. The needle is tiny, and there's usually plenty of loose skin over the stomach. You only have to break the skin to inject it. So I looked. I went inch by inch, searching for a tiny pinprick of a mark, but there was nothing." Ike sat back, tossing the last photo like a playing card face up at the sheriff. "But I kept looking, and there it is."

Fastwater picked up the photo for a closer inspection. "I don't get it. What is this?"

"The way I see it, my guess is that your friend put up a fight. She struggled, but her attacker managed to stab the syringe into the back of her neck." Ike turned sideways and rubbed his neck, high up under the hairline, showing Fastwater where the syringe had pierced the woman. "Even after she'd been injected, she probably continued to fight, acquiring at least some of these bruises in the struggle. But my argument is this: at some point the needle broke off and the syringe was removed from the scene. And as you can see, because it broke off under the hairline like that, the evidence was nearly impossible to detect."

Fastwater looked from the photo to his friend as the significance of Ike's words became clear. The pathologist leaned over the desk, resting his long torso on his forearms. He said, "When you put it all together—your arguments about the lack of minnows and her not wearing waders, these test results, and that photo of the broken needle—I can think of only one scenario that plays to all of it." He nodded at the sheriff, and said, "My guess is that the drowning and the lake were just a cover-up. I think you were right, Marlon, about your friend being murdered."

Fastwater slammed the desk with his fist and jumped to his feet, sending his chair clattering backwards across the floor. "I knew it!" he exclaimed.

With the sudden commotion, Gitch leapt to his feet, too, and even Ike sat back in a pose of self-defense. "Marlon," he said calmly, trying to counter the loud outburst. "Marlon, I'm serious, this has to stay right here between you and me." When Fastwater looked at him and when Ike felt he had his complete attention, he said, "I drove up here for a reason, you know. My phone may be tapped. It's easy to do down there in the city offices. I was ordered to drop the investigation, but I followed through on it because you asked me to. You've got what you need now, Marlon, so from here on I'm out of it."

Fastwater retrieved his chair and took his seat behind the desk. He said, "But it doesn't matter anymore where the evidence came from. You said it yourself, Ike. Rose was murdered."

"Actually, Marlon, you're the one who said that. I just got you the evidence. You still have to figure out the who and why."

Fastwater's eyes roamed over the desktop. "Believe me, I have a few ideas."

When Ike saw the sheriff reaching for the phone, he stopped him, saying, "This is my job we're talking about, Marlon. It's my career. You have to cover me on this."

Fastwater sat back, took a deep breath, and nodded. Standing up, he extended his hand, and said, "Okay, fair enough. I really appreciate this, Ike. No one will ever know, but I owe you one."

"Forget it. Keep the pictures and the lab reports. I don't ever want to see them again."

The sheriff gathered up the photographs, clipped them together, and slid them into the desk drawer. Then he shuffled the lab reports into a neat stack and set them aside. Ike sat in silence, watching his friend organize his desk, well aware of the gears spinning in Fastwater's head. Gitch closed his eyes as quiet settled over the small stone-and-timber office in the woods. When the phone rang, it took them all by surprise.

It was the sheriff's cell phone, buried on the desk somewhere. With feelings of dread once again pressing down on his chest, Fastwater shoved the clutter around until he located it. "Fastwater here," he answered.

"Marlon, something's happened out here at Mom's house." It was Leonard, talking fast and out of breath. "The door is broken in, and the power is out."

"Leonard, slow down. Is Arlene there?"

He could hear his nephew running through the house, interior doors banging open and closed. "Mom?" he yelled. "Arlene?" And then, into the phone, "The power is out, Marlon. Somebody cut it."

"Is Arlene there?"

"I can't find her. But all her stuff is here, I mean, her purse, car keys, and cell phone and stuff. I don't see anything missing. Oh, hell, the basement door is busted, too." Then Fastwater heard the sound of Leonard on the stairs.

"Leonard, you still there? It's probably a break in. Maybe they saw you and ran."

More heavy breathing. "Oh, shit."

"What? What is it?"

"I'm outside now. It looks like Mom drove her car right through the garage door. There's chunks of it all down the driveway, even out in the street."

"Are there lights on in the neighborhood? Are the streetlights on?"

"Yeah. There are lights everywhere except Mom's house. But, Marlon, how did she start the car without keys?"

"Her hybrid uses a smart-key."

"A what?"

"It's a keyless remote, Leonard. She leaves it in the car. You just push a button on the dash to start it. When she goes out, she's locks it up with the clicker." Fastwater stood up and paced behind the desk. "Listen, Leonard. Call the Duluth police. Get them out there to secure the place. Arlene must have been home and surprised the intruders when they broke in."

"I don't know, man. It's hard to picture Mom running from anyone."

"Listen, Leonard. I need you to get up here."

"Wait a minute, Marlon," Leonard interrupted. Fastwater heard him running again, breathing heavily into the phone. "Marlon? Marcy's car is here, parked around the side of the house."

The blood suddenly drained from Fastwater's face. "Are you sure?"

"I'm sure. And it's parked about three feet away from the curb, like she was in a hurry."

"What would she be doing up at Arlene's house?"

"I don't know. I saw her and Abby about an hour ago down at The Tempest. They were having some sort of argument with Randall, but they left when I showed up."

"Okay, Leonard. I'm calling in support." Fastwater glanced at Ike on the other side of the desk. As if distracted, he picked up the stack of lab reports, but then tossed them aside. "I've got the evidence now to show that Rose Bengston was murdered."

"What evidence? What happened?"

"Never mind that now. I'm going to have Randall and Jackie picked up, and anyone else hanging out with them."

"Jackie isn't in this, Marlon. She's out of town at the casino. I saw her board the bus earlier tonight."

"Oh, she's in it. But she'll be easier to pick up now that we know where she is. It's Abby I'm worried about. Where is she? Do you think Marcy dropped her off at Jackie's?"

"I don't know," Leonard said. "Hang on a minute, Marcy's car is unlocked." Fastwater heard the door opening, and a grunt as his nephew climbed in. "Nothing here, Marlon. Oh, wait. There is one thing. Ha! A Minnesota Twins baseball cap."

The sheriff didn't need to ask. Marcy never wore a cap, but Abby almost always did. "Call the police, Leonard. Wait until they get there, and then haul your ass up here."

"Want me to check out Randall's apartment?"

"No. I'll have the feds pick them up. If the girls are on the run, they'll be heading up here. Oh, and Leonard, when you come, take the back way. If Arlene is running, she'll be on the back roads."

EIGHTEEN

Arlene Fastwater

The blacktop ended just a few miles out of town, bouncing Arlene's car onto the narrow strip of gravel roadway leading north. For a while, all three women cast apprehensive glances behind them, anticipating the arrival of a big, black luxury sedan. It was dark here where the forest closed in tight against the lonely stretch of road. Not many people lived out here, but a few miles to the east, along the coast of Lake Superior, homes and cabins lined both sides of the highway. On the other hand, locals wanting to avoid the tourist traffic down on the shore used this old county road. Fishermen and hunters were also familiar with it, but after dark on a weekday it was mostly used by foraging deer, foxes, and the occasional meandering moose.

"Jeez, Arlene," Marcy complained. "Slow down a little. We're done for if you hit a deer. Running over a garage door is enough for one night."

Arlene laughed, but let up a bit on the gas pedal. Checking her rearview mirror for the hundredth time, she shook her head. It was a black void behind them, with dust from the tires on the gravel road swirling into the foggy darkness to create an impenetrable black cloud. Stars glittered overhead, though, bright pinholes of light pointing the way between tall pine tree pillars lining the old overland trail. The road was fairly straight, and in the light of day Arlene could've spotted a pursuer at quite a distance, but she doubted she'd be able to see anything tonight before it overtook them.

Then she caught Abby's eye in the mirror. Arlene adjusted her grip on the steering wheel, and asked, "What were you two talking to Randall about? And why are you being chased?"

Marcy turned enough to peek at Abby in the backseat. The girl looked so much older without the baseball cap. She had to remind herself that she wasn't much more than a child. Abby gave her a stern glare, so Marcy began carefully. "Well, you know, we found that paperwork. But Randall didn't much like discovering us in his office. He keeps it locked, you know. We only got in because Abby snuck off with her mother's key."

"I doubt he has the mafia chasing you because you were in his office."

Arlene watched Abby in the mirror until the girl finally looked at her. The silence between them became an uncomfortable war of wills. Then Abby said, "You saw that guy chasing us, and you know him. Who is he?"

If Marcy had been uncomfortable with the silence, these direct questions made her downright squeamish. She peered over at Arlene behind the steering wheel. Arlene was a professional, and her years of experience in public service had taught her how to hide her thoughts and emotions. As for herself, Marcy had no idea who the man was, except that he was the same guy she'd encountered in the casino. The second man was a complete mystery. The couple of times she'd seen him she'd been running away and he'd been in the background, obscured by shadows and darkness. So if Arlene knew either one of them, it would probably be from some trial or legal issue she'd prosecuted in the past.

Arlene said, "I told you, Abby, it was dark out. He kind of reminded me of someone I used to know. But it's been years. I really didn't get a good look at him, so I'd rather not say." She squinted off into the woods, and then checked the mirrors again. "But I'll wager ten to one he's part of that Chicago connection I told you two about."

"You really think so?" Marcy asked. "You mean I was chased by the mafia?"

"That's not a good thing, Marcy," Arlene pointed out. She opened the lid on her console storage compartment, but slammed it shut in frustration. "How did we ever survive the last thousand centuries without cell phones? I have to get word to Marlon. He needs to know about this guy."

"We're doing the best we can," Marcy offered. "We'll be home soon enough."

"I just don't understand what you did that warrants chasing you all around the countryside. Tell me word for word what you said to Randall."

"He was drunk," Abby said. "None of it made much sense." The look she gave Marcy contained a dire warning.

With Arlene watching Abby in the mirror, Marcy glanced outside into the black confusion of forest. Then she chuckled and turned back to Arlene. "Randall told us how much he loved Jackie. He said he didn't care about her gambling or the money she lost, that he could always get more money. I guess that's where the paperwork we found comes in."

"And I'm guessing," Arlene added, "that Randall and that paperwork are connected with this Chicago mob guy. Maybe Randall is laundering money for them, like you said." For a moment they sat quietly in thought, each with their own perspective on the evening's events. Then Arlene asked, "But Randall doesn't know you have the paperwork, does he?"

"No." Marcy grinned and looked back at Abby. "We were pretty slick about that, hey, girl?"

"Well then, why is he chasing you? There must be more to it."

Abby leaned against the door, avoiding Arlene's eyes in the rearview mirror. She wished everyone would just shut up for a while. She was exhausted and wanted to be home, sleeping in her own bed. She let her eyes close while her head rocked against the window.

"So you're telling me that all Randall talked about was Jackie and her gambling? He caught you breaking into his office, and all he says is how much he loves Jackie?"

"Well, no, not exactly," Marcy said. "He was mad, at least at first he was, but once we convinced him that we weren't up to anything and we hadn't stolen anything, he started in about fishing."

"Fishing? You mean like with a fishing pole? He must've been drunk."

"No kidding," Marcy laughed. "He went on about all the fish he'd caught with his father, and how he'd caught more fish than Abby ever will."

"But they were commercial fishermen. They used nets."

"I know! That's why it was so stupid. And then he rambled on about fishermen never telling where they catch their fish. Like he and Abby have some secret to hide, or something, because they're both fishermen." Marcy looked into the backseat at Abby propped against the door. She lowered her voice and concluded, "He was so loaded he even bragged about knowing where Ben is. He said the boy would be coming home soon."

Abby's eyes popped open.

Arlene began questioning Marcy about Ben, leaving Abby to drift along with her own thoughts. Had she been asleep? It felt like it, but on some level she'd absorbed the conversation in the front seat. There'd been talk about fishing and secrets, and that Ben would soon be found. And then the significance of Randall's secret washed over her, bubbling up out of her subconscious, flooding across her thoughts. It rolled her fatigue aside and buoyed up the burden of her personal tragedy. All of a sudden, she knew.

She sat up with a start, looking around. "Where are we?"

"Oh no," Arlene said, studying the rearview mirror. "We've got company."

Marcy spun around. "Maybe it's just somebody wanting to pass."

When the car sped up and rammed their rear bumper, Arlene clamped down on the steering wheel. "Yeah, I don't think so."

With the impact, Marcy screamed, "Faster, Arlene! That's the car. That's the guy!"

Even with Arlene's gas pedal floored, the big sedan tried getting up beside them. The little hybrid was engulfed in blinding light from their pursuer's headlights hard upon their rear window. "Damn it!" Arlene muttered. She should have known he'd be aware of this back road.

Marcy hung over the back of her seat, watching the race out the rear window. "Come on, Arlene! Faster!"

"Jeez, Marcy, cool it. Just a minute ago you told me to slow down." Arlene couldn't believe he actually meant to harm them, certainly not the girl. She wished she could assure her friends of that. Apparently, he intended to stop them, prevent them from getting to the authorities, although she knew it had to be for something more than the paperwork the girls had stolen. *That's it!* she thought. *He must be the Chicago connection!*

Arlene hunched her formidable bulk over the steering wheel, driving for all she was worth. As desperate as the man was to stop them, she was just as determined to keep going. Her car handled well, but loose gravel made for unpredictable traction, and the pursuing sedan out-muscled them with three times the horsepower. She scanned the speedometer and odometer, calculated their distance from Black Otter Bay, and said, "If we can just hold him off for few more miles."

Another jarring impact with the bumper drew another scream from Marcy. "We'll never make it like this," she yelled.

Arlene swerved to the left and back to the right, throwing up clouds of dust, trying every maneuver she could to keep the heavy sedan behind them. In the backseat, Abby studied the woods outside her window, and then checked on the stars above and ahead of them. Her mind was made up.

"Marcy," Arlene commanded. "Open the glove box."

Marcy did as she was told. When the lid dropped open, the handle of a nine-millimeter handgun stuck out at her. "What the . . ."

"Never mind. I have a permit. Give it to me."

Like handling dynamite with a lit fuse, Marcy gently pulled the gun out of the holster and handed it over.

"Just put it on my lap here," Arlene said.

Marcy carefully set the gun down. She glanced into the backseat at Abby, and then out the rear window just in time to see the headlights rushing down on them again. "Here he comes!" she screamed.

Before Arlene could swerve across the road, the sedan nosed in beside them, nudging up against the side of her rear fender. She felt the bumping once, twice, and then all control was lost as the big car spun them sideways over the gravel. The sedan suddenly backed off, but as Arlene tried to steer against the skid, her car swung violently back around in a wide fishtail. When they hit the thick ridge of loose gravel graded along the outside edge of the road, their speed and momentum flung them spinning in circles down the middle of the narrow lane. "Hang on!" Arlene yelled.

Round and round they went, and every time they spun full circle the sedan's headlights lit up their cowering, frightened faces. Marcy closed her eyes, ducked down on the seat, and wrapped her arms over her head. When their front tires slid into the ridge of gravel on the other side of the road, they were thrown headlong into the darkened depths of the soggy ditch. They bounced and teetered, but much of their momentum had been lost in the spinout, and they finally lurched to a wretched halt in ten inches of muddy snowmelt water. When they dared to open their eyes again, the relentless glare of the sedan's headlights from up on the roadway illuminated their predicament.

Arlene hit the gas pedal, but the car didn't budge. She shifted into reverse and revved again, but they were submerged to the floorboards and hung up on rocks and tree roots. Abby opened the car door on the side away from the road and fought to extricate herself from the seatbelt.

"Abby!" Arlene yelled. "It's okay. Shut the door."

An instant later the girl was outside, leaning back in the door. "Don't worry," she said. "I know where Ben is." And then she turned and ran, crouching low to keep the car between her and the road, using the headlights from the big sedan to pick her way over rocks and roots through the low, wet ground in the narrow ditch.

"Abby! Stop! Get back here!"

The girl disappeared in seconds, swallowed up in the shadows and darkness beyond the meager realm of temporary, artificial lighting provided by the headlights.

• • • • •

Arlene picked up the handgun, ejected the magazine, slammed it back in place, and then chambered a round. Marcy's eyes grew wide and round. "Oh, please, Arlene. Don't do that."

"It's okay." She looked out her window up at the roadway, directly into the glare of the headlights. The sedan sat wide and solid up on the embankment, perpendicular to the road, looking down on them like a sentinel on guard duty, or a cat playing with an injured mouse. Arlene turned off the car, allowing the silence of the night to fall down over them. The handgun rested easy on her lap. "You should get down, Marcy. Just scrunch down there until we see what's going to happen."

As Marcy curled up on the seat, Arlene tried to look through the swirling dust and debris. Her car sat parallel with the road, but off to the right and much lower down in the ditch. She really couldn't see anything. For all she knew, the man could be out of his car already, using the headlights to blind them while he snuck up unseen from behind. And it wasn't any better looking out the other windows, either. All she could see were shadows and forest leading off into the dark. The car gave her some sense of protection, though, like a battlefield bunker down in the trenches.

They sat there, helpless, Arlene stroking Marcy's head as her friend sniffled into the seat. "He's not going to hurt us," Arlene said.

Marcy raised her head. "Are you crazy? He just ran us off the road."

Arlene attempted a reassuring smile. "That's my point. If he wanted us dead, he would've done it already."

Marcy groaned and shoved her face back into the seat cushion. Arlene resumed her lookout duties, even though she could see nothing beyond a few feet. The cool weight of the gun was a comfort against her thigh. She had no desire to hurt him, either, but if she had to, she'd protect her friends to the end. As she tried in vain to see outside, the lighting inside the car suddenly shifted, panning across the interior like a silent movie. Arlene used a hand to shield her eyes against the glare. The sedan was moving, backing up, turning to get lined up straight again on the road. Now she could see it, broadside to them up on the grade. It paused there, thirty feet away, big and broad, strong and shiny, looking down on them as if to say, "I could finish you right here if I wanted."

Then the rear tires spun, spitting a spray of stones, and the car disappeared down the road in its own cloud of dust.

• • • • •

Abby ran with an exhilaration she hadn't felt in a long time. "Just try to catch me," she challenged. Cool evening air billowed through her lungs. Her pace wasn't steady; it couldn't be out here in the middle of the forest at night. She ran in dodging, darting spurts, interspersing carefully chosen footholds with bursts of straightforward speed. Her legs carried her over obstacles she couldn't actually see, but rather sensed beneath her feet.

She concentrated on the pounding of her heart, listening as it drowned out the residual noise of the city still clambering about in her head. She could almost feel the light from the stars overhead reaching down to touch the tips of gigantic cedar trees and white pines as she passed. The underbrush hadn't come up yet for the season, so the wilderness opened before her, welcoming her home over its soft, carpeted forest floor.

Abby wasn't certain of her exact location, but followed the land as it sloped gently downhill before her. She knew that ultimately it would lead her to the rocky shoreline of the big inland sea. Her eyes quickly adjusted to the dark, so that soon she was picking out shadows of individual trees cast in the moonlight. Her senses had been on high alert when she left her friends back at the car, but she'd heard nothing to suggest that pursuit was coming. She almost laughed out loud at the thought of some city slicker trying to catch her out here. Not even Arlene's mafia guy could match her in the woods. Now, already a mile or more from the road, she left her mind and senses open to absorb the wilderness rhythms around her.

At a break in the forest cover, she paused to catch her breath and slow her heart rate. The air here was perfumed with balsam fir, a wild north woods aroma that for her evoked the familiarity and comfort of home. She paced left and right in the clearing, hands on her hips, breathing deeply, her eyes turned up to the stars overhead. When she noticed the long, narrow regularity of the break in the treetops, she spun around and followed the same opening in the opposite direction. The Superior Hiking Trail!

She set out again at an easy lope along the path. It was well worn, mostly clear of rocks and ruts, and broad enough to be followed in the dark under the moonlight. A hairpin curve at the top of a steep incline over a feeder stream marked her location. She knew this place. She'd hiked here with Ben and her father.

Ben. How long had he been gone? Just two weeks? Three? It seemed so much longer. She stepped up her pace to race along the trail as it twisted back inland to detour around Black Otter Bay. All thoughts of exhaustion and sleep were gone. She had a pretty good hunch where Ben was, and if she could get there quickly enough, her little brother might be sleeping at home with them tonight.

The trail swung back toward the lake again, and by looking hard over her right shoulder she discerned the faint glow of lights from town receding behind her. This was where they'd crossed the trail when she skipped school with Ben to go fishing out at Big Island Lake. She had to pay close attention now. Boulder outcroppings and gigantic virgin white pines marked her way along the trail. To her they were like fire hydrants or telephone poles lining a city sidewalk, marking the way. And where city children had memories of riding bikes or rollerblading, Abby had her own memories: this was where she'd run a footrace with her father, and just back there was where they'd spotted a massive white-tailed buck resting on the ground. She'd wanted to take pictures, but her father told her to keep walking. "If you stop, he'll get spooked and run away," he'd said. So they'd walked until the deer was out of sight, and then they turned around and walked back. Three times they did this, with Abby clicking pictures each time they passed the resting animal.

She slowed to a walk now as the path led to the brink of a dark, gaping chasm. This was the place they called The Ladder, a thirty-foot vertical drop down the cliff face to the trail below. The Ladder was actually a series of breaks and cracks in the rock, probably formed thousands of years ago by the pounding of a narrow, powerful waterfall continuously fed by a receding glacier. It was an easy descent in daylight, with plenty of foot and handholds, and for Abby only slightly more challenging at night. Of course, if you didn't know it was there it could be deadly, and that was a big reason why her father discouraged hiking in the woods at night. But Abby climbed down The Ladder with ease, much like a teenage counterpart in the city toeing a skateboard.

The trail leading away from The Ladder traversed several acres of flat, boggy lowland. A boardwalk bridged some of the wettest spots, and her shoes clomping on the wood startled a few sleeping deer caught off guard by her unexpected appearance in the night. When the path began an ascent to higher ground, she paused for a moment to listen. Over the throbbing of her heart in her ears, she heard the distinct rumble of a semi as it accelerated northbound out of Black Otter Bay on Highway 61.

Once again Abby stepped off the trail to cut cross-country toward the sound of the truck and Lake Superior. Many of the larger trees had been thinned out here, forcing her to push through overgrown patches of dogwood, aspen saplings, and alder thickets. She worked her way forward, an eye always on the stars to maintain her heading. Finally, just when she began despairing over her slow, time-consuming pace, she saw a break in the forest ahead. Stepping through the last of the tangled maze of brush, Abby paused beside the ditch lining Highway 61.

In a crouch, she eased her way into the tall grass in the bottom of the ditch. The semi was long gone, just a faint hum in the distant background. To get her bearings, she scanned both directions on the highway, and then closed her eyes to clear her mind and focus her hearing on any sound that didn't belong in the nighttime woods. Convinced that everything was as it should be, she stood up for a closer inspection of the roadway, and a self-satisfied smile arose on her face as she realized she'd cross the blacktop within a couple hundred yards of where she wanted to be.

Abby slid forward to the furthest edge of her hiding spot. One last look revealed no one on the road, no glimmer of approaching headlights, and not a sound coming her way. She stood up, took a deep breath, and charged out of the ditch onto the roadway. The blacktop stretched out flat and smooth before her. Within seconds she was sprinting full speed, angling northeast across the road, running hard while searching the woods on the lake side for her destination. When she hit the narrow strip of shoulder at the far side, she continued running, racing along the painted white line edging the highway.

The opening she'd been looking for suddenly loomed out of the darkness. Barely slowing her pace, she turned off the highway, but didn't stop running until she located the sign that read, ROSIE'S BAIT SHOP—OPEN 24 HOURS.

• • • • •

Sheriff Fastwater had just hung up from talking to the authorities in Duluth when his cell phone erupted on the desk. He
grabbed it after one ring. "Fastwater," he answered.

"Uncle Marlon? I found Mom."

"Leonard? Where are you?"

Static and noise disrupted the connection, as if his nephew
had dropped the phone. More commotion and muffled voices,
and then in the background he heard his sister say, "Give me
that phone, Leonard."

The wrestling continued, and soon Fastwater was yelling
into his own phone. "Leonard? Arlene? Leonard!"

"They're okay," Leonard finally said, panting, like he was
jogging to keep the phone away from his mother.

"Where are you?"

"I found them on the back road, just like you said. Actually, they're not on the road, they're in the ditch, but everyone's
okay. We'll have to call the wrecker out here to yank them out."

"What the hell is she doing in the ditch?"

"Says some guy ran them off the road. I'll let her tell you
about that. I just wondered what you want me to do now."

Of all the things that could've happened tonight, this was
one the sheriff hadn't considered. He stood behind his desk,
silent, a thousand questions running through his mind. Finally,
Leonard spoke up again. "If you want to come out here, I could
head back to Duluth, you know, to help pick up Randall and
Jackie. Or, I thought maybe it would be best if I give the ladies
a ride up to your office. Marcy is pretty upset."

"Yeah, do that. Duluth will pick up Randall. As long as
Abby is safe and sound, we're all right."

"Abby isn't here, Marlon."

"What?"

"Mom said she took off into the woods when they hit the
ditch. Abby told her she knows where Ben is."

"Damn it, Leonard. Put Arlene on the phone."

"Yes, sir."

Another pause, more noise in his ear, then, "He's driving a big black car, Marlon. Something like you'd see in a *Godfather* movie."

"Arlene, what the hell happened? Where is Abby?"

"Abby took off. She has some notion of where her brother is. She never said where, but I'm guessing it's near town, because we're not that far away."

"How could you let her go? Why didn't you call me?"

"I don't have my phone. We were chased out of the house. Marcy is frantic scared right now."

Fastwater paced around the desk, running his heavy, thick fingers through his hair. Of course she didn't have a phone. He knew that. "Okay, Arlene. I'm sorry. How long ago did she take off?"

"Twenty minutes. Maybe a half hour."

"And you have no idea where she went?"

"No. She'd been talking to Randall earlier this evening. I guess he'd been drinking. Anyway, he told her that he knew where Ben was, and that he was safe. He said that her brother would be coming home soon. It must have been something he said, because it was like Abby suddenly figured it all out."

"Hmm."

"Listen to me, Marlon. He's driving a big, black, shiny sedan. If that car shows up in town it'll stick out like a sore thumb. Bust his ass, Marlon, but be careful. He's a pro, and I'm thinking he's the connection to Chicago that we've been looking for."

"Arlene . . . Really, you think the mob is working up here?"

"I'm serious as hell, Marlon."

The phone line was finally quiet for a moment. Fastwater couldn't believe this, but his sister worked in a totally different world than his. He said, "If you're right about this, you're lucky you just ended up in the ditch."

"It wasn't luck."

"Hey, these guys usually for play for keeps."

"Probably. But not this time, and not this guy."

"What are you talking about?"

"He had us dead to rights, but then he drove off. I'm pretty sure he had no intention of hurting us, he only wanted to stop us from getting to town."

"Why?"

"Because Abby figured out what's going on, and he had to stop her. The thing is, he doesn't know that I saw him, and I know who he is."

"You do?"

"Yup. And so do you, Marlon."

NINETEEN

Abby Simon

The fog rolled onshore shortly after sunset, blocking out the stars and moon and cloaking Lake Superior's rugged coast in a thick, damp shroud, like a sodden old woolen blanket. The temperature along the shore was a good twenty degrees cooler than just a quarter of a mile inland. Not a breeze stirred the fog as it settled in, hiding the rock-bound coast and ancient cedar forests in its grasp, while coating everything in a cold, clammy mist.

Abby crept along the bait shop driveway. She knew the way but stretched her hands out at arm's length for protection anyway, slowly groping along while trying to stay in the center of the lane. At slight breaks in the fog, a diffused glow of moonlight draped a haunting, surreal aura over the landscape. She didn't even notice the house at first; it just rose up beside her out of the fog. No lights, and no sound.

This had to be right, she thought. The search for Ben had been called off days ago, and all the volunteers and searchers had gone home, making the deserted bait shop an ideal place to hide Ben. It was convenient to the highway, but secluded a half mile outside of town. She remembered her mother saying that Randall had already signed over or sold Rose's property. If he planned to take credit for finding her brother, this would be a great place from which to orchestrate Ben's return. The house itself couldn't be used, as lights would be visible from up on the highway, but the bait shop, tucked in behind the house near the woods, was invisible from the road.

Abby stood near the house, listening. The absolute silence was spooky, like a hulking, unseen presence, a wolf watching from the shadows. The air was heavily scented here, as if the fog were perfumed. If she tried, Abby could smell the rot and decay in the old buildings, but overall it was the natural aroma of the forest that defined the night: wet driftwood down along the shore, the damp, cool fog, and the pungent scent of wet cedar and pine.

He must have gotten a fortune for this property, she thought, *enough to cover dozens of gambling debts.* Or, like her mother had suggested, more than enough to open a truly high-class art gallery, maybe in Chicago or New York. But was it enough for him to justify having his own mother removed from the picture? And, if so, how could Abby trust his word to keep Ben safe?

She looked from the vacant house into the quiet, somber forest. This just had to be the place. Everything fit. If Randall intended to release her brother, he'd have to bring him up here to keep him hidden until the time was right. She felt a nervous energy in the woods around her, maybe not so much like someone watching, but more like an expectant audience awaiting her arrival. Abby shivered. She wished she could just call out Ben's name, yell at the top of her lungs to break the tension and let her brother know that she was here.

Stepping away from the house, Abby crept along the driveway to where it circled around the back of the house in front of the bait shop. She moved slowly, listening for any sound that didn't belong. Finally, the darkened hulk of the bait shop loomed before her. Again, she didn't see any lights, but there was just the one window in the small door, and that could be covered up. Abby darted across the driveway to the large overhead door with the fishing mural Rose had painted on it years ago. She stood tightly against the door, an ear pressed to it, listening. She half expected the big yard light to come on, exposing her in the open with nowhere to hide.

The only sound was the soft rustling of young leaves in the aspen grove behind the shop. Abby stepped quickly across the front of the building to the smaller service door, trailing a hand along the rough-cut siding. She found that the window was indeed covered, blocked by a thick tarp draped over the door on the inside. Reaching for the doorknob, Abby glanced quickly over her shoulder, held her breath, and quietly turned the handle. Locked. She tried again, harder this time, and then stomped her foot and grunted in frustration. The bait shop had never been locked before, but then, if she was right and Ben was here, it would have to be locked.

She ran back to the overhead garage door, but that handle didn't budge, either. Frustrated and getting anxious, Abby listened again at a crack in the door panel, and then hissed Ben's name in a raspy whisper. Hiding in the shadows beneath the overhang, she alternated calling his name and listening. "Ben!"

Retracing her steps to the small door, Abby tried in vain to peer around the edges of the tarp. It seemed that all her efforts were being thwarted, and in desperation she began tapping on the window. Again she called Ben's name, louder this time, but all she got was a hollow echo and silence. She grabbed the door handle and rattled it hard, yanking the door against the frame.

Abby's anger heated up. She stood back, looked around again, and wondered how she could have gotten it so wrong. If Ben were here, he would have answered her call. She'd been so sure. Everything had pointed to the bait shop. She kicked the door, and then turned around to stare blindly up the driveway into the dark. He wasn't here. No one was here; the place was empty. She crammed her hands in her pockets against the chill and took a deep breath. *But then again, maybe he had been here,* she thought. Perhaps they'd just moved him, or maybe he was on his way up here even now. She spun back to the door with the decision that she had to get inside to look around.

Using the toe of her shoe to probe the ground for a rock, she suddenly remembered the woodpile beside the shop. A moment later Abby swung a split aspen log like a baseball bat, shattering the window against the tarp, where it clattered to the cement floor inside.

The crash of breaking glass destroyed the stillness of the night. Well, she thought, if anybody had been watching or waiting, they knew for sure that she was here now. Abby reached through the broken window and unlocked the door. Standing in the doorway, her hand automatically sought the light switch, until she remembered that all the fluorescent fixtures worked off switches on a wooden column behind the sales counter. With a last look over her shoulder up the driveway, she ducked into the bait shop and threaded her way from memory around the sales counter in the dark. Reaching the cash register, Abby suddenly stopped and jerked herself up straight to peer into the blackest corners of the building.

There it was again, that static-like feeling of nervous waiting, as if all the guests at a surprise party were hidden around the room, awaiting their cue to jump out and surprise her. The awful silence bore down on her until she realized why it was too quiet, even for a deserted building. The minnow tanks!

Abby reached for the light switches. Flicking through them resulted in nothing: no lights, no water pumps, nothing. She felt around for the telephone that also hung on the post, but the line was dead. With a sour smirk she realized that all the utilities had been shut off, and with her friends stranded back there in the ditch, she'd have to find another way to get them help. She wasn't worried about the man in the big car hurting her friends. After all, she was the one he was after. But when she thought of Arlene and her gun, a tight-lipped grin spread across her face. She had no doubt he'd get the bad end of that deal!

Abby continued rummaging around, opening the cash register and cabinet drawers. She found a heavy stainless steel flashlight that cast a brilliant arc of light around the room, and very conveniently fit like a war club in her hand.

She moved away from the counter area and followed the flashlight beam over to the minnow tanks. Dozens of little fish bodies floated belly-up in the dark water. When she plunged a hand beneath the surface, the water still felt cold, and tiny puckered mouths bounced against her hand looking for food. The other tanks were the same, leading Abby to believe the power hadn't been off too long. But what did that mean? Had Ben been here, or was she totally wrong about the whole thing?

Wandering around the room, she remembered Randall swatting the countertop displays off the cabinet in a fit of anger. Small packages of lures and tackle still littered the floor. She directed the light into the darker corners of the room, in among storage crates and obsolete gear. As far as she could tell, everything looked just as it had when she and Marcy stopped here after Rose's memorial service. It didn't look like anyone had been here since then, much less her kidnapped brother.

Abby leaned against the side of Rose's old pickup truck, where she and Marcy had hidden from Randall a week ago. It seemed so much longer than a mere week, and to confirm that the incident had really happened, she aimed the flashlight beam at the side wall of the bait shop to illuminate the bullet hole just a few feet above the truck bed. Whatever else it might prove, one thing was certain: Randall Bengston was crazy.

She opened the driver's door and climbed in, taking a seat behind the steering wheel. Exhaustion quickly took over, compounded by disappointment at not finding her brother. She'd been absolutely sure about this, so how could she have figured it so wrong? With the dome light on in the cab, she shut off the flashlight and fell back against the bench seat with a sigh. What had Randall meant by all that crap about fishing and secrets?

Abby let her eyes close with the thought that she'd put her friends' welfare in jeopardy over nothing. They'd tried to help her, and then she'd run out on them because of her stupid conclusions about Ben and the bait shop. He wasn't here, and it was obvious now that he never had been. She may not have understood the meaning behind Randall's rambling conversation, but she decided that it must have been either drunken nonsense or a bunch of lies. For all she knew, Ben could already be dead, although she still didn't believe that.

She opened her eyes to an exhaustion and despair she'd never known before. It was worse than the day her mother had left them, even tougher than the night she'd lost Ben. She wanted to go home, but couldn't muster the energy to climb out of the truck. Directly before her was Rose's old CB radio mounted under the dashboard. It had a whip-style antenna attached to the back of the truck bed, and Abby remembered Rose driving slowly through town, talking into the microphone, with the antenna rocking back and forth behind her.

Out of curiosity she reached out to turn the power knob. A little red light came on, but that was all. The microphone was clipped to a mount screwed into the face of the dash, and Abby reached out again to push the button several times. Nothing. She knew that CB radios weren't used much anymore since the onset of cell phones and computers, but this thing had to be working because the power light was on.

She sat forward to take a closer look. Turning the volume control produced a loud crackling of static. Once again she pushed the microphone button, and this time the static stopped. Intrigued, she unclipped the microphone, held it to her mouth, and pushed the button again. "Hello? Hello?"

No response. She turned the volume way up, pushed the button, and said, "Hello? Can anyone hear me?"

Nothing. Looking through the back window, she saw the antenna held down along the length of the truck box by a hook just behind the cab. She got out, unhooked the antenna, and let it whip upright from its base. Now she knew why Rose kept it clipped down; it was too tall to fit through the garage door.

She reached across the seat and grabbed the microphone again. "Hello? Hello? Is anybody out there? Can anyone hear me?"

The static resumed its noisy monologue. Abby climbed up to hook the microphone back on the dash when the CB suddenly roared in her face. "Breaker one-nine. Breaker one-niner."

Abby grabbed at the volume control and turned it down, then sat back, dumbfounded, staring at the little box mounted under the dash.

"Breaker one-nine," came a woman's voice again. "Are you still there? Over."

Abby couldn't hold back a grin. This old thing still worked!

"Breaker one-nine, this is Thunderbird. How about it out there, you still got your ears on?"

Abby picked up the microphone. She had no idea what to say. This was crazy! "Thunderbird?" she ventured. "Is that you, Mrs. Bean?"

"Ten-four, young lady. Abby?"

"Mrs. Bean! I'm so glad—"

"You have to hold the button down the whole time you talk, Abby. You're breaking up."

"Oh, sorry, Mrs. Bean, I mean, Thunderbird." Abby giggled. The name "Thunderbird" didn't exactly slide off her tongue, especially when addressing Mrs. Bean.

"What's your twenty, Abby? Where are you?"

Abby could barely hear again, so she turned up the volume. "I'm at the bait shop. The phone doesn't work here. Could you call Sheriff Fastwater to go pick up Arlene and Marcy? Our car went in the ditch on the back road up from Duluth. They're not too far from town."

"Is everybody okay?" The volume continued fading, so Abby kept turning it up.

"We're fine. I mean, I think so. I'm just really tired. Would you also call my dad to come get me?"

"Of course. Are you sure you're all right?"

Mrs. Bean's voice faded to a whisper as the radio drained the old truck battery. Abby turned the volume all the way up, but could barely even hear the static anymore.

"I'm losing power. Thanks for your help, Mrs. Bean." And then the radio was dead. Abby shut it off, replaced the microphone, and sat back again. At least she'd called for help for her friends. Mrs. Bean would know what to do.

Drawing a deep sigh, Abby felt the disappointment of the evening seeping into her, weighing her down and making it difficult to move. She slid off the truck seat and closed the door. Aiming the flashlight around the room one last time, she made a final inspection, looking for something she knew wasn't there, and then, feeling defeated, headed for the door to await her father's arrival. On the way she passed the minnow tanks sitting silently in the dark. Without water pumps, she figured they'd all be dead by morning.

Abby set the flashlight on the counter, and then stepped over to the door. Broken window glass crunched underfoot. She grabbed the tarp and lifted it to reach the door handle, but as she pushed it open she spotted the flash of headlights flickering against the treetops on the other side of the house.

She slammed the door and pulled just enough of the tarp aside to peer outside. A car was coming. By watching the lights among the trees, she could tell when the vehicle dropped off the highway to follow the driveway down around the house. As it approached, the glimmering lights played along the trees and brush, but when the car rounded the house, the headlights fell full on the bait shop.

Abby dropped the tarp and sucked in her breath. No need to lock the door, she'd already broken the window! Two quick steps brought her back to the counter, where she retrieved the flashlight and held it in both hands like a baseball bat. At the door again, she watched as the reflections from the headlights slid slowly across the tarp. Then it stopped.

A moment later it disappeared.

Abby stood behind the door, clutching the long, heavy flashlight like a weapon. She focused all her attention into listening. It was much too soon for her father's arrival, plus he would have left the lights on and the motor running. She couldn't hear anything, and when she couldn't stand it anymore, she once again reached for the tarp.

Not twenty feet away stood the big car, the same car she'd seen so long ago out at Big Island Lake, the car that had chased them up from Duluth. She wondered if the man's presence here meant he'd left Arlene and Marcy alone. The back road wound much farther up north before looping back down to Black Otter Bay, so it was entirely possible that she could have beaten him here on foot by cutting cross-country while he circled around up north on the back road.

Then another thought occurred to her: maybe Ben was in the car! Could she have been right after all? Was he just now being brought up here? She heard a car door close, quietly, like someone trying to be sneaky. In a sudden panic, she ran back around the counter to hide in the dark. Her heart resumed its frightened pounding, making it difficult to breathe or react sensibly. What was she thinking? She couldn't hide here. If that was indeed Ben outside and they brought him in here, she'd simply get caught and be of no use at all.

She stood up, scrunched her face into a grimace, and marched back around the counter to stand behind the door. She took a firm grip on the flashlight, wrapping her fingers around it tightly. Holding an ear at the edge of the tarp, she listened and waited while nervously gripping and kneading the flashlight, ready now to take the offensive.

A minute later she still couldn't hear anything. Then, silently and barely moving, with her resolve fading away, she inched the tarp aside to look out at the driveway. The big car sat there, a brooding menace outside the door. Then she saw a light out ahead of the car, and pulled the tarp away in time to stick her head through the broken window to see a lone figure carrying a bound and gagged body over his shoulder. Abby's thoughts immediately went back to Big Island Lake and the man in the waders carrying Rose's body. She watched as he followed his flashlight beam around the side of the bait shop.

The boathouse!

"Oh, my God!" Abby muttered out loud. Of course it was the boathouse! Nobody ever went down there anymore. She opened the door and stepped outside. With the flashlight still off and her eyes accustomed now to the dark, she scooted along the front of the bait shop to the path leading through the aspen grove to the beach. Up ahead, she spotted the bobbing glow of the man's flashlight as he unsteadily trekked along under the weight over his shoulder.

Abby paused as a million thoughts rambled through her exhausted brain. She was certain it was her brother on the man's shoulder, and he wasn't dead, because she'd clearly seen the duct tape over his mouth. She turned to look back at the bait shop doorway. She couldn't call for help because both the telephone and radio were dead, and there was no way of knowing how long it would take her father to get here. She aimed her flashlight back at the car. Nothing moved, no heads ducked out of the way. It was just a big, broad vehicle blocking the driveway.

Abby shut off the flashlight and took a deep breath. She realized now that she'd been right, that she really had figured out Randall's riddle. Something big was happening here tonight, and it included her little brother. She had no choice. She was completely alone, there was no help to be had, and this was her last chance to make it right with Ben.

She looked back at the footpath and the quickly disappearing light up ahead. After reaffirming her grip on the heavy flashlight, Abby set out on the narrow trail to the beach, trusting her memory to carry her safely over the rocky path in the dark to a reunion with her little brother. And this time she was determined that he wouldn't slip away.

• • • • •

Between the office phone and his cell phone, Sheriff Fastwater had taken more calls tonight then he usually received in a week.

"Fastwater," he said, grabbing the office phone off his desk.

"Marlon? I just talked to Abby."

"Mrs. Bean?"

"Abby is down at the bait shop. She said Arlene and Marcy are in the ditch out behind town."

Fastwater sat back. The bait shop! Why on earth would Abby think that Ben was down there? They'd searched that whole area a thousand times.

"Did you hear me, Marlon? Your sister went off the road."

"I know. Leonard is bringing them in."

"Abby called me on Rose's old CB radio."

"Did she say why she's down there?"

"No. But she asked me to call Matthew to pick her up."

"Can you raise her on the radio again?"

"No. It's dead."

Fastwater shoved his cell phone and car keys in his pockets, patted his utility belt, and let his gaze fall on Gitch, lying on his rug looking up at him expectantly. Into the phone, the sheriff said, "Okay then, thanks, Mrs. Bean. Go ahead and call Matthew if you want, but I'm on my way down to the bait shop now. I'll bring Abby home if he wants to wait for her there."

"Okay, Marlon. I'll call him."

Fastwater wanted to run, felt the need to find Abby as soon as possible, but when he reached out to hang up the phone, he heard the postmistress still talking.

"What? What's that, Mrs. Bean?"

"I was just asking if everything is okay."

"Everything's fine now. I'll just run down and pick up Abby. Leonard is bringing Arlene and Marcy in, and he'll get the wrecker out there to retrieve the car. I have to go now, Mrs. Bean. Thanks for helping." He didn't give her a chance to say more, but hung up and grabbed his SOO cap off the desk. "Come on, Gitch," he said. "Time to saddle up, buddy."

The big dog bounded to his feet and joined the sheriff already striding through the door. Outside, they found the fog piled up against the ridge like enemy armies amassing along a walled fortress.

"Jesus Christ," Fastwater muttered while opening the back door of the squad car for Gitch. He paused to look out into the black void over the lake. It was like the town below him and the stars above had completely disappeared. "What a night to go chasing around in the woods," he commented. And then he climbed in and pointed the big car down the hill. As an extra precaution, he turned on the emergency roof rack of lights, and they flitted silently through the deserted streets of town like a gaudy one-car parade on their way out to the bait shop down Highway 61.

· · · · ·

Abby shivered. It felt like the fog inundating the aspen grove had a weight to it, cold and wet, and almost smothering in its density. Young saplings crowded in against the path, further obscuring her line of travel in the dark. But she knew the twists and turns in the trail by memory, and her tired feet carried her over rocks and tree roots. The bobbing light up ahead was gone and she didn't dare turn on her own flashlight, so she carefully crept along in the dark, reaching out into the fog to feel her way forward.

Randall had said that Ben would soon return. She wondered if that meant he'd simply be set free from the boathouse, or if they'd haul him up into the forest somewhere to be found. And if Ben did come home safely, how could Randall expect that neither one of them would talk? She had to consider that once again Randall was lying, that he had no intention of letting her brother go. If Ben did come home, Randall's leverage over her would be lost. He couldn't risk either one of them talking to the authorities, which would explain the chase through Canal Park to Arlene's house and up the back road from Duluth.

No one ever used the back road anymore. Other than some locals, no one even knew it existed, so how had the man in the big car found them? There were just too many questions without answers, making it too risky to leave Ben's fate in the hands of Randall. With a frown, she admitted to herself that the one thing she knew for sure was that none of this would have happened if she hadn't made Ben skip school to go fishing.

An exposed tree root caught her toe and sent her careening down the path, the flashlight clattering to the ground as she swung her arms to keep from falling. Finally regaining her balance, she crouched in the pathway, silently berating herself. *Pay attention, dummy!*

She paused to listen, but the forest maintained its brooding silence. From down on the shore Abby heard the incoming surf splashing over the beach. It was a gentle lapping, with the soft sound easily carried to her through the fog. She backtracked a few steps, feeling around on the damp ground for the flashlight. Ready again, she continued on her way, treading slowly along the twisting pathway leading to the boathouse.

Lake Superior acted like a natural air conditioner down here along the shore, and the sweat she'd worked up running through the woods from the back road had dried against her skin so that she trembled now in the damp fog. She heard voices up ahead, and the banging around of equipment being moved in the boathouse. The square-hewn log structure soon materialized out of the fog, but with no windows to peek through, Abby just slid her fingertips along the well-worn logs and tried to listen.

The voices were a jumble of words against the surf. The open wall facing the lake provided the only access, so she crept forward over slippery rocks, letting her fingers lead the way along the smooth log surface. Reaching the front corner, she squatted sideways against the building to listen. She could smell the lake here, the cold, deep water, wet rocks, and driftwood underfoot. And then a hand slipped around her face and a mighty force yanked her off her feet.

Abby fought and kicked, twisted and squirmed, but the big hand over her mouth choked off her breath, leaving her helpless to fight back. Within seconds, she quit struggling and went limp, settling back against the bulky form behind her.

"Hello, Abigail," a voice close in her ear said.

That voice! The day Ben was taken she'd heard that voice on the telephone.

"I had a feeling we'd meet face to face one day," he said, and a moment later she was heaved around the front of the building and set down inside. A large open boat with a center console, unlike anything Abby had seen before, rested on the boat ramp. Light from an overhead lantern reflected off a glittering metal-flake fiberglass finish. The prop from an enormous outboard motor protruded into the water. Randall stood in the boat behind the console, a coil of rope in one hand, the gun in the other, wearing a huge grin on his face. In the bow of the boat sat Ben, duct tape wound around his head to cover his mouth. His hands were tied behind him. He jumped to his feet at the sight of Abby, but Randall casually swung the gun up and leveled it at his face.

"Sit down," he commanded.

Abby jerked against her assailant, but the large man clamped down on her with a vise-like grip. At a nod from Randall the hand over her mouth was removed, but still he held her body tight against him, restraining her arms at her sides with his overpowering size and grip.

Randall leaned over the far side and handed down the coil of rope. "Come over here and help secure our guest," he commanded. When he stood up and looked back at her, he smiled. "This is just wonderful, Abby. How nice of you to drop in on us."

Abby interjected, "How did you get here so fast? I just saw you in Duluth."

Randall chuckled. "On the water it's less than fifty miles as the crow flies." He patted the leather-wrapped, oversized steering wheel. "I made it up here in just over half an hour." He wore his thinning shoulder-length hair tied back in a short ponytail under a Greek fisherman's cap. Abby thought he looked like a middle-aged father taking his family on vacation up north. "Come on, Danny," he called again to the third man in the boathouse. "Get over here and lend a hand."

Abby looked at her brother, who watched everything with an incredulous, wide-eyed stare, but she nearly choked up when his gaze fell on her. He wore his tear-stained, naïve little brother expression, and the glitter of expectation in his eyes said that he believed she could fix all this. He frowned at Randall's friend coming around the front of the boat and leaned away when the man reached over the railing to pat his shoulder. When Abby finally saw the man, she gasped out loud, "Uncle Dan!"

He looked up at Randall in the boat. "Let them go," he said. "That was the deal, Randall: no harm to the kids."

So that was how they knew about the back road! Abby studied her uncle. She hadn't seen him in a long while, years probably. He'd always been the fun one, the adult bending all the rules, the family vagabond blowing through town with outlandish stories and silly gifts. Despite the present circumstances, she couldn't hold back a little thrill at seeing him. He wore his old brown leather jacket over khaki trousers, and his thick hair, dappled with gray now, was brushed back in a tousled, carefree style. He still reminded her of the old Indiana Jones character.

Daniel Simon stood close to her, and she could feel the intensity rattling through him as he directed his glare at Randall. The set of his jaw was just like her father's. She'd recognize the family resemblance anywhere, no matter how many years he stayed away.

Randall seemed to be enjoying his position of leadership, standing above everyone high up in the boat. He ignored Daniel's request, instead smiling down at the girl. "I knew you'd show up, Abby. I always told your mother that you're a clever one."

"Come on, Randall," Dan interrupted. "Let them go."

Randall nodded at Abby's captor. "Tie her up, Eddie. This chit-chat is fun, but we don't have the luxury of time."

Dan persisted. "We had a deal, Randall."

Randall turned on him. "And now the deal is done," he growled. "Your guys got the property, and I finally have the money I should have gotten years ago for this place. You have no idea what a rotten life I had here. My father, the local fishing hero, was a tyrant. Even my own mother," he sneered, "wouldn't stand up to him."

Daniel Simon approached the side of the boat and looked up at Randall. He lowered his voice, as if in confidentiality, but in the narrow, enclosed room Abby could hear every word. "After these bozos screwed things up for you, I promised to help. You said no one else would get hurt. The kids got in the way, but you promised to keep them safe." He grabbed the boat railing and shook it violently. "You're not going to hurt these kids."

Randall smirked and leaned toward the railing, cocking the handgun and pointing it at Abby's uncle. "You're a fool, Dan Simon. Just like your brother and all the other low-brows in town." He looked at Eddie and barked, "Tie her up!"

Abby gave her uncle a pleading look, and then glared at Randall in the boat, but with the arm around her waist suddenly loosening, her anger exploded in freedom. Taking a step forward, she spun on the balls of her feet, swinging the flashlight like a baseball player swinging for the fences. The heavy stainless steel flashlight connected with a solid "thwack" against the side of Eddie's head. He never saw it coming, and quietly crumpled in a pile at her feet. Abby stumbled backwards as her uncle dropped to the ground, grabbing at the handgun in Eddie's waistband. Spinning in a crouch, he used both hands to steady his aim at Randall. When she looked up in the boat, however, she found her brother clutched close in Randall's arm, the gun pressed tight against the boy's temple.

"It's over now," Randall announced, his calm voice more unnerving than an outburst. "Abby, get up here in the boat, and Daniel, go ahead and drop the gun." When her uncle didn't move, Randall dragged Ben to the boat railing and sneered, "If you try anything stupid, I'll drop this whole affair in Jackie's lap, and yours, too. Think about it, Danny-boy. You're up to your neck in the Ardito family. They'll put you away forever, and you'll never see these kids again."

"What are you going to do?" Dan asked.

"We're going for a little boat ride." He held Ben in front of him like a shield, leaving no opening for an attack. "Toss that gun outside. Go on, Danny, throw it out the door into the lake."

Dan hesitated, staring at his adversary, until Randall said, "Your choice, Danny. Toss it, or I can just as easily shoot now and dump them later. It's your call."

Abby watched as her uncle pitched the gun underhand through the doorway. It landed with a heavy splash in the surf.

Randall grinned at his apparent victory. Nodding at Daniel, he said, "Thanks to you and Eddie, I finally got paid for those god-awful years working the nets. No one knows of my involvement in this, and Danny, I really don't think you're stupid enough to say anything yourself. I mean, how would that look? Your own nephew and niece." He pressed the muzzle of his gun hard against Ben's head and looked at Abby. "Now, for the last time, get in the boat."

Daniel asked, "Where are you going?"

"Far away, but it starts with a simple forty-mile boat ride to the south shore of Wisconsin." Once again he displayed his cruel-hearted smirk. "If we don't all make it across, well, you know what they say: Lake Superior never gives up its dead."

Abby reached for a handhold on the railing at the side of the boat directly across from Ben, when a painful groan attracted everyone's attention to the ground near Daniel's feet. Eddie held the side of his head and tried to sit up.

"Get in the boat now, Abby," Randall commanded.

She hoisted herself up, straddled the railing, and looked behind her again. Eddie was on his feet, dazed and unsteady, but when he spotted the gun in Randall's hand, he reached behind him for his own. Suddenly everyone began yelling and scrambling for cover. Eddie charged the boat, screaming, "What, were you planning to just leave me here?"

The gun in Randall's hand jumped, sending a reverberating explosion through the small room. Eddie staggered backward and sat down again on the cobblestone beach floor, this time with a stain of blood blossoming across his chest. He reached behind him in a daze, groping for the gun that wasn't there. Daniel knelt beside him, steadying the wounded man. By the time they looked back up at the boat, however, Randall had pulled the release lever, and the heavy boat dropped swiftly down the tracks into the water. The sudden movement flipped Abby over the railing, where she disappeared into the bottom of the boat.

A moment later, the big outboard motor fired up with a lusty rumble. Daniel lunged for the boat, charging into the water, but quickly lost his footing on the slippery underwater rocks. By clutching the bow of the boat he finally regained his balance, only to be knocked aside by another form leaping over the railing. In the darkness beyond the reach of the boathouse lantern, it looked like a wolf hurtling through the air. The animal barely grazed the railing before crashing into the interior of the boat. It all became clear when Sheriff Fastwater stepped around the side of the boathouse, using two hands to level his massive .44 Magnum at the drifting vessel. Over the grumbling of the idling engine, he yelled, "Shut her down, Randall. Shut her down or I'll blow it out of the water."

To everyone's surprise, Randall laughed, cranked the steering wheel around, and shoved the throttle lever full forward. Fastwater's .44 began to speak, a deafening roar that knocked the knees out from under everyone. One shot, and then two. Abby fell on top of Ben, covering him with her body as sparks flew from the outboard motor housing. Three shots, four. Pieces of metal and plastic ricocheted through the night. Gitch leaped up to maul Randall where he stood clutching the center console. Five shots, six. The motor sputtered, coughed, ran again, then suddenly died. The next wave rolled under them broadside and Randall and Gitch, locked in a bear hug, tumbled to the floor. By now, Daniel was out to his waist in the lake, but managed to grab hold of the free-floating rig.

Retrieving Abby's flashlight, Sheriff Fastwater played it over the scene out on the water. Henry Bengston's old breakwater of stacked boulders created a grinding, screeching wail as it punched at the hull of the boat. Abby got to her feet first and, looking every bit like an all-star third baseman, flung Randall's gun as hard as she could out to sea. Ben struggled to get up, and she held his arm to support him while working at the tape over his mouth. There was still a commotion in the back of the boat, but a moment later Gitch's big head stuck over the side to look at the sheriff, and then he raised himself up on his paws on the railing, tongue lolling and tail wagging, just like he did on the windowsill in the sheriff's office.

"Good boy, Gitch," Fastwater called while using his speed loader to insert fresh rounds into the gun. Daniel walked the boat back to shore, secured it to the ramp cable at the water's edge, and prepared to help the kids over the side when Ben suddenly blurted, "Dad!"

Everyone turned to look at the tall man in the plaid flannel shirt scrambling down to the waterfront. He gave his brother the briefest look and then waded into the cold, black lake to grab Ben in both arms, hauling him over the railing. He clutched his son in a desperate embrace, rubbing the boy's back with his huge hands and snuggling his face against his son's neck. When he finally set him down on shore, Abby saw tears in her father's eyes reflecting off the boathouse lantern light. She'd never seen her father cry before, not even when Jackie left, so when he spotted her still standing in the boat, she couldn't hold back her own tears of exhaustion and relief. He came to her and cupped her cheeks in his big, rough hands. All she could think to say was, "Poppa."

TWENTY

Black Otter Bay

The Black Otter Bay Café had taken on a party atmosphere by late Sunday morning. Rumor had it that Matthew Simon and his children would be stopping in soon. For the past few days they'd been in Duluth, where authorities had questioned them vigorously in an effort to piece together the components of Randall's illegal business dealings. But the family was back in town now, and the locals were eager to hear their first-hand accounts regarding the events of the past few weeks.

The story of Ben's miraculous return had made the front page of the Duluth newspaper, as well as all the regional news broadcasts and even several national media outlets. For a day or two the town had been overrun with well-dressed, exotic-looking journalists and reporters, but now that they were all gone, the locals were patiently awaiting the opportunity to personally congratulate their hometown heroes.

The Simon family, minus Jackie, had attended church that morning, but of course the townsfolk were too polite and shy to corner them for specifics, especially in a house of worship. Pastor John Petersen had mentioned it, though. From his pulpit in the tiny country church overlooking the shore of Lake Superior, he'd centered his weekly homily on the joys of a loving family and caring friends. He publicly applauded the outpouring of support from the tight-knit community. And it appealed to the townsfolk's sense of fair play when the good pastor offered up a prayer for the well being of the wounded man recovering in a Duluth hospital.

Marcy Soderstrom had returned to work, and her participation in the arrest of Randall Bengston, however peripheral it may have been, attracted a lot of attention in the absence of the Simon family. Today, anticipating a busy day of serving customers, she wore a fresh coat of fire-engine red fingernail polish to match her high-top red tennis shoes.

She paused for a moment in her rounds to look out over the crowded café. Arlene Fastwater had been here all morning, entertaining everyone with her legal opinions regarding Randall's case. Her amusing anecdotes and outrageous laughter contributed to the festive atmosphere in the café. Marcy kept looking at the door, awaiting the arrival of Matthew and his family. She told herself that she was just excited to see them, like everyone else in town, and the thought that it could be something more than that was simply crazy. With a weary sigh, Marcy once again glanced at the door, and then cruised the counter refilling coffee cups. At the end of the line she set the empty carafe aside, grabbed a freshly brewed pot, and wandered out among the tables.

"Hey, Marcy," Red Tollefson called when he spotted her coming his way. He shared a table with Arlene, Owen Porter, and Mrs. Virginia Bean. As Marcy approached, he said, "Tell us again about getting run off the road. Your version is a lot more exciting than Arlene's."

Marcy's breath caught in her throat at the reminder of that horrible night on the back road. She paused near the table, eyeing their coffee cups but seeing the fog and confusion in the front seat of Arlene's speeding, spinning car. She looked at the sheriff's sister, so calm and elegant. Her raw silk caftan lit up the room with its cheerful red and pink floral designs.

Red said, "Arlene claims you guys almost rolled over out there."

Marcy's eyes popped wide open. "We did?"

Owen Porter burst out laughing. "Are you sure you were there, Marcy?"

Mrs. Bean said, "Now, Owen . . ."

Arlene's voice carried over the laughter. "Hey, come on, you guys, it's not her fault she doesn't remember. Her eyes were closed through most of it."

Marcy cringed with the new round of laughter. She wasn't used to being on this end of the joke. Seeing her embarrassment, Arlene added, "But Abby would never have gotten out of Duluth without Marcy's quick thinking. Plus, she discovered the hard evidence they'll need to prosecute Randall."

With the laughter finally fading away, Red said, "I can't believe Dan Simon tried to kill you. He knew who was in the car, didn't he?"

"Of course he did," Marcy said. "He saw me in Duluth. He knew who was in the car, and that Abby was with us."

Red fingered his coffee cup and shook his head in disgust.

"But there must be some sort of loyalty left in the man," Arlene said. "Because I'm convinced he wasn't trying to hurt us. He only wanted to keep Abby from getting to town."

"How can you say that?" Marcy argued. "Jeez, Arlene, it was the middle of the night and he ran us off the road. You said yourself we almost rolled over in the ditch."

"And that's why, honey, if I get him in a court of law, I'm going to roast his scrawny little hide. But he never intended to hurt us."

Marcy rolled her eyes and leaned around Owen to top off their coffee cups.

Red pushed his cup forward, saying, "I read in the newspaper that the sheriff stopped Randall's getaway by shooting his boat." He looked at Owen with a skeptical grin. "You ever heard of such a thing? He didn't even shoot holes in the hull, but disabled the motor instead. And he wasn't using a shotgun or rifle, either, just his service revolver."

"Have you ever seen the sheriff's handgun?" Owen countered.

Red puffed himself up for a good argument. "It sure sounds like a stretch to me. I mean, think about it. The boat was out in the water, and it was pitch black and foggy outside. And don't forget that those kids were in the boat, too." His voice grew louder while he made his argument. "It would take quite a shot with a handgun just to hit the boat, much less the motor. No, sir, if it actually happened that way, it was nothing but pure luck." Too late, he realized the café had fallen silent. People were looking at him, and his words seemed to linger in the air.

He looked around and found Marcy standing by the counter, still holding the coffee pot while staring at the door. Red let his eyes wander over the crowd to the entrance, where he saw Sheriff Fastwater standing in the doorway looking at him. It seemed everyone in the room was staring at him now. The big lawman peeled off his sunglasses, fired a last dismissive glare at Red, and then stepped toward the counter, where Marcy began pouring his coffee.

Folks let out a collective sigh, and Mrs. Bean leaned across the table to quietly address Red. "Oh, he shot it all right. Marlon told me so. He blew that outboard motor to pieces," she added, jabbing an index finger at the table in front of Red to emphasize her point. She stood up, used a hand adorned with an amethyst ring and matching bracelet to smooth out her dress, and with a snooty parting nod at Red, joined the sheriff at the counter.

A murmur went through the room now, and when Red once again looked at the door, he saw Matthew Simon standing just inside, with Abby and Ben in front of him. Marcy immediately slapped the coffee pot down on the counter and went to them, in her haste looking like a worried mother intent on the safety of her family. Matthew's white shirt was buttoned tight around his neck, giving him a stiff, awkward appearance, and making his presence in the crowd look even more uncomfortable than usual.

Leonard Fastwater was with them. He stood off to one side, thumbs hooked in the pockets of his blue jeans, his thick black hair plaited into twin braids that hung over his shoulders. He smiled with pleasure at the chorus of greetings called out to the Simon family.

A few of the more outgoing townsfolk came forward to meet them at the door with handshakes and pats of congratulation. Marcy slid her arms around the shoulders of the children and led them to a table, with their father straggling behind, acknowledging the well-wishers with nods and timid smiles.

Owen Porter stood up, tall and gangly, to shake his friend's hand as Matthew passed. "We're really happy for you, Matt," he said.

"I appreciate that, Owen." Matthew paused at their table, working his neck uncomfortably in the tight shirt, and added, "We want to thank all of you for your help and support." The words sounded strange coming from such a taciturn man, and even though the short phrase was probably rehearsed, the words rang with genuine sincerity.

He turned to leave when Red suddenly spoke up. "Sorry to hear about your brother."

Matt stopped and looked back at him with a puzzled expression. "But my brother is fine," he said. "It was that other guy that got shot." He looked at Arlene and Owen, offering a confused shrug.

Red persisted. "But didn't he kidnap Ben?"

Matt laughed. "Good heavens, no. He was working undercover on an investigation into the Ardito family in Chicago. He didn't get involved in this part of it until after Ben was taken. He kept an eye on him to be sure he was safe while continuing the investigation." Matthew looked down at his shoes. This was more talking than he was used to. He gave the impression of wanting to leave, but then he looked at them again, and said, "Of course, it would have been nice if he'd let me know that, but I guess under the circumstances that wasn't an option."

Stepping away, Matt nodded again at Arlene and Owen, and then joined his family at the next table, where friends surrounded Abby and Ben. Marcy scurried off to the counter for soft drinks and coffee.

Red turned to Arlene, shaking his head in confusion. "What kind of circumstances is he talking about? I could have sworn I heard a reporter say that Ben was held hostage in Disney World. Now Matt says Dan was in Chicago."

Arlene snorted. "Ben was in Chicago, but they convinced him that Navy Pier was actually Disney World. That way, when they released him, he wouldn't be able to point out where he'd been."

Red sat back, incredulous.

"Come on, think about it," Arlene said. "He's only eight years old, and he's never been away from Black Otter Bay before. He's got his uncle with him, and besides, what does he know about Disney World? Hell, you can go ask him right now and he'll probably tell you he's never been to Chicago in his life."

"Well, if you're going to get kidnapped," Owen interjected, "I guess that would be the way to go."

Mrs. Bean returned to her seat at the table, with Sheriff Fastwater and Leonard hauling along extra chairs for themselves. Arlene adjusted the place setting in front of her, then tightened up the dangling bracelets on her wrist while studying her brother. When he was settled in next to the postmistress, Arlene said, "So let me see if I have this right. Dan Simon was working undercover in the Ardito family in Chicago when he heard about the kidnapping. He promised Randall a quick deal on the Bengston property in exchange for Ben's safety."

Red cleared his throat and said, "What I want to know is, how in the hell did Dan ever get involved with the mafia in the first place?"

"He wasn't in the mafia," Owen explained, not even trying to hide his exasperation. "Haven't you been listening? He was working undercover."

"Dan always was a little wild," Arlene said, eyeing the sheriff. "He'd been in Chicago for years, so it was just a matter of time before he hooked up with the wrong crowd."

"You don't know that," Sheriff Fastwater said.

Arlene sat back, unaccustomed to having her viewpoint questioned. Then she folded her hands on the table before her and tightened her expression into a professional scowl. Like a teacher addressing a class, she said, "The Chicago mob has worked Duluth for a long time, but always in the background, through politics or the trade unions. Recently, they've become more active, and we've been on the lookout for the person working this end."

Before she could continue, Mrs. Bean asked, "Did Dan say he was that person?"

"Of course not." Sarcasm oozed from Arlene's lips. "What's he going to say? 'Oh, by the way, I joined the mafia and here are my contacts.'" She directed a haughty look at the postmistress. "It's obvious he's the connection. He knows Duluth and the people up here—he's perfect for the role. Besides," she added, looking at her brother, "he didn't have to confess, because your honorable constable here arrested him."

The sheriff took a leisurely sip of his coffee and eyed her over the rim of the cup. "For the record, Arlene, I didn't arrest him. There aren't any charges against him. He's explaining things to the authorities in Duluth, and then he's free to go."

"Free to go? Are you out of your mind?"

Fastwater held his hands out as if deflecting her anger. "Hey, you've got the Ardito family now. You know that Eddie Ardito was laundering money through Randall's businesses and that his family intended to develop the Bengston property, which, by the way, is now going to the state. It'll become a roadside rest area, with a public picnic spot on the shore."

"Dan Simon is the connection," Arlene insisted. "He's part of it."

"You know," Mrs. Bean said in a conciliatory manner, "it's a long way from running underwear up the post office flagpole to working for the mafia. He's Matthew's brother, after all, and he deserves our patience."

"He ran us off the road," Arlene argued. "He could have killed us."

Fastwater sipped his coffee, looked around the table, and said, "Or he could have been trying to keep you out of harm's way."

Arlene sat up straight, thrusting her large frame into the argument. "Well, that would be a pretty stupid way to keep us safe," she sneered.

The sheriff sat forward, leaning on his forearms to speak privately to his sister, but aware that everyone at the table was listening. His black eyes glistened as he said, "You're wrong about him, Arlene. Randall is your connection. Dan was working undercover. He's been with the feds since his Army discharge. They're hiding him in Duluth, keeping him out of the public eye to preserve his cover."

Silence. Arlene's mind whirled through the facts. She could see by the look on her brother's face that he was telling the truth, but she remained skeptical. Everyone at the table expected her to refute his words, and she tried to speak, but the implications of what he'd said held her in check. Before she could launch another argument, Abby quietly appeared at Mrs. Bean's side. The girl looked around the table, saw the faces hovering in anticipation of something, and knew that she was interrupting.

Abby's braid had been brushed out for church, and her thick black hair hung in a gentle ripple down her back. She'd recovered her Minnesota Twins baseball cap, however, and she wore it now to hold the heavy waves in place. Ben stood at her side.

Arlene's frown still dominated the table, but with no one speaking up, Abby finally looked down at Mrs. Bean. "I just wanted to thank you," she said.

The postmistress grabbed Abby's hand and squeezed it affectionately. "Why, whatever for, dear?"

"Well, for being there when I called for help on the radio."

The postmistress laughed, causing her violet-blue eyes to twinkle with delight. "I should be the one thanking you," she said, patting Abby's hand. "Most nights I only get calls from sleepy truck drivers looking for someone to talk to. For at least one night you justified Thunderbird's existence."

Owen and Red chuckled, and even the sheriff brightened up with the apparent change of subject.

But then Arlene asked, "How is your Uncle Dan? Did you see much of him down in Duluth?"

Sheriff Fastwater leaned forward again. "Come on, Arlene. This isn't a courtroom."

"Uncle Dan is fine," Abby said. "It was lucky Randall didn't shoot him, too."

"Well, there's no honor among thieves," Arlene said.

"Oh, Uncle Dan isn't a thief," Abby replied. "He's a U.S. Marshal. I just wish he could go fishing with us, but he can't get away right now."

"Yeah, I bet," Arlene muttered under her breath, but contrition softened her expression as she looked at her grinning brother.

Marcy was taking a break at the next table, sitting with Matthew and eavesdropping on Abby's conversation, along with almost everyone else in the café. Her elbows were on the table, her chin resting in her hands, and now she leaned toward Matthew to say, "Red told me the walleye fishing is picking up. Where are you guys going?"

Matthew was slow to answer. Marcy could see his thoughts wandering far away. With both hands, he held his coffee cup in front of his face, as if hiding in the bushes while spying on Abby. His eyes squinted over at Marcy, flicked back to his daughter, and then out of the blue, he said, "My little girl is suddenly so grown up. She's going to be even more beautiful than her mother. How am I ever going to get through this?"

Marcy laughed. "Are you kidding me? Abby's a great kid. I think the bigger question is, what's she going to do with you?"

Matthew smiled, set his cup down, and leaned back. Running a finger under the collar of his shirt, he exhaled a deep sigh while continuing to study his daughter. Folks at the next table were getting up, gathering their belongings and preparing to leave. "We had a trip planned up to Lake Oja before all this happened," he said. "The kids still want to go, so I guess we'll set up camp out there for a couple of nights." His gaze went around the room, and he nodded at Owen and Red as they stood up to leave. It almost seemed like an accident when his roaming eyes landed on Marcy again. "Want to come along?" he asked.

The blush rose on her face so fast she had to look away. Her breath stuck in her throat, and she'd suddenly lost all control over the pounding of her heart. She started to get up, but then sat down again. Arlene's flowing gown caught her eye, as did the surge of customers making to leave. Then she spotted the old lake trout over the door, and she focused her attention on the greasy mat of dust along its back.

Matthew stood up. "It's okay if you can't go. I know it's kind of short notice."

"Oh, no, it's just fine," Marcy stammered, and then she banged her knee on the table leg while trying to get up. Matt hadn't noticed, and she winced at the pain while limping behind him toward the door. Her thoughts and emotions were all mixed up, and it didn't help that the trauma of last week's adventures still lingered so close beneath the surface. She couldn't seem to look away from the big fish on the wall. It was like it was watching her, too, and saying, "So now what? Are you planning to leave us again?"

Marcy wanted with all her heart to go camping, but at the same time she desperately needed to be home, to immerse herself in the routines of the café while forgetting about the nightmare of last week. She wanted to greet the morning regulars again, and listen to their bantering and stupid jokes. Who knows, maybe she'd even get the ladder out and clean that old lake trout.

Near the door, Matthew stopped and turned around to face her. From the anguish on her face, he knew she wasn't going camping. He took her hand, saying, "It's okay."

"I'll be here when you get back."

He smiled. "I know."

A round of laughter erupted outside, and they stepped through the door to join everyone on the large front landing. Ben pointed over the rooftops of town. "Look, Dad!" he called.

People moved aside to make room for them. Some of the folks pointed and chattered, but all of them were grinning and laughing. Matthew and Marcy stepped between the sheriff and Mrs. Bean, following their gaze out over the town. It took a moment, but they burst into laughter when they saw it: from the highest flagpole over the post office fluttered the tattered remnants of a faded red union suit.

THE END

Acknowledgements

A word of thanks to the talented folks at North Star Press; Corinne, Anne, and Curtis, who make it look so effortless. A special thank you to Lorna Landvik; you've been an inspiration, mentor, and friend for twenty-five years. And to Jane St. Anthony, for all the advice and counsel along the way.

I'm grateful for all the words of encouragement from family and friends, and a sincere shout-out to everyone in the Nokomis neighborhood; it's so great to be a part of this community.